"WHAT'S YOUR TAKE ON THIS, HAL?"

"I'm sorry, General, but I believe Admiral Stone is right. We aren't at war with China. For U.S. military personnel to board the *Wuhan* without hard evidence of illegal action under international law would be an act of war."

General Blake slammed his fist on the table. "Damn it! We can't stop her and we can't board her. What the hell are we supposed to do, just sit here and do nothing?"

"I didn't say we can't board her," Hal Brognola stated, "just that we can't use United States military men. That's a very dangerous area the *Wuhan* is sailing in. Piracy is rife. Anything might happen to a ship with a valuable cargo. I say we board her. We will just have to be sure we maintain plausible deniability."

"Can you arrange that, Mr. Brognola?" the CIA director asked.

"I believe I can. I'll have to talk to the President."

DON PENDLETON'S

STONY

AMERICA'S ULTRA-COVERT INTELLIGENCE AGENCY

MAN

STATE OF
AGGRESSION

A GOLD EAGLE BOOK FROM
W⊕RLDWIDE.

TORONTO • NEW YORK • LONDON
AMSTERDAM • PARIS • SYDNEY • HAMBURG
STOCKHOLM • ATHENS • TOKYO • MILAN
MADRID • WARSAW • BUDAPEST • AUCKLAND

First edition December 2001

ISBN 0-373-61940-5

STATE OF AGGRESSION

Special thanks and acknowledgment to
Pat Rogers for his contribution to this work.

Printed in U.S.A.

STATE OF
AGGRESSION

PROLOGUE

The White House, Washington, D.C.

Hal Brognola sat outside the Oval Office and waited. At the moment, the President was tied up in a meeting with the Joint Chiefs of Staff. The news was full of crises and disasters, and U.S. military resources were stretched thin. The President was going to have to make some hard choices and make them quickly.

Brognola glanced around the waiting room. There were other people waiting. Perhaps they would give him a clue. He saw an Army major general wearing the dagger patch of SOCOM, the Special Operations Command, on his left shoulder. An Air Force brigadier general and two men in civilian dress sat nearby. The Army general looked familiar. Brognola had seen him on TV, but he didn't remember his name. He couldn't place the Air Force general, which wasn't surprising. Washington, D.C. had more generals and admirals per square mile than any other place on the face of the Earth. There was no way of telling if their presence had anything to do with him or not.

The door to the Oval Office opened, and the Joint Chiefs came out, five admirals and generals, each with four stars gleaming on their shoulders. The Joint

Chiefs didn't look happy. Whatever the subject of their meeting with the President had been, the meeting hadn't been pleasant.

The President's secretary smiled beautifully. "Ambassador Locke, General Blake, General Saunders, Dr. Hatch, Mr. Brognola, the President will see you now."

Hal Brognola grinned as the group filed into the Oval Office. The President's secretary might be new, but she was one of the shrewdest people in Washington. She could calculate anyone's political clout instantly, and she was seldom wrong. He was at the bottom of the pecking order as far as she was concerned. That didn't bother Brognola. The less people knew about him and what he really did, the better.

The President was sitting behind his big desk, staring at a stack of papers. He glanced up and smiled thinly as the group came in, but he had a haggard look. There was one other person in the Oval Office, a tall, distinguished-looking man in an elegant gray suit sitting in one of the guest chairs.

The President motioned for them to be seated.

"This is John Marlowe from the State Department. He is acting for the secretary of state," the President said.

Marlowe smiled and nodded as the President made the introductions.

"Now, then, Mr. Marlowe, time is critical. Please proceed with the briefing."

"At once, sir," Marlowe responded.

"Mr. President, gentlemen," Marlowe said. "Let me have your attention, please. I am the assistant secretary of state for counterinsurgency and antiterrorism. This meeting is classified top secret, special access required. If anyone present does not have this clearance or has not had the related briefings, they must leave this meeting immediately. I will also remind you that anyone who discloses any information that they learn in this meeting in any manner whatsoever to an unauthorized person is subject to the full penalties of the Espionage Act.''

"General Blake is the commander of the Special Operations Command. His clearance has been faxed to your agency, Mr. Marlowe, and I will vouch for Mr. Brognola,'' the President said. "I trust that that will be satisfactory. Please brief them immediately.''

"I recognize General Blake's importance for this meeting, but I don't understand Mr. Brognola's need to know. May I inquire what his role is?''

"Mr. Brognola is an expert on certain points of international law, which may be very important in this situation,'' the President said smoothly.

This was certainly news to Brognola, but he wasn't about to contradict the President. He looked at John Marlowe and smiled modestly.

Marlowe nodded to Ambassador Locke, who immediately opened a plastic case and took out a slide projector.

"Gentlemen, this is Paul Locke, our ambassador to Australia.''

Locke cleared his throat. "Gentlemen, I have received information from the Australian government that leads me to believe that a major crisis is developing in the southwest Pacific. The Australians believe that some outside force is attempting to destabilize the government of Indonesia. Their apparent objective is to destroy the Republic of Indonesia and divide it into a number of smaller nations. Naturally, this is a matter of great concern to the Australian government. I flew here to brief the President at the personal request of the prime minister of Australia.''

He paused for a second and threw a switch. The lights dimmed, and a map appeared on the wall screen. Brognola knew what he was seeing. The map showed Australia and the long chain of islands that comprised the Republic of Indonesia, stretching east and west close to the northern coast of Australia.

General Blake raised his hand. ''Question, Mr. Ambassador. Why is this such a big deal for the Australians? They've been worried about the Indonesians for thirty years. They've fought the Indonesians several times in the past few years, small fights, but people on both sides got killed. I would think the Australians would be glad to see the Indonesian government fall.''

''You're right, General. But if that happens and Indonesia falls apart, who picks up the pieces? Australia and Indonesia are less than one hundred miles apart in some places. If a major power takes over, Australia is threatened, and we are pledged to support Australia if she is attacked. There already is a crisis in that area. Indonesia and Australia are quarreling over the future of Papua New Guinea. Both nations are very important to United States foreign policy. Indonesia is the fourth most populous nation in the world. Australia is one of our oldest allies. They are asking for our support. I think we must give it to them.''

''How do we know that East Timor isn't just an isolated incident?'' General Saunders asked.

The President frowned.

''It isn't, General,'' the ambassador responded.

"The CIA reports that there's an active independence movement on Sumatra. This morning, a mob attacked government buildings in the province of Aceh. Indonesian troops fired on them. Thirty civilians were killed. The UN Security Council is having an emergency meeting this afternoon. We have to start taking action. Now."

The President glanced at his watch.

"All right, gentlemen, thank you for attending the meeting. I have to think this over. I'll make a decision in a few hours. In the meantime, I want to keep all our options open. General Blake, prepare an emergency contingency plan to commit U.S. troops to East Timor. I want one battalion on the ground within twenty-four hours."

The group stood and began to file out of the Oval Office.

"Just a minute, Mr. Brognola," the President said. "If you will please stay for a minute, I have a few questions I would like to ask you."

Hal Brognola sat down abruptly. He no longer wondered why he had been asked to attend the meeting. He knew.

The President looked at the clock on his desk and smiled.

"Time passes quickly when you're having fun. We have to make this quick. I have to welcome the Chinese trade delegation in thirty minutes. To be frank, I have to do something about this situation, and it looks like any conventional solution just won't work. I had a briefing from the CIA this morning. They're afraid that our intelligence agencies have been penetrated. I'd like you to find out what's really going on. I need information from people on the scene I can really trust. Send in your people, and find out what's really going on as soon as possible.''

Brognola thought for a minute.

''Phoenix Force is primarily a counterterrorist organization, sir. This really isn't our type of mission,'' he said quietly.

''No? Your people are the best we have for a covert mission. The job has to be done, and I'm asking you and your people to do it. You'll have my full support. All the resources you may need will be immediately available to you—people, money, military support, whatever you need. However, I expect you to get the job done quickly.''

It wasn't a request Hal Brognola could refuse.

''All right, Mr. President,'' he said formally, ''we'll take care of it. I'll get the ball rolling immediately.''

CHAPTER ONE

Kupang, West Timor, Indonesia

Mack Bolan woke up. He had been dozing in his seat, recovering from the effects of ten thousand miles of high-speed travel across the Pacific Ocean. The Air Merpati Airlines Boeing 707 was losing altitude steadily, flying along the northern coast of the island of Timor. Bolan glanced at his watch. It was too soon for them to be landing in East Timor. The 707's intercom began to chime. A man began to speak in Indonesian. It meant nothing to Bolan, but some of the passengers groaned. The voice shifted smoothly to English.

"Ladies and gentlemen, this is the captain speaking. I regret to inform you that our flight has been diverted. United Nations Peacekeeping force air-traffic control has informed us that due to heavy UN air traffic, we cannot land at Dili Airport in East Timor as scheduled. We will be landing at the Kupang Airport in West Timor in fifteen minutes. Air Merpati Airlines sincerely regrets any inconvenience this may cause you. We will make every effort to book you on a later flight or arrange alternate ground transportation."

Bolan glanced toward the aisle and saw that David McCarter was glaring at the intercom speaker. If looks could kill, the speaker would have been instantly reduced to smoking rubble. Gadgets Schwarz seemed unconcerned. He still had his nose buried in a tourist's guide to Indonesia. He had been reading it since the plane took off from Java, pausing only to try his newly learned Indonesian phrases on the smiling flight attendants.

An Air Merpati Airline flight attendant walked down the aisle and offered Bolan a refreshing hot towel with a smile. He smiled back. She was a very attractive young lady and very attentive. She leaned over him casually and pointed out the window.

"There is Kupang, Mr. Belasko. We will be touching down in a few minutes. If there is anything you would like, now or after we land, I will be very happy to see that you get it."

Mack Bolan waited a few seconds and motioned to Schwarz. He nodded, stepped across the aisle and took the seat next to Bolan.

"We're landing in West Timor. That's Indonesian territory. Stay by your equipment and delay going through customs as long as you can. If there's no one from the UN there to meet us, we may have a little trouble explaining some of your gear."

"Got it, Striker. If worse comes to worst, I'll tell them I'm the producer of a TV show and offer to take their pictures."

Bolan looked out the window. The plane was making a low turn over Kupang. From the air, at least, it looked very nice, a small city with old white stone buildings and a brilliant blue coastline surrounded by dark green, forest-covered hills. Sixty years ago, it was part of the Dutch East Indies. Since 1948, it had been part of the Republic of Indonesia. It looked attractive from the air, but it wasn't where they needed to be. It was the transportation hub and the main point of legal entry for travelers coming to Timor, but it was 120 miles from Dili in East Timor.

The airport was west of the city. The pilot made a smooth landing and taxied toward the terminal. Bolan looked intently out the window as the 707 moved slowly down the runway. Kupang was a civilian airfield, not a military base, but the Indonesian military was there in force. Several needle-nosed Indonesian jet fighters were parked in sandbag revetments at one side of the runway. He recognized Lockheed-Martin F-16s, and they weren't there for show. Bolan could see Sidewinder air-to-air missiles, and five-hundred-pound bombs mounted under the fighters' short, stubby wings.

The planes were guarded by heavily armed soldiers in camouflage uniforms, carrying M-16 rifles and wearing bright orange berets. Bolan knew who they were—KOPASSUS, the elite Indonesian army commandos. The last time he had seen them, they had been pursuing him through the jungles of New Guinea.

When the Air Merpati 707 parked in front of the terminal, the airline ground crew rolled out the exit ramp. Bolan picked up his hand luggage and followed McCarter down the aisle. The Briton was still seething. He was the team leader, and his mission plan had just been disrupted.

Bolan felt the heat as he and McCarter deplaned. It was one o'clock in the afternoon, and the sun was blazing down from a bright blue sky. The temperature was nearly ninety degrees. The terminal wasn't air conditioned, and he could feel himself starting to sweat. They walked into the terminal building, showed their passports to the immigration authorities and moved quickly toward the customs desk. McCarter strode off, looking for a place to have a quiet smoke.

Bolan walked on toward the customs desk. This stopover could pose a real problem. In Dili, the UN peacekeeping force was in control of the airport. There, they could have whisked through customs no matter what weapons and gear they were carrying. Here, they were in Indonesia, and the Indonesian government wouldn't be amused by the weapons, ammunition and electronics equipment in their luggage. He had heard that Indonesian customs men cheerfully accepted bribes. He would have to find out just how true that was.

He picked out the senior Indonesian customs official and showed him his passport. The official smiled when he saw the bright blue ten-thousand-rupiah bill that Bolan had slipped inside his passport. This wasn't one of those American idiots who expected all sorts of special services without paying for them!

"Welcome to Kupang Airport, Mr. Belasko. I hope your will enjoy your stay here. Is there any way I can assist you?"

Bolan smiled back. "I have landed here unexpectedly, but there may be someone here to meet me from the American consul's office. If not, could you assist me in obtaining helicopter or ground transportation to Dili?"

"There is no one here from the American government, but there are people waiting for you from the

Indonesian government. I am sure that they can arrange transport for you.''

Bolan frowned. He wasn't expecting a welcoming committee from the Indonesian government. The customs official smiled and pointed. A tall, well-built young woman wearing a white linen suit and wraparound sunglasses was walking briskly toward him. She was certainly worth looking at, but Bolan was more interested in the man in uniform by her side.

He wasn't tall by American standards, but he radiated confidence and what soldiers call ''command presence.'' He was dressed in a British disruptive-pattern camouflage uniform and a purple beret. The gold insignia of an Indonesian major gleamed on his collar. Bolan wasn't impressed by fancy uniforms, but the badges on the major's chest were remarkable. He wore a name tag and the U.S. Navy SEAL qualification badge over his right jacket pocket, and over his left pocket were paratrooper's jump wings, an expert marksman's badge and a gold badge with the letters KIPAM. What looked like a 9 mm Browning Hi-Power pistol was holstered at his right side.

The tall young woman held out her hand and smiled. Bolan shook it. He noticed that she carried a large dark brown leather purse over her left shoulder. It looked heavy and she carried it a secure fashion, her left hand grasping the shoulder strap. Obviously, there was something more than lipstick and a compact in her purse. Still, the island of Timor wasn't a safe place, and she was a government official. It might be perfectly normal for her to be carrying a gun.

''I am Mara Tharin from the Foreign Ministry. I am here to assist you in carrying out your mission.

This is Major Abdul Salim. He has been assigned to provide security and coordinate military affairs.''

They shook hands. Major Salim gave Mack Bolan a cold smile and held out his hand. Bolan had the distinct feeling that the major didn't like him, or perhaps he simply disliked all Americans.

McCarter joined the group.

''I am glad to meet you, Mr. Green,'' she said, using the Briton's cover name. ''Now, where is the rest of your party, Mr. Belasko?'' Mara Tharin asked.

Bolan wanted to know how she knew who they were. She hadn't spoken to the customs official, so she had to have seen photographs before she came to the airport.

''Is your party ready to depart, Mr. Green?'' Tharin asked, flashing her lovely smile and perfect white teeth again. McCarter looked around. Jack Grimaldi had passed through customs easily. There was nothing in his nylon flight bag to arouse suspicion, but Gadgets Schwarz was surrounded by an excited group of customs officers.

''Perhaps you could assist Mr. Sower, Miss Tharin. He is our electronics and communications expert. He has quite a lot of technical equipment. I would appreciate it if his things were handled very carefully and as quickly as possible. As soon as he's through customs, we will be ready to go with you,'' McCarter replied.

''Of course. I am sure that Major Salim can assist him.''

Salim strode over to the customs official like a hungry tiger ready to pounce.

''Take care of this man at once! Do not disturb his

equipment. He is here to work on an important government project," he snapped.

The customs official turned pale. Whatever organization Major Salim was from, the customs man wanted to avoid trouble with him at all costs.

"I will see to it at once, sir, at once! If there is anything else I can do to assist you, do not hesitate to call on me."

Major Salim smiled coldly. "See that you do."

The customs official scurried over to Gadgets Schwarz. His subordinates began to complete their examination with remarkable speed and efficiency.

"Follow me, gentlemen," Tharin said, sounding amused. Most likely she had worked with the major before.

Bolan and McCarter followed her toward the terminal door, keeping an eye on the porters who were handling their baggage. Jack Grimaldi joined them casually.

"Major Salim seems to be a very efficient soldier," McCarter said politely.

Tharin smiled again.

"Yes, he is very efficient, but do not call him that. He does not like it. He is not a soldier, he is a marine. He is from KIPAM, the amphibious reconnaissance paratroop commandos. They are an elite unit, and they do not like to be called soldiers."

McCarter smiled. Marines were the same the whole world over. He could remember getting that same lecture from a colonel of the Royal Marine Commandos. Very well, he would call Salim whatever the major liked.

Three cabs were waiting outside the terminal. They climbed aboard and drove toward the main road. The ride to downtown Kupang had been uneventful. If anyone was following them, Bolan couldn't detect it.

They were driving through the downtown area now, along one of Kupang's four main streets. The streets were full of Timorese tribesmen in colorful clothing, Chinese shopkeepers, Indonesian bureaucrats and policemen, and other colorful individuals Bolan couldn't begin to identify. They kept going until they reached a small improvised military base on the outskirts of the town. The base was surrounded by barbed wire, and several carefully sighted machine guns in sandbag revetments protected the fence. The sentry at the gate took one look at the major's uniform and insignia of rank and waved them through.

"Do not worry, gentlemen," Tharin said. "Our security is quite good, but everyone knows Major Salim."

The cabs pulled up by a series of helicopter pads. Salim led them toward two green-and-brown-mottled helicopters at one end of the flight line. Bolan smiled at their old, familiar configuration. They were modern updated versions of the old Bell Hueys he had seen so often in Vietnam. They were marked with the red-and-white Indonesian army insignia. On either side, a pale blue square marked UN had been added. He could see a small weapons pod mounted on each side of the two helicopters. The muzzle of a .30-caliber machine gun protruded from the center of each pod, and four light rocket-launcher tubes were mounted below the gun. They didn't make the Huey a gunship, but they gave it some firepower.

The sergeant in charge saluted Salim, and two crewmen led by a corporal opened the passenger compartment doors. Bolan, McCarter and Mara Tharin climbed in and took seats in the passenger compartment. The major took the copilot's seat next to the pilot. Mack Bolan glanced out a side window. Grimaldi and Gadgets Schwarz had boarded the second chopper. Their pilot started the twin turbine engines, and they whined into life. The rotor blades rotated faster and faster, and the Huey lifted off. They were on the way to Dili.

CHAPTER TWO

Over West Timor

The Indonesian pilot pushed his throttles forward, and the whine of the twin Lycoming turbine engines deepened as the Bell 412 helicopter began to climb. The second helicopter lifted off and followed it into the air. Mack Bolan looked down as the chopper began to fly east over Kupang toward East Timor. The pilot was climbing steadily to clear the range of dark green hills that circled the landward side of Kupang, gaining altitude at a steady five hundred feet per minute. Bolan looked at the map. Most of the island's cities and main roads were along the coasts. Except for a few small towns, the interior was a vast expanse of mountains, hills and forests that was sparsely inhabited. It wasn't really a jungle. It was a thick tropical rain forest, good guerrilla country. A small army could be hidden under those trees. It didn't look the safest country in the world to fly over. The sound of the engines changed as the pilot leveled off and went to economical cruise speed. They were flying due east now, along the coast. The border between East and West Timor was about fifty miles away.

Major Salim leaned back from the copilot's seat.

"We should be on the ground in Dili about an hour and a half, gentlemen," he announced.

Bolan nodded. There was nothing for him to do but sit and look out the window at the tropical rain forest below. There wasn't much else to see.

The helicopter droned on. Bolan was almost dozing in his seat when he heard the sound of the engine change and felt the helicopter turn as the pilot increased power and started to descend. He looked out the window. There was still nothing to see but the dark green tops of trees.

Salim stepped back into the passenger compartment.

"Something has happened, gentlemen. One of our army patrols near the border has been ambushed. They are heavily outnumbered and under attack. They have called for air support, but it will take time to get there. We must go help them."

Bolan didn't like the change in plan. The two Bell 412 helicopters weren't gunships. They were slow, unarmored and lightly armed. Still, he couldn't fault the major. If it had been American troops in the trap and he had been calling the shots, he would have gone in, too.

Salim exchanged a few words in Indonesian with Mara Tharin, and the woman shrugged. Whatever the major had said, she didn't seem to care. Salim turned to Bolan and McCarter again.

"We will be making firing runs. We are flying with a reduced crew, so we can carry your party and all your baggage. I need someone to man the right-hand door gun. Are either of you gentlemen familiar with belt-fed machine guns?"

"I am, Major," the Executioner replied, "and I've

been a door gunner on a Huey more times than I like to remember. Just check me out on the gun, and I'll see what I can do.''

''He's better at shooting from a helicopter than I am,'' McCarter stated, ''but I've fired a machine gun once or twice. I'll give him a hand.''

Salim really smiled for the first time since they had met him. He had been sure the big American and the tall Englishman were soldiers. Something in the way they moved and talked told him that, but there were paper soldiers and there were combat soldiers. He really respected only men who were willing to fight.

He nodded and led them to the right-hand door. Bolan slipped into the web harness that allowed the gunner to lean out the door to fire without falling out. Salim took an ugly-looking black plastic-and-steel .30-caliber machine gun from a rack and handed it to Bolan. Then he set out several steel ammunition boxes for McCarter.

Salim opened the door. The slipstream was howling by as the pilot flew at full power. Bolan placed the gun in the pivoting pintle mount and opened the weapon's feed cover. McCarter inserted a belt of gleaming brass cartridges in the feedway. Bolan closed the cover and worked the bolt. All it took now was a few pounds of pressure on the trigger. He was ready to fire.

The Executioner looked over his shoulder. The Indonesian corporal was mounting the left door gun. Mara Tharin stood next to him, ready to hand him a long belt of linked cartridges. That was interesting. Bolan didn't think that the average young woman who worked for the Foreign Ministry would be that familiar with machine guns. He would worry about that later. Right now, he had other things on his mind.

The major was back in the copilot's seat. His voice crackled in the intercom.

"We are going to make a quick pass over the target area."

Bolan looked ahead. He could see four military jeeps in a line along a dirt road. One of them was burning. Men in bright orange berets lay in the drainage ditches along the road. They were firing rifles and machine guns at targets concealed in the trees.

The helicopter was attracting attention as it shot over the ambush. Bolan could see yellow muzzle-flashes as the attackers fired short bursts at the aircraft. He put his sights on the target and squeezed the trigger. The black machine gun vibrated, and he could see red tracers flash toward the ground. He fired another burst and then another. Behind him, he could hear the left door gun hammering away.

They probably weren't hitting anything. It was difficult to achieve pinpoint accuracy firing a handheld gun with iron sights from a moving helicopter. However, the purpose of a helicopter door gun was to lay down suppressive fire. The sound of bullets hissing past their heads would spoil the ground gunners' aim. Bolan ceased fire. They had flown beyond the target area, and there was no use wasting ammunition when he could see nothing to shoot at. He opened the machine gun's feedway cover, and McCarter snapped a fresh belt into place. They had better be ready. Salim was a fighter, and Bolan knew he was going in again.

Bolan heard Salim speaking rapidly in Indonesian.

"He is telling the other helicopter to attack now," McCarter said. Bolan wondered how the Briton knew that. As far as he knew, McCarter couldn't speak Indonesian, but this was no time for questions. The engines howled as their pilot pulled their helicopter in a hard left turn.

Bolan could see the other helicopter slanting in as it made a firing run. The pilot understood what he was doing. He triggered his two pod-mounted machine guns and sent twin swarms of red tracers into his target area. He was dead-on. Halos of orange fire wreathed the helicopter's weapons pods as eight deadly 2.75-inch rockets shot out and flashed toward the ground. Bolan saw the yellow-orange flashes as the rockets struck and their warheads detonated. The chopper pulled up and started to leave the target area.

Several streams of green tracers clawed upward at the departing helicopter. The two Hueys had no armor. A few well-aimed bursts of light machine gun bullets could shoot them down. Major Salim could see the situation clearly.

"Stand by for a firing run!" Major Salim ordered.

The twin turbine engines howled again as the pilot went to full emergency war power, and the helicopter headed straight for the concentration of hostile machine guns. The helicopter vibrated as the two pod-mounted machine guns opened fire. Bolan could no longer see the target. The nose of the aircraft blocked his view as the Huey flew straight at it. He concentrated on his suppressive fire, snapping off short bursts at hostile muzzle-flashes. Suddenly, the fuselage was shrouded in orange fire as Major Salim launched the 2.75-inch rockets. The pilot pulled up and started out of the ambush area.

Suddenly a stream of bright green tracers flashed toward the Huey. Large tracers. Someone was firing at them with a heavy weapon, a .50- or .60-caliber machine gun.

"Flak at two o'clock," he snapped into his microphone.

The pilot didn't waste time asking questions. He pulled the Bell 412 into a hard right turn. Bolan saw a swarm of bright green dots streak by, passing through the space their helicopter had occupied a few seconds before. He heard the sound of ripping, tearing metal as a another burst of heavy bullets tore into the Bell's upper fuselage.

The pilot twisted hard left, trying to throw off the aim of the gunner below them, but it was no use. He was firing burst after burst of heavy machine-gun fire. The aircraft shuddered and shook as it was hit again and again. Bolan heard a grinding howl as the engines began to vibrate. Another burst ripped through the passenger compartment. He could see the tracers as bright green blurs as the bullets ripped through one side of the helicopter and out the other. A giant's hand seemed to slap the FN machine gun out of Bolan's grip, shattering the ball mount and sending the ruined gun spinning away out the door. The helicopter's fuselage started to shudder, and acrid gray smoke began to fill the passenger compartment.

As the pilot fought the controls, there was nothing Bolan could do but hang on. Another burst streaked past the nose as the pilot dived desperately toward the ground. The bright green tracers seemingly missed the Bell by inches. The ground seemed to rush up at them with incredible speed. The stricken helicopter began to fishtail from left to right. If Bolan hadn't been strapped in, he would have been thrown out the door. The engine's howl rose to a shriek of tortured metal.

They were close to the ground now; there was no time to hover. They were going in. The dying helicopter touched treetops and crashed toward the ground, its landing skids tearing branches from the trees as it went.

"Hang on!" Major Salim yelled as the Bell 412 smashed through the branches. The rotors tore away with loud ripping noises. The nose struck a tree trunk and crumpled as the smoking fuselage ground to a halt. The pilot's hands flew to the control panel as he cut power and activated the fire-extinguishing system.

Bolan staggered to his feet and toward the cockpit. Salim and the pilot were gone. They had jumped out through the cockpit doors. Black acrid smoke poured into the cockpit. McCarter had been slammed against the side of the fuselage, but he was getting up. He looked quickly at the opposite door. Mara Tharin had disappeared, and the Indonesian corporal was lying on the floor in a pool of blood. Bolan hesitated for a split second. He didn't see any flames, and he was damned if he was going to leave their weapons and equipment. He lunged back into the passenger compartment. The black smoke was thicker there. It seemed to be coming down from a hole in the ceiling.

Smoke was billowing from the helicopter's upper fuselage. Bolan could see dozens of large bullet holes in the engine and transmission housings. He knew the aircraft would never fly again. The Executioner remembered what the forest had looked like from above, and the people who had shot them down were probably headed for the crash site. He had to get their weapons and their survival kits. It might be a matter of life or death.

He slipped back into the cargo compartment, groping for the plastic cases that held their weapons, slid them out the door, then grabbed the packs and the black nylon cases that held their equipment and lunged out the door. He dropped to his knees, gasping and coughing, trying desperately to clear his lungs.

Bolan heard a whomp as the helicopter burst into flames. McCarter pulled him to his feet. "Run, Striker," he shouted. "It's going to blow up any minute now!" They staggered through the trees as fast as they could run, dragging their weapons cases. There was a dull roar behind them, and the helicopter vanished in a ball of orange fire.

CHAPTER THREE

West Timor, near the Border with East Timor

Mack Bolan threw himself down as metal fragments hissed by and flaming debris rained down to the jungle floor. He brushed a smoldering fragment from his sleeve and looked back. There was nothing left of their helicopter but a column of thick, black, greasy smoke climbing upward into the sky. He got to his feet and moved forward, dragging two heavy plastic cases. McCarter stumbled along behind him. There was no time for conversation. The column of smoke was like a beacon. Someone was almost certainly coming, and Bolan didn't want to greet a Timorese guerrilla welcoming committee standing in the open.

Running in the heat and humidity with the heavy equipment cases was brutal. They had traveled about four hundred yards and were both gasping for breath when McCarter signaled a halt. They dropped to the ground. The thought of just lying there and resting was tempting, but they might have company at any time. They had to be ready.

Bolan snapped open his personal equipment case and pulled out his M-4 Ranger carbine. The weight of the dull black weapon was reassuring. The M-4 carbine was a wicked weapon, a shorter and lighter version of the M-16 rifle with a lethal M-203 40 mm grenade launcher clipped under its barrel. He pulled a 30-round magazine from the case, snapped it into the carbine and worked the bolt to chamber a round. He swept the carbine's muzzle in an arc around them but saw nothing to shoot. If the enemy was coming, they weren't there yet.

He reached deeper into the case and drew out an olive-drab U.S. Army web belt with four triple 30-round magazine pouches attached, which he buckled around his waist. There was a brown leather holster on the right side of the belt. Bolan drew his .44 Magnum Desert Eagle, pulled back the slide, chambered a round and set the safety. Now he was ready to fight. He glanced at McCarter. The Briton was just as ready with his M-4 Ranger carbine in his hands and his ammunition belt around his waist. McCarter stood and pointed in the direction they had been going. Bolan nodded and got to his feet. Time to move out.

They headed through the trees rapidly, halting at the edge of a large clearing perhaps a hundred yards across. About fifty yards ahead of them was a shallow dip in the ground. As Bolan watched, a man's head and shoulders suddenly appeared as he fired a flat black automatic weapon at some target the big American couldn't see. He recognized Major Salim's distinctive purple beret. Dust and dirt suddenly spouted as a burst of machine-gun bullets missed Salim by inches.

Most of the hostile fire was coming from a low ridge at the opposite side of the clearing. Bolan took up a prone position. He set his carbine's selector lever to semiautomatic and looked for targets, but he couldn't spot anyone. The enemy was taking advantage of all available cover and concealment.

McCarter was scanning the trees at the other end of the clearing. Suddenly, he stopped and studied one place intently. He handed Bolan the binoculars.

"Look, Striker! Near the top of that tall tree. Someone's playing Tarzan."

The branches of the big tree were stirring near the top, but there was no wind. Someone was climbing the tree, most likely a sniper. Once he got to the top, Salim was a dead man. He had no cover from a rifleman firing down from the treetops, and his 9 mm pistol was no match for a high-powered rifle at a hundred yards.

The Executioner heard a metallic click. McCarter was loading a 40 mm high-explosive round into the breech of his M-203 grenade launcher. He flipped up the grenade launcher sight and aimed carefully at the top of the big tree.

"Spot for me, Striker."

Mack Bolan peered through the crystal-clear lenses of his ranging binoculars. He pushed the button, and two red numbers appeared at the bottom of the picture.

"Ninety-four meters," he said.

McCarter smiled, but it wasn't pleasant. He hated terrorists.

"Piece of cake, Striker. I'll teach the bloody bastard not to climb trees."

Bolan heard the odd *blup* sound as the M-203 fired. The low-velocity grenade arched through the air and disappeared into the branches. The top of the tree suddenly exploded. Leaves and branches flew, and a man's body fell heavily to the ground.

"I don't think you need anyone to spot for you, David."

"I think not, Striker. I bloody well put paid to his account, but now they know we're here. We better get moving."

Bolan nodded. The smaller trees at the edge of the clearing gave them concealment, but not cover. It hid them until they fired again, but if the enemy could locate them, the small tree trunks wouldn't stop rifle and machine-gun bullets. He scanned the area quickly. There was no good cover in sight except Salim's position. To get there, they would have to cross fifty yards of open ground. Riflemen might have trouble hitting moving targets, but a good machine gunner could cut them to pieces.

He kept his head down as a light machine gun opened fire. Full-metal-jacketed bullets tore through the air three feet above the ground. The gunner didn't know exactly where they were; he was simply laying down suppressive fire along the clearing edge. Bolan and McCarter kept low. There are such things as lucky hits, and they could kill a man just as dead as a precisely aimed sniper's bullet. The machine gunner traversed his weapon again, and bullets ripped through the trees.

"Time to go," Bolan said. "You go first, and I'll cover you."

Bolan flipped up his grenade launcher sight and loaded a 40 mm smoke grenade into the M-203's breech. To his left he heard the metallic click-click that told him McCarter had loaded his M-203.

"Ready, Striker."

Bolan nodded. "On my count. Three, two, one, fire!"

The two grenade launchers fired together. Bolan snapped a second smoke round into his M-203, and they fired again. In a smooth, unbroken rhythm, they loaded HE grenades, fired, reloaded and fired again.

The smoke grenades struck first, and clouds of gray-white smoke spread through the area. The four HE grenades shot into the smoke and detonated, sending lethal fragments hissing through the smoke. Eight 40 mm grenades weren't exactly an artillery barrage, but the enemy gunners would keep their heads down for a few seconds.

McCarter was crouched and ready.

Bolan shouldered his M-4 carbine, took aim and shouted, ''Go!''

The Briton shot to his feet and sprinted toward Major Salim's position.

Bolan pulled the trigger of his M-4 and sent a series of short bursts into the smoke. It was providing a fair amount of cover, but the smoke from the four grenades was beginning to dissipate. He saw a red dot suddenly flash toward the little ridge. The last cartridge in the M-4's 30-round magazine was a tracer. His M-4 was empty. Bolan snapped a fresh magazine into his carbine. He risked a quick look and saw McCarter leap into the shallow fold in the ground that protected Major Salim.

There was no time to lose. The smoke was noticeably thinner, not providing as much cover as before. The soldier leaped to his feet and raced after McCarter, zigzagging from side to side. The dirt suddenly flew behind him as an AK-47 bullet smashed into the ground. Damn! Someone could obviously see him. He didn't try to shoot back. To stop and fire back would be suicidal. Bolan kept on running. He heard the snarling bark of an M-4 carbine and the repeated crack of a 9 mm pistol as McCarter and Salim opened fire.

The man with the AK-47 fired another burst, missing by inches. Bolan put everything he had into one last rush. He threw himself down and slid for the lip of the ditch like a base runner trying to steal third. As he slid into the ditch, he slammed into McCarter.

"I really wish you would watch where you are going, Striker," McCarter said dryly. "It is simply not polite to run into someone you know."

Bolan glared at him. He had no breath to waste dealing with McCarter's odd British sense of humor. Major Salim stared at them both. He had heard that Americans and Englishmen were crazy. Apparently, it was true.

"If you two gentlemen are through greeting each other, we have a few minor problems," Salim said. "I think our friends are getting ready to try something. It will take them a few minutes to reorganize, but I think then they will be coming."

McCarter nodded. "Too right, Major. You are the expert here. What do you think we should do?"

"Gentlemen," Salim told them, "I suggest you reload. There are a lot of them. We will need every round if they rush us. Have either of you any 9 mm cartridges you can spare? I have only one full magazine left."

McCarter took out two flat brown boxes of cartridges. "One hundred rounds of 9 mm NATO high velocity. That should do the trick."

Salim looked relieved. Like all combat soldiers, he dreaded running out of ammunition in the middle of a firefight. He began to press cartridges into his empty magazines.

Bolan reached into his equipment case and pulled out a thick black cylinder, which he placed on top of his M-4 carbine, then carefully tightened the mounting clamps. He peered through the sight. The temperature was about ninety degrees. A man's body temperature was nearly nine degrees higher. He couldn't see sharp images through the foliage that gave the enemy cover, but he saw many ghostly white blobs moving toward the edge of the trees.

"I can see a few feet into the trees. Get ready. They'll be coming in a minute."

Bolan had a full 30-round magazine in his carbine. He slipped a 40 mm HE grenade into the M-203 grenade launcher below the carbine's barrel. He was as ready as he would ever be. If they couldn't stop the guerrillas' rush, he intended to take as many of them with him as he could.

He waited tensely. Then a whistle blew, loud and shrill. Twenty or thirty men rushed out of the trees. They were short, stocky, brown-skinned men dressed in dark blue or black clothes. They were shouting something in Indonesian that Bolan couldn't understand. Most of them were clutching AK-47s or Russian SKS rifles.

He pulled the trigger on his grenade launcher and fired a grenade into the center of the rush. As he pulled the trigger of his M-4 carbine and sent five short bursts into the charging men as fast as he could fire, he heard McCarter fire a grenade. The two bombs struck and detonated, filling the air with deadly fragments. Bolan could hear men screaming. Many of the attackers were down, but the rest surged forward, firing their rifles from the hips.

There was no time to reload. Bolan saw two men running forward. They seemed to have no weapons. Then he saw the grenades in their hands.

"Grenades!" he shouted, and drew his .44 Magnum Desert Eagle from its holster in one fast fluid motion. He fired twice as soon as his sights were on. The big pistol bucked and roared. Two heavy bullets smashed into the first grenadier, and he went down instantly. Bolan swung his sights smoothly, aiming at the second grenadier. Too late! His arm was already moving forward as he completed his throw. Bolan saw the black blur of the grenade as it flew through the air straight toward him.

The grenade landed three feet short, but it was still moving forward. Instinctively, he thrust his Desert Eagle at the grenade. There was no time to aim. He simply pulled the trigger twice. The dirt geysered up in front of the grenade. Bolan saw it bounce into the air and fall back toward the guerrilla grenadier. The Executioner dropped below the edge of the ditch. The grenade exploded, and lethal fragments whined overhead. Bolan snapped a fresh magazine into his big .44 Magnum and risked a quick look. He could see nine or ten bodies lying on the ground. The rest of the attackers were in full retreat, running back toward the trees. McCarter was encouraging them with some fast semiautomatic fire.

"I think they've bloody well had enough, Striker. They won't try that again."

Bolan loaded a fresh magazine into his carbine. McCarter was probably right. Their attackers were amateurish, but they had been brave and determined. The problem was, what would they try next?

An hour crawled by. The heat and the humidity were stifling, but Bolan was determined not to be caught off guard. He looked through his carbine's thermal sight, slowly scanning the low ridge where the enemy was concentrated. He stopped his scanning suddenly and stared at one spot near the center of the ridge, where he could see a group of white ghostly figures moving through the foliage.

"Targets!" he said. "Four or five people moving forward toward the edge of the trees. They're up to something. Let's give them a warm welcome!"

McCarter smiled grimly as he slipped an HE grenade into his grenade launcher.

"Too right, Striker, it's the only proper thing to do."

Bolan's M-203 was already loaded. He watched carefully as the ghostly figures in his infrared sight moved to the edge of the trees and stopped. It was hard to figure what they were doing. A four-man charge would be suicidal. He and McCarter would cut them to pieces before they had gone ten yards. It didn't matter what they were doing. They had stopped, and they were stupid enough to have bunched up.

"On my count, fire HE. Three, two—"

"Hold your fire!" Salim shouted. "Don't shoot. White flag!"

A piece of cloth would be the same temperature as the background of trees and branches. It wouldn't show up well in infrared. Bolan and McCarter peered over the tops of their thermal sights. Salim was right.

Someone was waving a large white piece of cloth tied to a branch.

"What do you think they are up to, Major?" McCarter asked.

"God knows, but I do not," Salim said. "Perhaps they want to surrender."

McCarter snorted. "Not bloody likely!"

Someone shouted from the trees, "Hold your fire. We want to talk to you."

"We have nothing to say to you unless you wish to surrender," Salim replied. "In that case, I can promise you that you will not be shot. You will be arrested and given a fair trial. Just lay down your weapons and come out."

The man in the trees wasn't amused. "You are in no position to make demands. We are. We have your pretty whore, Mara Tharin, here and we will kill her if you do not surrender immediately."

"How do I know you are telling the truth? You may have killed her already."

"Oh, I think we can convince you. Sing for your friends, bitch. Sing loud. They want to hear your lovely voice."

There was a moment of silence. Then a woman screamed in wordless agony.

The guerrillas obviously had a woman there, but how did they know it was really Mara Tharin? The white flag proved nothing. They could have killed the woman and taken her skirt from her dead body.

"Bring her out where I can see her. If she is alive, we will talk. If not, you can go to hell! We will have nothing to talk about," Salim said coldly.

"Very well. Hold your fire. We are coming out,

and we will bring the woman with us. But I warn you, any treachery and she dies instantly.''

Four men emerged from the trees and moved forward. One of them waved the white flag. Two others carried AK-47s ready in their hands. The fourth man shoved Mara Tharin in front of him.

Mack Bolan looked through the optical sight of his M-4 carbine. He could have killed the man with the flag and the two riflemen in three short, quick bursts, but he couldn't shoot the man behind Tharin without taking a chance of killing her. McCarter was studying the advancing group through his optical sight.

"Do you have a clear shot at the man holding Mara?" Bolan asked quietly. He didn't want to risk being overheard by the approaching men.

"Negative, Striker. I can take the other three, but not the leader. Miss Tharin is in my line of fire."

Salim was listening. "We cannot trust these murderous bastards. They mean to kill us all. If either of you get a clear shot at him, take it, and then kill the others immediately."

Bolan and McCarter nodded. They weren't playing games. A quick surgical strike was the only chance they had to save Mara Tharin's life.

The four guerrillas advanced slowly until they were ten yards away from the ditch. Mara Tharin slowed them. It is hard to walk rapidly when someone was pressing a sharp knife against your throat. McCarter stared at her and her captor. Her face was bruised and her lips were swollen. She was naked below the waist except for her black stretch panties. Her long bare legs would have been attractive under other circumstances. Now they made her look helpless and vulnerable.

The man holding Tharin seemed to be the leader. The party stopped about ten yards from their position. The leader kept his body behind the woman's as much as possible with his knife pressed against her throat. That was smart, but he was larger than she was. Bolan put the crosshairs of his optical sight two inches to the right of Tharin's ear. If the man holding her made a mistake, he was a dead man. It wouldn't be fair, but Bolan didn't care. If the guerrillas had killed Tharin in a firefight, that was one thing. To take her prisoner and torture her was another.

"Let her go," Salim said. "She is just a civilian."

"I have no time to waste. I have read her ID. She is an intelligence agent," the guerrilla leader said. "Come out now and negotiate. Otherwise, I will kill her."

"How do I know you will not shoot me as soon as I stand up?" Salim asked.

"We are FRETILIN. We are not murderers like you Indonesians. We have not killed the girl. We will not kill you if you surrender. Throw down your weapons and come out, or we will kill the bitch!"

"FRETILIN?" McCarter asked.

"The Revolutionary Front for an Independent East Timor. A grand title for a bunch of filthy scum and murderers. Do not believe them. They are murderous bastards. They will kill us, and then they will kill her, too." Salim glared furiously at the man who held Tharin. If looks could kill, the man would have died where he stood.

"We can't just stay here and let them kill her," McCarter said.

Salim started to get to his feet. "You are right. Time to go talk to the bastards. Cover me," he said.

"I think not. You shouldn't go," McCarter objected.

Salim was startled. He wasn't used to being contradicted.

"Think about it. You are obviously the one they are after. They want to kill you, not Striker or me. They can have no idea who or what we are. Your uniform tells them who you are. They may have a sniper ready to kill you the instant you expose yourself. You stay here. I'll go."

Salim nodded. He didn't like it, but he knew the Briton was right.

"Go with God, then. Striker and I will cover you."

McCarter slowly stood up. His skin crawled as he waited for a sniper's shot, but no one fired. He turned to Bolan. "One thing, Striker. If they kill me, don't let any of them get away alive."

Bolan nodded as McCarter stepped up over the lip of the ditch and strode toward the group of guerrillas. He held his Ranger carbine low, muzzle down, ready to snap up and fire.

The enemy leader looked surprised. He stared at the big Englishman.

"I thought the KIPAM officer was in command. Are you authorized to negotiate with me?"

"Too right I am," McCarter said in an ice-cold voice, "and these are my terms. You release Miss Tharin immediately, and I'll let you go back to your position alive. Otherwise, if you hurt her or kill her, you're a dead man. I'll shoot you down where you stand."

The guerrilla leader stared at McCarter. There was something about the look in McCarter's green eyes and the tone of his voice that carried total conviction.

Still, he couldn't just release Mara Tharin and slink back to his men. The loss of face would be intolerable.

"You are bluffing. You will surrender, or I will kill her very slowly and very painfully. I will cut her pretty face, and you can stand there and listen to her scream."

He took the knife away from Tharin's throat and pressed the sharp point lightly against her cheek. The woman moaned and the guerrilla who held her smiled cruelly. He pressed the point of his knife a little harder. A drop of blood trickled down Tharin's cheek.

"I am not bluffing. I will count to three, and then I will cut her. I will slash her pretty face to the bone. One, two—"

He had forgotten one thing. The razor-sharp edge of his knife was no longer against Mara Tharin's throat. Suddenly, she twisted her head and bit his wrist, sinking in her strong white teeth as deeply as she could. He screamed in pain and surprise. His other arm held her tightly, but she managed to twist to the left. For a second or two, part of his head and chest were exposed. McCarter snapped up his carbine and fired. A 3-round burst tore through his chest. He dropped his knife and staggered backward. That was the last thing he did. Bolan had a clear shot, and he put a burst through the terrorist's head. He was dead before his body hit the ground.

McCarter pivoted smoothly and cut down the man with the white flag and the rifleman beside him in two fast bursts. He whirled to shoot the other rifleman. Too slow! The gunner had raised his AK-47, but Bolan's M-4 carbine snarled before he could pull the trigger. Six full-metal-jacketed bullets ripped through the rifleman's body. He lost all interest in shooting McCarter and went down hard.

The whole affair had taken three or four seconds. There was a sudden silence. The other guerrillas back on the ridge were stunned by the sudden shooting, but that wouldn't last long. Mara Tharin was reaching for the ground, grabbing her purse and an AK-47 rifle. Whatever the woman was trying to do, McCarter knew there was no time for it.

"Run!" he shouted in his best command voice. He took his own advice and dived for the lip of the ditch as a machine gun opened fire behind them. He heard the rapid crackling sound of Bolan's M-4 as he fired repeated bursts of covering fire at the edge of the trees. Tharin was a step in front of him. They tumbled into the ditch together as machine-gun bullets shrieked overhead.

The silence was deafening as both sides ceased fire. Bolan took a quick look around. McCarter and Tharin looked all right. The woman looked faintly ridiculous crouching in her torn top and panties, but she was busily checking the AK-47 she had snatched up. She didn't like the way the guerrillas had treated her and planned to kill the first one she got in her sights.

Bolan didn't like the situation. The heat and humidity were brutal. They had no food or water, and they were using up their ammunition rapidly. But he could see no easy way out. There was no chance of their getting away during daylight. He glanced at his watch. Sunset was still several hours away.

"It looks like we're in trouble," he said to Salim.

"Someone is about to get in trouble, but I do not think it is us. Listen!" the major said with an evil grin.

Bolan listened intently. At first, he heard nothing. He had been exposed to a lot of shooting in the past hour, and he was slightly deaf. Then he heard it. A low steady whine from the west. Jet engines. The Indonesian air force was on the way! The other helicopter had to have made it back and reported the attack. The rumbling whine grew louder and louder, and four needle-nosed F-16s flashed over the clearing. Bolan could see the sunlight reflected off their polished aluminum wings and the darker olive-drab shapes of the five-hundred-pound bombs under each wing.

The F-16s flew in a wide turn and made a second pass over the clearing.

Mara Tharin was puzzled. "What are they waiting for? Why don't they bomb those filthy bastards to hell?"

Bolan knew. "They can't be sure where we are. They have to know exactly where we are before they make their bombing runs. Otherwise, they might blow us to hell along with the enemy."

He turned to Salim. "Are there any standard Indonesian recognition signals? Any way we can mark the targets for them?"

The major shook his head. "No, if this were a normal patrol, I would have a radio, and I would tell them where we are. Without a radio, I am not sure what we can do."

"Excuse me, Major, but if a radio is what you need, I have one."

Mara Tharin opened the flap of her large brown purse and took out a small black radio. Bolan smiled in amazement. There seemed to be no limit to what she carried in her purse. She handed the small radio to Salim.

"It is set on the standard emergency frequency, Major. They should be monitoring that," Tharin stated.

Salim extended the antenna and began to speak rapidly in Indonesian.

Bolan watched as the flight of F-16s turned away and started to lose altitude in a shallow dive. They seemed to be leaving the area, but he wasn't concerned. He had seen enough fighter strikes on ground targets to know they were preparing to attack coming in fast and low.

The four F-16s flew across the treetops, their Pratt & Whitney F100 engines howling as they flashed toward their target at five hundred miles per hour. Bolan was painfully aware that he was standing only two hundred yards from the target point. McCarter and Tharin were hugging the ground like sensible people.

Bolan would have loved to join them, but Salim was standing, watching calmly as if he were observing an exercise, and Bolan would be damned if he blinked first.

He kept his binoculars on the Indonesian planes. The Indonesian air force pilots were determined to show the KIPAM major what they could do. Bolan was willing to be impressed, but he disliked intensely the idea of being hit by friendly fire. He didn't have any more time to worry about it. The wings of the F-16s were suddenly haloed in orange fire as their rocket launchers ripple-fired lethal showers of 2.75-inch air-to-ground rockets. The rockets shot overhead, trailing orange flame and gray-white smoke.

Bolan watched, fascinated, as the rockets began to strike and detonate. The low, rocky ridge seemed to vanish in fountains of sand and the gray smoke of burning high explosives. Each F-16 had launched thirty-eight rockets in a few seconds. The results were very impressive.

Salim smiled. The stocky Indonesian major seemed to be enjoying himself immensely. "The first attack is for defense suppression, Mr. Belasko. It confuses and demoralizes the enemy. Now, the—" Salim's words were lost in an ear shattering shriek as the four F-16s flashed by less than two hundred feet overhead.

Salim's smile broadened. "As I was saying, the second flight will deliver the main attack. Here they come."

Bolan swung his binoculars. Four more F-16s were coming, flying even lower than the first four. The big American could see the noses of their bombs, ominous, hanging in olive-drab clusters under their wings and fuselages. "Each of them carries four 250-kilogram—or as you would say, 550-pound—bombs," Salim remarked, "and 20 mm Gatling guns also. They will—"

Whatever else Salim was going to say was lost in the roar of jet engines and the sudden sustained snarling roar of 20 mm Gatling guns firing 100 rounds per second. Bolan saw the bombs drop away as the F-16s shrieked overhead. Retarding fins snapped open to delay the bombs' fall and give the F-16s just enough time to clear the area before their bombs struck and exploded. The target area disappeared in smoke and dust, shattered branches flew, and the ground shuddered as the bombs struck and detonated.

The aircraft shrieked away and were gone. Bolan

was glad they were on his side. He was completely convinced that the Indonesian air force knew how to fly close-support missions.

"What's that?" Salim shouted over the howl of the F-16s' engines.

Gray-white smoke streaked from the left side of the target area and shot up after the four F-16s. Bolan could see the small dull green missile flashing toward the last jet. The Indonesian pilot saw it, too. His only chance was to outfly it, but the missile was locked on. He pulled his F-16 into a hard right turn, but the missile had been designed to kill maneuvering targets. It struck the tailpipe of the jet and vanished in a ball of yellow fire. It was too low for the pilot to eject. The stricken jet smashed into the ground and exploded in great burst of orange fire.

Major Salim swore bitterly. That was all anyone could do. There was no use searching through the wreckage. The pilot had died instantly. There was nothing for them to do but wait for the other helicopter to pick them up.

CHAPTER FOUR

The General's Headquarters

The general was asleep when the phone rang. He hadn't slept for sixteen hours. He swore at the insistent ringing as he slowly woke up. He glanced at the clock—two o'clock in the morning. There was no one he wanted to talk to, but the call had to be important. He had left strict orders not to be disturbed unless it was a real emergency or very important. Obviously, someone thought it was.

He wasn't in a mood to be polite.

"Hello," he rasped.

"Pardon me for disturbing you, sir, but the marshal is on the line. He says it is most urgent. He must speak to you immediately."

That got the adrenaline flowing. The marshal was the only officer he reported to directly. He was an old man who liked his sleep. If he was calling at 2:00 a.m., something was up. The general recognized the voice of his chief of staff. A good man, not easily rattled.

"Do you know the subject of the call?" he asked.

"No, sir, only that the marshal says that it is urgent and he must speak to you personally."

"Very well, connect him."

The general looked at the base of his phone. A green light was blinking rapidly. The built-in mini-computer was checking to confirm that the line was secure. The light stopped blinking and shone a steady green. There was a click, and he heard the marshal's familiar voice.

"I am sorry to call you at this late hour, but I must meet with the president and the war council in a few hours. How are things going in Indonesia?"

The general relaxed slightly. The marshal wanted information. There had been no disaster while he slept.

"Things are going well, sir. We have begun preliminary operations. We have staged attacks on the Australians in East Timor and the Indonesians in West Timor. Most of the attacks have been successful. Some of our groups have suffered casualties, but that is only to be expected. We have ships with supplies and reinforcements ready to enter the area. We can escalate the conflict at any time. We are forcing the Indonesians to commit their reserves to West Timor. When we start phase two, they will find it difficult to oppose us."

"Good, but there is something you may not know. The Americans are committing troops in East Timor. A battalion of Rangers and a reinforced battalion of Marines. They will be in position in less than twelve hours. How do you evaluate this?"

The general took a deep breath. His career might well depend on what happened next. It was one thing to try to destabilize Indonesia but quite another to risk war between his country and the United States.

"Two battalions? I do not think that is significant,

sir. The Americans are only making a cheap gesture to reassure their allies. I do not think they have the will to fight a real battle. I recommend that we proceed at once with phase two.''

The line was silent for a few seconds. Then the marshal spoke slowly and clearly. "Very well, General, you have my full authorization. Execute Red Dragon Rising immediately!''

Dili, East Timor

BOLAN AND McCARTER walked down Juan de Calmera Street. Downtown Dili was a mess. The capital of East Timor showed signs of heavy fighting and looting everywhere. Half of the buildings were burned-out shells, and their walls were pockmarked with bullet holes. The East Timorese and the Indonesian militias had obviously gone at it hot and heavy before the UN peacekeeping force had arrived. The streets were peaceful enough. People were going quietly about their business, but Bolan's practiced eye noted several patrols of heavily armed Australian soldiers watching the crowds.

They passed a burned-out Chinese temple and saw a squat, nearly intact building ahead, the American flag flying from the flagpole in front. A hastily painted sign proclaimed that this was the United States Consulate. The approach to the building's entrance was neatly sandbagged, and four United States Marines were standing guard. They weren't there for show. They were dressed in green combat fatigues and held M-16 A-2 rifles.

The sergeant in command spoke politely as Bolan

and McCarter walked up. "Can I help you, gentlemen?"

McCarter reached slowly and carefully into his pocket. He didn't want to startle men holding automatic rifles. He pulled out his passport and handed it to the sergeant.

"I'm David Green," McCarter said, using his current alias. "I am a British citizen. This is my associate, Mr. Michael Belasko. He's an American citizen, a special observer from your Department of Justice. We're here to attend a briefing. The assistant cultural attaché is expecting us."

The sergeant checked his clipboard. "Right. Sanchez, these are the men the Swede wants to see. You can tell they're really interested in Indonesian culture. Escort them up."

Bolan didn't mind the sarcasm. He supposed that there must be some real cultural attachés somewhere in the U.S. diplomatic service, but all that he had ever met were CIA agents. They followed Corporal Sanchez into the building, which was jammed with cluttered desks manned by people talking on telephones or shuffling papers. They went up a flight of stairs and stopped at a closed office door. Sanchez rapped on the door.

"Mr. Belasko and Mr. Green to see you, ma'am."

A woman's voice said, "Come in. Please close the door behind you."

They went in. A very tall, pale-skinned woman sat behind a cluttered desk. A sign on the desk said Ingrid Johannsen. They didn't have to ask. She was obviously the Swede, and she didn't waste time on pleasantries. She stared at them with her bright blue eyes. "What is the challenge?" she asked.

"The sun is rising in the west," McCarter responded.

Johannsen nodded. "Correct. The response is 'Who knows where it will set?' I am Viking. Authenticate."

McCarter smiled thinly. He thought the CIA's challenge-and-response system was bloody silly, but that was how the game was played. "Dagger," he said, "and my friend is Striker."

"Very well. Gentlemen, I am the acting station chief for East Timor. I don't know who you are or who you work for, but I have orders from the station chief at the Jakarta embassy to give you all possible assistance in performance of your mission." She paused and smiled at them cynically. "Whatever that may be."

She wasn't happy with mysterious people appearing in her area of operations with no idea of what they were there to do.

"We could tell you, but then, of course, we would have to kill you," McCarter told her.

It was an old joke, but it conveyed a message. Ingrid Johannsen wasn't cleared to know about Stony Man, and she probably never would be. She shrugged.

"All right, I understand. I don't like it, but I do understand. What can I do to assist you, Mr. Green?"

"We need a secure satellite communications system. We need to communicate with our mission control center."

"I'll have someone take you there immediately," she announced to McCarter.

She smiled at Mack Bolan. "Please stay, Mr. Belasko. I've ordered a fresh pot of coffee, and there are a few more questions I'd like to ask you."

McCARTER WAITED until the door was closed and locked. The Dili secure communications room wasn't very impressive, but at least it had a satellite communications system set up and running. Two glowing green lights told him the satcom was ready to transmit and receive. That was good, but it was CIA equipment. He wondered what else it might be ready to do. He reached into his pocket and pulled out what looked like a TV remote controller. For all he knew, it might actually be able to control a TV set, but Gadgets Schwarz had added a number of special features.

McCarter turned it on and slowly scanned the CIA satcom. Two red lights came on. The equipment was bugged. He looked carefully under the keyboard. He wasn't an electronics genius, but he had listened very carefully when Schwarz had explained the equipment. There were two miniaturized electronic devices attached to the bottom of the keyboard. One was a voice recorder. Every word he said would be recorded. The other was more subtle. It was a keystroke recorder. If he chose to type a message for coded transmission, every key he pushed would be recorded. Someone was very curious about messages that might be sent or received by the satcom. McCarter smiled cynically. He would bet a month's pay that somebody's name was Johannsen.

He pushed two buttons on Schwarz's device. Nothing seemed to happen, but the two red lights flickered and went out. If anyone was monitoring them, it would look as if they were having severe technical problems. There was nothing their owners could do about it. They could hardly burst in and say, ''Please don't transmit until we replace our recorders.''

McCarter pressed the transmit button.

"Granite Home, this is Phoenix One. Acknowledge, Granite Home."

His voice flashed upward into space and was instantly transmitted to a second relay satellite over the United States and down to the antennae at the Stony Man Farm operations center. The operations center's satcom radios were monitored twenty-four hours a day when the Stony Man team was deployed.

"Stand by, Phoenix One."

McCarter waited for a few seconds, then heard a familiar voice. Barbara Price's voice was as clear as if she were standing a few feet away.

"Glad to hear from you, David. We were beginning to get a little worried. What happened?"

"Striker and I are now in the American consulate in Dili. I thought I should report to you as soon as possible. Here's what happened."

McCarter told her everything that had happened after their plane had landed in West Timor. He tried to cover everything precisely, with no omissions or exaggerations.

"There's one other thing I should tell you. Striker and I examined the weapons left behind by the guerrillas. They were all Russian-type infantry weapons, but they weren't Russian manufacture. The AK-47s were Hungarian. The SKSs were made in Bulgaria. Also, they were almost brand-new. Few signs of use. Most of them looked like they were just out of their shipping grease. The Bear will be interested in that. Someone definitely is shipping weapons into Timor."

"He certainly will. That's the first piece of hard evidence anyone has turned up."

"That's all I have to report. Do you have any questions?"

"Yes. Where's Striker?"

McCarter grinned. "At the moment, he is drinking coffee with a lovely seven-foot-tall blonde who says her name is Viking."

There were ten seconds of silence. Then Price spoke with a cool tone in her voice. "Is that a joke?"

"Certainly not, Barbara. A slight exaggeration perhaps. She is only six foot six and not all that pretty. She's the acting CIA chief of station in Dili. She is trying to get Striker's life story out of him. I'm sure he's enjoying the coffee and telling outrageous lies. Seriously, ask Aaron to find out as much as you can about her. She had this room bugged, but Gadgets's latest toy scrambled her equipment."

"Understood, we'll check her out. Here's Aaron, now. He wants to talk to you."

"David, I understand you have been having a little excitement," Aaron Kurtzman, Stony Man's computer expert, stated.

"A little. I've filled Barbara in. Do you have any words of wisdom for us?"

"As a matter of fact, I do. 'There is no bear, but there are many snakes.'"

"Pardon me," McCarter said, "your transmission not understood." It wasn't true that he had no sense of humor, but it was a very British sense of humor. He didn't always understand things that the others on the Stony Man team thought extremely funny. Still, it wasn't like Kurtzman to make jokes when he was communicating via satcom.

Kurtzman chuckled. "Sorry about that. I'm just back from a high-level intelligence meeting at the

Pentagon. Those are the latest Washington buzz words, and they are relevant to your mission. They mean that the Soviet Union has gone away, so there's no bear. There are a number of countries and groups hostile to the United States. They're the snakes.''

''Concept understood, but what is the relevance to our current mission?'' McCarter asked.

''The purpose of the meeting was to compare available data and try to determine which snake is trying to destabilize Indonesia.''

''Were they successful?''

''No, but they have come up with a short list— Russia, China, North Korea, Vietnam and India. They are going to concentrate on them and have another meeting tomorrow.''

McCarter wasn't impressed by the list. Surely the cream of U.S. intelligence could do better than that. ''What do you think?''

''Well, I'd take India off the list. The government is completely occupied with Pakistan. North Korea doesn't have the resources. The Russians do, of course, but they have troubles of their own. Still, it could be them, but most of the spooks seem to think it's China or Vietnam.''

McCarter understood, but it wasn't all that helpful. They were still fighting shadows.

''Any other developments since we deployed?''

''Yes. There have been several serious incidents in the Indonesian province of Aceh. That's the northwest tip of the island of Sumatra. There have been major riots, clashes between armed separatist groups and the army and police. Over one hundred civilians dead and thirty soldiers. The Indonesian government has declared martial law. A group calling itself the Free Sumatra Movement says the Indonesian army is committing horrible atrocities. The UN Security Council is meeting tomorrow. All this is making the President unhappy. It sounds like whoever is trying to destabilize Indonesia has shifted into high gear.''

"It sounds like East Timor all over again. What's the U.S. government doing about it?''

"Deploying more military forces to Indonesia. An aircraft carrier and its battle group are moving down from Taiwan. A reinforced Army brigade will start deploying to East Timor tomorrow. We're building up ground troops there, because the Indonesians don't want foreign troops on Indonesian soil. At least, not yet.

"Speaking of reinforcements, the rest of the team will be flying out tomorrow. They'll meet you in Dili. By the way, I checked with some CIA contacts concerning Miss Johannsen. I thought you might run into her if you got to Dili. They say she is a first-class agent, loyal to the CIA and the United States. They use words like 'self-starter' and 'hard charger.' She has very high efficiency reports.

"That's the good news. The bad news is that she's extremely ambitious. A lot of people who know her say they don't trust her. They say she'd sell out her own mother to get ahead. Watch your back when she's around.''

"Understood. Is there any change in our mission?''

"Not yet, but Hal's meeting with the President tomorrow. I'll contact you if there is anything new. Continue investigating the situation on Timor. Any questions?''

"Negative. Your message understood. Phoenix One out.''

McCarter turned off the satcom. He put Schwarz's little electronic marvel in his pocket and opened the comm room door. Mack Bolan was waiting for him.

"I've just talked to Barbara and Aaron. They said—"

"Tell me on the way. We're off to see the Wizard."

McCarter cocked an eyebrow.

"The Wizard. He runs the CIA agents network in East Timor. He's an old friend of yours. He'll be glad to see you. Let's go."

CHAPTER FIVE

The Maya Beach Hotel, Dili, East Timor

Mack Bolan and David McCarter walked slowly down the street. The sun was going down and it was a little cooler, but no one else was walking fast, and they didn't want to attract attention. Both of them carried nylon zipper flight bags, loaded with submachine guns and a dozen magazines.

McCarter waited until they were a block away from the American consulate, then asked the big American, "What did you tell the fair Miss Johannsen, Striker?"

"The censored story of my life. She's a very understanding young woman. She knows that none of it is my fault. I'm just an innocent victim of society."

McCarter snorted. That simply didn't deserve a reply.

"What did she tell you?"

"Not much. Don't trust Mara Tharin. She works for Indonesian counterintelligence. She'll probably have us both shot as spies next week. Don't trust you. You're an Englishman, after all."

They reached the Maya Beach Hotel and went inside. They didn't stop at the desk, and they stayed away from the elevators.

As they walked down the third-floor hall to room 316, Bolan was alert. He kept his hand close to the butt of his .44 Magnum Desert Eagle, but saw nothing. He knocked carefully on the door of room 316, remembering that the man they were going to see was fond of 12-gauge shotguns and .357 Magnum revolvers and believed in shooting first whenever possible. The soldier was careful not to stand in front of the door when he knocked, just in case the Wizard was feeling nervous.

Fred Byrnes looked through the peephole, unlocked the door and let them in. Bolan smelled the familiar scent of gun-cleaning fluid. A 12-gauge Remington pump shotgun was lying on a small table, its gaping muzzle pointing towards the door. Byrnes held a .357 Magnum Colt Python revolver in his right hand.

Bolan raised an eyebrow. "Expecting trouble, Fred?"

Byrnes grinned. "I always expect trouble when I'm in the field, Striker. I figure I'll live a lot longer that way. Besides, you have to clean and oil your guns once a day in this goddamned climate, or you'll end up with a pile of rust. Sit down, and I'll pour you a cool one. You can have anything you like, as long as it's beer or Jack Daniel's."

Bolan saw a young African American woman sitting quietly at a small table. A notepad computer was open in front of her.

Byrnes noticed Bolan's glance. "That's Amy Andrews. She's our resident computer genius. She's so new she hasn't got a code name, but I'm working on getting her one. Amy, this is Striker, and the other one is... What name are you using this time?"

"My passport says David Green," McCarter replied.

"Pleased to meet you, gentlemen," Amy said softly.

"Now, how about that beer before we get down to business?"

Bolan thought for a second. He drank very little, if at all, when he was on a mission. It wasn't that he had anything against drinking, but anything that reduced his awareness or slowed his reflexes could be fatal. Still, he remembered that being hospitable was important to Fred Byrnes.

"I'll have a beer," he replied.

"I will, as well," McCarter added.

Byrnes smiled and pulled three bottles from the small hotel-room refrigerator and passed them around.

"Amy doesn't drink. She was very strictly brought up, but I'm working on corrupting her morals. Any CIA field agent has got to drink. It goes with the job."

Byrnes sipped his beer and smiled. "Well," he said cheerfully, "things are going to start heating up now that you and Green are here, Striker."

Amy smiled again. "That's all right. Things are getting exciting. I like it. It's just like a movie. It makes me feel like a real spy."

Byrnes chuckled. "That's a dirty word, Amy. A nice girl like you shouldn't say it. Remember, other countries have spies. We have agents."

Bolan smiled. He had heard those words a thousand times before. Perhaps the CIA really believed them.

Bolan sipped his beer. "How are you, Fred? It's been a while."

"Damned right it has, Striker. Still living a life of travel and adventure?"

Bolan took out a small flat black box that Gadgets Schwarz had given him. He turned it on and scanned the room. No red lights came on. If any bugs were in the room, they weren't the electronic variety.

"I'm doing all right, Fred. What about you? The last time I saw you, you were down in Bolivia and talking about retiring again. I'm surprised to see you here in Indonesia."

"You know how it is. When you've done this kind of work as long as I have, retirement can get awfully boring, awfully fast. Think about it. What the hell would you do if you retired?"

Bolan frowned. He did know how it was. When you had risked your life a thousand times, peace and quiet could be unendurable. He couldn't imagine what he would do if retirement was an option.

"I was back in Washington when I was contacted by the assistant director of operations. He said he had real problems. The CIA had to step up their efforts in Indonesia. The CIA has too many satellite jockeys and computer geniuses and not enough old hands like me. He said he badly needed someone in Timor who had a lot of experience operating in the field and establishing networks of local agents rapidly. Everybody back at headquarters thought old Fred was the only man for the job."

Byrnes smiled cynically. "I knew they were shining me on, but what the hell. I wanted to get back in the field, so here I am. How about you? Still working for the same people?"

"Yeah," he replied. "Sometimes."

Byrnes sighed. He had the natural curiosity of a good intelligence agent, but he knew that sustained probing by the CIA's Jakarta station had not been able to find out who the two men really were or whom they worked for. He would only find out if they decided he needed know and decided to tell him. He took another sip of beer and changed the subject.

"How well do you know Johannsen? Do you trust her?"

That was interesting. Maybe Byrnes knew something Bolan didn't.

"I just met her today, so I don't know her very well, but I don't have any reason not to trust her. Do you?"

Byrnes scowled. "Nothing concrete, but there are quite a few people in the CIA who don't trust her. We'd better keep an eye on her."

Bolan was puzzled. That sounded like CIA paranoia, but maybe Byrnes had survived thirty years as an agent in the field because he suspected everybody. Still, that left one obvious question.

"If you don't trust her, Fred, why is she your contact?"

Byrnes snorted. "Because she's all I could get. Indonesia was a backwater as far as the Company was concerned until last month. The Jakarta station is a joke, and the Indonesians know everyone we have stationed there."

Bolan knew that was true and he knew why, but it wasn't the time to discuss it if he and Byrnes were going to work together. Maybe he was getting paranoid, but could he trust Fred Byrnes? Probably. The Bolivian drug cartel hadn't been able to buy him. Unless the man had changed in the past couple of years, he wouldn't sell out now.

Bolan set down his glass. "Maybe we should get down to business."

"All right," Byrnes agreed. "What do you know about my operation, Striker?"

"Not much. My organization told me you are in charge of CIA operations in Dili. They gave me your location and the contact phrases. That's all I really know. Why don't you fill me in?"

"All right. About two months ago, the President put pressure on the CIA to do a lot more in Indonesia. The director of operations knew he had very little field capability there. He sent a group of people down here to get things going. I'm handling East Timor, trying to develop a network of agents that can provide human intelligence capability. My objectives are to locate any evidence of foreign intervention, arms shipments, secret bases, and to gather information on the local Indonesian leaders and find out if any of them have sold out to separatist movements or foreign powers."

Amy Andrews looked puzzled. She had only been working with Fred Byrnes for a few days, and he was a real field agent. It was exciting, but a lot of what he said was incomprehensible to her.

"What do you mean when you say you're developing a network of agents? Doesn't the CIA have plenty of agents they can send in?"

Byrnes chuckled. "You've been seeing too many movies, Amy. Things don't work that way. CIA agents don't do the actual spying. Look at me or Striker, or you, for that matter. Could any of us pass for Indonesians? Even if we could, none of us speaks Indonesian. No, what we have do is recruit people who live in the country we are going to operate in. CIA agents like me control these people and direct their operations."

"I don't understand. How can you just come in here and recruit Indonesians to spy for the CIA?"

Byrnes smiled cynically. "You can. You can always find people who will do it if you know how to look. Cocaine production is big business. A lot of people are involved. Where there are a lot of people, some of them are always unhappy. Some of them want something very badly, to get rich, to change the government, to get revenge because they think they were treated badly."

Andrews looked both fascinated and repelled. She had found out how things really work, and she didn't like it. Bolan understood how she felt. It sounded ruthless. Byrnes seemed to think of the people he recruited as pawns on a chessboard, not real human beings. If some of them were killed, he would shrug his shoulders and recruit replacements. Bolan knew that most intelligence services worked that way. It was why he had never really trusted any of them, American or foreign. Byrnes didn't see anything wrong with it. After thirty years with the CIA, it seemed as natural to him as breathing.

Byrnes hadn't noticed Andrews's look. He wouldn't have understood what bothered her if he had. It would never have occurred to him that anyone would be upset by standard CIA operating methods.

"Getting any results?" Bolan asked.

"Yes. Not as much as I'd like, but I'm starting to get some. My real problem is time and the pressure I'm getting from those desk jockeys in Washington. They think anything can be done the day before yesterday if they throw enough money at it. Now, if I'd had a few months to recruit my agents, things would be running smoothly. But I've only had four weeks, and I couldn't start slowly. Washington is screaming for results right now. The President is after the director, and he's after me. I don't really know the people I've recruited. Some of them may have been sent by Indonesian intelligence to find out what I'm up to. That means I've got to be careful not to blow my cover. Anyway, let me show you what I've got so far.''

Andrews tapped her computer's keys. A map of the island of Timor appeared on the screen. Yellow dots appeared in a dozen places, and yellow lines crisscrossed the ocean around the island. Byrnes pointed at the display.

''Yellow dots are where my agents report arms shipments. The yellow lines are the paths of ships that could have delivered the weapons. That's based on satellite surveillance data I got from Washington. Amy put that data into the computer. There's not much she can't do with a computer.''

Andrews blushed. It meant a great deal to her to be praised by the legendary Fred Byrnes.

Bolan was impressed. It was a neat piece of work, but he had a few questions.

''What do you think it means, Fred?''

''Well, Washington is right. Someone is pouring shiploads of weapons into East Timor, and West Timor, too. Notice that four of the twelve dots are in West Timor. I don't think they're just stockpiling weapons for a rainy day. All those landings took place in the last two months. Somebody is planning to do something serious, and they are going to do it soon.''

Bolan nodded. It was hard to come to any other conclusion.

"Do all of the suspect ships originate from the same country, Fred?"

"No, dammit. That's the problem. Some of them came from North Korea, some from China and others from Vietnam and Russia. And remember what I said, these ships could have delivered weapons, but some of them didn't. The U.S. doesn't have continuous satellite surveillance in this area. We've never actually spotted a ship unloading. That may be because the people who are doing this are smart enough to plot the orbits of our surveillance satellites and only unload a ship when they know there's a gap in our coverage."

McCarter had been listening quietly.

"Suppose we raided one of these sites, Fred. If we dropped in unannounced, we might learn a great deal," he suggested.

Bolan liked McCarter's idea, but he could see one big problem.

"How fresh is your data, Fred? It doesn't take that long to unload infantry weapons from a ship."

Byrnes smiled wryly and shook his head. "You're a hard man to get ahead of, Striker, but you're right. That's the problem. I'm depending on the human agents, not some superscientific nonsense. I don't dare let most of my agents carry radios. They'd be shot immediately if they were caught with one, so I have to wait until they have been out to the site and then get back and report in person. My latest information on these sites is three to four days old."

Bolan frowned. He knew from bitter personal experience that a raid based on three-day-old intelligence could be disastrous.

Byrnes noticed Bolan's expression.

"I'm sorry. Striker. I know what you need, but so far I haven't been able to get it. If we could get better satellite coverage and an instant alert from Washington, then maybe we could do it."

The Executioner thought it over. Hal Brognola had seemed sure he could get any kind of support they needed. Bolan would get in touch with Barbara Price and Aaron Kurtzman and see what they could arrange. He was about to say what he might be able to do when someone knocked at the door rapidly and insistently.

Byrnes picked up his 12-gauge shotgun and pointed it at the door.

"Who is it?" he asked.

Bolan heard a woman's voice. A voice he ought to have known, but he couldn't be sure.

"Wizard, this is Viking. I have an urgent message for you from headquarters. Open the door."

Ingrid Johannsen stood in the doorway. She was flushed and obviously excited.

Byrnes turned white. He stared at her as if he had seen a ghost.

"What the hell are you doing here?" he snarled.

Johannsen was so excited she didn't notice the tone of Byrnes's voice.

"I just got a message from Washington. It's straight from the director's office! All hell is breaking out in Sumatra. The director wants me to go immediately to Sumatra and take charge. He says you are to go to there and set up a network of agents. We are to report directly to his office. Think of that, Fred. We're going to be working directly for the director!"

Byrnes glared at her. He turned red and nearly shook with fury.

"You stupid bitch! You came her to tell me that? Haven't you got a brain in your goddamned head? You stand out like a sore thumb in Dili! Don't you think people know you're CIA? Don't you know the consulate is under surveillance? Christ! A six-year-old child could follow you. I don't give a damn if you get yourself killed, but you've blown my cover. You've lead them right here to me. You may have blown my whole damned network."

"I'm sorry, Fred," Johannsen said meekly.

"You'll be a hell of a lot sorrier if there's an assassination team on the way. We've got to get out of here. Amy, get your backup computer disks and—"

There was a sudden knocking on the door to the hall. Bolan instantly swung his .44 Magnum Desert Eagle to cover the entrance. Someone knocked again, loudly and insistently. The soldier frowned. Gadgets Schwarz and Jack Grimaldi would have spoken up and identified themselves. He didn't know anyone else in East Timor. It could be someone from the hotel, but Bolan hadn't lived this long by taking things for granted. He was careful not to stand in line with the door as he thumbed off the safety.

He heard the hiss of a large zipper being opened behind him. McCarter was lying prone on the floor just to the left of the large sofa. He opened his nylon flight bag and pulled out a 9 mm Heckler & Koch MP-5 silenced submachine gun. It would never win a long-range shooting match, but it was incredibly deadly at close range.

Whoever was outside knocked again. Bolan thought for a second. The lights were on, and they had been talking freely. No one was going to believe the room was empty. He gestured to Fred Byrnes with his left hand. Whoever was out there wasn't going to go away. Bolan moved to stand alongside the door.

"Who is it?" Byrnes called. He tried to sound groggy, like a man who had been out late last night and had been sound asleep.

"Mr. Byrnes, I am from the East Timor Directorate of Immigration. There is a serious problem with your passport. Open the door. I must speak to you immediately!"

Byrnes said nothing. He picked up his 12-gauge shotgun, pushed off the safety and pointed it at the door.

"Something's wrong, Striker," he whispered softly. "My passport says my name is Fred Barnes. There's no way they should know my real name. We're in trouble, real trouble."

CHAPTER SIX

The Maya Beach Hotel, Dili, East Timor

"All right, all right! Just a minute while I slip on some clothes," Byrnes said casually.

That should buy them a few seconds. Bolan stayed against the wall and stretched forward until the fingertips of his left hand touched the doorknob. He pushed lightly, and the knob started to turn. The door suddenly seemed to explode. The flimsy wood ripped and tore. Splinters flew as a burst of full-metal-jacketed bullets slammed through the door. There was no sound of shooting, just the ripping sounds of bullets tearing through the door. If Byrnes had been standing in front of it, he would have been a dead man.

Byrnes was more than willing to return the favor. The room vibrated to the roar of his shotgun as he fired three shots as fast as he could pull the trigger and pump the action. He had loaded the weapon with Magnum buckshot loads. Thirty-six-round lead buckshot smashed through the door as if it were tissue paper. Someone outside screamed as the heavy buckshot hissed out into the hall.

Bolan heard the boom of a shotgun from the hall.

The doorknob and lock were suddenly shattered. The door suddenly erupted, and splinters flew again as McCarter put a burst of heavy subsonic 9 mm rounds through it. If the people outside were thinking about rushing into the room, that would discourage them.

The Executioner dropped to the floor and rolled to his nylon flight bag. He pulled out two cylindrical grenades and held them up so that McCarter and Byrnes could see them. The men nodded their understanding. They knew what he was about to do, and they would cover him. He rolled back to the door, staying down. He pulled the pin on one grenade and held down the safety lever. He reached up with his left hand and suddenly pulled the remnants of the door wide open. The men outside were taken off guard. The last thing they expected was that the people in the room would try to come out.

Bolan released the safety lever and heard a soft pop as the fuse ignited. He still held on to the grenade. Its fuse had a three-second burning time, and Bolan wasn't about to toss it until the last desperate second. It would ruin his whole day if someone outside had the time to pick it up and throw the grenade back before it detonated. He counted down the numbers, then threw the grenade and closed his eyes tightly. He heard an incredibly loud bang, and even through his closed eyelids saw the blaze of light as the flash-bang grenade exploded.

McCarter rushed the door and swept the hallway with sustained bursts from his MP-5. He didn't stop shooting until he had emptied his magazine. He reloaded instantly.

"Good show, Striker! That took care of the whole bloody lot!"

Byrnes looked relieved, but he still shoved three red Winchester plastic shells into his shotgun. He was an old hand and wanted to have a full magazine in case anything else was about to happen.

Bolan stepped to the door and looked up and down the hall. McCarter had indeed taken care of the enemy.

Bolan thought quickly. They had made a hell of a lot of noise, but it would be a few minutes before the police or a UN patrol got there. The hotel staff and the other guests weren't going to run toward the sounds of a gunfight. Thousands of people had been killed in and around Dili before the Australians had arrived. People who had lived through the killings were going to mind their own business. They probably had time to make a run for it if they moved quickly.

"Let's get the hell out of here, Fred," Bolan said.

Byrnes was more than willing to go, but he was a true professional. He wouldn't leave classified information behind where the enemy could seize it. He turned to Andrews who looked stunned by what she had just witnessed.

"Do you have your computer and all your data disks?" he asked quickly.

The woman nodded. She might forget anything else but not her precious computer and her backup data disks.

"Do you have a gun?"

Andrews reached into her purse and pulled out a snub-nosed Smith & Wesson .38 Special. She held as if it were a live, squirming snake, but at least she had it.

"Ever learned how to shoot it?"

"I fired fifty rounds for familiarization at the CIA school. That's the only time I've ever shot a gun. I guess I'm not a very good shot."

Byrnes sighed. There was a good deal he could have said about that. Sending Andrews into danger was like sending a babe to the slaughter, but he had no time for swearing.

"That's fine, Amy. You go first. I don't think they can have seen you before. I'll be about ten feet behind you. Don't worry, I'll cover you. They probably don't know what I look like, either. Keep your pistol in your purse. If you see anything you don't like, just turn around and walk back to the room. Got it?"

The woman nodded. It was simple enough. It gave her a thrill to think about it. She was in the field and acting like a real agent, and best of all it showed that Fred Byrnes trusted her.

"All right, Striker, you and Ingrid follow me. You take my shotgun, Ingrid. I can't look like a tourist carrying it. Green, you have the best weapon. You bring up the rear. If we run into trouble in the hall, you cover us as we fall back on my room."

Byrnes paused for a second, realizing that he had assumed command.

"That all right with you, Striker?"

Bolan nodded. It wasn't a perfect plan, but he couldn't think of a better one. Byrnes was making use of the people he had, and he probably knew far more about escaping from buildings than any of the rest of them.

Byrnes glanced out the window. "It's starting to get dark. If we can get out of the hotel and get to my car, I think we'll be all right. Okay, let's go!"

Andrews stepped out into the hall. Nothing happened. She began walking down the hall, followed by Byrnes. He looked like an innocent tourist, but his hand was close to his .357 Magnum gun. Bolan waited a few seconds, then stepped into the hall. It seemed to be all right. Now, if they could get down the stairs and into the lobby and— He heard a distinct loud metal click, a sound that he'd heard a thousand times before. The sound of an AK-47's safety being pushed off.

"Down! Get down!" he yelled, and drew his Desert Eagle as he dropped to the floor.

Andrews froze. Byrnes instantly threw himself into the woman's long legs and pushed her to the floor. Just in time. Bolan heard the distinctive sound of AK-47s firing on full automatic. Bullets hissed through the air where they had been standing two seconds ago.

Gunners were cutting loose from the top of the stairs. The big Desert Eagle roared and bucked in the Executioner's hands as he fired four quick shots down the hall. The AKs kept firing.

"Fall back, Striker, and keep low!" McCarter shouted as he poured in short quick bursts from his submachine gun.

Bolan snapped in a fresh magazine. The volume of fire from the stairs entrance seemed to be falling off.

"Come on! Go! Go! Go!" McCarter yelled.

Bolan jumped to his feet and raced back toward Byrnes's room, staying close to the wall. Byrnes was in front of him, shoving Andrews along. An AK-47 fired from down the hall. Bolan heard a fast series of booming roars as Ingrid Johannsen emptied Fred Byrnes's 12-gauge shotgun. As buckshot whistled past his head, he hoped that she knew what she was doing. He would hate to be killed by friendly fire in a hotel hallway. He reached the open door to Byrnes's room and dived inside.

McCarter was shoving a fresh 30-round magazine into his submachine gun. "What took you so long, Striker?"

Bolan shoulder rolled to his flight bag and took out his Beretta 93-R. He had a dismal feeling that he was going to need all the firepower he could get.

McCarter leaned out around the corner of the doorjamb and fired two quick bursts down the hall. His silenced weapon made only faint hissing noises, but Bolan could see the smoking brass cases cascading out of its breech.

Suddenly, Ingrid Johannsen lunged through the doorway. She had Byrnes's empty shotgun in one hand and a flat black automatic pistol in the other. Perhaps they had underestimated her. She seemed to be some use in a firefight, after all.

McCarter suddenly yelled out, "They're coming. Get down and get ready."

They all dropped to the floor, even Amy Andrews. She was a bright young woman, and she seemed to be starting to grasp the basic rules of survival in a close-range firefight. She rolled behind a heavy leather chair. None too soon. Half a dozen automatic rifles snarled into life out in the hall.

The world seemed to explode. The hall was filled with the roar of AK-47s on full-auto, and dozens of full-metal-jacketed rifle bullets sprayed into the room beyond. The mirror on the back wall shattered. The heavy woven rattan sofa shuddered under the heavy metal assault. The firing seemed to go on and on endlessly. Bolan stayed down. Had he had been standing in line with the door, he would have died instantly.

There was a momentary lull in the firing. Bolan could hear Amy Andrews moaning softly behind her chair. He had no time to worry about her. She would probably be all right as long as she had sense enough to stay down. He risked a quick glance through the shattered window. It was nearly dark outside. He reached up to the light switch and snapped off the lights. The room went dark. He dropped to the floor and rolled away from the wall, being sure to stay well clear of the door. He brought up his Berreta 93-R in a hard two-handed grip and covered the door.

He was almost certain he knew what was coming next. A man dived into the room and lay prone. He didn't shoot; neither did Bolan. He knew that trick. There were certain basic tactics for attacking or defending a room, and they were the same the whole world over. The attacker was waiting for a defender to fire, and he would shoot at the muzzle-flash. Bolan aimed at the man, the soft green glow of his Beretta's night sights centered on the man's body.

Perhaps two seconds had gone by. The AK-47s roared into life again. Two men were firing. Bolan could see them as they were illuminated by the bright flickering yellow light of their muzzle-flashes. One man was at each side of the door. They raked the back wall and blasted both corners of the room. They weren't wasting ammunition. They were using standard room-clearing tactics. The room vibrated with the continuous roaring as the firing seemed to go on forever.

Bolan wasn't the only person who could see them. David McCarter didn't know who the men were, but he had no doubt that they were hostile. He had no friends in the hall. He took out the man to the left of the door with a short burst to his chest. Half a dozen heavy subsonic 9 mm bullets tore into the attacker, and he went down instantly.

Now, though, the man waiting on the floor had located David McCarter. The muzzle-flash of the Briton's submachine gun had given his position away. The man swung his AK-47 toward him, but Bolan was ready. He triggered the Berreta twice, and six 9 mm hollowpoint bullets smashed into the hardman's side. He twitched once and lay still.

Bolan heard the hiss of McCarter's silenced MP-5 as he fired a short burst through the open door. Someone outside fired back, raking the room with a series of rifle blasts. Bolan hoped his comrade wasn't hit, but he had no time to look. He was getting extremely tired of being outgunned. He rolled to the side of the man he had just shot and ripped the AK-47 from his dead hands.

Bolan knew AK-47s almost as well as his own familiar weapons. Some people said the AK-47 was the deadliest weapon in the world in close combat. The soldier wasn't sure he believed that, but it was deadly enough, and the solid weight of the rifle in his hands was extremely comforting.

The men outside were determined to kill everyone in the room. Only the threat of David McCarter's MP-5 was stopping them from rushing in. One of them began to fire around the right side of the door into the room, one burst after another. They were trying to get McCarter to return their fire so that they could pinpoint his position and cut him to pieces. The Briton took the bait and fired back, one burst, then two as he traded bursts with the rifleman. Bolan heard a hollow clunk as the bolt of McCarter's submachine gun slammed home on an empty chamber.

He wasn't the only one who heard. A second man had been waiting just outside the door. With a snarl of triumph, he took a step forward and swung the muzzle of his shotgun toward the Phoenix Force leader. McCarter scrambled desperately for a fresh magazine, but he wasn't going to make it.

Bolan could see the black bulk of the shotgun in the intruder's hands. He took a flash sight picture, his sights silhouetted against the dim light in the hall. He aimed at the center of the man's body and pulled the trigger. Bolan's assault rifle roared and vibrated in his hands. Four rifle slugs ripped into the center of the man's body. His snarl of triumph changed abruptly into a shriek of agony. He staggered forward, his hands convulsing on his weapon, the rounds firing harmlessly into the ceiling as he collapsed to the floor.

Another attacker charged into the room. He didn't seem to see Bolan. He ran past him, bringing up his rifle. Byrnes was starting to reload his shotgun. He was looking down at the weapon, trying to see the loading port in the near darkness. Bolan could see the attacker's silhouette in the dim light from the doorway. He tried to twist into a firing position, but the angle was bad.

"Look out, Fred," Amy Andrews screamed.

Bolan heard five quick cracks as she emptied her little Smith & Wesson as fast as she could pull the trigger. She was a poor shot, but she was firing at point blank range. Their attacker staggered and almost fell. He snapped up his AK-47 and fired a short burst at Andrews, but that was the last thing he ever did.

Byrnes put six high-velocity .357 Magnum bullets through his chest. He was dead before he hit the floor.

Bolan heard the *klatch-klatch* of a 12-gauge shotgun being pumped. Byrnes was reloaded and ready to fire. There were several men still outside in the hall, but they had lost their enthusiasm for rushing through the door. McCarter was reloaded now, and Bolan and Byrnes were ready to fire again. The cross fire from three deadly weapons made the room's door a death trap for anyone who tried to charge through it. But that worked both ways. They were still trapped inside the room. If the attackers had grenades, they were doomed.

Bolan thought furiously, but he could think of nothing they could do but stay in the room and shoot it out. Stalemate. For a long moment, there was silence, each side waiting for the other to make a move. Then Bolan heard shouting in the hall in an Indonesian tongue and then the echoing roar of sustained firing. Someone was blasting away with full-auto rifle fire. A gunner outside the door screamed in pain. Then everything was quiet.

Bolan listened intently. He was still a little deaf from the concentrated blasts of automatic weapons fired in a closed room. At first he couldn't be certain, but then he was sure. People were moving slowly and carefully down the hall in his direction. He kept his sights on the door, ready to fire, and waited tensely.

"We are friends. Hold your fire!" someone shouted.

A stocky man in the purple beret and camouflage uniform of the Indonesian Marines stepped into the room. Bolan recognized Major Salim, who looked around the shattered room and shook his head.

"You cannot say I did not warn you, Mr. Belasko. East Timor is not the safest place in the world."

He couldn't argue with that, but he was still curious about one thing.

"We were very glad to see you, Major, but how did you know where we were?"

"Thank Mara Tharin for that. Our intelligence service maintains continuous surveillance of your consulate."

His smile broadened. "Only to protect American citizens in Dili, of course. Mara took the precaution of having you followed. Her agent was in the lobby of the hotel. He saw suspicious armed men entering the lobby and going upstairs. He called Mara, and she called me. So here we are. The Marines to the rescue!"

McCarter looked around the room impatiently. He didn't think that this was the time or the place for long conversations. An Australian patrol was likely to arrive at any minute, and he didn't want to be there to try to explain a miniature battlefield.

"Everyone all right? Good. Let's get the hell out of here! We can have a nice chat when we are in a safe place!" McCarter snapped.

Bolan took a quick look around the room. "Where are Amy and Ingrid?"

"Over here behind the big chair. Amy's bleeding. She's been hit. I'm afraid it's bad," Johannsen called.

Bolan was behind the chair in a flash. McCarter snatched a first-aid kit from his flight bag and followed him. Fred Byrnes was already there. Johannsen was on her knees, desperately trying to stop the blood flowing from Andrews's chest. She looked bad, multiple gunshot wounds in her chest and a trickle of blood oozing from one corner of her mouth. She was dazed by the shock of being hit several times, but she still seemed conscious. Byrnes dropped down by Johannsen. McCarter tore open a military trauma dressing. It probably wasn't going to do any good, but they had to try.

Byrnes tore open her blouse. There were four bullet holes just below her bra. McCarter pressed the trauma dressing to the wounds, but Bolan could see the look on his face. They had both seen too many wounds like that to have any illusions. Andrews was going to die, and there was nothing they could do about.

Byrnes pushed Johannsen aside and cradled Andrews gently in his arms.

"Hang on, Amy. You're hit, but we'll get you to a hospital. You're going to be all right," he said in a low husky voice. Bolan had been in some tight spots with the man, but he had never heard him sound like that.

"I'm sorry, Fred," she said very softly. "I screwed up again. I thought that man was going to kill you. I tried to shoot him. I guess I missed him. I'm useless. I—"

Andrews coughed, a hard, racking cough and began to bleed heavily from her mouth.

"Don't talk like a fool, Amy. You did the right thing. You hit the bastard twice. You saved my life. You can be my backup anytime."

The woman smiled at him. Then she coughed again and went limp.

"Hang on, Amy. Hang on."

"I'm sorry, Fred," McCarter said softly. "She can't hear you. She's gone."

"I am sorry she is dead, gentlemen, but we cannot stay here," Major Salim said. "It is time to go."

CHAPTER SEVEN

The White House, Washington, D.C.

Hal Brognola sat in the Oval Office and listened as the assistant secretary for Southeast Asia droned on and on. He might be the government's supreme expert on Southeast Asia, but he was a lousy public speaker. Brognola glanced around the room. It was a small meeting. There were only seven men in the room, including the President, but six of them were very important men, indeed. The Joint Chiefs of Staff were there, gleaming with silver-and-gold insignia of rank and the brightly colored ribbons of their decorations. All of them looked bored. If the assistant secretary said "Indonesia's fragile new democracy" one more time, there might be a military mutiny. They couldn't have cared less about Indonesian politics. They were there to tell the President what the armed forces could do and set the troops in motion if the President gave the orders.

The door to the Oval Office suddenly opened, and the director of the CIA rushed in.

"I'm sorry to be late, sir, but I've just been talking to the section chief in Indonesia. I have the latest information on the situation there," he said quickly.

"Good. Don't keep us waiting. You have the floor."

The director didn't like the tone in the President's voice, but at least he had fresh information.

"At once, Mr. President. There has been a large demonstration today in Medan. That's the capital of Northern Sumatra. The demonstrators were protesting the civilian deaths in the first demonstration. No one is sure what really happened, but the Indonesian government says the demonstrators fired on their troops without provocation. They shot back immediately. Over a hundred demonstrators and six Indonesian soldiers were killed. The demonstrators deny that they fired on the army. They say this is more brutal repression by the Indonesian government. There's a march going on right now in downtown Medan. It's peaceful so far, but the demonstrators are carrying signs saying, Indonesia Out Of Sumatra and Blood For Blood. Leaflets are being passed out calling for another big demonstration tomorrow. There have been two attacks on Indonesian police patrols in the city. I think the pot is about to boil over."

Everyone looked grim. The United States government was trying to restore peace and stability in Indonesia. So far, it hadn't been doing a very good job.

"You say you got all this from your man in Jakarta? That's on Java, a thousand miles from Sumatra. What do you get directly from Sumatra?"

"Well, sir, as you know, we have been focusing our attention on the situation in East Timor. Most of our resources are concentrated there. We have very few people on the ground in Sumatra."

The President frowned.

"I have taken immediate action to solve the problem,'' the director said quickly. "I'm deploying some of our best people from Timor to Sumatra. They're on their way now in an Air Force jet. They should be there in two hours. As soon as they get their feet on the ground, we will start getting direct reports by satcom."

The President turned to the assistant secretary. "You're the expert on Indonesia. How seriously should we take this?"

"Very seriously, sir. Many Sumatrans resent the Indonesian government being run by people from the island of Java. Sumatra was an independent kingdom before the Dutch came. A lot of Sumatrans remember that. There was even a rebellion against the central government in 1958. The government had to send in the army to put it down. If the Free Sumatra Movement is active again, they'll have a lot of followers."

The President looked at the Joint Chiefs. "What military assets do we have in the area?"

"Almost none, sir. Everything we have in the area is covering East Timor," responded General Blaine, Chairman of the Joint Chiefs. He didn't appear happy despite his exalted title, but he had been asked a direct question and had told the truth.

"And there's another problem, sir. Indonesia hasn't asked for U.S. forces on her soil. We can't move in troops or planes without their approval."

"All right, I understand that. Has anyone got any ideas about what we can do?"

The chief of naval operations saw his opportunity. The Armed Forces were supposed to be unified, but he always liked a chance to make the Navy look good at the expense of the Army and the Air Force.

"We have a few ideas, Mr. President. I checked

our ship dispositions just before I came over here. The *Enterprise* and her battle group are in Singapore. She's a nuclear-powered aircraft carrier. There are eight surface combat ships and two nuclear attack submarines with her. Singapore is close to Sumatra. The *Enterprise* group can be on station off Medan in ten hours if you give the order.''

"Do it! Anyone else have any ideas?''

"Yes, sir,'' General Blaine said. "We have had fairly good relations with the Indonesian military. Let's tell the Indonesians we want to have joint maneuvers with them. That way, their politicians don't have to take the heat for stationing U.S. troops in Indonesia.''

"All right, let's get on it immediately. But before you leave, Mr. Brognola has a team in Indonesia. Let's hear what they've found out.''

Hal Brognola spoke cautiously, choosing his words with care. He wanted to give the meeting the significant information Stony Man had, but he didn't want to reveal anything about their operations.

"My team has been in Indonesia for forty-eight hours, operating in East and West Timor. They report that there are several well-armed groups operating against Indonesian forces and the United Nations peacekeeping forces. They were involved in two armed clashes with these groups. They report that these groups are well armed with brand-new Russian-designed weapons.''

Blaine whistled softly. "Russian weapons? Are you sure?''

"Russian-designed weapons, General. Most of them were made in former Soviet-bloc countries.

Only a few were actually manufactured in Russia itself.''

Brognola noticed that the CIA director looked startled and annoyed. Some organization he had never heard of was conducting paramilitary and intelligence operations in the CIA's backyard. He glared at Brognola.

''Why hasn't this information been shared with other interested agencies?''

Brognola smiled disarmingly. ''It was briefed to the CIA's acting station chief in East Timor twenty-four hours ago. The information has probably not reached your office yet.''

The director had nothing more to say, but he made a mental note. He was going to find out just who and what Hal Brognola was and find out fast.

The President looked around the room. No one else had anything to say.

''Very well, the meeting is over. Let's get things moving. Now!''

U.S. Air Force Transport, over Northern Sumatra

THE BIG U.S. Air Force C-17 droned on, its four huge jet engines moving it steadily along at 550 miles per hour. Mack Bolan sat in a seat near the tail and looked quietly around the huge cargo compartment. The C-17 was carrying only a hundred or so people from Dili to northern Sumatra. They were a diverse group, UN bureaucrats, military men from the UN peace-keeping force and a number of media people from half a dozen countries. The official word wasn't out yet, but the smart money was betting that the UN would be going into Sumatra. Bolan and his companions easily blended in.

They were grouped together in the tail area. McCarter was telling Jack Grimaldi and Gadgets Schwarz about the action they had missed in Dili. Major Salim and Mara Tharin sat opposite Bolan. The major sat silent and subdued. He looked out of place wearing plain green fatigues and a blue UN beret. Bolan thought he was worried about something, but he didn't know Salim well enough to ask him about it. Mara Tharin had her nose in a book. Ingrid Johannsen sat pale and silent. She hadn't spoken to anyone since the C-17 took off. Fred Byrnes was in the front of the aircraft. He was up to something. Bolan wasn't sure what.

An Air Force crewman came down the aisle offering coffee to the passengers. Major Salim took two cups and sat next to Bolan. He handed the Executioner a cup.

"Sumatran Litong is one of the finest coffees in the world. Try some. You will like it."

Bolan took a sip. It was excellent coffee, and it was nice of Salim to offer him a cup, but he knew that Salim seldom did anything without a purpose. He smiled and waited to see what it was.

"I am afraid I have been neglecting my duties as a host, Mr. Belasko. Is there anything I can do for you?"

Bolan thought for a moment.

"There is one thing. I've never been to Sumatra, and I know next to nothing about it. Could you fill me in on the situation there? I haven't had time to have a briefing, and I don't want to bother Miss Johannsen."

Salim looked across the aisle. "Yes, I think she blames herself for the death of the young woman at the hotel. There is no need to bother her. I am a Sumatran. I can tell you anything you want to know."

"I would appreciate it. Just keep it simple. Just tell me what I need to know."

"It is simple, really. It all boils down to one thing. There are forty million Sumatrans, but 115 million people live on Java. That is half the population of Indonesia. I do not have to tell you who has the political power. The Javanese control the government. They have controlled it since we gained our independence in 1948. Many Indonesians who are not Javanese resent that bitterly. Nowhere is that resentment stronger than on Sumatra. We were an independent nation for a thousand years before the Dutch came. Many of us do not see any reason why we should be ruled by Java today. That is not what we fought the Japanese and the Dutch for.

"That is what makes this situation so serious. If Sumatra fights for its independence, there will be civil war. East Timor means nothing. It was never part of Indonesia. It was a Portuguese colony with less than two million people. We just took it over when the Portuguese left it in 1975. If we lose it, it will be merely an annoyance. But if Sumatra goes, Indonesia is finished. That is why what is going on in Sumatra is a major crisis, the biggest crisis Indonesia has ever had to face."

Salim took a sip of his coffee.

"If you don't mind my asking, you are a Sumatran. How do you feel about this?"

Salim stared at Bolan for a moment. "That is a personal question, but we have fought together. I will tell you how I feel. Do you remember your American Civil War?''

Bolan smiled. "Not personally. It was a little before my time, but I've read about it. What are you getting at?''

"Let us imagine it is 1861. You are an officer in the American army, a major, perhaps. You are from Virginia. It is seceding from the United States. You know there will be war. What do you have to decide?''

"Who am I going to fight for, the United States or Virginia?''

"Exactly, and that is the position I am in. Do I fight for Indonesia or Sumatra? It is not an easy choice. If there is civil war, it will be a long and bloody battle.''

Bolan was puzzled. "If they outnumber Sumatra three to one, how can it be a long fight?'' he asked.

"It would not be as easy as it sounds. Indonesia does not have a large army. There are about 220,000 soldiers, mostly infantry. There are about seventy battalions. That is not many for a country with 210 million people, and it is divided up between the islands. There are only eight of the battalions stationed on Sumatra, less than seven thousand men. If the government wants to occupy Sumatra in force, they will have to strip troops from Java and all the other islands and get them there. That would not be easy. Indonesia does not have much of a navy.''

Mack Bolan hadn't known that. It made it easy to see why Washington was worried. If there were two or three simultaneous uprisings, the Indonesian government wouldn't be able to handle them all at the same time. Someone else knew that, and they were

supplying weapons to any independence movement
who wanted them.

"That is the big picture. My problem is much simpler. If war comes, I will be fighting against my
friends whatever I decide. If I go with Sumatra, I must
fight against my friends in the army and the marines.
If I stay with the government, I must fight against my
friends, even my relatives, in Sumatra. It is a terrible
decision. You Americans have a saying, 'I am
damned if I do and damned if I don't.' "

Bolan nodded. It was a terrible situation that Salim
faced. Bolan was sympathetic, but there was nothing
he could say. Salim would have to make up his mind.

The major started to say something else but
stopped. Fred Byrnes was coming down the aisle. He
had two cameras slung around his neck. He was playing his old role of newspaper correspondent. Apparently, he was fooling the other UN passengers, but
Bolan wouldn't have bet a month's pay that he was
fooling Mara Tharin. She was shrewd. It had probably
occurred to her that Amy Andrews had been far too
young to be running a CIA operation. Byrnes had a
cup of coffee in his hand. He sat next to Ingrid Johannsen and handed her the cup.

"Here, drink this. You look like you need it."

Johannsen looked down at the cup listlessly. "I
don't want it, Fred. My stomach is tied up in knots.
I keep seeing Amy's face as she died."

Byrnes stared at her. Major Salim excused himself
and walked forward toward the nose of the C-17. Perhaps he was going to compare notes with Mara
Tharin. Byrnes waited until Salim could no longer
hear what he said. Then he spoke in a cold hard voice.

"Stop sitting there sniveling like a little girl and

feeling sorry for yourself, Johannsen. You're a CIA officer in the field. When this plane lands, you are going to be the senior CIA officer in Sumatra. Start acting like it!''

Johannsen flinched from Byrnes as if she had been slapped.

"I'm sorry, Fred, but it was all my fault. I was so excited, I just didn't think. I just rushed over to your hotel, and I got Amy killed. I don't know if I can live with that.''

"You're damned well going to have to live with it, Ingrid, and still do your job! When we land, I'm going to have disappear into the woodwork and start recruiting agents. You're the one who's going to have to meet with the generals and the politicians. This is a Muslim country. They won't be thrilled that the U.S. sent a woman in such a critical job. You'll have to show them that you can handle it. There isn't anyone else available. You're here. You speak Indonesian. You've got to do it.''

"I don't know if I can, Fred. I made a stupid mistake, and I got Amy killed. You don't know how I feel.''

Bolan had been sitting quietly. It wasn't his fight. He was going to stay out of it, but he was surprised to see Byrnes smile.

"You think I don't know what it's like, Ingrid? Welcome to the club! I've been a field agent for thirty years. I've made a lot of mistakes. A lot of my agents got killed. Sometimes it was my fault because I made a mistake. I didn't like it, but I kept going. How you feel doesn't count. First, last and always the mission comes first!''

Johannsen stared at him for a minute. "You're

right, Fred. I've got to do it. There isn't anyone else. How do I start?''

Byrnes smiled at her. "That's the spirit, Ingrid! Go wash your face and comb your hair. Get ready to show those Indonesians who's running things for the CIA. Make them think they're lucky to be getting you. Now, get going. We'll be landing in a few minutes.''

Johannsen smiled faintly. She still looked pale, but she got up and went down the aisle toward one of the C-17's Spartan rest rooms.

Bolan looked at Byrnes. "Maybe you were a little too hard on her, Fred. She's never seen anyone killed before,'' he remarked quietly.

"Somebody had to straighten her out. No matter how bad Ingrid feels about Amy, she's still got to do her job. No one held a gun to her head and made her join the CIA. I don't care about her emotional upsets. The mission comes first.''

Bolan nodded. Byrnes was a hard man, but he was probably right.

He didn't have any time to worry about it. He could hear the steady hum of the engines change as the pilot throttled back and started down. He looked around for the rest of the team. McCarter and Salim were standing by an emergency exit, looking out its window. The Briton beckoned urgently. Something was up. Bolan got up and moved down the aisle.

"You need to see this, Striker. This is Medan. It doesn't look good down there. We may be too late,'' McCarter said.

Bolan looked out the window. They were still a few thousand feet up, but he could see the city spread out below them. It was much bigger than he had thought, but that was not what McCarter had wanted him to see. Several columns of dark black smoke were rising into the air, marking the large fires burning in the city.

CHAPTER EIGHT

Medan, Northern Sumatra

The big C-17 landed with a squeal of brakes and taxied down the runway toward the Medan airport terminal. The terminal area was crowded. Several airliners were unloading passengers. It looked peaceful enough, but Mack Bolan noticed several Australian and Indonesian military transports unloading soldiers. The C-17 taxied up to a ramp and stopped. The passengers started deplaning. Major Salim got up and walked for the doors, followed by Mara Tharin, saying that they were going to check arrangements for ground transportation.

McCarter and Bolan got up and picked up their equipment cases. Fred Byrnes signaled them to wait. He had a clipboard in his hands. Anyone looking at them would have thought they were being interviewed.

"As soon as we get inside the terminal, I've got to split. I don't want to go anywhere near an Indonesian military headquarters. I'll tag along with these UN big wheels. They all think I'm a real reporter, and they are going to be extra nice to me if they think I can get their names in the papers. I'll contact you as soon as I can. Have fun with the Indonesian brass, and take care of Ingrid. I think she'll be all right, but she can use all the help she can get.''

Bolan stuck out his hand. ''Good luck, Fred. By the way, is there anything I can do for you?''

Byrnes smiled cynically. ''Sure, there is, Striker. I need an experienced agent who can speak perfect Indonesian, has years of experience in-country, can pass for an Indonesian national, understands covert operations and can catch the next plane to Sumatra. Just wave your magic wand and produce him, and I'll buy you a case of whatever it is you drink. Maybe two cases. Think you can do that?''

Bolan nodded. ''I don't think that's much of a problem, Fred. I think I can get someone who fills the bill here in forty-eight hours, maybe less.''

Byrnes was a hard man to astonish, but he stared at Bolan in amazement. One thing he knew for certain—it wasn't a joke.

''Just how the hell can you do that, Striker? Do you work directly for God?''

Bolan smiled at the man and said nothing.

''I know, I know. If you tell me, you'll have to kill me.''

''You know how I'd hate to have to do that, Fred.''

Ingrid Johannsen was back from the rest room. She still looked pale, but she seemed to have her confidence back.

Jack Grimaldi came rapidly down the aisle. ''Come on, Striker. Your Indonesian girlfriend is in a big hurry. Some general wants to see Mr. Green.''

THEY FOLLOWED Mara Tharin into the building. It looked normal enough, but everywhere McCarter and

Bolan looked they saw men in uniform moving in pairs. They were keeping a wary eye on the crowd. McCarter was quite good at recognizing Indonesian uniforms, but he had never seen anything like this. They wore black berets, belts, boots and holsters, and most of them carried 9 mm submachine guns ready in their hands.

"Who are those soldiers, Mara?" McCarter asked.

"Soldiers? Oh, you mean the men in the black berets. They are not soldiers. They are the police."

McCarter looked surprised. "The police?"

Tharin smiled. She thought Englishmen were a bit odd, but she liked McCarter.

"Yes, they are from BRIMOB, the Police Mobile Brigade. They are the national police force, specialists in counterterrorism and riot control. They are very effective, but people are afraid of them. They are not known for being gentle. If they are here in force, it means that the government takes this trouble seriously."

Major Salim hurried up. Bolan noticed that he had replaced his blue UN beret with the purple beret of the Indonesian Marine Commandos.

"There is trouble in the city. I have arranged a military escort. They are waiting. Let us go now."

They followed Salim out of the terminal. Several jeeps were waiting, their engines idling. Two large six-wheeled armored cars were standing by. Bolan recognized the type. The British Saladins were serious fighting machines, mounting large cannons in armored turrets, more like light tanks than police vehicles. Salim didn't waste any time. He had the party and their gear quickly loaded in four of the jeeps and gave the signal to the commander of the escort. They moved out smoothly, one of the armored cars leading, followed by a jeep mounting a belt-fed machine gun and manned by BRIMOB officers. They made an impressive group. Bolan thought if he were a demonstrator he would leave them strictly alone.

McCarter, Bolan and Salim were in the second jeep.

"We are going to the headquarters of the First Regional Command. The general wants to see us," Salim said. He had nothing more to say. Bolan knew he had a lot on his mind. The civil war he feared seemed about to break out. Still, the streets seemed peaceful as they drove toward the central city. McCarter commented on that. Salim smiled.

"Yes, if you are an Indonesian, you know better than to start trouble with BRIMOB. If you start trouble with them, they will finish it. You will be lucky if you live to go to prison."

McCarter could believe that. The heavily armed BRIMOB officers looked ready for anything. They moved quickly toward the center of Medan. There was almost no traffic. Twice they passed burned-out cars and groups of Indonesian soldiers guarding intersections. They were in the center of the city now. Groups of people were standing on the sidewalks. Some of them were carrying signs and glared at the passing jeeps, but no one tried to interfere with their passage. The cannons and machine guns of the escort were a powerful argument for law and order.

They came to a stop in front of a large stone building. The red and white Indonesian flag hung from a flagpole in front of the building. Its entrance was protected by sandbags and barbed wire. The soldiers who guarded the entrance wore camouflage uniforms and full battle gear. Salim showed his ID and hustled his charges inside. A sentry checked Salim's ID again and ushered them inside a large conference room, which was set up as an operations center. A large map of Sumatra covered one wall. A tall thin man was staring at the map. He wore the three gold stars of an Indonesian lieutenant general on his shoulders.

Salim saluted smartly. "Major Salim reporting as ordered, General Rahman. This is the observation group you wished to see." He made the introductions quickly.

The general smiled. "I am glad to see you again, Salim. You always seem to turn up where there is trouble. I am pleased to meet the rest of you, also. Step over to the map, and I will explain the situation."

Bolan looked at the map. He was surprised to see just how big Sumatra was. It was a long oval island, nine hundred miles long and two hundred miles wide, slanting upward from its southern tip at a forty-five-degree angle to the north.

General Rahman picked up a pointer. "As you can see, Sumatra is a large island, the largest in Indonesia. Because of its size, it is divided into two military commands. You are here in Medan. It is the headquarters of the First Command. I am its commanding officer."

He pointed to the northern tip. "My responsibility runs from here to 450 miles to the south. I have six battalions of infantry and a few helicopters to control the sector. Controlling the entire area is an impossible task, but I must try to do it. I have—"

Rahman stopped and glared at Gadgets Schwarz,

who was staring at a small, flat black box in front of him.

"Mr. Sower," he said, he said, using Schwarz's cover name, "is that a tape recorder you have? This is a classified meeting. The information I am presenting is very sensitive. You must not record it."

Schwarz reached down and pushed a button on the black box. A green light began to flash.

"I'm not recording, General, but somebody is. There is an electronic surveillance device behind the left-hand corner of your map. I'm jamming it. Whoever is listening thinks they've just had a sensor failure."

Schwarz walked over to the wall and lifted the corner of the map. A small black cylinder had been inserted in a small round hole neatly drilled into the wall. He carefully pulled it out and examined it closely.

"That's a neat little device. It's a voice-actuated recorder. When it's turned off, it's almost impossible to detect. It turns on whenever anyone is speaking. It has been recording every word that's been said in here ever since it was installed. It's jammed right now, but it will be recording again as soon as I turn off my box."

Rahman looked stunned. "My God, I hold my staff meetings in this room. You are saying that someone knows all our plans."

Schwarz shrugged. "I'm afraid so, General. Do you want me to put it back or take it out?"

"Destroy the damned thing!"

Mara Tharin had been sitting quietly. Now she spoke softly.

"Perhaps that might not be wise, sir. If Mr. Sower

can keep it neutralized during the meeting, let's leave it in place. That way we may find out who put it there, or you can use it to give the enemy false information.''

The general smiled. He liked the way Mara Tharin thought. Use the enemy's weapons against him.

"Very well, Mr. Sower. We will do as Miss Tharin suggests."

He moved back to the map and pointed to the northern tip of Sumatra. "This is Aceh Province. It all started there in 1998. People calling themselves the Free Aceh Movement began protests. At first, they were peaceful. Then a year later, there were small-scale armed attacks on military and police patrols. The army managed to contain that, but there were the usual accusations, killings of innocent civilians, rape and torture. It might have died down, but then came that damned business in East Timor. The government allowed a vote there on independence, and the United Nations moved in. Now people in Aceh say they should be allowed to vote for independence and the UN should protect them. The government refused to allow it. Aceh is not like East Timor. It has always been part of Indonesia."

"There is another factor, sir," Salim said. "Aceh is the richest province in Indonesia. The loss of its natural resources would be a staggering blow to the Indonesian economy."

"Ah, yes, I had forgotten that Major Salim comes from Aceh. Well, he is right. Indonesia cannot afford to lose Aceh, much less all of Sumatra."

"What is the government doing to maintain control, General?" McCarter asked.

The general looked unhappy. "Yes, Mr. Green.

That is the important question. I have only six battalions of infantry to control the northern half of Sumatra. I have three battalions in Aceh and three here in Medan. I have asked for reinforcements. The government has sent me two thousand BRIMOB officers and one battalion of paratroops. I am happy to get them, but now we are having massive demonstrations here in Medan. My troops are stretched to the limit. I have nothing in reserve. If anything happens in some other place, I do not know what I will do.''

He walked across the room and picked up a rifle. Bolan recognized it instantly as an AK-47. It looked like a standard weapon, except that it had a second pistol grip in front of the magazine. The general handed it to McCarter. Bolan saw that the weapon was nearly new.

"This is what our peaceful protesters are carrying these days,'' the general said wryly. "Have you ever seen one like it?''

McCarter examined the rifle closely. "Quite a few, actually. We were attacked by a large party of guerrillas on Timor yesterday. Many of them had rifles exactly like this. Hungarian-made AK-47s, new out of the box.''

Rahman looked skeptical. "Are you certain Mr. Green? Why should new Hungarian rifles be appearing in Sumatra?''

"Quite certain, sir. I have seen a great many AK-47s in my time. Most of them were pointed at me, but I have learned something about them. People who are fanciers of AK-47s say the Hungarian rifles are the best AK-47s ever made. As to why, well, someone has bought them on the open market and is shipping them to any antigovernment group in your country. If a Free Bali movement were to spring up, I would bet a hundred pounds you would find Hungarian AKs there in a week or two."

"He is right, General," Mara Tharin agreed. "I had pictures of the weapons we captured on Timor sent to Jakarta for analysis. Our experts there said exactly the same things Mr. Green is saying."

"It is worse than that, General," Salim announced. "I called for air support during the fight when these weapons were captured. One of our F-16s was shot down with a shoulder-fired surface-to-air missile. It is not just rifles we have to worry about, sir. I feel certain that antiarmor and antiaircraft weapons are being smuggled into the country."

Ingrid Johannsen had been listening quietly. Now, she had something to say.

"I was the acting CIA section chief in Dili before I was reassigned here, General. My people were running computer analyses of illegal-arms flows into East and West Timor. They concluded that it's not just a few dozen rifles being smuggled in fishing boats. Weapons like this are being smuggled in by the shipload."

Rahman looked grave. "What you are telling me is very bad. Any group that opposes the government can get first-class weapons from whoever is doing this just by asking. The guerrillas will be as well armed as my soldiers. This is war. I must call Jakarta at once. They must stop stalling and send me reinforcements immediately."

Someone knocked loudly and insistently at the door. An Indonesian captain came in and saluted the general. He spoke rapidly in Indonesian. The general listened and then barked an order. The captain saluted and hurried out of the room. Rahman went to his desk and opened a drawer. He took out a black leather belt and pistol holster and buckled them around his waist.

"I am afraid this meeting is over. The captain has just told me that a large demonstration is forming near the city center. It is supposed to be a peaceful protest, but already two police cars have been set on fire. BRIMOB is guarding the city center and the government buildings there. They say that there are far too many demonstrators for them to stop. They are calling for military assistance. I must go. Come along if you like, gentlemen, and see how we do things here. But I warn you, it may get very exciting."

CHAPTER NINE

The City Center, Medan, Sumatra

General Rahman's command car stopped next to a group of jeeps parked near the west edge of the city center. McCarter and Bolan looked around the large public square. They saw pockets of BRIMOB officers keeping a wary eye on small groups of demonstrators who were marching back and forth, waving signs and chanting slogans. There were several hundred BRIMOB officers dressed in riot gear posted around the square. The situation didn't look particularly threatening to Bolan, and he said as much to McCarter.

"We need to know more about what's going on," McCarter said. "Let's put Gadgets and Grimaldi up on top of one of those buildings. They'll have a good field of view there. You arrange that with Major Salim. I will see what I can find out from the general."

McCarter strolled over to the command car. The general was a busy man. He was conferring with two BRIMOB officers and four military officers who wore dark orange berets. Mara Tharin and Ingrid Johannsen were standing quietly behind the general, listening to every word that was being said. McCarter had spent many years in the British army. He was too old a hand to speak to a general who was giving his pre-combat orders.

He heard the rumble of many diesel engines. Long columns of Indonesian army trucks were entering the square, escorted by four Saladin armored cars. The trucks pulled to a stop. Sergeants shouted orders, and groups of men in camouflage uniforms and dark orange berets began to climb quickly out of the trucks. They were in full combat gear and carried American M-16 rifles slung over their shoulders. McCarter recognized the uniform. They were KOSTRAD, elite army paratroopers. The four paratroop officers moved out to join their men and began to form a line across the square. The four Saladin armored cars moved in behind them, menacing the far side of the square with their 76 mm guns.

It was an impressive display of military power, but McCarter knew the real question was the Indonesian government's willingness to use it to maintain control of Medan.

The general glanced at McCarter.

"There you are, Mr. Green. Miss Tharin has been telling me all about you. She says that you had a great deal of crowd-control experience in Northern Ireland. I am not too proud to take good advice. Have you any suggestions?"

"Let me be sure I understand the situation, General. Do you have authorization to use all necessary force to control this demonstration?"

Rahman shook his head. "No, I do not. I have contacted Jakarta several times. They will not give me the authority to declare martial law. Instead, they say

I must use minimum force and do everything in my power to limit civilian casualties. Of course, they say I must also maintain complete control of Medan at all costs. With friends like our politicians, I do not need enemies.''

McCarter nodded. Rahman wasn't the first soldier to be given contradictory orders by men who didn't understand the situation and wouldn't be there to do the fighting if things went wrong.

''Well, sir, if I were you, I would put some sharpshooters with snipers' rifles up on the roofs of those buildings. Order them to shoot anyone in the mob they see with weapons or hand grenades. Also, you need more men. You really don't have enough men to hold the square against a determined mob.''

''The sharpshooters are a good idea, Mr. Green. I will order it done. You are right. I do not have enough men here. I am bringing in reinforcements from other parts of the city. I only hope they get here in time.''

Someone shouted a warning to the general. McCarter looked across the square and saw a large crowd of people pouring into the area, more and more of them, waving signs and chanting. There were thousands of them already, and more were crowding in. The situation was getting ominous. The paratroop officers shouted an order. A ripple seemed to run along the paratrooper's line as they fixed bayonets.

McCarter turned to Ingrid Johannsen. ''I'm afraid the party is about to get rough, Ingrid. Perhaps it would be wise for you to leave the area while you still can.''

The woman smiled and lifted her right arm. She was wearing a blue armband. White letters proclaimed Press in English and Indonesian. She had a television camcorder slung over her shoulder. "I'll be all right, Green. Major Salim got me these. He says the demonstrators want publicity. I'll be perfectly safe if they think I'm from the media."

McCarter shrugged. He wasn't so sure that she was right, but she was a grown woman and a CIA agent. She could make her own decisions. He opened his bag and took out his silenced 9 mm Heckler & Koch submachine gun, snapped in a magazine and chambered a round. He had no idea what was going to happen next, so it was best to be prepared for anything. Bolan hurried up. McCarter saw that he was wearing his miniature earphones and microphone of his tactical radio.

"Gadgets and Jack are on the roof. They're on tactical channel two."

McCarter took out his own headset and slipped it on. He pushed the button.

"What do you see, Gadgets?" he asked.

Schwarz's voice came through loud and clear. "Half the people in the world seem to be heading into the square."

"Could you be a little more precise, Gadgets? Give me a rough count, if you please."

"Damned if I know. They are jammed up shoulder to shoulder as far as I can see. There must be thousands of them headed this way—five or ten thousand. I can't be sure. They seem to be well controlled. Whoever is doing this knows what they're doing. You had better be careful down there. And look pretty. The media is arriving. I think you're about to be on television."

"Roger, Gadgets. Call me immediately if you see anything new. McCarter out."

Bolan was staring at the swarms of demonstrators fanning out across the square. Slowly but steadily, they were beginning to move forward toward the thin line of soldiers and policemen.

Bolan shook his head. "The people running this show must be crazy, David. If General Rahman has to order his men to open fire, hundreds of people will be killed. Can't they see that?"

"Nothing could make the leaders of this demonstration happier. They want martyrs. Lots of martyrs. One of the main reasons they're doing all this is to get worldwide media attention. If Rahman's men kill several hundred civilians, it'll be on television all over the world tonight. It will be East Timor all over again. The United Nations Security Council will meet and vote to deploy a UN peacekeeping force to Sumatra. Then it will be a UN-sponsored election to vote on Sumatran independence."

"They'd get hundreds of their own people killed just for that?"

"You are bloody well right they would. This may be the start of a revolution, Striker. People get killed in revolutions. You can't make an omelette without breaking eggs. And if the Australians are right and a foreign power is trying to break up Indonesia, then they don't care how many Sumatrans get killed. You can bet your last dollar on that!"

Bolan didn't like what McCarter said. It sounded heartless and cruel, but it was probably true. McCarter was one of the most intelligent men he knew, and when he analyzed a situation, his conclusions were usually right. He watched as the demonstrators moved slowly forward and came to a halt fifty yards in front of the line of paratroopers. They stood there chanting their slogans and waving their signs.

"They don't like those bayonets, Striker. They don't know if the soldiers will shoot them or not, but they are bloody well sure what will happen to the people in front if they try to push through."

Bolan knew that McCarter was right, but the party wasn't over. Whoever was controlling the demonstrators wasn't going to turn them around and march quietly back out of the square. Rahman took advantage of the pause. He climbed up on the hood of his command vehicle and spoke into a bullhorn. His amplified voice rang through the square. It was an exposed position. McCarter noticed that Salim was standing near the general with an AK-47 ready in his hands. Ingrid Johannsen was using her camcorder, taking pictures of the nearest demonstrators.

"What's Rahman saying?" Bolan asked her.

"He's reading them the riot act, Belasko. He's telling them they have made their point. The government is aware of their grievances, but this demonstration has gone too far. It is now an illegal assembly. They should disperse before someone is injured."

An ugly roar swept through the crowd of demonstrators, who made no move to disperse. People began to throw rocks at the paratroopers. The leading edge of the demonstrators began to creep forward.

Gadgets Schwarz's voice whispered in McCarter's ear. "Watch out, guys. There's a group of a dozen men just behind the demonstrators in front. They're right in front of you and the general. I can't be sure from here, but I think they have weapons. Be careful."

"Thanks, Gadgets. Count on it," McCarter acknowledged.

The demonstrators were steadily moving closer. They were only about thirty yards away from the line of paratroopers. General Rahman was tired of waiting. He snapped an order. The BRIMOB officers moved forward, passing through the line of paratroops. They formed a thin line, standing in groups of three or four. The crowd roared louder, screaming threats and curses. They might resent the Indonesian army, but they hated the elite riot police.

The BRIMOB officers were pulling grenades from their belts, aluminum cylinders like small silvery beer cans. They pulled the safety pins, held the grenades for a second to be sure the fuses were burning properly and then hurled them into the ranks of the demonstrators.

"My God, Green!" Ingrid Johannsen was horrified. "What are they doing? They'll kill hundreds of people."

The grenades struck. They didn't explode but began to spray clouds of gray-white smoke.

"Tear gas," McCarter said tersely. "CS tear gas, I believe. What the media likes to call pepper gas. Now, we will see how serious these people really are."

The BRIMOB officers drew more gas grenades from their pouches. Before they could throw them, the crowd rushed forward, shouting furiously. Some of them were tearing the signs from their long poles and brandishing them as weapons as they charged the BRIMOB officers. The riot police drew their batons and defended themselves as they fell back on the line of supporting paratroopers. McCarter admired their response. Even under direct attack, they weren't going to shoot until the order was given.

The line of paratroopers fell back slowly. Some of the BRIMOB officers had retreated behind their lines and were lobbing more tear-gas grenades over the paratroopers' heads. Rocks and bottles showered down on them as the demonstrators retaliated.

"Get ready, Striker, and don't hesitate to shoot the bloody bastards if they break through because they seem to be unarmed. As my old nanny used to say, 'Sticks and stones may break your bones,' and if you are knocked down, you'll very probably be trampled to death."

Bolan nodded and pushed the safety selector switch on his 9 mm Beretta 93-R to bursts.

The demonstrators surged forward as if they were one giant monster. The paratroops were being pushed back. Their line was broken in two or three places. Rahman was shouting orders. Something seemed to suddenly snatch the bullhorn out of his hands and send it spinning away. A rock sailed out of the crowd and struck him in the forehead. He staggered and fell. Salim whirled and caught him before he hit the ground.

The major didn't hesitate. He shouted as loud as he could, his voice ringing with the tones of command. The paratroopers shouted with savage glee and lunged forward, thrusting with their bayonets and striking with the metal-shod butts of their rifles. Bolan heard shrieks and screams, but his attention was concentrated on a gap in the paratroopers line right in front of him. He remembered Schwarz's warning and brought his Beretta smoothly to his shoulder. There! A group of ten or twelve men in dull black clothing rushed through the gap and charged toward the command car.

One of them had a flat black automatic pistol with a long black cylinder screwed onto its barrel. He was swinging it up, aiming at the general and Salim. Bolan sighted on the center of the man's chest and squeezed the Beretta's trigger. Three 9 mm hollow-point rounds drilled into the man's chest, staggering him. Another well-placed burst punched him to the ground.

Ingrid Johannsen suddenly screamed. Three men were running toward her with long-bladed chopping knives in their hands. She hurled the camcorder into one man's face and tried frantically to draw her pistol. Snarling in triumph, the second man rushed at her, the twenty-inch blade poised above his head for a blow that would split her skull. Bolan had no time for fancy shooting. He snapped up the Beretta and fired as soon as he could see the flat black rectangle of his front sight outlined against the man's side. Three 9 mm hollowpoint rounds struck the knife wielder's side and tore through his body. The knife fell from his hand, and he dropped heavily to the ground.

The first man staggered to his feet, dazed from the impact of Johannsen's camcorder. He still had his big knife in one hand, and he lunged toward her. He held the point of the long blade low, ready to rip open the woman's belly, but he had made the fatal error of bringing a knife to a gunfight. Johannsen had her SIG-Sauer P-226 pistol in her hands. She pulled the trigger repeatedly, firing one 9 mm bullet after another into her attacker. The P-226 held fifteen rounds, and she fired them all. The last few rounds struck the man in the head and shoulders as he fell. It was over-kill, but Johannsen didn't like the idea of a sharp knife being driven through her body.

The survivors of the group who had attacked turned and ran back for the safety of the crowd. McCarter saw that the paratroopers had closed the gaps in their line. He could see blood staining the blades of some of their bayonets, and three demonstrators' bodies sprawled on the ground. He glanced at Johannsen. She was pale and shaken, holding her empty pistol in her trembling hand. It was the first time she had ever killed someone.

"Good shooting, Ingrid," McCarter said, "but don't just stand there. Reload! They may be coming again."

She heard the ring of command in McCarter's voice, fumbled for a spare magazine and pressed it into the butt of her SIG. She pushed the slide release, and the SIG's slide shot forward, chambering a fresh round.

"Good girl!" McCarter said approvingly. He was glad she seemed to be holding together. He knew everyone was afraid in close combat. What counted was that you did what you had to, despite the fear.

McCarter looked around the square. The paratroopers and BRIMOB had stopped the first attack, but there simply weren't enough of them to clear the square. He glanced toward the command car. General Rahman was on his feet, bleeding from a small cut on his forehead. He was speaking rapidly into the microphone of a tactical radio. McCarter heard the unmistakable sound of helicopters flying low and fast. He looked up. Four Indonesian army helicopters were sweeping low over the square. They carried silver tanks under their stub wings. As they passed over the edge of the crowd, they began to spew clouds of ominous gray-white smoke. The thick clouds spread and began to cover the crowds. The BRIMOB officers shouted gleefully and threw more tear gas grenades into the crowd. McCarter heard cries of panic as the demonstrators turned and frantically started to run from the square.

Rahman gave an order. The paratroopers cheered and began to move forward slowly but steadily. The people on the edge of the crowd saw their gleaming bayonet blades coming closer and closer and began to push frantically to the rear. The paratroopers advanced triumphantly as the demonstrators poured out of the square.

Bolan was surprised that the gas from the helicopters seemed to have little effect on most of the demonstrators. Here and there, some people were writhing on the ground or stumbling around rubbing their eyes. Groups of BRIMOB officers were rounding them up and putting them in handcuffs.

The BRIMOB officers were separating the men they had arrested from the women. The men were already being loaded into a truck. The dozen women were huddled together near the command car. Some looked angry, but others were beginning to look fearful as the BRIMOB officers began to search them. One of the men smiled and held up something in his hand.

"This one has a radio. She will tell us all sorts of interesting things!"

"Good," Salim said. "Twenty prisoners. If any of them were leaders, we may find out something worth knowing."

"Do you think they'll talk?" Bolan asked.

"I think they will. BRIMOB is not known for its gentle interrogations. They will soon have those women begging to tell them everything they know. And that reminds me, I have what you Americans call a date with a young lady. I cannot keep her waiting."

It seemed an odd time for Salim to be worried about his love life. Bolan shrugged his shoulders. Different countries, different customs. He wondered what they should do next. McCarter was talking to General Rahman. Ingrid Johannsen was listening.

"Good idea to spray gas from your helicopters, General, but what kind of gas was it? It does not seem to have disabled many of them."

"I must confess that I have been a little deceitful, Mr. Green. Our helicopters have no tear-gas-spraying equipment. They are only equipped to lay down smoke screens. That was simply smoke. It was a gamble, but it worked. There was the smell of pepper gas in the air from the BRIMOB grenades, and some people had been hit by the real gas. It was easy enough to persuade our friends that they were being gassed on a grand scale. It was not completely honest of me, but at least it made them run, and I did not have to order my men to fire. I am sure God will forgive me. After all, many lives were saved."

"Remind me never to play poker with you, General."

"I am glad you approve, but I must remember my manners. I owe you and my friends my life. I will not forget that."

Being thanked in public embarrassed McCarter. "Only doing our job, General," he muttered. He looked around the square. "Things seem under control here. What's our next move?"

Rahman nodded. McCarter was a wise man. He saw that they had won a battle, but the war wasn't over yet.

"We have one more thing to do here. Then we will go back to headquarters and lay our plans. Ah, here is Major Salim now."

McCarter looked behind him. Salim was climbing out of the back of the command vehicle. Mara Tharin was with him, and she didn't look happy. She had changed into a T-shirt and skin-tight jeans. It made her look younger and somehow more vulnerable. Her eyes were red and swollen, and her face was streaked with tears. There were bruises on her arms, and her lips were swollen. Salim was pulling her along by her long black hair. She stumbled along awkwardly. Her hands were handcuffed behind her back. McCarter could smell the sharp scent of pepper gas from her clothes.

Salim pulled her along cruelly toward the group of female prisoners.

"Come along, bitch. Your friends are waiting for you!"

Tharin shrieked angrily in Indonesian, but she followed Salim helplessly. The pain in her scalp was too strong for her to resist. Salim paid no attention to her protests. He pulled her along and shoved her into the group of cowed women. Tharin stood up as he released her hair and spit at him. The major slapped her hard several times across her face. Tharin's head rocked back and forth on her shoulders, and her long black hair thrashed from side to side from the force of the blows. The woman shrieked louder.

"What's she saying?" McCarter asked Ingrid Johannsen.

"That he is a filthy fascist beast. She says he has beaten her and raped her in perverse and unnatural ways. She says he will pay for it, he and all the other pigs who work for the government."

Salim smiled cruelly, mocking Tharin's helpless rage. He said something to her in a gloating tone of voice.

"He says he is looking forward to interrogating her. He will use an electric cattle prod. He will teach her to be obedient and submissive. She will beg him to rape her before he is through with her."

Salim slapped Tharin again. The BRIMOB officers shoved her and the other women prisoners into a truck and drove them away. Johannsen was beaming. "That was great! What a wonderful piece of tradecraft!"

"Yeah, but what a hard way for Mara to gather intelligence," McCarter commented quietly.

"A shocking example of police brutality," someone said from several feet behind him. McCarter knew that voice. Fred Byrnes was standing there looking every inch the dashing reporter.

"Gentlemen, I'm with Multi Media. I'd like to do an in-depth interview if you are free this evening. I need to get the British point of view. I would appreciate it if you and your friends would meet me at my hotel. Dinner will be on me, of course, and I think I can find some good whiskey."

McCarter smiled. "It will be my pleasure. Riot control is thirsty work. I could use a little good whiskey!"

CHAPTER TEN

The Tiara Medan Hotel, Medan, Sumatra

McCarter led the way through the lobby of the Tiara Medan Hotel. It was an impressive place with polished wood floors and Sumatran native works of art decorating the walls. Uniformed wait staff were scurrying around, carrying trays of drinks to the crowded floor and handling the guests' baggage. McCarter led the group past a bar decorated with tropical flowers. Pretty young women in skimpy dresses that left little to the imagination were serving exotic tropical drinks to the patrons.

Fred Byrnes had said they should meet in his room. The hotel's bar and restaurant were too public for classified conversations. That was a pity. McCarter enjoyed exotic drinks and pretty young women, but duty called. He looked casually around the lobby as they moved toward the elevators. No one seemed to be following them or paying any special attention except for two expensively dressed Indonesian men who were eyeing Ingrid Johannsen speculatively. That was only natural. Six-foot-tall natural blondes were rare in Indonesia.

They walked into the elevator. McCarter pushed

the button for the fourth floor, then looked at his watch. It was a little before seven o'clock. Byrnes should be in his room. They reached the fourth floor, and the elevator doors opened. Gadgets Schwarz used a small hand mirror to scan the hall without stepping out. He gave McCarter the all-clear sign. McCarter led the way to room 408 and rapped on the door. He had keen hearing, and he heard the unmistakable click of a revolver being cocked.

"Who is it?" Byrnes called.

"Green and friends. We're a few minutes early."

McCarter heard the rattle of the door chain being taken off, and the door opened. Byrnes uncocked his .357 Magnum Colt Python and slipped it into an inside-the-waistband holster.

"Come right in. There's a wet bar. Help yourself to whatever you like."

He smiled at Ingrid Johannsen. "You were very good today at that damned demonstration, Ingrid. I saw you kill that man who ran at you with the big knife. That was damned good shooting!"

"I don't know, Fred. I fired sixteen shots, and I only hit him six times. I'm not sure that was very good shooting."

"You're alive and he's dead, Ingrid. I think that's good enough. There are no second-place winners in a gunfight. If you don't believe me, ask Striker."

Byrnes looked around. "Where's Mara Tharin, McCarter?"

"I'm afraid she was unavoidably detained. She is in the maximum-security wing of the Medan women's prison. I fear she isn't having a very pleasant evening."

The CIA agent nodded. He knew how it was. An intelligence agent's life wasn't always a happy one.

"Well, help yourselves to drinks, and we'll order dinner."

"Good idea, Fred, but first there's something I have to do. Gadgets, if you please."

Schwarz nodded and opened the black plastic suitcase he had been carrying. He took out and unfolded a complex piece of electronic equipment.

Byrnes stared at Gadgets Schwarz's latest high-tech marvel.

"What in the hell is that, Gadgets?"

Schwarz smiled. "This little thing, Fred? It's just the latest and greatest man-portable satcom, a Raytheon PSC-5 Spitfire. It makes that crude stuff we were using last year totally obsolete. It will transmit in code or clear voice messages, send fax or video transmissions and allow multiple-user conference calls. I haven't been able to program it to mix drinks yet, but I'm working on it."

Byrnes shook his head. It seemed impossible that one small man-portable device could do all those things, but he had worked with Schwarz before. If he said it would, Byrnes knew it would.

"And all I've got is a cell phone. I'd sell my soul for one of those!"

Schwarz grinned evilly. "Sorry, Fred, but you've been in the CIA for thirty years. I'm afraid your soul's not worth much anymore."

McCarter checked the frequency setting on the Spitfire satcom and pushed the send-and-receive button. Instantly, a narrow radio beam flashed up into space at the speed of light. An American communications satellite received it and relayed it down toward an antenna in Virginia. McCarter glanced around the room. Byrnes and Johannsen seemed casual and relaxed, sipping their drinks and talking about the day's events, but McCarter was very good at reading body language. It had kept him alive more than once. They were listening intently, ready to pick up any clue to McCarter and Bolan's mysterious organization. They weren't hostile, but their CIA training instinctively led them to try to penetrate the secrets of any other secret organization, American or foreign. It was part of their tradecraft.

Perhaps he was about to show them that the Stony Man team had some tradecraft of its own. A green light lit up on the Spitfire's control panel. The communications link was up and working.

"Home Base, this is Diagonal. I say again, Home Base, this is Diagonal."

McCarter heard Barbara Price's cool voice as clearly as if she were standing next to him in the room. Good! Price would understand the special call sign, Diagonal, he had just used and know what it meant. Someone who wasn't a member of the Stony Man team could hear what McCarter was saying and her answers. She would be careful not to reveal anything when she replied.

"Diagonal, this is Home Base. What is your situation?"

McCarter briefed Price.

"So, we are here in the Tiara Medan Hotel except for Jack. He's at the airport, picking up the special package. Wizard and Viking are with us. They and the Indonesian authorities are cooperating with us. No complaints there. What is going on at your end?"

"The Bear is at NRO arranging for more satellite

surveillance support. The big Fed is at the Pentagon meeting with the brass. I'll contact you later and tell you what they found out.''

"Roger, Home Base. Your message understood.''

"Any problems at your end we might be able to help you with?''

"As a matter of fact, there is. We are fighting in the dark, Home Base. We aren't finding the enemy's weak points and striking them as we usually do. Instead, they're calling the tune, and we're reacting to their moves. If we are to accomplish anything, we need better intelligence. Without it, we can't take the initiative. Find us one of these arms-smuggling ships, and we'll capture it or destroy it. Otherwise, we aren't going to accomplish a bloody thing.''

Price paused for a moment. She could sense McCarter's frustration, and it was probable that the rest of the team in Sumatra felt the same way. She was the mission controller. One of her duties was to keep up morale when the team was deployed. She never tried to put a spin on things. It was up to her to support the team and get them what they needed, whether it was hardware or information.

"I understand, Diagonal. All available resources are being used to solve the problem. The White House is deploying additional military resources to the Indonesian area. The National Reconnaissance Office is conducting extensive satellite surveillance of the area. They have identified eight suspect ships. The Navy has deployed six nuclear attack submarines on the sea lanes to northern Indonesia. They will pick up and shadow any of the ships that appear to be heading for Indonesia. I'll inform you immediately when we have more information. In the meantime, continue your activities in Sumatra.''

"Roger, Home Base. Your message received and understood.''

"Anything else, Diagonal?''

"Yes. Striker wishes to speak to you on a matter he says is quite important. Wait a moment, and I'll put him on.''

"What can I do for you, Striker?''

"Go to the witness-protection files. Look under *D*. Contact the person who is in Hilo, Hawaii. Tell her that Striker wants to see the Dragon Lady in Sumatra. If she agrees, get her here as soon as possible.''

Price didn't have the slightest idea who or what the Dragon Lady was, but she was the Stony Man mission controller. If Bolan wanted to see the Dragon Lady in Sumatra, Price would do her damnedest to get her there.

"Roger, Striker. Message understood. Will comply. Home Base out.''

USS La Jolla, *off the Northern Coast of Sumatra*

COMMANDER JOHN ADAMS WAS dead to the world, sleeping the deep sleep of exhaustion. He had been on watch four hours on duty followed by four hours of rest and then another four hours on duty for the past three days. He had been asleep for an hour when someone rapped urgently on his door. He suppressed the desire to kill whoever was knocking at his door. "Come.''

"Sorry to wake you up, Captain, but the XO said to tell you that we have one of the suspect ships on sonar. He has changed course to intercept her. The

XO estimates we will be in visual range within twenty minutes.''

No rest for the wicked. He slipped on his shoes and reached for his cap.

"Tell the executive officer I'll be right there."

He walked down the narrow corridor and stepped into the attack center, the *La Jolla*'s nerve center. He glanced quickly at the panels that covered the left side of the attack centers. Each display board showed an array of green lights. Good. Green boards showed that there were no emergencies or problems. All the *La Jolla*'s systems were working properly.

Captain Adams looked at the symbols on his attack display. The computer was showing him the tactical situation for two hundred miles around him. Blue symbols showed friendly vessels, while yellow showed neutrals. There were no red symbols. Those were reserved for hostile ships or submarines. The United States wasn't at war at the moment, but Adams knew that that could change at any moment.

He turned to the chief petty officer, who sat at the weapons-control console. "How are we loaded, Chief?"

"Harpoon ASMs in one and three, Mark 48s in two and four, Captain."

All four of *La Jolla*'s torpedo tubes were loaded. Two long-range antiship missiles and two torpedoes loaded and ready to fire. The *La Jolla* was ready for action. If it came down to it, either Harpoons or Mark 48s could blow the *Wuhan* out of the water.

La Jolla was running in total emission control. None of her electronic systems were radiating. She was being extremely quiet, but her sonar operators and electronic systems were listening intently. Adams

looked at his close in attack display. The *Wuhan*
should be in easy visual range. He stepped to the periscope and pushed a button. The periscope slid
smoothly upward. He stared through the periscope's
eyepieces. There she was, steaming along at fifteen
knots. There was nothing unusual about her. She
looked like hundreds of other small freighters that
sailed the South China Sea.

Adams spoke over his shoulder to his executive
officer. "That's the *Wuhan,* all right. Call Washington
and tell them we've found her. Then ask them politely
just what the hell they want us to do next."

The Situation Room, the Pentagon

HAL BROGNOLA LISTENED quietly as the CIA representative finished his briefing.

Admiral Stone looked at the map and made a few
quick calculations.

"All right, gentlemen, I think I understand the situation. The first part of what you want is quite easy.
The *Wuhan* is a freighter, small, old and slow. *La
Jolla* can intercept her in a half an hour, but the problem is just what do we tell her to do then?"

General Blake looked puzzled. He wasn't about to
tell a U.S. Navy admiral how to operate his submarines, but the answer seemed obvious to him.

"Force her to stop her engines and heave to, Admiral. Then, have *La Jolla*'s crew board her and
search her, find the weapons and order her into an
Indonesian port. A ship full of AK-47s ought to convince even the damned UN!"

Stone shook his head. "I wish it was that easy, but
it's not. I can have Captain Adams sink the *Wuhan*

easily, but I'm not sure he can make her stop and be boarded.''

Blake was puzzled. The *Wuhan* was a freighter. Surely, there was nothing she could do to resist a modern U.S. Navy nuclear attack submarine.

''I don't understand, Admiral. What's the problem?'' he demanded.

''International law and *La Jolla*'s weapons capability,'' Stone said. ''You tell me you think there is a large shipment of weapons on board the freighter. I think you're probably right, but you don't know that for certain. We have no evidence of any illegal activity. The *Wuhan* may not be carrying anything but a cargo of rice. She's a Chinese merchant ship, proceeding on the high seas. Her captain can argue that we have no right to stop him, and legally, he's right. Any captain who is approached by a strange submarine is likely to radio an emergency message immediately. If the message is received by the Chinese authorities, we're going to have an ugly international incident. There's another problem. We are neither armed nor equipped to stop and board a ship on the high seas. The *La Jolla*'s crew has no training for that kind of operation.''

''If you stop her, why can't you board her?'' Blake persisted.

''I'm not sure *La Jolla* can stop her,'' Stone said.

''I beg your pardon, Admiral, but I don't understand,'' Blake continued. ''Surely, you can fire a shot across her bow and stop her. If we find the weapons there, they won't dare protest. If we don't, we let her go and let the lawyers argue.''

''*La Jolla* can't put a shot across her bows. I wish she could, but she can't. U.S. Navy attack submarines haven't carried cannons for fifty years. The biggest guns on board the sub are M-16 rifles. *La Jolla* is armed with four 21-inch torpedo tubes. She carries two kinds of antiship weapons, Harpoon missiles and Mark 48 torpedoes. Give the order, and she can blow the *Wuhan* out of the water from fifty miles away with Harpoons or sink her with Mark 48 torpedoes closer in, but I can't just damage her. If we intercept the freighter and *La Jolla* surfaces and orders her to stop, her captain just may say 'To hell with you' and keep on steaming. If that happens, we either sink her or let her go.''

"You can't just damage her enough to make her stop?" Brognola asked.

Stone shook his head. "She's a cargo ship, and she's not very large, only about twelve thousand tons. There's no way to control the exact spot a Harpoon missile or a Mark 48 torpedo will hit her. Both are very powerful antiship weapons. One hit with either one of them will probably sink her. I'm not willing to order *La Jolla* to attack without positive evidence she's involved in illegal acts.''

Blake frowned. The admiral's legal scruples didn't bother him. He saw no difference between killing the enemies of the United States with rifles or torpedoes, but sinking the *Wuhan* with missiles or torpedoes would destroy the evidence. There had to be some other solution. He stared at the situation map.

"You've got an amphibious assault ship off the coast of Sumatra with a battalion of Marines on board. Why not order her to intercept the *Wuhan* and have the marines board her?"

Stone shook his head. "It's still the same damned problem, General. Under international law, we have no right to stop and search a ship belonging to a foreign power. That's an act of war. I can't order anyone to do it without a direct order from the President, and he's tied up for hours with the prime minister of India.''

Blake turned to Hal Brognola. "You haven't said anything, Mr. Brognola. I remember the President said you are an expert on international law. What do think?''

"I'm sorry, General, but I believe Admiral Stone is right. We aren't at war with China. For U.S. military personnel to board the *Wuhan* without hard evidence of illegal action under international law would be an act of war.''

Blake slammed his fist on the table. "Goddammit! We can't stop her and we can't board her. What the hell are we supposed to do, just sit here and do nothing?''

"I didn't say we can't board her,'' Brognola said. "Just that we can't use United States military men. That's a very dangerous area the *Wuhan* is sailing in. Piracy is rife. Anything might happen to a ship with a valuable cargo. I say we board her. We will just have to be sure we maintain plausible deniability.''

The CIA representative chuckled. He knew instantly what Brognola meant. Perhaps people from the Department of Justice were smarter than he thought.

"Can you arrange that, Mr. Brognola?'' he asked.

"I believe I can. I'll have to talk to the President.''

The Marshal's Situation Room

NINE THOUSAND MILES away another group of men was discussing the situation. A large map of the South

China Sea hung on one wall of the situation room. Dozens of small colored flags were attached to the map showing the positions of ships and submarines, some theirs, some those of the hated Americans.

A tall thin man in a dark blue naval uniform was concluding his briefing. He wore the insignia of an admiral on his shoulder straps.

"So you see, here are the eleven cargo ships directly assigned to Operation Red Dragon. These flags show the position of our submarines. Those two groups of blue flags represent the two American battle groups. Each has a large aircraft carrier that carries approximately eighty fighters and attack planes. Each group also has a dozen surface combat ships. Their main role is to protect the carrier. The yellow flags along the coast of Indonesia are Indonesian warships. They are not large or powerful, but they could be used to intercept the Red Dragon cargo ships if the role of any of them is discovered. Are there any question?"

"Yes. Where are our surface ships? Surely, our new cruise missile armed destroyers would be a serious threat to the American carriers."

"They would, Marshal, but they will not be deployed without authorization from the highest levels. The American satellites would detect them as soon as they moved toward their carriers. Who knows how they would react! My orders were to do nothing to provoke a direct clash with the Americans. That is why I am relying on our submarines. The American satellites cannot see them as long as they remain submerged."

"If the Americans detect them, cannot they tell that the submarines are ours?"

"They cannot be certain, sir. It is true that each

class of submarine has its own distinct sonar signature. The submarines I have deployed are Russian-built Kilo class. The Russians have sold Kilo-class submarines to many countries. The Americans will know they have detected a Kilo-class submarine, but they cannot be sure whose Kilo it is. I think that they will be reluctant to fire unless we fire first.''

The marshal knew very little about naval warfare. He had done his fighting on land for fifty years. Still, he was satisfied. The admiral seemed competent, and his planning was thorough. He nodded to the general sitting quietly by his side.

''Give us your assessment, General. How do you evaluate the most recent events?''

The general strode to the map and pointed to Sumatra. ''As you know, our actions in Timor are a feint to distract the Americans and keep them off balance. Western Sumatra is our main objective. In general, things are going well there. We have established contact with all the dissident groups who are working for Sumatran independence. We are supplying arms to any group who wants them. We are using them to conduct guerrilla warfare against the Indonesian forces on Sumatra.''

A man in an expensive gray suit held up his hand. ''Are you saying that everything is going well? That there are no problems?''

The general had never met the man in the gray suit, but he knew who he was. He wished that he hadn't been asked to the meeting, but the premier had sent him.

''No, sir. There are always problems in any large paramilitary operation.''

"Perhaps you will enlighten us, General. What are these problems?"

"The Americans are reacting strongly. They do not know the details of our plan. They are not certain who we are. But they know someone is working against them. They are bringing in military resources and sending aid to the Indonesians. Perhaps more threatening, they are moving intelligence resources into Sumatra to try and discover our plans. I will show you an example."

He touched a button, the lights dimmed and a projection screen slid down in front of the map. A picture of a tall blond woman walking down a street appeared on the screen. The projector clicked, and a close-up of the woman's face appeared on the screen.

"This is Ingrid Johannsen. She was the CIA's principal operative in East Timor. They have transferred her to Sumatra. She is in charge of the CIA's operations there."

"Surely, there must be some mistake, General," the man in the gray suit said. "Why would the Americans put a woman in such an important position? If they are seriously concerned, why do they not send in a team of experienced agents?"

"Because the Americans have very few experienced agents who can speak Indonesian. She is the best person who is available. Do not be deceived by her sex and her strange appearance. Our agents say that although she lacks experience in the field, she is highly intelligent and reasonably competent. Also, look at this next picture. We suspect that the Americans have sent in an assassination team to support her."

A picture of Mack Bolan and David McCarter flashed on the screen.

"These men suddenly appeared on the scene in East Timor. They are supposed to be an observation team of some sort. Perhaps so, but they are extremely competent with their weapons. We almost succeeded in killing Johannsen in East Timor. These men saved her. Now they have accompanied her to Sumatra. I do not believe in coincidences. I suspect they are part of a CIA paramilitary team."

"You are probably right. What do you intend to do about it?"

The marshal interrupted smoothly. "Do not worry about them. West Sumatra is a dangerous place. I fear that they will all have a serious accident."

He glanced around the conference table. "Are there any more questions? No? Then Red Dragon will proceed as planned. This meeting is adjourned."

The marshal stared at the map. He would rather have had this battle on land. He had sent hundreds of thousands of his country's soldiers into battle many times. Now, he was old and had to sit behind a desk while younger men did the fighting. Perhaps now was the time to think about retiring. He noticed that he wasn't alone. The general was standing at his shoulder.

"Is there something else, General?" the marshal inquired.

"Sir," the general formally, "I wish to make a personal request."

The marshal kept his face impassive, but he was worried. If the general was losing his nerve and was unable to stand the stress, he was in trouble. It would be impossible to replace him on short notice.

"What is your request?" he responded quietly.

"Sir, I am concerned about the situation in Sumatra, more than I was willing to say in the meeting. If we are defeated in Sumatra, I am afraid the government will not continue Red Dragon. Our officers in Sumatra are good men, but they are young and inexperienced. I, at least, have been in combat. Send me to take command in Sumatra. I will win or I will not return."

The marshal smiled. That was the kind of man he liked to have in his command.

"No, you are responsible for all the other operations, too, not just the ones in Indonesia. I cannot spare you, but you are right. Sumatra is critical. We must have a skilled commander on the spot. Pick your best colonel, and send him. What about your operations officer? He seems to be an able man."

"Colonel Chun? Yes, sir. He is an excellent officer, and he has been in combat before."

"Good, send him at once. If the Americans are really starting to move, we have no time to spare."

CHAPTER ELEVEN

Military Headquarters, Medan, Western Sumatra

General Rahman looked up from his desk as Mack Bolan, David McCarter and Major Salim were ushered into his office. The general seemed to be in a cheerful mood.

"Good morning, gentlemen. I trust you had a pleasant evening. As you Americans say, there is good news and bad news, but at least some of the news was good for a change. The demonstration here yesterday has put the fear of God into the government in Java. They have decided to send me some reinforcements, three battalions of infantry and a battalion of Marines. It is not everything I need, but it will let me keep the lid on here and immediately reinforce our troops in Aceh Province."

"Is there more trouble in Aceh, sir?" Salim asked quickly.

"Yes, that is the bad news. Guerrilla attacks on our troops and police have been increasing steadily. Our intelligence believes that there will be large-scale demonstrations in the near future. Aceh has always had several strong groups who are opposed to the central government. New Russian-type weapons are starting to turn up. If they can get good weapons in quantity, I am afraid that there may be serious fighting.''

Rahman strode to the map of Sumatra on the wall. He pointed at the western end of the big island.

''There is the city of Banda Aceh, the capital of Aceh Province. There was a large demonstration there three days ago. A mob attacked government buildings. My troops there were forced to fire on them, and thirty civilians were killed. The UN Security Council has an investigating committee on the scene. We must take action to defuse this situation before it blows up in our faces.''

He paused for a moment and looked at McCarter and Bolan.

''Banda Aceh is where the action will be for the next few days, gentlemen. I am dispatching Major Salim and Miss Tharin there immediately. Do you wish to accompany them or stay here?''

McCarter looked at Mack Bolan. Bolan nodded. If the action was going to be in Aceh Province, that was where they wanted to be.

''We will be glad to go with them, General. In fact, we can provide some first-class transportation. We have a high-performance military helicopter waiting at the airport. We flew in on a C-17 last night. It can fly to Banda Aceh in an hour, carrying the entire party and their gear.''

''Very well, gentlemen. Is there anything else you require?''

''Yes, sir. I need your order to BRIMOB to release Mara Tharin in my custody,'' Salim said.

The general smiled. ''How is Mara? I do not think she has been enjoying her stay with BRIMOB?''

"No, they think she is a rebel, and they are treating her harshly. They whipped her a few times, but she will be all right. She will have no permanent scars. In a week or two, she will be as good as new."

McCarter thought that was a rotten way to treat a young woman, but he was leading a mission in a foreign country. He kept his mouth shut.

An aide abruptly entered the office and spoke to the general. "Sir, there is a very tall American woman outside. She says she works for the American government. She says she has a message for you from the United States, which you must hear at once."

"A message for me from the American government? I did not think that they knew that I existed. Show her in immediately."

Johannsen bustled in, her face flushed with excitement.

"General, I have just received a direct message from CIA headquarters on satcom. I think you should see it immediately."

She took an envelope marked Classified and handed it to him. Rahman opened the envelope and read the message rapidly.

"The message says that your NSA has intercepted and partly decoded a radio message originating in the South China Sea. A Colonel Chun is on the way to assume command in Red Area. I am sure that this is very interesting, Miss Johannsen, but it is not very enlightening. Who is this mysterious colonel? Where is he coming from? And where is Red Area?"

"The computers at NSA weren't able to decipher all of this message, General, because it was in a fairly advanced code developed in China, but they were able to decipher enough so that the information could be compared with our surveillance satellite intelligence. It was about six hours ago that they were able to decipher that was in cipher.''

Rahman was starting to feel impatient, but he smiled tolerantly. He could remember the first briefing he had given to a group of generals long ago. Besides, he was always courteous to women, especially those representing friendly foreign nations. Let her have her moment of glory.

''I am afraid you have lost me, Miss Johannsen. I am a simple soldier. I do not understand. Is not code, code? If your NSA can read part of it, why can they not read it all?''

Johannsen was startled. Surely, everyone knew the difference between codes and ciphers. Still, perhaps generals didn't bother with the small details.

''In cipher, the sender types the message in normal language, and the machine puts it in cipher, substituting letters or numbers for the spelling of the actual words. It was the cipher that the NSA computers were able to decode, but they also used code in some places. It's impossible to crack the code, because they use substitute words that only the people receiving the message know. We can deduce that Red Area is a place. However, we can't tell from the message what or where it is.''

Rahman frowned. If that were true, what use was the message?

Johannsen continued quickly. ''However, the really good news is that our satellites were able to pinpoint the replies to the original message. They detected seven of them, all on the same frequency, and all using the same code. Six of the replies came from within Indonesia. Three of the six are in Sumatra. One of these signed its reply 'Red Area.' Our satellite data tells us that Red Area transmitted from a site forty miles east of Banda Aceh. We can locate that site with an accuracy of three miles.''

Salim grasped instantly what the woman was saying.

"God is great! He has delivered them into our hands. Let us pay this Red Area headquarters a visit. It would make me very happy to meet the enemy face-to-face.''

"Great work, Ingrid!" McCarter said. "But I have one question. You said seven sites replied, but one wasn't in Indonesia. Where is it?''

"In the South China Sea. NSA has checked with the Navy. Their data indicates that the source is one of our suspect ships, the freighter *Wuhan* out of Hong Kong. If she maintains her present course, she will be off Sumatra in twenty-four hours. And one more thing. A U.S. Navy attack submarine is shadowing her. When she reaches Sumatra, we'll know exactly where they are going to land the weapons!''

The general's aide reentered the office and spoke quietly to the general.

Rahman smiled sardonically. "Duty calls. Captain Ajeng informs me that a United Nations human rights committee is here to investigate me for my brutal violations of human rights. They have heard of my brutal repression of innocent Sumatran citizens who want only to peacefully protest the actions of the government. Who knows? The next time you see me, I may be on trial for war crimes. You had better go before you, too, are indicted. Go with God.''

Over Western Sumatra

JACK GRIMALDI SLIPPED into the MH-60K Black Hawk's pilot seat with a smile on his face. He had felt like a fifth wheel on this mission so far, missing the action and not having any clear function. Now he had his bird and he was ready to fly. Grimaldi was a master pilot, and he was back in his element. The fuselage of the Black Hawk shook as the rest of the Stony Man team loaded themselves and their equipment into the passenger compartment. Fred Byrnes and Ingrid Johannsen were already on board. They were all there except for Mack Bolan. He had gone to the airport's civilian terminal to pick up Gary Manning and meet some mysterious diplomatic courier.

Grimaldi looked out his side window. Major Salim was standing outside looking impatiently at his watch. A police jeep pulled up manned by two BRIMOB officers. They pulled Mara Tharin out of the back seat and shoved her roughly toward the major. The woman looked as if they had been giving her a hard time. Her face was bruised and her T-shirt was ripped and torn. She had a gag in her mouth, and she limped as she tried to walk with her hands handcuffed behind her. One of the BRIMOB officers handed Salim a clipboard. He studied the papers on it, nodded and signed his name several times. The BRIMOB officer departed as the major helped Tharin into the chopper.

Grimaldi saw Bolan and Manning walking rapidly toward the Black Hawk. There was a woman walking with them, a stranger, but someone the Stony Man pilot thought he ought to know. He was always interested in attractive women, and whoever she was, she certainly made the grade. She had long legs, long dark black hair and walked with an easy feline grace as if she were relaxed but ready to spring into action at a moment's notice.

Grimaldi grinned. He certainly needed to get to know her better. He hoped she was one of those charming women who were impressed by intrepid birdmen.

"Let's go, Jack," McCarter said. "Everyone is on board. We've wasted enough time here. Let's go!"

Major Salim strapped himself into the copilot's seat and started to check out the weapons and sensors. Grimaldi pushed the starter switches and felt the Black Hawk shudder as the twin T700-GE-701 turbine engines began to whine. He looked at the major, who was checking with the control tower. Salim nodded, and Grimaldi advanced his throttles. The engines' whine deepened to a howl as he went to full power and lifted the chopper smoothly into the air. He climbed to four hundred feet and leveled off. Below, he could see the rooftops of Medan. Almost instantly, they had passed the city's boundaries and were skimming low and fast over a carpet of green trees. He checked his displays. Both engines were running smoothly. All the other indicators were green.

Salim was speaking rapidly in Indonesian to the Medan airport tower. Grimaldi couldn't understand a word he said, but the tone in Salim's voice told him something was going on.

"What's up, Major?" Grimaldi asked quickly.

"I am not sure. It may be merely a coincidence, but a commercial helicopter took off immediately after we did and is following us now. It was some kind of commercial Bell Huey. It is registered to a Medan air-taxi service."

Grimaldi looked to the rear end. He was surprised

to see that the other helicopter was following very closely, maintaining its position a few hundred yards behind them. It was an Augusta Bell version of the Huey, like the Indonesian army choppers they had flown in on Timor. It wasn't camouflaged like the army birds. It sported a bright blue-and-white paint job. Probably a civilian helicopter, but Grimaldi knew that it was easy to mount weapons on any variety of Huey. He could see two teardrop-shaped objects mounted on either side of its fuselage. They were probably extra fuel tanks, but they could be weapons pods.

"I don't like it. It sure as hell looks like it's following us."

Salim shrugged. "Perhaps so, but there is no way to be sure. We are on the direct route to Banda Aceh. Many people fly there every day. Perhaps it is merely a coincidence."

Maybe so, but Grimaldi didn't like coincidences when he was on a mission. He concentrated on his flying. He kept his eyes on his multifunctional display. The MFD converted the data from the MH-60K's infrared sensors and radar into a clear picture of the scene ahead. Even in broad daylight, the infrared sensors could see through dust and haze far better than the human eye. He would use their capabilities to keep the Black Hawk down near the treetops. If the helicopter behind them was actually following them, he just might see how good their pilot was down at a hundred feet.

Just in case, it was time to arm the Black Hawk's weapons systems. Grimaldi threw five switches. A row of green lights on the weapons control console came on. The Black Hawk was carrying two, 19-

round, 2.75-inch multiple rocket launchers under each stubby External Stores Support System wing. They were ready to fire. Grimaldi checked the fixed .50-caliber machine gun he controlled. It was loaded and on safe. He could fire it with the flick of a switch.

Salim was watching closely. "I thought Black Hawks were troop transports. This one seems to be heavily armed."

"You're right, Major. Most Black Hawks are transports, but this is one of the MH-60K Special Operations Command versions. It has the weapons and sensors to do a little fighting. Speaking of that, do me a favor. Go back to the passenger compartment and tell Gadgets he's needed up front. If we are going to fight, I'll need him to operate the countermeasures. Ask Striker to have someone mount the door guns. Tell everybody else to be sure they're strapped in tight. We may have to do some fancy maneuvering. I don't want to break anyone's neck."

Salim stared at Grimaldi for a second. Was he joking? No. Salim had never seen anyone fly a helicopter like that, but the pilot seemed certain that he could do it. He unfastened his seat belt and stepped into the passenger compartment. The rest of the party was sitting on the hard troop transport seats. Since all the Black Hawk's sensors and weapons were operated from the cockpit, they really had nothing to do but stare at one another for the next hour.

Ingrid Johannsen looked at the mysterious woman Striker had brought on board. The woman sat opposite her, as relaxed, cool and calm as if she rode on special-operations helicopters often. Johannsen was curious. She wanted to know who and what this woman was. It might give her another clue to who and what Striker was. She decided to try the warm-and-polite approach.

"Hello. Striker forgot to introduce you. I'm Ingrid Johannsen. I work for the U.S. government. Striker said you are a special courier for the State Department. That sounds like an interesting job."

The woman took off her stylish wraparound sunglasses and stared coolly at Ingrid for a moment.

"I am Meiko Tanaka. I am not a diplomatic courier. That is merely my cover story. I am here because Striker sent for me. I owe him a debt of honor. I could not refuse."

Johannsen gazed at the woman's face. It was totally impassive. For all the emotion she showed, she might have said, "The sun is shining brightly."

"So you and Striker are old friends, Meiko?"

The woman looked annoyed. "I did not say that. I know him, of course, but I do not know him well. Two years ago, I was in great trouble here in Indonesia. Striker helped me. He got me out of the country and arranged for me to get U.S. citizenship. Naturally, I was grateful. I said, 'If you or your team ever need the services of a person with my limited talents and small skills, call me, Striker, and I will come.' That was a promise, a debt of honor. My ancestors have been samurai for a thousand years. I will keep that promise or die trying. If you are a person of honor, you will understand that."

Johannsen stared at her. "Death before dishonor" was a trite and foolish phrase unless the person who said it really meant it.

Tanaka took a flat black 9 mm pistol out of the brown leather case at her feet and checked it carefully, then put it back. The conversation was obviously over. Johannsen felt she had been judged and found wanting. Perhaps the warm-and-polite approach hadn't been a good idea. The woman was very polite in her choice of words, but she didn't seem to be the friendly sort. The CIA agent watched, fascinated, as Tanaka casually pulled up her short skirt and drew a .25-caliber Beretta from a thigh holster. Johannsen wasn't an expert on firearms, but she knew that the black cylinder attached to the little pistol's muzzle was a sound suppressor. Tanaka checked the weapon and returned it to its holster.

Gadgets Schwarz slipped into the copilot's seat and buckled his harness.

"What do you think, Jack? Is that helicopter after us?" Schwarz asked.

Grimaldi shrugged. "I'm not sure, but I'm damned well going to find out. I've been going straight for Banda Aceh. Now I'm going to change course and fly off the direct route. If he goes on straight for Banda Aceh, he's probably legitimate. If he follows us, things are going to get a bit hot. Better check out your countermeasures."

He brought the nose of the helicopter smoothly around thirty degrees toward the south. Now the ball was in the other team's court.

Schwarz looked out the cockpit's right side window. He held a pair of gyroscopically stabilized binoculars in his hands and stared at the blue and white helicopter behind them.

"No reaction so far, Jack. He's maintaining his previous course and speed. No, wait. He's turning, changing course. He's staying right behind us."

Schwarz continued to scan the other helicopter.

"See anything else?" Grimaldi asked.

"Damned right I do! Those two things mounted on the sides of the fuselage aren't extra fuel tanks. I think they're weapons pods. I can see two machine-gun barrels sticking out the front of the closest. I can't be sure about the other one, but I think that it's got rockets or is a missile pod. Whoever they are, I don't think they're the local welcoming committee."

The countermeasures control panel suddenly beeped. A red light began to blink steadily.

"Look out, Jack! They've turned on a fire-control radar. They're locked on!"

Grimaldi didn't hesitate. He pushed his throttles forward. The Black Hawk's twin turbines howled as they went to full war emergency. Bolan and Manning had mounted the .30-caliber GE Minigun doorguns. Now it was time for tactics.

If the Augusta Bell helicopter carried air-to-air missiles, they outranged the Black Hawk's 2.75-inch rockets. Better to get in close, and do it now. Grimaldi grinned fiercely as he suddenly pulled the nose of the Black Hawk into a hard left turn and went straight at the blue-and-white helicopter. Whatever the trailing helicopter's pilot had expected, it wasn't that.

Fortunately, the Black Hawk had been designed to go in harm's way. Its engine-exhaust ducts were fitted with infrared suppression kits to reduce their infrared signature and make it harder for infrared homing missiles to lock on. The MH-60K had an ALQ-144 infrared jammer and a flare dispenser. If the other helicopter had air-to-air missiles, they would have to depend on them.

Bolan's voice crackled on the intercom. "Heads up, Jack! They're coming in!"

Grimaldi saw them, too. "All right, we're going in.

Gary, Striker, open the doors! Stand by to engage targets to either side. Gadgets, stand by to fire rockets on my command, and give me infrared counter-measures now!''

Schwarz pushed a button, and the ALQ-144 began to pulse, emitting incredibly bright flashes of infrared light. The flashes were almost invisible to the human eye, but they were blinding to the seekers on the in-frared missiles trying to home in on the Black Hawk.

Manning was ready, crouched behind the gun in the Black Hawk's right-hand door. He saw some yel-low tracers flashing from the side of the other heli-copter. He aimed the minigun and fired. The squat, cylindrical Gatling gun exploded into life. Swarms of red tracers shot out from the helicopter's side and flashed toward the blue-and-white aircraft. Manning had set the firing rate to the maximum of 6,000 rounds per minute. He fired only a three second burst as the Black Hawk swept by the target area, but in those three seconds the minigun poured 300 rounds at the enemy bird.

The MH-60K shuddered as it absorbed the mini-gun's recoil. Grimaldi fought his controls to maintain his course and speed. He pulled the chopper around in a hard left turn that would have made its designers extremely nervous.

"Ready to fire rockets!" He lined up the MH-60K's nose straight on the cockpit of the hostile helicopter and went straight at it as the enemy aircraft returned fire. Yellow tracers clawed at the Black Hawk and flashed past Grimaldi's windscreen. He squeezed the trigger and sent a burst of .50-caliber, armor-piercing, incendiary machine-gun bullets in re-ply. The cylindrical rocket launchers under the Black

Hawk's stub wings were suddenly wreathed with halos of orange fire as Schwarz began launching the 2.75-inch rockets.

Grimaldi saw the orange burning dots of the rocket motors as the rockets accelerated away, trailing lines of white smoke. Each of the four rocket launcher pods could fire a rocket every second.

"Look out, Jack!" Schwarz yelled. They were getting too close for comfort. Grimaldi pulled the Black Hawk's nose up and felt the dull black helicopter shudder as Manning fired another burst.

Manning's voice crackled in Grimaldi's headset. "Missile launch at six o'clock!"

Schwarz didn't wait for orders. Instantly, he pushed the button, and the Black Hawk's ALE-39 flare dispenser began to shoot infrared flares into its wake. Grimaldi could see the missile flashing toward them in his rearview mirror, streaming gray smoke behind it as its solid-propellant rocket motor burned. He knew the missile's infrared guidance unit was searching for a heat source, trying to lock on and home in on the Black Hawk. He was too low to take evasive action, and he knew that his chopper could never outfly the missile. All he could do was depend on the helicopter's countermeasures and pray.

The missile shot toward the Black Hawk. Its guidance unit searched ahead, looking for its target, which wasn't a strong infrared source. The bright pulses from its infrared jammer and the explosions of light from the flares dazzled and confused it. The guidance unit expanded its search pattern. There! Down and to the left was a clear, unambiguous target. The missile locked on, flashed forward, struck the heat source and detonated.

Grimaldi didn't want to give the other helicopter's crew a chance to launch again. He turned hard and pulled the Black Hawk's nose up. He saw the blue-and-white helicopter lined up in his sights as its pilot tried to twist aside. Grimaldi pressed the trigger. The Black Hawk vibrated as the big .50-caliber Browning machine gun roared into life. Grimaldi saw a stream of red tracers flash toward the enemy aircraft.

The .50-caliber Browning was one of the most powerful heavy machine guns in the world. Its half-inch-diameter, armor-piercing, incendiary bullets were five times heavier than those fired by a .30-caliber military rifle. They were designed to tear through metal and start fires, and they did their job. They ripped through the hostile helicopter's skin as if it were made of tissue paper. Grimaldi could see the yellow-white flashes of high-velocity bullets striking metal.

The blue-and-white helicopter shuddered and went down, trailing light gray smoke. Grimaldi lined up his sights and fired again. He wasn't particularly vindictive, but the other helicopter's crew had just tried to kill him. He wasn't going to give them a chance to try again. Grimaldi pressed his trigger, and the big Browning roared again. Metal shards flew from the enemy aircraft's fuselage. Dark gray smoke began to pour from the transmission housing.

Grimaldi heard McCarter's voice in his headset. "What's going on up there, Jack?"

Grimaldi knew that the people in the passenger compartment couldn't see what was happening straight ahead.

"I've hit them with the .50-caliber Browning. They

are damaged, under control, but they're going down. One more burst and they're finished.''

"Hold your fire! Let them land if they can. Major Salim wants to take prisoners. Even if they are all dead, we may find out something when we search the wreckage. Keep ready to shoot and follow them down.''

"Roger. Will comply.''

CHAPTER TWELVE

Aceh Province, Western Sumatra

Grimaldi kept the other helicopter in his sights and followed it down. Whoever the other pilot was, he was good, fighting his controls to keep his stricken bird in a shallow dive. There was a large clearing in the trees ahead. The crippled helicopter headed toward it, trailing a thick plume of dark gray smoke. It clipped the upper branches as it barely cleared the trees on the near edge of the clearing, touched down hard and skidded across the open ground in a cloud of dust.

Grimaldi slowed and hovered a hundred feet off the ground and fifty yards away from the smoking wreck. Its rotors were torn off, but its fuselage was mostly intact. McCarter was right. Anyone whom the bursts of .50-caliber machine gun fire hadn't killed could well have survived the crash. He had better be careful. The Augusta Bell's door machine guns might still be working, and the hovering Black Hawk would be an easy target.

He pivoted the fuselage so that Manning's door-mounted Gatling gun could cover the wreck. Anyone who tried to match a single-barreled machine gun against Manning's Gatling would soon discover the error of his ways.

McCarter's voice crackled in Grimaldi's headset. "All right, Jack. Set her down, and we'll pay our friends a little call."

Grimaldi reduced power and the Black Hawk slowly settled to the ground. Manning's .30-caliber Gatling was still pointing at the wreck, but there was no hostile reaction.

"Good show, Jack. Striker, Major Salim and I are on the way. Keep us covered."

Grimaldi looked out the side cockpit window. They were advancing carefully. Bolan and McCarter had their M-4 Ranger carbines ready. Salim had an AK-47 gripped in his hands. Meiko Tanaka was going along. McCarter hadn't said she was going. The woman had probably invited herself. She seemed unarmed, but Grimaldi wasn't deceived. The woman was deadly.

Bolan and McCarter led the way toward the smoldering wreck. Most of the smoke from the transmission area had dissipated. As they got closer, they could smell the acrid chemical odor from the wrecked helicopter's automatic fire-extinguisher system. The fuselage was tipped a bit to the right. Bolan could see the long black barrel of a .30-caliber machine gun pointing out the side door. He snapped up his M-4 carbine, but there was no need to fire. The door gunner's body was hanging limp in his web harness.

Bolan and McCarter moved cautiously closer. Tanaka followed them and looked over their shoulders. The door gunner had stopped half a dozen big .50-caliber bullets. His chest was soaked with blood.

"Notice something interesting? This chap is Oriental. Chinese, I would say at a guess," McCarter said.

"You're right, David. That might be significant."

"As for his being Chinese, three million ethnic Chinese live in Indonesia. Some Chinese families have lived in Indonesia for more than three hundred years. Do not jump to conclusions!" Tanaka warned.

"Sorry about that, Meiko," McCarter said with a grin. "I'll try to do better in the future."

Tanaka drew her pistol and moved carefully along the fuselage toward the cockpit door, cautiously looking through the cockpit window.

"There is blood on the pilot's seat, Striker, but there is no one here. The door on the other side is partway open. They must have left. Perhaps they made for the trees."

Bolan and McCarter joined her. The pilot's seat was soaked with blood, and the windscreen in front of it was riddled with bullet holes.

"This's odd," McCarter said. "I don't think they made a run for the trees. Jack would have seen them as he was setting down. Could they be hiding in the passenger compartment? Perhaps we should carefully go see and—"

"Look out!" Tanaka yelled before throwing herself down. A black metal object shaped like a large egg was sailing over the top of the fuselage and dropping toward them.

McCarter had fast reflexes. "Grenade!" he shouted, and dropped to the ground.

Bolan was a fraction of a second behind him. The grenade struck the ground and detonated. The explosion of a real hand grenade wasn't impressive, but Bolan knew it wasn't the blast that killed. It was the shower of metal fragments. Bolan felt three hard blows like a boxer's jabs on his left side as he went down.

He wasn't sure if he was wounded or not; he had no time to think about it. He heard shouting in a language he didn't understand, and three men rushed around the nose of the downed helicopter with AK-47s in their hands. Bolan twisted onto his side, trying to bring his sights on. He could see the cold black muzzle of the first man's rifle swing toward him. At point-blank range, the AK-47's steel-jacketed bullets would easily tear through the soft body armor he wore under his shirt.

Bolan heard the flat, repeated crack of a 9 mm pistol as Tanaka fired as fast as she could pull the trigger. The Executioner saw the winking yellow muzzle-flashes as the AK spit a 6-round burst. The dirt fountained upward as the steel-jacketed bullets smashed into the ground a foot from Mack Bolan's head. Tanaka shrieked a wordless battle cry and kept shooting. The AK-47's muzzle swung toward Bolan's face. The gunner suddenly jerked and shuddered as two of Tanaka's 9 mm hollowpoint rounds tore through his shoulder. He pivoted and fired a short burst at her. She was twisting desperately to one side as the AK-47 fired. The burst of steel-jacketed bullets missed her by inches. He aimed again, but time had run out for him. Bolan's sights were aimed at the center of his chest, and he pressed the trigger. His M-4 carbine snarled and drilled six high-velocity bullets through the man's chest. He staggered, sagged and collapsed to the ground.

Bolan heard the snarl of AK-47s firing rapidly to his left and the higher-pitched crackle of an M-4 carbine replying. He swung his carbine to the left, but there was no one left for him to shoot. McCarter had cut down one man, and Salim had riddled the other. Everything was suddenly still.

"Is everyone all right?" McCarter called. Everyone seemed to be.

Tanaka slipped a fresh magazine into her CZ-75. She was in a cold self-contained rage, hissing with anger and humiliation.

"I apologize for my miserable shooting, Striker. I am not skilled at this kind of shooting. Please forgive me."

"Consider yourself forgiven, Meiko. You hit him. That's all that counts. If you hadn't hit him, he would have killed me."

Tanaka looked dubious. "I will try hard to do better next time, Striker, I will—" She suddenly snapped up her pistol. "Look out! There is someone moving behind the nose of the helicopter!"

Bolan brought his M-4 carbine to his shoulder. McCarter followed suit.

A woman stepped around the nose of the wrecked helicopter. She trembled as she looked into the muzzles of three deadly weapons pointed straight at her.

"Please do not kill me. Please, I surrender. I did not want to do anything wrong. They made me do it," she sobbed. Bolan centered his sights on her chest. She didn't look Indonesian; she had distinctly Oriental features.

"Throw down your gun!" Tanaka ordered. "Do it now, or I will kill you!"

The woman dropped the flat black pistol as if it were red-hot. Tanaka sprang forward.

"Put your hands behind your head! Spread your legs! Do not move a muscle!"

Tanaka ran her hands over the trembling woman's body. It was a very thorough search. All she found was a small nylon wallet in one pocket of the woman's jeans. Major Salim had moved to stand close behind the woman. The sight of his camouflaged uniform and purple beret seemed to frighten her even more. Tanaka handed him the woman's wallet. Salim threw it to the ground without looking at it. He grasped the woman's long black hair and pulled her down on her knees.

"I do not care who she is. She has tried to kill an Indonesian military officer in the performance of his duties. She has attacked representatives of a friendly foreign power. The penalty for both of those offenses is death. She is obviously guilty. I will carry out that sentence now!"

He pushed the hard cold muzzle of his AK-47 against the cringing woman's neck.

"I will give you ten seconds to say your prayers. Then I will send you to your ancestors. Ten, nine, eight—"

"Please, do not kill me. Please, I am innocent. I have not had a trial," she sobbed.

Salim smiled cruelly. "Seven, six, five—"

"Hold on," McCarter said quickly. "She may be telling the truth. She hasn't had a trial. Even an accused murderer has some rights. You can't just kill her in cold blood."

"I can't? Watch me!"

"Wait, Major, Green may be right. But if she is a rebel, she may have valuable information," Tanaka declared. "Take her to Aceh, and let me interrogate her. Get a whip, and I will have her begging to tell you everything she knows in half an hour.''

It was a perfect example of the old "good cop, bad cop" routine, and Salim, McCarter and Tanaka were playing their parts to perfection.

Salim snapped on his AK-47's safety. He managed to look disappointed.

"Very well. She deserves to die, but your arguments have convinced me. Let us search the wreckage and leave this place. We have been here too long.''

Near Red Area, Western Sumatra

COLONEL CHUN FINISHED putting on and checking his equipment when the inner door to the special compartment opened and the Airbus 340's crew chief came in.

"Is your equipment ready, sir?'' he inquired. Colonel Chun nodded. "The captain says to inform you we are on final approach for the drop zone. Our course and location are confirmed by the satellite global positioning system.''

That was good. It would be extremely embarrassing if he came floating down fifty miles from the right place in the middle of an Indonesian army post.

Chun told himself to be calm. A high-altitude, low-opening parachute jump wasn't the safest activity in the world. He had done it before, of course, but he had never jumped from a commercial aircraft. That worried him. He knew there were no unimportant details in a HALO jump. Small mistakes could kill you. The steady whine of the big plane's four turbofan jet engines changed as the pilot throttled back and leveled off.

A green light began to blink.

"Five-minute warning, sir. The captain says be ready," the crew chief's voice echoed through the cramped compartment, loud and clear over the whine of the engines. The crew chief gestured upward with both hands.

"Get ready, sir. Stand...up!"

Chun groaned as he heaved himself up. He was carrying 150 pounds of parachutes, weapons, combat equipment and survival gear, and he could feel the shoulder straps of his parachute harness cutting deeper into his shoulders. He had no time to worry over minor discomforts.

"Final equipment check. Prepare for compartment depressurization!" the crew chief shouted.

Quickly, Chun checked his equipment. Now, for the critical step. Everyone in the troop compartment had to go on oxygen. The big aircraft was flying at thirty-six thousand feet. The Airbus 340's aft compartment had to be depressurized now. The HALO jump required opening the special tail door. If the pressure inside the troop compartment didn't match that of the thin outside air, a hurricane of air would blast through the compartment the instant the door was opened. Chun had to start to breathe oxygen from the bailout bottle strapped to this parachute harnesses before the door was opened. The bottle could supply thirty minutes of oxygen. His bailout bottle and his oxygen mask would keep him alive until he dropped below ten thousand feet.

The three-minute-warning light was on. Chun was now breathing from his bailout bottle. The crew chief gave him a final equipment check. He looked closely at Chun's head and face to be sure that they were covered by his jump helmet and oxygen mask. His boots, gloves and insulated jumpsuit protected the rest of his body. It was sixty degrees below zero outside, and the air would be howling past the fuselage at 150 knots when he jumped. It was going to be like stepping into an icy hurricane. Any unprotected skin meant instant frostbite.

Chun gave the ready-to-go signal. The crew chief nodded and pointed toward the rear. Slowly, careful not to tangle his equipment, Chun moved toward the tail door.

The two-minute-warning light came on. Chun was standing three feet from the tail door. When it opened, there would be nothing below him but thirty-six thousand feet of air. The pilot was waiting until the last moment to open the door. The crew chief signaled for the final oxygen check. The red final-warning light came on, and Chun heard the high-pitched whine of hydraulic motors as the special tail door was opened and locked open in the ready position. Instantly, icy outside air filled the small compartment. He stared into the bright blue sky outside.

One-minute warning! Chun looked back and made the ready-to-go gesture to the crew chief. He returned the gesture with his own signal. Colonel Chun was not having breathing problems or any other trouble with his other equipment. He was ready to go.

Colonel Chun felt a sudden surge of adrenaline. There was nothing left for him to do now but go out the door. He had never frozen in the door, and he never would. The loss of face would be intolerable. Suddenly, the go light was on.

He heard the crew chief shouting, "Go! Go! Go!"

The colonel took one long stride and dived out the

open door into the icy air outside. Instantly, he was in free fall. The slipstream buffeted and spun his body, turning him over and over like a rag doll. Looking back, he could see the bright sunlight flash from the big wings and fuselage of the aircraft as it pulled away. Chun used his arms and legs to stop his spinning and turn his body to a facedown position.

Now came the hard part. He was falling faster and faster toward the earth below. The only sounds were the sighing of the air as it rushed past him and the harsh, rasping noise of his own breathing inside his oxygen mask. He looked down. All he could see were the tops of a thick layer of clouds below. The scene didn't seem to change. The colonel knew he was falling several hundred feet each second toward the ground below, but he seemed to be suspended in space. He found free fall from high altitudes most unpleasant, but his plan called for opening this parachute at three thousand feet. Until then, he would have to grit his teeth and bear it.

Now, where was the beacon? There it was! From the edge of a wide, flat patch of ground near the small stream, the beacon began to blink, sending out pulse after pulse of infrared light. It would have been invisible to the naked eye, but Chun's night-vision goggles showed him the steady series of bright, flashing pulses. The beacon's light was shrouded by a funnel-shaped shield. Even with infrared vision equipment, it would be invisible to anyone on the ground.

The beacon was putting out a steady, rhythmic series of infrared pulses. That was the go code. If the operator thought the landing zone wasn't secure, he would have been pushing the warning button, and the beacon's output would be a series of faster, flickering pulses. It was a standard special-operations clandestine beacon. His Free Sumatra Movement contact had to be at the landing zone. Now, to concentrate on his landing. He was a bit to the left of the landing zone, but his ram-air canopy parachute could be flown like a hang glider, allowing time to come down at angles as great as forty-five degrees. He should touch down close to the blinking infrared beacon that marked the center of the landing zone.

He checked his altimeter—three thousand feet. He kept his eye on his altimeter dial and grasped the rip cord's D-ring. He was counting to himself without thinking as he glanced quickly to the left and right. All clear. Three! Two! One! Chun pulled his rip cord. His pilot chute deployed, pulling the special high-performance, ram-air canopy out of its pack and into the air. The canopy blossomed, and Chun felt a bone-jarring jolt as it filled with air and abruptly slowed his fall. Quickly, he slipped his hands into his steering loops, ready to maneuver if he had to. Now, it was time to concentrate on his own landing.

He pulled on his parachute's steering loops and began to move to the left, toward the steadily blinking beacon. He had to make a good parachute landing fall now. Long ago, when he had first trained as parachutist, his instructors had drilled it into him again and again, no operational jump was any good unless you make a good PLF. A broken knee or ankle deep inside Sumatra was likely to be just as fatal as a burst from a well-aimed Indonesian M-16 rifle.

Chun knew that his knees and elbows were the most vulnerable points in a parachute landing fall. He tensed and slightly bent his knees. He kept his hands in the steering loops with his elbows turned inward, close to his chest. The ground was getting closer and closer. Now, he was almost on top of the beacon. He released his equipment rucksack. It dropped away and dangled twenty feet below him on the end of its heavy nylon line.

He pulled on the steering loops and went to full brake. His forward motion stopped immediately, and he went straight down. He felt a heavy jar through the nylon line as his rucksack hit the ground. Now! Feet together and roll! Chun felt a jolt through every bone in his body as he struck the ground in the controlled crash landing of a heavily loaded military parachutist. He did a forward roll and came to a stop. Everything seemed to be in one piece. He felt a surge of relief! He was down and safe.

No time to rejoice. First things first. He had to be ready to fight before he worried about anything else. He reached for the nylon weapons case under his left arm, snapped it open and pulled out his dull black AKS-47, the deadly, folding-stock, lighter version of the AK-47 rifle. There was a round in the chamber, and a full 30-round magazine was inserted in the receiver. Chun flicked the AKS's selector switch to automatic. Now he was ready to fight if he had to. He would worry about getting out of his parachute harness when he was sure the landing zone was secure.

He saw a flicker of motion in his night-vision goggles. A group of three or four men was crouching in a cluster of bushes fifty feet away. One of them held a pistol ready in one hand and an infrared flashlight in the other. It certainly looked as if they had to be his contacts, but he had better make certain. He dropped to a prone position and covered them with his AK-47. He kept his finger in the trigger guard, but he was careful not touch his trigger. It would be a great loss of face if he accidentally shot his Free Sumatra Movement contact.

"The time is now!" Chun whispered the challenge.

"And the dragon is rising," the leader of the group responded.

The colonel felt the tension drain away. That was the correct response. He had done it. He was down safe and in the right place. Now, let the Americans and Indonesians beware!

CHAPTER THIRTEEN

Banda Aceh, Western Sumatra

Jack Grimaldi flew low over Banda Aceh. It was a sprawling city on the northwestern tip of Sumatra. Mack Bolan looked down through one of the Black Hawk's side windows. Seen from the air, Banda Aceh was an interesting city. It was an odd mixture of faded grandeur and modern architecture. The city was divided in two by a river that ran from north to south through the center of the city. Three miles to the west, he could see Uleh-leh, Banda Aceh's port area. The harbor seemed full of merchant ships and two Indonesian navy frigates. Major Salim was proud of Banda Aceh. His family had lived near it for six hundred years. He had told the party that it was a splendid cosmopolitan city with many outstanding sights to see.

"And you must meet my Uncle Ismail. He is a real hero. Everyone in Aceh Province respects him. He will like you."

Bolan looked out the window. He believed Major Salim, but he didn't think he would be touring many museums or old mosques or meeting local heroes. He had traveled to many parts of the world since he had

taken on his War Everlasting, but he seldom had time
for sight-seeing. At least, Banda Aceh seemed to be
in good condition. He saw none of the shattered,
burned-out buildings that were so common in the
towns and cities of East Timor. The only signs of
trouble that he could spot were barricades across
some streets manned by police and soldiers, and here
and there armored cars patrolled the streets.

Grimaldi brought the Black Hawk smoothly around
and began his final approach. The airport was
crowded. There were few civilian aircraft, but Indonesian jet fighters and helicopters were parked in revetments along the sides of the runway. Two gigantic
U.S. Air Force C-17 transports were unloading, their
huge nose and tail doors gaping open as Indonesian
paratroops filed out and lined up along the runway.

Grimaldi made a perfect landing on a helicopter
pad. Two jeeps were waiting on the edge of the pad.
As soon as the helicopter's rotor blades whined to a
stop, an Indonesian army officer walked rapidly to the
side door. Salim stepped outside. The officer saluted
smartly and spoke rapidly in Indonesian. Ingrid Johannsen was looking over Mack Bolan's shoulder, listening intently.

"It looks like we're popular here, too, Striker.
There's no rest for the wicked. General Sudarso wants
to see us immediately."

Fred Byrnes stepped off the Black Hawk.

"Well, I don't imagine he wants to see me. Thanks
for the ride, men. I'll do you a favor sometime. See
you around."

Salim motioned to the waiting jeeps.

They rode down the streets. Everything seemed
peaceful, but Bolan noticed that the escorting para-

troopers kept their rifles in their hands. They kept their eyes on the people moving up and down the sidewalks. They pulled up at the entrance of a large heavily guarded building.

"Military headquarters for Aceh Province," Salim said. "Follow me. I will take you to the general's office."

General Isi Sudarso was a small, compactly built man. He was wearing a camouflage uniform and an Indonesian paratrooper's red beret with the winged-gold-badge insignia that showed his airborne status. Bolan noticed his web equipment and M-16 rifle hanging from a hook behind his desk. Sudarso wasn't a paper pusher. He was ready to fight and personally lead his men at a moment's notice.

Salim saluted and made the introductions. The general motioned for them to be seated.

"We are fighting a guerrilla war. Do you gentlemen know what that means?" Sudarso began.

McCarter smiled wryly. He had done several tours of duty in Northern Ireland, fighting the IRA.

"I think so, General. I believe it was Winston Churchill who once said, 'You send out a hundred men and they see nothing. You send out ten men, and they don't come back.'"

"Your Mr. Churchill was a wise man. He was right. I do not dare send out less than a platoon, thirty or forty men, on patrol. That means that the rebels control large areas of the countryside. What I need is two full infantry divisions, and I know that is impossible. Also, I need more information. I need to know where the rebels' bases are located and who their leaders are. Speaking of that, have you learned anything from the woman you captured?"

Salim looked inquiringly at Mara Tharin.

"We turned her over to BRIMOB, sir. I just called them. She is dead. She had a cyanide capsule hidden in her mouth. She bit down on it when they started to question her. She was dead in thirty seconds. She was either a fanatic or she was more afraid of her own people thinking she was a traitor than she was of us."

McCarter didn't say anything, but he did not like what Tharin had said. Cyanide capsules told him they were up against some serious people indeed.

Sudarso shrugged. "Well, enough of my troubles. General Rahman told me that you are on a most important mission and asked me to give you all the assistance I can. He also said that you were bringing me some very important information, so important that it cannot be discussed on the radio. Can you give me a briefing on this?"

"Miss Johannsen has that information, General. Perhaps she will be so kind as to give the briefing," McCarter said smoothly.

She quickly repeated the briefing she had given to General Rahman in Medan. Sudarso was obviously impressed.

"Your NSA has done remarkable work, Miss Johannsen. This is very valuable information. We must decide how we can use it to our maximum advantage."

Johannsen smiled and accepted the compliment without comment. Of course, it was not her NSA. She worked for the CIA, and the NSA and the CIA despised each other. However, this didn't seem like the time or place to discuss that. She did not comment on operational decisions. That wasn't her department.

"What do you think, Salim? You know the terrain. What do you recommend?"

"We must strike their headquarters. Now, we know where their headquarters is to within three or four miles. But if I was their commander, I would move my headquarters regularly. Once it moves, we may never find it again. We must kill or capture this Colonel Chun while we have the chance. He is their new leader. If we take him out, the rebels' morale may collapse."

General Sudarso rubbed his chin thoughtfully. "I think you are right, Major. If you cut off a snake's head, the body may thrash around for a while, but it will surely die. What do you think, gentlemen?"

"It is an excellent idea, General," McCarter replied. "I see only one problem. How do we do it? It isn't as simple as it seems. We have no idea who or what is at Red Area headquarters. It may be just a communications facility. On the other hand, it may be a base for their main force guerrilla combat units. Colonel Chun is almost certainly somewhere in Red Area at this very moment, but because their radio transmitter is there does not mean that he is."

Sudarso frowned. "You are right, Mr. Green. Perhaps we need a more direct approach. There is a squadron of F-16s at Medan, and we have two battalions of paratroops here. Suppose we stage an air strike and follow it by an airdrop of several hundred paratroopers? That will take care even of Mr. Green's worst case. If there is a large guerrilla force there, so much the better. We will wipe them out and kill or capture Colonel Chun if he is there."

The general paused and looked around the room. Ingrid Johannsen said nothing. It was an operational decision. Intelligence was her field. She knew nothing about strategy and tactics, but Mack Bolan did. He had been letting McCarter carry the ball. But this was a subject that Bolan knew a great deal about.

"The basic concept is all right, General, but I see a few problems. How many F-16s could you get?"

Sudarso thought for a moment. "Certainly twelve, perhaps sixteen, but no more than that. Our air force is stretched as thin as our army."

Bolan was familiar with F-16s. They were the most common fighters in the U.S. Air Force.

"At the most, they could carry four 500-pound bombs apiece. We're talking about an area five miles in diameter. Two hundred B-52s couldn't saturate it, and a battalion of paratroops would take days to search it. What we need to do is make a covert reconnaissance of the area, see what's there and conduct a surgical strike."

"An excellent plan, Mr. Belasko, but how are we to accomplish it?"

"Our team has a lot of experience in this kind of mission, General. With your permission, we'll drop in on Red Area. Keep your F-16s on runway alert, just in case. We would like to take Major Salim with us. He speaks the language and knows the terrain. We'll be ready to leave in two hours."

Sudarso liked the plan. The American team was assuming most of the risks. If they failed, his losses would be minimal. He was ready to agree, but he wasn't sure just what the command arrangements were on the American team.

"What do you think, Mr. Green?" he asked politely.

"Excellent plan, General. Let's go pay a visit to Red Area."

Red Area Headquarters, Aceh Province, Sumatra

FORTY MILES AWAY, Colonel Chun was also about to conduct an important briefing. It was his first meeting with the key personnel of the Red Area command group. Five men looked at him expectantly as he entered the small room. Chun knew that this meeting was critical. If he had come to assume command of a well-trained regiment of paratroopers, he would have had few problems, but this was different. These people were not well-trained, experienced combat troops.

They were all volunteers, citizens who had taken up arms because they believed in the cause they were fighting for, an independent Aceh or a free Sumatra. They weren't professional soldiers. He couldn't simply give them orders and expect them to obey him without question. He had to lead by persuasion and example.

They were looking at him expectantly. He knew that they were impressed by his simple khaki uniform and the AKS-47 that he kept close at hand. Hamed was in charge. He introduced the three group leaders by first name only. Colonel Chun approved of that. No matter how severely you were interrogated, you couldn't tell your captors what you didn't know. The fifth man was ethnic Chinese. He was tall and thin and wore gold-rimmed glasses. He was better dressed than the other men and looked out of place in this cave in the hills. Hamed introduced him as Dr. Chang.

A mature Chinese woman entered the room. She

carried a brass tray with a intricately carved brass teapot and cups. She poured tea for everyone and then sat at the table. That was interesting. She was obviously not a servant but a member of the command group.

"This is Mrs. Wu, Colonel," Abdul said. "She is the head of intelligence. We are all here now, Colonel. How do you wish to proceed?"

"Conduct your standard briefing. I am here to learn."

The three combat leaders spoke first. Each had about 150 men in his group and was responsible for operations in a particular part of Aceh Province. Each described the raids and ambushes they had conducted in the past two days. They were following typical guerrilla tactics, attacking small parties of Indonesian soldiers and police while avoiding combat with larger groups. Chun nodded his approval. These were classic guerrilla-war tactics. He had learned them long ago when he was a young lieutenant.

Dr. Chang spoke next. He was in charge of supplies. He quickly ran down the inventory of weapons, ammunition and supplies. Now it was Mrs. Wu's turn. She spoke well, concentrating on the numbers and deployment of the government in Aceh Province.

"Our latest information is that General Sudarso is being reinforced. A battalion of paratroopers is arriving today. A battalion of Royal Marine Commandos is expected tomorrow. The Americans are transporting government troops to Sumatra in their large jet transport planes."

She paused and looked around the room. No one had any questions, but the three combat group leaders looked grave. It wasn't good news that the enemy forces were being reinforced by two thousand elite fighting men.

"You should be encouraged by this. It demonstrates that your operations are a success. If you were not doing well, they would not be reinforcing General Sudarso," Chun said.

Mrs. Wu smiled. She liked the way Colonel Chun thought.

"In the counterintelligence area, the Americans are increasing their efforts in Aceh Province. Their new acting station chief, a woman named Johannsen, is in Banda Aceh. She is accompanied by a small party of men who appear to be a paramilitary team. They were with her at the demonstration in Medan. We are not sure what their mission is, but we will keep them under observation. There is also evidence that the Americans are trying to recruit agents in Banda Aceh. I have assigned four of our people there to infiltrate their organization. If the Americans appear to threaten us, we have two teams in the city who can be ordered to take them out."

Chun nodded and sipped his tea. He wasn't disturbed by her reports of the American actions. He didn't like Americans, but he didn't underestimate them. They were formidable opponents.

Hamed looked at Chun. "Do you have any questions, sir?" he asked respectfully.

"No, you seem to be well organized and to be following the proper tactics."

Chun paused and looked around the table. The members of the command group were smiling, happy that they had made a good impression on their formidable new commander. Now, it was time for him to make a good impression on them.

"Now, tell me what problems do you have, and do you have any recommendations for our future actions?"

"We need more weapons, Colonel," Hamed responded quickly. "More recruits are coming in daily. We have few good weapons to give them. Some of our men are carrying old Japanese rifles. And the army is using more armored cars. We cannot knock them out with rifles. We need weapons that are effective against them."

Chun agreed. Few things were more demoralizing than having to face hostile armored vehicles with weapons that weren't effective against them.

"I understand, and I have good news for you. There is a cargo ship, the *Wuhan,* off the coast of Sumatra. She is steaming toward Aceh Province now and should be here in twenty-four hours. She has four thousand new rifles and many mortars and machine guns on board. Also light antitank and antiaircraft missiles. As soon as those weapons have been landed, our fighting power will be greatly increased.

"Are there any other recommendations?" he asked.

Dr. Chang raised his hand. "Yes, Colonel. I believe we must make new efforts to strike the enemy harder blows. We need to carry the war into Banda Aceh. I believe we should mount a bombing campaign against government targets in Aceh Province. Let us construct large bombs and put them in cars and trucks. We can use them against enemy headquarters, barracks, police stations and airfields. Let Mrs. Wu prepare a recommended target list for your approval, Colonel. We can cripple their military efforts and demoralize their troops. I recommend we begin immediately."

"Can you construct these weapon, Doctor?" Chun asked.

"Be sure that he can, Colonel. Dr. Chang is a professor of chemistry. The small bombs he has built for us have worked perfectly," Hamed announced proudly.

"Excellent. Begin work immediately, Doctor. It is about time we carried the war into the enemy's rear areas."

Near Red Area, Aceh Province, Sumatra

THE SUN WAS SETTING and a light rain falling as Jack Grimaldi brought the Black Hawk down into a small clearing, drifting low over the treetops through the twilight like a dull black ghost. The helicopter's side doors were already open as the chopper gently touched the ground. Mack Bolan and Major Salim were out the door in a flash, rifles ready to fire and crouching low as they moved quickly under the arc of the idling rotors. Their eyes and the black muzzles of their rifles swept the trees at the edge of the clearing. There was nothing to shoot. The clearing seemed deserted.

No time to waste. Bolan gave the all-clear signal. McCarter and Gadgets Schwarz, followed by Meiko Tanaka and Mara Tharin, exited through the door. Bolan waited until Gary Manning carefully lowered several large black plastic cases out the door and followed them to the ground. He made sure Grimaldi could see him, then he pointed upward into the fading light. Grimaldi saluted and pushed his throttles forward. The Black Hawk's twin engines whined, and the dull black helicopter lifted off and vanished almost instantly into the gathering darkness.

Bolan motioned to the cases. Everyone picked one up. He pointed toward the trees and led the way, keeping his M-4 carbine up and ready. The trees around the clearing seemed deserted, but a really clever enemy might wait until everyone was out of the helicopter and catch them by surprise. Bolan was still alive because he never underestimated his enemies. There were some extremely competent soldiers all around the world, and a lot of them didn't wear American uniforms.

He relaxed a little when everyone was into the trees. The rain seemed to be slacking off. Schwarz and Manning rigged a small shelter, using two camouflaged plastic ground sheets. That was for Schwarz's equipment. The party would just have to get wet. The electronics expert rigged a few intrusion alarms around the perimeter and vanished into the shelter, taking the black plastic cases inside with him.

Major Salim seemed satisfied with the arrangements. He joined Bolan and McCarter, who were sitting with their backs to the trunk of a large tree. Their M-4 carbines were across their thighs as they looked back toward the clearing.

"Your friend Jack is an excellent pilot. I could not ask for a better insertion. We are probably safe here tonight provided we are careful. Mara Tharin is unhappy. She would like a small fire and some hot tea. I told her that a fire in enemy territory is too dangerous. I added that she had to learn to endure a little hardship when she is in the field. It may shock you to hear that she swore at me."

Salim paused and chuckled. "Your Meiko, on the other hand, told me that her ancestors have been samurai for a thousand years. She says she laughs at hardship and smiles at danger. The frightening thing about her is that I do not believe that she is joking.''

"No," McCarter said. "I've seen Meiko in action before, Major. She's a serious young lady.''

"I must tell you that I have a concern. I looked at the map just before we landed. We are about twelve miles from the target area. I am afraid that we are too far from our objective. I do not see how we can get there, reconnoiter and be back before sunrise. What is your plan?''

"Gadgets is getting ready to take care of that, Major," Bolan said. "The miracles of modern technology will solve our problems.''

Salim smiled skeptically. He had seen more than one miracle weapon that failed miserably when used in combat.

Bolan looked at his watch. "Gadgets should be ready now. Let's go take a look at his latest gadget. Mind the store, David. Major Salim and I are going to watch Gadgets perform minor miracles.''

Schwarz was almost ready. He was making his final preflight tests. In front of the improvised shelter, he had set up a large metal tripod with a long metal rail installed at its peak. On the rail sat what looked for all the world like a large model airplane. Its fuselage was about five feet long with a four foot wingspan. It had two tail booms and a propeller pointing to the rear between them. The only really unusual thing was a large round sphere mounted in the nose.

Salim wasn't impressed. "It looks like a toy, a very complicated and expensive toy, but still a toy. How will it solve our problems?''

"It may look like a model airplane, Major, but it's ten orders of magnitude more capable than that. It's a UAV, an Unmanned Aerial Vehicle. That ball in the nose mounts an advanced infrared thermal imager. It's got a low-probability-of-intercept data link, a computerized guidance system, a hybrid electric-gasoline engine and terrain-avoidance radar.''

Salim looked blank; Schwarz had lost him with his first sentence.

''I am sure all that is true, but what does it do?''

''Anything we tell it to. See that black box that Meiko's holding? Once we get it launched and in stable flight, all you have to do is push the right buttons and it will go exactly where you tell it to. When it's flying in the dark, it's almost impossible to detect. And when it gets there, it will send back sharp high-resolution pictures in real time. And it will do it day or night.''

Tanaka was sitting cross-legged nearby, staring at what looked like a laptop lying across her thighs. She had an expression of intense concentration on her face as she stared at its flat-screen display. A thin black cable snaked its way from the back of the computer to a connector on the side of the miniplane.

''All right, Meiko. Turn the power switch from external power to internal.''

The woman seemed fascinated by what she was doing. She turned the power-source selection switch and stared at the lights on the control board.

''Power on internal. All lights green. Preflight checks complete. Ready for launch!'' she reported.

Schwarz disconnected the cable from the small aircraft and peered over Tanaka's shoulder.

''You can do the honors, Meiko. Engine to full flight power! Safe-arm switch to arm! Stand clear, everybody. All right, Meiko. Three, two, one, *launch!*''

Tanaka pushed the launch button. Bolan heard a soft hissing noise from the launcher, and the UAV shot forward along the launcher rail and vanished into the darkness.

Schwarz stared at the control panel. This was the tricky part. Once the UAV reached flight speed and leveled off, he could relax, but there was nothing he could do to help it. If something went wrong and it crashed, the nearest replacement was six thousand miles away.

"Green light!" Tanaka announced. "Flight speed achieved. Flying level at one thousand feet on course forty-six degrees. All systems go. Waiting for commands."

Schwarz sighed with relief. He looked over her shoulder and checked the control panel displays.

"The target area should be in sight in nine minutes. In the meantime, we'll give you a show. Crowd around and look at the pictures. Okay, Meiko. Sensor on. Standard display."

A picture suddenly appeared on the flat-screen display, showing the tops of trees and a narrow dirt road in crisp black-and-white. It was startlingly clear and stable. They might have been looking out the window of a light plane flying low over the forest.

"Now, I am impressed, Mr. Sower," Salim said. "I can see why your friends call you Gadgets. I do have a question, though. Why is the picture in black-and-white? Surely, such a marvelous device should have pictures in glowing color?"

"There isn't any color it can see, Major. It's sending us infrared images. The sensor sees differences in temperature. It can distinguish differences as small as two degrees. Hot things show up as white. Cooler things are black. Where your eyes would just see the dark, the sensor sees a clear picture. By the way, the sensor can zoom. If you want to look at something close up, just let me know.''

The Able Team warrior was in his glory, but Bolan had something he had to do. He stepped outside the improvised shelter. Manning had set up and aligned the Spitfire satcom. He was sitting beside it, wiping down his Heckler & Koch sniper's rifle. Gadgets loved his high-tech gear, and Gary loved his rifles. They were both good men to have with you when you went in harm's way. Bolan picked up the satcom's microphone and pushed a button. Two glowing green lights told him the satcom was ready to transmit and receive.

Bolan pressed the transmit button. "Granite Home, this is Striker. Acknowledge, Granite Home."

His voice flashed upward into space and was transmitted at the speed of light to a second relay satellite over the United States and down to the receiving antennae at the Stony Man Farm operations center. Stony Man's operations center's satcom radios were monitored twenty-four hours a day when the team was deployed.

"Stand by, Striker."

Bolan waited for a few seconds and smiled as he heard a familiar voice. Barbara Price sounded as clear as if she were standing next to him.

"Glad to hear from you, Striker. What's going on?"

"Team has successfully inserted in target zone. The bird has flown. It will be on target in approximately seven minutes. We have reason to believe our friend may be there. Uncertain how many hostiles may be in target area. Depending on what we see, we pay him a call or direct fast movers standing by to strike the target area. Jack is standing by in case we need to extract suddenly. Will advise you of outcome.''

It would hardly pass for sparkling conversation, but Bolan didn't like long radio conversations when he was in the field. He had been told that it was almost impossible to intercept a satcom transmission, but the word *almost* stayed in his memory. After all, Colonel Chun also probably thought his communications were secure.

"That's all I have to report, Granite Home. Do you have any questions?''

"Negative, Striker.''

"Have there been any other developments we should know about?''

"Hal is in Washington. Big meetings tomorrow. Aaron says it's down to China and North Korea. He would bet on China, but some people are making a good argument for North Korea. We haven't found anything about Colonel Chun. The CIA is working on it. The problem is that there are a lot of Chuns in northern China and North Korea.''

Bolan shrugged. It would be interesting to know more about the mysterious colonel, but his nationality didn't change tonight's mission. They would still take him out if they could.

"Understood, Granite Home. Is there any change in our mission?''

"Not yet, but Hal is meeting with the President

tomorrow. I'll contact you if there is anything new. Any questions, Striker?''

''Negative, Granite Home. Your message understood. Striker out.''

Bolan turned off the satcom. Now it was time to try to ruin Colonel Chun's visit to scenic Sumatra.

CHAPTER FOURTEEN

The Situation Room, the Pentagon

Hal Brognola listened quietly as Jack North, the CIA representative, started his briefing. Brognola wasn't sure that he could trust North. He was a little too curious about just who Brognola was and what his mysterious organization did. North had called the meeting on short notice. It would be interesting to hear what he had to say.

"Gentlemen, we have a problem. I have just been talking to our section chief in Jakarta. He tells me that the Indonesian government is starting to panic about the situation in Sumatra. They're planning a new political initiative in Aceh Province, but their latest intelligence reports say that the Free Sumatra Movement is close to starting an all-out armed rebellion. The only thing holding them back is a shortage of modern weapons. They feel that they must take immediate action to stop the *Wuhan* from unloading her cargo of weapons in Sumatra."

That was interesting. "How do they plan to do that?" Brognola asked.

"They have two Indonesian navy warships in the harbor at Banda Aceh. They'll be sent to intercept the

Wuhan and board her. If they find arms on board, they'll order her into Banda Aceh and confiscate the weapons.''

"Is that legal? Didn't you tell us, Stone, that we can't stop a Chinese merchant ship on the high seas? You said her captain can just say that they have no right to stop him, and legally he would be right. What happens if the *Wuhan* just refuses to stop?'' General Blake demanded.

"The Indonesian captains will say she was stopped in Indonesian territorial waters inside the twelve-mile limit whether she was or not,'' Admiral Stone replied. "That will make it legal. If her captain won't stop, the Indonesian captains have orders to use force to stop her or sink her.''

"I thought you said *La Jolla* couldn't damage the *Wuhan* enough to make her stop, Admiral. If a modern nuclear attack submarine can't do it, what makes you think these Indonesian warships can?''

"They are surface warships, General, frigates. That means they are small destroyers. They're old, but they're faster than the *Wuhan*, and they mount 120 mm guns and 21-inch torpedo tubes. They can stop her or sink her.''

"Well, suppose they do sink her. Doesn't that solve our problem? Why should we give a damn if they do?''

The State Department representative shook his head. General Blake might be a brilliant soldier, but he just didn't understand international law.

"If she's sunk, that will destroy the evidence, and it might create a serious crisis between Indonesia and China. It would be better to capture the ship and the weapons intact.''

General Blake turned to Hal Brognola. "You said at the last meeting that you thought you could do that, Brognola. I remember you said you thought you could do it if the President would authorize a covert operation. What's become of that?"

"The President gave the go-ahead. My chief of operations is trying to work out the plan. There are two main problems. The first is how to get our team on board the *Wuhan* while she is at sea. We think we see two or three ways to do that, but we need very accurate scale drawings of the freighter's deck and bridge area."

"That's no problem. We will have them to you in the next two hours," the CIA representative said quickly.

Brognola smiled. Perhaps the CIA was good for something after all.

"Thanks, that will be a big help."

"You'll get them! Your friendly CIA is always happy to be of service!"

Yes, Brognola thought cynically, as long as the Company thought it would pay, but this wasn't the time or place to share that opinion.

"You said two problems. What's the other one?"

"How will we get them back off the ship if we have to, General? Ideally, they will seize the ship, capture the crew and order the captain to take the *Wuhan* into the harbor at Banda Aceh. Realistically, it may not work out that way. The ship may be badly damaged, or the crew may be dead. None of my team are experts on operating cargo ships. If she can't be moved, they'll rig explosive charges and blow her to hell. Before that happens, however, we need to get them off the ship."

"I may be able to help you with that, Brognola," Stone offered. "The *Hornet* and her escort group are operating off the north coast of Sumatra. They are about six hours away from the *Wuhan*. I can order them to close in and stand by to support your people. If they have to abandon ship, the *Hornet* group will pick them up."

"The *Hornet* is an aircraft carrier?" General Blake asked.

"No, it's a large amphibious assault ship. She carries a Marine Expeditionary Unit. That's a reinforced battalion of Marines, a Marine helicopter support group and a few specialized Marine support aircraft."

"Aircraft? I thought you said she wasn't an aircraft carrier."

Stone sighed. It all seemed so simple to him, but after all, he was an admiral.

"She isn't a carrier, gentlemen. She has a large flight deck, but she lacks the equipment to launch conventional jet aircraft. She can operate helicopters and vertical-takeoff-and-land jet aircraft. She's carrying eight Marine Corps Hawker Harriers. They aren't supersonic, but they're very effective attack aircraft. If necessary, they can easily sink the *Wuhan*." He paused. "After Mr. Brognola's team has been safely withdrawn. What do you say, Brognola? Shall I order the *Hornet* group to intercept the *Wuhan*? They can stand off just over the horizon until you are ready to go in. Can you tell me approximately when that will be?"

"That sounds like a good plan, Admiral," Brognola responded. "There is a problem, however. My team is tied up at the moment. They're conducting an operation in Aceh Province and won't be available for the next few hours."

"What are they doing that's more important than this?" Blake questioned.

Brognola glanced at his watch. "You remember those messages the NSA intercepted? The one about Colonel Chun going to Red Area to take command? Right now, my team is a few miles from Red Area and is conducting a reconnaissance. If they decide that Chun is probably at this location, they'll go in and capture or kill him. If it doesn't appear possible for them to penetrate Red Area, they'll call in Indonesian air force jets who'll bomb the hell out of it. They're right in the middle of the operation. I can't pull them out right now, but I'm sure they can take care of the *Wuhan* as soon as they have completed this operation."

Blake whistled softly. "Jesus, Brognola, you're certainly putting your people in harm's way. They had better be a really first-class team."

"They are, General. Believe me, they are."

Near Red Area, Aceh Province, Sumatra

MACK BOLAN SET the satcom to the standby mode. He knew that Barbara Price had given him all the information she had available. If anything new came up, she would contact him immediately, but he couldn't avoid the feeling that they were playing everything by ear back in Washington. Things seemed to change every hour. He liked missions that were well-planned and directed against specific targets. Well, he had one specific target, Red Area and Colonel Chun. He'd take care of that now and worry about other things later.

He was about to brief McCarter when Gadgets Schwarz stuck his head out of the improvised shelter.

"Striker, we've picked up something I think you need to see."

Schwarz didn't sound worried. The UAV's mission had to still be going well, but it might have spotted something that affected their planning. Bolan slipped back inside the shelter. The black-and-white images on the display showed the slowly unrolling treetops of the forest and a narrow dirt road that slanted across the picture. Meiko Tanaka and Gary Manning were staring intently at the screen. Major Salim was looking over the woman's shoulder. He seemed to be fascinated by the UAV's capabilities.

"What have you seen?" Bolan asked.

"Trucks, Striker, and jeeps, and they all seem to be going toward Red Area. Look, here are three more. Zoom in, Meiko."

Tanaka touched a button, and the center of the picture seemed to grow as the UAV's sensor's zoom lens magnified the center of the image. Manning was right. Bolan could see three trucks moving slowly down the dirt road. Each of them seemed to have a bright white glow from the truck's hood. That made sense. The UAV's sensor was a thermal imager. It detected differences in temperature. If the trucks had been driving for a while, the heat from their engines would have made the hoods hotter than the rest of the trucks.

"How many vehicles have you seen, Gary?"

"At least fifteen, and they're all going toward Red Area. Something is sure as hell going on, but it doesn't make any sense, Striker. Guerrilla movements are supposed to be covert secret operations. How can they be driving trucks all over the place? What happens if they're stopped by government patrols?''

"They probably won't be. General Sudarso is so short of troops that he's not going to be sending out random patrols at night forty miles from Banda Aceh. And suppose one of the trucks is stopped? I'll bet a month's pay that all those trucks are empty and their drivers have a good cover story. I think they are collecting those trucks for an important operation. Something that's important enough that they are willing to take a few risks.''

Manning was skeptical. "What is that important to them, Striker?''

"Weapons. Indonesian intelligence says the rebels are recruiting a lot of people since so many were killed by government troops during the demonstrations in Sumatra. If you have got a lot of new recruits, you have to get weapons to arm them. They won't get very far trying to fight the Indonesian army with pitchforks.''

"All right, I'll buy that, Striker. But where are they going to get all these weapons?''

"Remember that ship we have been hearing about, Gary, the *Wuhan?* Even a small freighter can carry thousands of weapons. She'll anchor just offshore, and she can unload in a few hours. Now, put yourself in the guerrilla leader's place. You have to move those weapons, take them where they are needed and distribute them to your combat units. You aren't going to do that with oxcarts. You need a lot of trucks. They know that, and they are getting them together.''

"There is another factor we must consider,'' Tanaka said quietly. She pointed to four flickering red numbers on the UAV control panel. "That is the time-of-flight indicator. The UAV has been flying for sixteen minutes, and we have seen fifteen trucks. There were probably many more that have arrived in Red Area before we could observe them."

Bolan didn't like that thought, but Tanaka was probably right.

"All right. What do we do about it?" Manning asked. "Go out and ambush trucks?"

"That would not be logical, Gary," Tanaka replied. "The rebels have many trucks. If we destroyed a hundred, they could get more, but there is only one Colonel Chun. We came here to kill him. Let us do that, and we may stop this war before it starts."

"Okay, Gary. Let's get everybody together. We have a little planning to do," Bolan said.

Ten minutes later, the members of the team sat around the shelter. Gadgets Schwarz listened from inside and kept his eyes on the pictures flowing back from the UAV. Bolan gave a quick briefing. He kept it short and to the point.

"I think they are planning to bring in the ship and unload the weapons tomorrow night. If we are going to do anything, we have to do it tonight. Any questions?"

McCarter spoke up. "We do have one problem you haven't addressed, Striker. We suspect that Colonel Chun is in Red Area, but we don't know that for a fact. Assuming he *is* there, we don't know his precise location."

"Now that we understand the problem, does anyone have any suggestions?" Bolan inquired.

"I've been thinking about the data we've seen from the UAV," Manning answered. "This Red Area isn't very heavily defended. We haven't seen any trenches or barbed wire. There are just small teams of guards patrolling the perimeter. I'm sure we've got better night-vision gear than they have. I think we could slip into the base without being detected. There's probably some sort of headquarters area. If we can find that, Colonel Chun will probably be there.''

"I don't see that there's any way we can find out whether he's there or not unless we go and see," Bolan replied. "Has anyone else got any other ideas?''

"Perhaps I might offer a small suggestion," Tanaka offered. "Our problem is to locate Colonel Chun. Suppose we go to Red Area and persuade the guerrillas to take us to him.''

"Just how do you propose we do that?" McCarter asked.

"We'll capture a truck. Major Salim will drive it to the entrance. Mara Tharin and I will go with him. When we reach the entrance, the major will say he picked us up on the road, trying to get to Red Area. Mara will say that she escaped from the BRIMOB jail in Banda Aceh and that I aided her. She can show them the marks where the BRIMOB officers beat her. That will make them believe her. She'll say that she has urgent information for Colonel Chun. The Americans are planning to attack Red Area within the next few hours. The fact that she knows his name will convince them. If he is there, they'll take us to him.''

"Wait a minute, Meiko," Manning objected. "You're Japanese, not Chinese. Won't they take one look at you and know you're lying?''

"I do not think so. I do not look particularly Japanese. Remember the first time you saw me in New

Guinea, Gary? I was playing a lovesick airline stewardess panting to get in bed with you. You suspected that I was up to something, but did you think I was Japanese the moment you saw me?''

"All right, Meiko, I'll admit that I didn't, but Colonel Chun's Chinese. Will you fool him so easily?''

"I believe so. Back in the 1930s, before the Japanese invasion of China, Japanese military intelligence conducted a detailed study of using Japanese agents in China. They concluded that twenty-five percent of Japanese women could pass for Chinese. I am one of that twenty-five percent. I have passed for Chinese before. I can do it again.''

Manning shrugged. "All right, Meiko, it's your neck.''

"I believe it has a very good chance of working,'' McCarter remarked. "Gadgets can stay here to operate the UAV and the satcom. He'll notify base when our attack occurs. Everyone else goes. We're going to need all the firepower we can get. Any questions?'' McCarter concluded. There was none.

"Very well, then. Come on, Striker. Let's go get Meiko a truck.''

TWENTY MINUTES LATER the ambush was set. Bolan had chosen a bend in the road where trees grew close to the edge on each side. He and McCarter lay quietly in the edge of the trees. The Briton had his silenced .22 Walther PPK. Bolan had fitted a sound suppressor to his Beretta 93-R. Both weapons lacked the range and accuracy of their M-4 carbines, but they were lethal at close range. Major Salim waited patiently with them. He had his Hungarian AK-47 ready for action. There was no way to silence it, but if they needed backup firepower, Salim could provide it. Manning was on the other side of the road with his sniper's rifle. If something went wrong, he'd make sure that no one escaped the ambush to spread the alarm.

McCarter whistled softly. Bolan listened for a few seconds and heard a truck engine. Someone was about to drive into their trap. Tanaka stepped out into the road. She pulled Mara Tharin after her with one hand and lifted the other over her head in a universal signal for the driver of the truck to stop. A gray truck came around the bend in the road. Bolan could see two men inside the cab. Tanaka stood in the beam of the headlights and gestured urgently for them to stop.

The driver of the truck slammed on his brakes, and the doors flew open. The passenger stayed back, covered by the car. Bolan saw an AKS-47. The driver drew his pistols and moved forward quickly toward the two women. Tanaka kept a smile on her face and spoke quickly in Indonesian. There was a short conversation as she told her cover story. The driver seemed to believe her and led the way toward the truck.

The driver opened the truck's front door and pulled out a small two-way radio. Bolan didn't hesitate. To let him send a radio message could be fatal. He pulled the trigger, and his Beretta 93-R coughed discreetly as he fired a lethal burst of 9 mm Parabellum rounds into the man's chest, slamming him back against the truck's side.

He swung the Beretta 93-R on the other man, and saw the yellow flash of bullets striking metal as the man dived for cover behind the truck, firing a quick burst as he went. The volley of steel-jacketed .30-

caliber bullets ripped through the foliage above the soldier's head, leaves and twigs raining to the ground. Bolan tried to align his sights and get in another shot, but the man was skillfully using the body of the truck for cover.

The Executioner saw a flash of movement and started to tighten his finger on his trigger. The man staggered around the corner of the truck, his AKS-47 dropping from his hands. Bolan saw his body jerk and sway as McCarter hit him again with three more silenced shots. He fell and lay still. The Briton came around the truck with his Walther poised and ready, but the fight was over. Automatically, Bolan reloaded, slipping a fresh 20-round magazine into his Beretta.

"We must go quickly, Striker, before another truck comes," Tanaka said. Her voice was hoarse with excitement.

Bolan knew she was right, but there were a few details they had to attend to first. It would be foolish to leave the bodies of the two men sprawled in the road. The next truck that came along would see them and sound the alarm. He and McCarter dragged the bodies a few feet into the trees. Anyone searching the road carefully would find them, but someone driving by wouldn't.

Major Salim slipped his purple beret inside his jacket, helped Mara Tharin into the truck's cab and slid behind the wheel. Tanaka climbed in beside her. Some boxes stood in the back of the truck, covered with a canvas tarpaulin. Bolan and McCarter threw the boxes into the bushes and slipped under the tarp. Gary Manning joined them. They would certainly be found if someone searched the truck, but a casual observer looking in the back wouldn't see them.

Salim started the engine, put the truck into gear and drove down the dirt road toward Red Area as fast as he dared.

"Be ready," Tanaka called to the Stony Man team. "I can see the entrance to the camp ahead."

Salim pulled the truck to a stop. Bolan heard a man's voice challenging him in Indonesian. The doors opened and Salim stepped out. Three men were guarding the entrance, which was barricaded by wooden crates. They had AK-47 rifles slung over their shoulders, and they seemed alert but not suspicious.

"Who are you?" one of them asked.

"I am Abdul from Banda Aceh. I have driven this damned truck forty miles to this accursed place. Now, I am hungry and I would like a place to sleep."

The men relaxed as they heard Salim's Sumatran accent. He sounded like one of them.

"I think we can find you something to eat, but you will have to sleep in your truck. This is not a hotel, friend."

"God knows that that is true."

One of the other men looked into the cab. He shone a flashlight on Tanaka and Tharin.

"Your assistants are very pretty. Doubtless, they are fine company on a long drive."

"Do not speak like a fool. I am a pious man. I do not carouse with women when I am on duty. I picked them up on the road. They were on their way here when their car broke down. They said they have urgent information for your commanders. It sounded important to me, so I brought them here."

The guard looked at Major Salim with a wicked grin.

"This Chinese woman has a nice figure. Are you

sure you did not stop on the way and spread her legs?''

Salim laughed. ''God forbid that your impious words should come to my wife's ears! If she should hear you, I would have to quit the rebellion if I wanted any peace in my house.''

The leader laughed. ''Your wife is a jealous woman?''

''Of course,'' Salim replied with a modest smile. ''Any woman who is lucky enough to have such a handsome and virile husband as I am is bound to be madly jealous.''

''Of course. I can see that we will have to lock up all the women in camp while you are here.''

The leader turned to Tanaka. ''What is this important information, woman, and how do you know the way to Red Area?''

''My sister and I run a safehouse in Banda Aceh. This woman escaped the BRIMOB jail and came there. She asked for help. She knew our address and the password, so we took her in. She told us she had learned valuable information while she was a prisoner. The government knows the location of Red Area and is planning to destroy it and kill Colonel Chun. I thought the command group must be warned, so I brought her here.''

The leader stared at her suspiciously. ''What do you know about Colonel Chun, woman?''

''Nothing but what she told me, sir, but the government thinks he is a key man, and they plan to kill him. There is a lot of activity at the airport. More jet fighters have flown in from Medan. I suspect that they are planning an air strike in the morning, but I cannot be certain.''

The leader looked grave. This was sobering news. If the air force staged a bombing raid on the camp, he would be in the middle of it.

He turned to one of the guards. "Take these women to headquarters. They will know what to do with them there."

He and the other guard moved the crates out of the way. Salim put the truck in gear and drove smoothly through the gate.

"They did not seem to suspect anything. Stay hidden. We will be near the center of the base in five minutes."

Salim was creeping along, driving slowly and carefully. The last thing in the world he wanted to do was attract attention. At last, the major stopped the truck and cut off the engine. Bolan lifted one corner of the tarp and took a quick look around. They had no time to waste. They had to get out of the truck without being seen and follow Tanaka and Tharin to the headquarters area.

"WE MAY HAVE to leave in a hurry. I think we need another vehicle, Striker," McCarter declared.

That made sense. Half a dozen cars and trucks were parked under the trees. Two of them were armed patrol vehicles, jeeps with a heavy machine gun on a pedestal mount. Bolan went quickly to the closest one and pulled the canvas cover off the weapon. The dull gray weapon was an American .50-caliber Browning M-2 heavy machine gun. A long, linked belt of armor-piercing, incendiary ammunition was inserted in the feed-way. It was a superb weapon. Its .50-caliber bullets would destroy anything short of a tank or an armored car. If they had to shoot their way out, here was the gun that could do it.

As Manning and Salim moved quietly to a second jeep, McCarter got behind the wheel of the first. Bolan climbed into the back and grasped the big Browning's grips. McCarter started the engine and drove slowly through the dark, using only his blackout lights, careful to avoid anything that might attract attention. Anyone who stopped them would be in for a big surprise.

THE GUARD ESCORTED Mara Tharin and Meiko Tanaka to the entrance of the headquarters cave. He explained his business to the sentry on duty there. The sentry went inside to inform the commanders. It occurred to the guard who had escorted them from the camp entrance that he might have forgotten something. He had been a guerrilla fighter for only three months. It was hard to remember everything a soldier was supposed to know.

"Are either of you armed? You must hand over your weapons before you are allowed inside."

Tanaka smiled. "You should have asked me sooner. Now, do not be startled. I am going to reach under the back of my blouse."

She slowly drew out a flat black 9 mm pistol.

"Here. Be careful. It is loaded and cocked. The safety is set, but still, be careful. We will both be very embarrassed if my pistol is accidentally fired in front of headquarters."

The sentry reappeared. "Commander Hamed will see them now. Go back to your duties."

The sentry handed over Meiko's pistol.

"Here, this belongs to the Chinese woman. Give it

back to her if Hamed decides she is all right. God be with you!''

The sentry motioned to the two women. ''Go inside. Do not make any sudden motions. I would hate to have to shoot you and find out later that it was all a mistake.''

The women moved slowly into the cave. It was brightly lit by two Coleman lanterns. To someone who had been outside in the dark, their light was dazzling.

Tanaka looked around her at the seven people who sat at the rough wooden table. Three of them were ethnic Chinese. One was a woman. She couldn't be Colonel Chun. The others were all possible targets. She relaxed her tense muscles and waited to hear what they would say. She knew that important men find it difficult to pretend to be unimportant. She steeled herself to be as patient as a tigress waiting for her prey, waiting for Chun to reveal himself.

CHAPTER FIFTEEN

Red Area Headquarters, Aceh Province, Sumatra

The man who sat at the head of the table was obviously an Indonesian. He wore no uniform, but he had a quiet air of authority.

"Who are you? And why are you here?" he inquired

"I am Anna Chou. This woman is Mara Tharin. My sister and I run a safehouse in Banda Aceh. This woman escaped the BRIMOB jail and came to us. She asked for our help. She knew our address and the password, so we took her in. She told us she had learned valuable information while she was a prisoner. The government knows the location of Red Area and is planning to destroy it and kill Colonel Chun. I thought the command group must be warned, so I brought her here."

Hamed stared at her suspiciously. "What do you know about Colonel Chun?"

Tanaka could tell that the man was suspicious. She was a fine actress when she needed to be. She would show respect and dedication to the rebel cause.

"Nothing but what this woman told me, sir, but the government thinks the colonel is an important man, and they intend to kill him. There is a great deal of activity at the Banda Aceh airport. More jet fighters have flown in from Medan. I suspect that they are planning an air strike in the morning, but I cannot be certain.''

That was important information if it were true. Hamed had survived three years in the Free Sumatra Movement because he was careful and suspicious. He had to question her closely.

He picked up Tanaka's pistol from the table and looked at it closely.

"This is a 9 mm Browning, a government pistol. Where did you get it?"

"From a BRIMOB officer. He thought I was pretty, and he was much more interested in raping me than arresting me.''

Tanaka reached beneath the lustrous black fall of her hair and drew a small knife with a six-inch triangular blade. The lantern light reflected from the polished steel.

"He held me down and was enjoying tearing off my clothes. I put the blade in under his jaw and thrust upward. There are no bones there, you know. He died instantly. I regret that. I would have been happy to see him die slowly.''

Tanaka wasn't making that up. She had killed a man this way, many years ago and in another country, but it wasn't something she would be likely to forget.

"He didn't need his pistol anymore, so I kept it. It is a useful weapon for a woman who is a rebel.''

Everyone stared at her. Even Hamed was startled by the cold, deadly tone in the woman's voice.

"Where did you learn to do such things?" Mrs. Wu asked her.

"My brother is a kung fu master. He taught me a great many things he said a young woman should know."

"Very well. I believe you. I will return your pistol to you before you leave. There is something about your story that bothers me, however. You say this woman came to your house with the story that she had been held in the BRIMOB jail and escaped, and you immediately believed her. You are obviously an intelligent woman. Did it not occur to you that she might be a BRIMOB agent? Why did you believe her?"

"Not because of what she said, but because of what she showed me. Mara, show them the marks."

Mara Tharin blushed deeply. "I am ashamed to do such a thing in front of these strange men."

"Do it, anyway, Mara. It is for the cause."

Tharin stood, faced the wall, unsnapped her jeans and pulled them and her panties down below her knees. Mrs. Wu gasped. One of the men swore softly. Everyone stared. Mara's bare buttocks and thighs were covered with thin, raised purple welts.

"Who did this to you?" Hamed asked quietly.

"BRIMOB officers. I would not tell them who had organized the demonstration in Medan. They stripped me naked and said that they would whip me until I begged to tell them everything I knew. I screamed and begged. I swore that I knew nothing, but they kept on whipping me. That was not the worst thing they did. They used an electrical cattle prod on me. It was horrible. I am afraid that I would have told them everything I knew, but they kept on doing it until I fainted. They became afraid that I might die, so they threw me back in the cells with the other women. I escaped, and I am here.''

The woman pulled up her jeans.

Tanaka glanced casually around the table. Every member of the command group seemed convinced. Good. Now, if only Colonel Chun would say something that would serve to identify him.

''What do you think, Mrs. Wu?'' Hamed asked.

Mrs. Wu turned to Tanaka. ''Anna, you said that there are more jet fighters at the airport than usual. Did you see this yourself? How many jet fighters?''

''I saw them. Usually there are twelve fighters stationed at the Banda Aceh airport. Late this afternoon, there were eight more. There may be more now. They are all the same kind. American planes. The pilots call them F-16s.''

Mrs. Wu nodded. ''Twenty or more F-16s! They must be planning a large attack, but not until tomorrow morning. Indonesian air force F-16s have no night-attack capability.''

Hamed frowned. ''That is so, but twenty jet fighters! Each of them can carry several bombs, and they will have cannon and rockets.''

He looked at his watch. ''We have five hours until dawn, but we have no time to waste. We must make a decision quickly. What shall we do, Colonel?''

Tanaka kept her face impassive. The man in the khaki uniform was Colonel Chun!

''You are right, Hamed. There are several things we must decide and decide quickly. Do we evacuate the camp? Do we still have the *Wuhan* deliver the weapons? Can we mount any kind of effective defense?'' Chun spoke calmly but with authority.

''We have several Russian heavy machine guns

and a few shoulder-fired antiaircraft missiles, but that is not much against twenty F-16s,'' Hamed replied.

"Still, if skillfully used, we might shoot down several aircraft. If they are going to destroy our camp, I should like to make them pay,'' Chun declared. He glanced at his empty teacup.

"Planning battles is thirsty work. May we ask you to bring us some fresh tea, Mrs. Wu?''

"Of course, Colonel. I will prepare some immediately.''

She stood and turned to leave the cave. Tanaka stood immediately. "I would be glad to assist you if I may,'' she said quickly.

Hamed smiled and nodded. He had been a farmer before he became a guerrilla leader. He didn't approve of modern young women. He was pleased to see that the woman had some manners and respect for her elders.

Gadgets Schwarz had stressed that Tanaka had to be outside when she used the small device he had given her. Now, all she needed was a few minutes of privacy.

"I would like to ask a small favor,'' Tanaka asked once outside the cave. "I would have been embarrassed to ask it in front of all those men. I have been traveling for hours. Is there a toilet? I need to relieve myself.''

Mrs. Wu smiled. It was a relief to see that the young woman could be embarrassed and had normal human frailties.

She pointed to a small canvas shelter by the side of the path. "There. I am afraid you will not find it to be modern, but it is what we have.''

Tanaka slipped into the shelter and closed the flap.

She would use the facility in case Mrs. Wu was listening carefully, but she had more-important things to do. She sat on the wooden seat and took a small silver pin from her blouse. It had been a typical piece of Sumatran jewelry until Gadgets Schwarz had modified it. A single small button protruded from the back. Tanaka paused and mentally reviewed the simple code that he had given her. She pushed the tiny button and held it down for three seconds, and a silent, almost undetectable radio pulse was emitted. She waited for a count of five and pushed the button twice again. The low-powered radio signal flashed up and was relayed to Schwarz by the circling UAV.

TWELVE MILES AWAY Schwarz stared at the UAV control panel as a red light began to blink on and off.

"One, Colonel Chun is on the base."

"Two, he is in the cave in the small hills at the center of the base."

"Four, rebels have accepted our cover story."

"Six, will need assistance to complete mission and withdraw."

Schwarz watched the red code-receive light on his control panel blink on and off each time Meiko pushed her button. He felt a pardonable glow of pride. It always made him happy when one of his devices worked.

He pushed the transmit-receive button on the satcom and spoke into the microphone. "Viking, this is Gadgets. Come in, Viking."

There was a short pause, and then Schwarz heard Ingrid Johannsen's voice.

"Gadgets, this is Viking. Reading you loud and clear."

"Viking, our team has penetrated Red Area. Dragon Lady reports that our target is on the base. He is in the cave in the small hills at the center of the base. We will need assistance to complete the mission and withdraw. Request air strikes as soon as possible."

"Message understood. Fighters will take off at first light. Anything else?"

"Tell them to be careful. Our people are going to be in the middle of the target area. Will inform you if the situation changes. Gadgets out."

Now to tell McCarter and Bolan. He picked up his tactical radio and spoke urgently into the microphone.

TANAKA FOLLOWED Mrs. Wu back into the cave and helped her pour the steaming tea. Colonel Chun and the command group were deep in conversation. Tanaka listened carefully. She had no way to communicate with the rest of the team, but she still might learn something useful.

Chun set down his cup and began to speak in the formal style of a commander giving orders.

"Very well. We will leave one group here with all the shoulder-fired antiaircraft missiles. They will be dispersed around the camp and will evacuate as soon as they have launched the missiles. All other personnel will be evacuated using the trucks. We will shift command to the alternate site. I suspect that they will send in paratroops after the air attacks. We will not attempt to ambush them. Guerrillas do not fight big battles with regular troops."

Mrs. Wu poured another cup of tea for the colonel. He sipped it, then continued.

"Mrs. Wu will collect all valuable papers and burn

the rest. She will prepare the large radio for movement. Take these women with you. That will take one truck. Hamed will select the most valuable weapons and equipment and have them loaded on the remaining trucks. Does everyone understand? Good. Let us move rapidly. Except for the missile teams, we must be far away when the F-16s arrive.''

The members of the command group picked up their weapons and filed out. Hamed took an AK-47 from a rack, handed it to Mrs. Wu and followed the group. Mrs. Wu handled the weapon awkwardly. Tanaka smiled faintly. She had had no chance to kill Colonel Chun, but she knew she could disarm Mrs. Wu easily. Then, she would control the cave and the radio. With that, she could communicate.

She waited until her adversary was facing away from her, taking maps down from the wall. She unsnapped the fly of her jeans and drew her small, silenced .25-caliber Beretta from the holster nestled against the top of her left thigh. It wasn't a powerful weapon, but she had practiced with it and used it for many years. At short range, she wasn't going to miss.

Mrs. Wu turned and stared horrified at the muzzle of the other woman's Beretta.

"Freeze! Do not move! Be quiet or I will kill you!"

Mrs. Wu seemed paralyzed by the shock. She looked around her and took a deep breath. "You do not dare shoot. The guard outside will hear it."

Tanaka smiled. She shifted her aim slightly and pulled the trigger. The Beretta hissed faintly, and splinters flew a foot from Mrs. Wu's face.

"The next one goes through your head. Take her

rifle, Mara, and watch the entrance. I will contact Striker.''

"How can you do this, Anna? You are betraying your own people," Mrs. Wu moaned.

"You are not my people. I am neither Indonesian nor Chinese. I am an American citizen. I am serving my country!''

Tanaka moved to the radio. She turned it on and carefully adjusted the frequency. "Striker, this is M. Come in, Striker.''

"This is Striker, M. What's your situation?''

"We control the cave. I am using their main radio. I have one prisoner, but Target has left the cave. They think an air strike is coming in the morning. They are evacuating the base. Shall I stay here or come out and join you? It might be wise if we left this place.''

"All right. They're running around all over the place, getting ready to pull out. We ought to be able to make it out of here during the confusion. Stand by. We have two vehicles and will pick you at the cave. Striker out.''

Tanaka thought quickly. She had a few minutes until Striker arrived and would put them to good use. She hadn't had a chance to shoot Colonel Chun, but any information she could obtain on the rebels' plans would be valuable to General Sudarso. She would take all the maps and any papers that looked interesting. She told Mara to search through the papers while she moved close to the entrance to the cave. There was at least one guard outside, which could be a problem.

The guard challenged someone, then she heard Major Salim replying.

"Mrs. Wu, there is a man here with a message from Colonel Chun."

"Mrs. Wu is using the radio. She says to bring him in," Tanaka said.

Major Salim came through the entrance, followed by the guard, who had his AK-47 in his hands. He seemed alert but not suspicious. Salim moved to the center of the room. The guard looked around. He could see the radio.

"What is going on here? Where is Mrs. Wu?" he demanded.

His expression changed, and he started to lift his weapon.

Salim lunged forward like a tiger. He grabbed the barrel of the guard's rifle and with all his strength drove the edge of his hand down across the side of the guard's neck. It was a paralyzing blow. The guard went down and stayed down.

"Is Striker here with the vehicles?" Tanaka asked.

Salim nodded. He saw Mrs. Wu cowering in a corner.

"Who is this woman?"

"A prisoner with valuable information. Bind and gag her, and we will take her with us."

Salim tore several strips of cloth from the table cover. He tied Mrs. Wu efficiently, forced a wadded piece into her mouth, then threw the woman over one shoulder and led the way out of the cave.

Tanaka climbed into the back of the first jeep, while Major Salim put Mrs. Wu into the passenger seat of the second jeep and got into the back behind the big .50-caliber machine gun. Mara Tharin joined him. They were ready to go.

Bolan took a quick look around. He saw men and

vehicles here and there as the rebels got ready to evacuate their base. Everyone seemed busy. No one was paying any attention to them. Time to go before that changed.

"Let's go," he said.

McCarter put his engine in gear and headed for the main entrance. It was taking a chance, but it was the only way to reach the road quickly, and Bolan wanted to move as far and as fast as he could before they abandoned the vehicles. He checked the .50-caliber machine gun. A 105-round belt was loaded in the ammunition box on the side of the gun. He pushed the bolt latch release and pulled back the bolt-retracting lever and let it go forward, feeding the first cartridge into the chamber. The big machine gun was ready to fire. All he had to do was push down on the thumb trigger.

A light truck carrying several men passed them going the other way, but it didn't try to stop them. In the dim light, they looked like any other vehicle leaving Red Area. They were out of the center of the base now. Bolan looked ahead toward the main gate. He could see dim lights, and he caught a flicker of movement. The gate was still guarded. Three large wooden crates formed an improvised barricade. McCarter saw it, too. He slowed and looked over his shoulder.

"Here's the gate, Striker," he said quickly. "What do you want me to do?"

Bolan thought for a second. Both their vehicles had four-wheel drive. Maybe they could surprise the guards by avoiding the gate, and going around the side of the road. No, that was too big a risk. They knew nothing about the terrain. They might hit a tree or break an axle. If one of their two vehicles was disabled, they would be in a lot of trouble.

The hardest decision was easy when you had only one choice.

"All right, through the gate. Let's go!"

McCarter put the jeep in gear and drove forward. He had been driving with only the blackout lights on. Now he turned on his headlights and illuminated the gate. Bolan didn't like what he saw. Two vehicles were parked just inside the gate, one on either side of the road. Both looked like jeeps. Bolan could see a light machine gun mounted on each, but they weren't as large or powerful as his. He swiveled the big Browning to point at the left-hand vehicle.

They were close now. Some kind of wooden traffic-control arm dropped from one side of the gate, blocking the road. A man with an AK-47 stepped in front of the barrier and signaled for McCarter to stop. They couldn't risk that. If the guard looked into their vehicles, they were finished. There was no possible way they could pass for Indonesian guerrillas. McCarter kept going. The man in front of the barrier shouted something, and Bolan saw the men in the two vehicles start to swing their light machine guns toward him.

He pushed the thumb trigger, and the Browning roared into life. A swarm of red tracers flashed at the enemy vehicle. Bolan saw bright yellow flashes as the .50-caliber bullets punched into the jeep. The bullets from the big Browning could penetrate more than an inch of solid armor plate at close range. They tore through the jeep's light steel body as if it were made of tissue paper.

One of the huge, armor-piercing, incendiary bullets

pierced the jeep's gas tank. The vehicle burst into bright orange flames. Its crew bailed out and ran for their lives as flaming debris rained to the ground.

Bolan fired another burst, this time at the second jeep. Something struck the roof of the cab in front of Bolan and screamed away. The gunner on the second jeep had the range and was firing rapidly. Green tracers streaked past the Executioner's head as he aimed the Browning carefully. The Indonesian gunner was firing high, but that wouldn't last long. McCarter floorboarded the accelerator, and his vehicle roared as it shot forward. Bolan saw a swarm of green tracers streak by them as the enemy gunner fired where they had just been. Bolan didn't make that mistake. He took a proper lead and pressed the Browning's trigger. He fired a long burst, saw his tracers strike the hood of the second jeep, corrected his aim and fired again.

He couldn't shoot with total precision as he fired from the back of the swaying vehicle, but a jeep at short range was a big target. Bright, yellow flashes illuminated the area as a dozen .50-caliber armor-piercing, incendiary bullets shrieked into the jeep. Its engine began to smoke and burn. The gunner stopped firing abruptly. One of the heavy .50-caliber bullets had struck him in the chest.

McCarter kept the gas pedal to the floor, and the jeep roared forward. The guard standing in the road stared at it as if he were hypnotized, watching the Briton drive straight at him. He threw himself to one side at the last desperate instant as McCarter rammed the barricade. Bolan heard a splintering crash, and wood splinters flew through the dark as their vehicle shot through. He reversed the Browning on its mount, ready to fire behind if he had to, but he saw nothing to shoot. They were racing down the road into the night. He could see the headlights of Gary Manning's jeep behind them, but there were no signs of pursuit.

Bolan kept his eyes to the rear, looking for any signs of pursuit. Their attack on the gate guards had been so fast that it was hard for the rebels to react. All the enemy could know was that there had been shooting at the camp's gate. In the rush and confusion of the evacuation, it wasn't likely that anyone could organize a pursuit.

They drove on until they reached the turnoff to the clearing where they originally had landed in the Black Hawk. Gadgets Schwarz was waiting with his M-4 carbine ready.

He smiled as McCarter braked the jeep to a stop. "I hope you guys have been having fun. I radioed Jack. He's on the way."

"Good. The sooner we're out of here the better," Bolan responded.

He heard the sound of helicopter rotors overhead, and the Black Hawk seemed to materialize out of the dark. Grimaldi settled down smoothly. He kept the Black Hawk's engines idling, ready for a fast takeoff.

Tanaka collected the intelligence material she had taken from the cave.

"Bring her, and let us get on board," she said.

Major Salim stared coldly at Mrs. Wu. "We know this woman is a traitor. Why waste time with a trial? We should execute her here and now!"

"Remember, she has valuable information," Tanaka said.

"Go ahead and shoot me. I would never get a fair trial anyway," Mrs. Wu gasped.

Despite her brave words, she sounded terrified. Tanaka smiled. Good, she would work on that.

"We will not shoot you. That would be too quick and easy. We will take you back to Banda Aceh. The BRIMOB interrogators there are renowned for their skill. After they have questioned you for an hour, you will beg them to be allowed to tell them everything you know."

CHAPTER SIXTEEN

Banda Aceh, Western Sumatra

Rafael Encizo was yawning as a paratroop sergeant ushered him to General Sudarso's operations room. He looked a little the worse for wear after an all-night flight from Washington on an Air Force jet transport. They didn't call flights like that "red-eyes" for nothing.

"Better have a cup of coffee, Rafe," Gary Manning observed. "You sure look like you could use some."

Encizo smiled and took a cup. "Thanks, Gary, but that's the pot calling the kettle black. You guys have looked a lot better. What did you do, spend all last night partying?"

"You might say that. The party lasted all night, and we had fireworks at the end. Loud, bright fireworks! But that was then, and this is now. Did you bring the data?" McCarter responded.

"I didn't fly nine thousand miles just for fun!"

Encizo opened his slim black briefcase and took out a stack of drawings. "Here's the latest drawings and photographs of the *Wuhan*, courtesy of our friends at the CIA. And here's a computer CD-ROM disk for you, Gadgets. Now, if you don't mind, I'll curl up in a corner and sleep for the next twelve hours."

Mack Bolan chuckled. "Sorry, Rafe, but you're our nautical expert. We need your advice. Hang in there. You can catch some sleep in forty-eight hours."

Encizo groaned.

"You know what they say, Rafe. 'There's no rest for the wicked,' and you are one of the wickedest people I know," McCarter remarked. "Let's get to work. I think we're all going to take an ocean cruise, and you're invited."

"With friends like you, I don't need enemies," Encizo retorted as he spread out the drawings. "This is a side view and an overhead view of the *Wuhan*. She's not a very exciting ship. She was built in Korea twelve years ago for a Chinese trading company, and underwent an overhaul three years ago in Shanghai. She displaces about twelve thousand tons, has a crew of thirty or forty officers and sailors, and has a top speed of eighteen knots."

McCarter peered at the drawings intently. "What are these red circles and arrows?"

"I had a one-on-one meeting with the merchant ship's expert at the CIA. Those red marks indicate interesting modifications made to the *Wuhan* when she was overhauled. Those arrows there show new radio antennas. There isn't anything unusual in that except that it looks like they installed some high-powered long-range radios. That's peculiar in a small merchant ship. This circle indicates a new surface-search radar installed during her overhaul. Again, that's not a particularly unusual thing in itself, but it looks like a long-range, high-performance military model.''

Bolan looked closely at the drawings. "That leaves these four red circles, Rafe. One at the bow, one at the stern and one on each side of the bridge. What does your CIA friend say they are?''

"He didn't know, Striker. Damned if I do, either, but he said we had better be careful if we go in. These four things have always been covered when we have observed the *Wuhan*. There aren't any satellite sensors that can see through a canvas cover, but our friend checked with a CIA weapons expert. He said he couldn't be sure, but the size and shape are consistent with pedestal-mounted automatic weapons, .50-caliber machine guns or 20 mm cannon.''

McCarter and Bolan looked grave. Either one could blast the Black Hawk out of the sky with a few well-aimed bursts.

"Where's Jack?'' Encizo inquired.

"At the airport. He's putting some stuff on the Black Hawk. He'll be here as soon as he gets that done,'' Bolan reported.

"Speak of the devil,'' McCarter said.

Grimaldi walked in the door. He made straight for the coffee and poured himself a cup.

"How's it going, Jack?'' Encizo asked.

"Just fine, if you like flying all night and working on the bird next morning.''

"We all appreciate your sterling efforts, Jack,'' McCarter said soothingly. "Is the Black Hawk ready to go? I think it is about time we welcomed the *Wuhan* to Sumatra.''

"She's fueled and checked out. I've checked the weather in the search area. It's clear, with light winds in the search area. We can leave whenever you're ready. I'll find her, no sweat, but you geniuses had better figure out what we are going to do when I do. How are you going to get aboard her?"

"I had rather thought that we would use our parachutes and drop in unannounced," McCarter said with a grin.

"Don't forget, a ship at sea is a moving target. Suppose the *Wuhan*'s captain sees you jumping and decides to make a sharp turn? You'll land in the water. I'll try to fish you out, but we would be close to the ship. If they have machine guns on the freighter, the Black Hawk would be a sitting duck. I doubt that we'd make it."

McCarter frowned. Grimaldi seemed to be a bundle of cheer this morning.

"What do you think, Striker?" he asked.

Bolan looked at the diagrams of the freighter. Grimaldi was the best pilot he knew. There ought to be some solution to the problem.

"If we take them by surprise, Jack, couldn't you land here, on the center of the main deck?"

"Maybe, let's see." Grimaldi took a small ruler from his pocket and measured carefully.

"It would be close, Striker, damned close. The diameter of the Black Hawk's main rotors is fifty-three feet eight inches. There's a little clearance but not very much. Remember, the ship will be moving. It may be rolling, and the wind may be blowing. All I have to do is make a small mistake and break a rotor blade on one of those cargo hoist masts. Then we crash-land. And with a broken rotor blade, we won't be able to take off again."

Bolan thought hard. Everything Grimaldi had said was true, but there had to be some way to do it.

McCarter's frown turned into a smile. "I have it! We will simply rappel down. All Jack has to do is hold the Black Hawk steady, and we simply climb down ropes to the deck. Piece of cake, really."

Grimaldi nodded. "It just might work. I'll borrow a few things from the Indonesian fly boys and put them under the stub wings. I'll be ready to lift off in two hours. Meanwhile, you two military geniuses figure out the plan."

The Wuhan, *off the Coast of Sumatra*

MACK BOLAN SAT in the Black Hawk's copilot's seat. He looked out of the plastic canopy, scanning the *Wuhan* with twelve-power gyrostabilized binoculars. She was a dull gray with a red-and-yellow stripe painted around her hull. Large black letters proclaimed that she was the *Wuhan* out of Shanghai. The soldier was impressed by her sheer size.

The Executioner didn't like the odds. What had the CIA man told Encizo? She would carry a crew of thirty or forty officers and men, but she could have a lot more men on board belowdecks where no satellite sensors could see. Grimaldi was looking at the infrared images on the multifunctional display. The infrared images were black-and-white, but they would reveal any unusual heat sources that would be invisible to the naked eye.

"Negative scan," Grimaldi reported. "You see anything, Sarge?"

Bolan took one last look. Nothing was going on. The *Wuhan* and her crew seemed busy with their normal routine. He could see two of the four canvas-covered objects. They might well be heavy machine guns or light automatic cannon, but there was no way to tell.

"Negative, Jack. It's a go."

Grimaldi began to throw switches on his control panels.

"All right, Sarge. Get Ingrid back up here. I need to go over the communications and countermeasures controls with her one more time. Check out everything in back. The lookouts on the *Wuhan* have certainly seen us by now, but helicopters aren't that unusual along the coast. But once we go in, they're going to know something is up." The team had needed one more body for the mission, and Ingrid Johannsen was the only person available.

"Roger," Bolan replied. He had nothing more to say and no orders to give. It was up to Grimaldi now. He was in charge until the raiding party hit the freighter's deck. The soldier stepped back into the passenger compartment. There was a bustle of orderly confusion as everyone completed last-minute weapons and equipment checks. Gary Manning and Major Salim manned the two .30-caliber Gatling door guns. McCarter, Encizo, Schwarz and Tanaka took their positions and waited for the order to go.

Bolan took a second to check Meiko. She had never done this before and might be getting nervous. It was hard to read her expression. Her face was impassive. She had remembered to sling her silenced Heckler & Koch submachine gun across her back, which left both of her hands free to manage the rappelling rope. She had her harness and leather gloves on. She looked ready to go. Bolan smiled to encourage her.

"All set?"

The woman nodded.

"Remember, it's important to get down before the smoke clears, but don't try to go too fast. Keep everything under control and make a nice, smooth descent. Remember what Wyatt Earp said. 'Take all the time you need, but take it rapidly!' Understand?"

Tanaka stared at him blankly. "I understand most of what you said, Striker, but who is Wyatt Earp?"

Bolan thought for a second. It was not a good time to discuss the history of the American West.

"A famous American samurai, very skilled with his weapons."

He picked up the intercom mike and moved to his position by the left-hand door. "Ready back here, Jack."

"All right, Sarge," Grimaldi pronounced, and Bolan heard the sound of the Black Hawk's twin turbine engines change from a whine to a howl as the Stony Man pilot pushed his throttles and went to full emergency power. "Here we go!"

The floor suddenly tilted downward as Grimaldi put the Black Hawk's nose down into a shallow dive and slanted toward the freighter. Bolan slid the door back and latched it open. Manning grinned and pivoted the .30-caliber M-134 Gatling until it pointed menacingly out the door. On the other side of the compartment, McCarter and Salim were doing the same thing with the right-hand gun.

The *Wuhan* loomed up ahead, seeming to grow larger and larger as the Black Hawk flattened out and streaked toward the Chinese freighter's stern. Grimaldi threw two switches. Gray-white smoke began to stream out of the two tanks under the Black

Hawk's stub wings. The chopper leveled out and flashed along the deck. It seemed to Bolan that they cleared the tops of the ship's cargo-handling masts by mere inches.

Ahead, Bolan could see some of the crew dashing across the deck, like ants whose anthill has been disturbed. The Black Hawk shot over the bow, and Grimaldi pulled the aircraft in a hard right turn. He leveled out and streaked back along the deck, spraying more thick gray-white smoke. The vessel seemed to disappear, shrouded in the cloud of smoke. All Bolan could see were the tops of the cargo-handling masts and some of the antennae mounted on the bridge.

Grimaldi brought the Black Hawk around and slid smoothly into the gap between the masts and hovered. Now, all he had to do was maintain that position, but it wasn't as simple as that. The ship was moving through the water at ten knots. The pilot kept his eyes on the forward mast and held the Black Hawk as motionless as he could, maintaining the interval to the mast.

"Go! Go! Go!" Grimaldi shouted into his microphone.

Bolan had already slipped the rope through the loops on his harness. He took a deep breath and stepped out of the door. He hung a few feet below the helicopter's fuselage and took a quick look around. The smoke they had sprayed was designed to lay down smoke screens for land warfare. It was heavier than air and clung to the *Wuhan*'s deck. She couldn't just steam out of it, but the motion of the ship and the light breeze would disperse the smoke fairly rapidly.

Straight below him, the smoke was thinner, partially blown away by the downwash from the Black Hawk's rotors. Time to go. He released the friction brake and started down, controlling the rope with his hands and the tension on his friction brake. It was hard going. At least, the sea was calm. The ship was steaming along as steady as a rock.

Bolan hadn't wanted to try to make the climb down the rope with a rifle in his hands. If there was trouble before he was on the deck, he would have to depend on his pistols. He slipped the safety straps of their holsters over their grips, grabbed the rope and began to descend. When his boots touched the deck, the soldier paused for a second and looked around quickly. The smoke was just beginning to clear. The *Wuhan* was a typical Asian-trade small freighter. She had a superstructure forward that contained her bridge and another aft. The bridge was critical. Whoever held the bridge controlled the ship. Between them was the flat main deck with hatches that led down to the cargo holds. There had to be a deck watch somewhere, but he didn't see anyone.

Bolan heard the sudden bark of heavy machine-gun firing from the direction of the bridge and the ripping snarl of an M-134 .30-caliber Gatling gun replying. No one seemed to be shooting at him, but he took no chances and dropped prone on the deck. He could see several large boxes of deck cargo lashed to the deck about twelve feet to his right. He tugged twice on the rappelling rope with his left hand and drew his .44 Magnum Desert Eagle with his right.

The Executioner felt a quick pull on the rope as McCarter answered the signal. He slipped through the smoke like a ghost and took cover behind the big boxes of cargo. It was up to him to cover the rest of the party as they climbed down the rope. He took a firm two-handed grip on his .44 and scanned the deck. Nothing was moving. He waited tensely. The seconds seemed to crawl by. Then he saw a black shape appear over this head. It was McCarter, who slipped quietly down onto the deck and moved to join Bolan behind the boxes.

The Briton unslung his M-4 carbine and checked it carefully. "Meiko's coming down next," he said quietly.

Bolan nodded and unslung and checked his M-4 carbine and its 40 mm M-203 grenade launcher. McCarter covered the deck. Bolan checked his watch. Where was Meiko? She should be on deck by now. He slipped quietly back to the rope and looked up. The woman was nearing the bottom of the rope, but she was climbing down slowly, clinging to the rope. The wind and the motions of the ship were giving her trouble. He reached up with his left hand, caught the end of the rope and held it steady as she slid down the last few feet to the deck.

Someone suddenly shouted behind him in Chinese. Across the deck, a man in a sailor's uniform was looking toward the boxes and yelling loudly. The sailor's hand flashed to his side as he drew a flat black pistol. Mack Bolan whirled. With no time to aim precisely, he put the carbine's front sight against the man's chest and pulled the trigger, firing two short bursts as fast as he could pull the trigger.

The man collapsed to the deck. It was good shooting, but it wasn't quiet. The crackling snarl echoed along the deck. He heard men shouting, and an alarm bell began to ring. The crew had been taken completely by surprise. Most of them still weren't sure what was happening, but like any well-trained crew they were rushing to their battle stations. They would be armed, too. The South China Sea was infested with pirates. No sensible captain sailed his ship there without a well-armed crew.

A light machine gun mounted on the forward superstructure opened fire and began to search the deck. Bolan heard the rapid crackling sound of McCarter's M-4 carbine as he raked the superstructure with two fast bursts. Sparks flew as the full-metal-jacketed rounds struck the steel structure and shrieked away. McCarter fired again, and the machine gun suddenly stopped.

Bolan heard men yelling and feet pounding on the deck behind him. Tanaka hadn't waited for orders. She had turned quickly to cover their backs. He heard the soft hiss of her silenced 9 mm Heckler & Koch as she raked the aft deck with three quick bursts.

"Cover me, Striker," Encizo called from the rail.

"Go!" Bolan shouted. The little Cuban sprinted across the deck. Bolan raked the forward superstructure with three short bursts. Bullets struck the deck two feet behind Encizo and screamed away from the steel surface. He threw himself down and rolled behind the cargo boxes. Splinters flew as another burst smashed into the big wooden boxes.

Bolan risked a quick glance behind him. Tanaka was in a steady prone position. She had switched her Heckler & Koch to semiautomatic fire and was pinning down the people behind them with rapid-fired single shots. Encizo tapped Bolan's shoulder and pushed his M-4 Ranger carbine into his hands. Bolan took a split second to slip a fresh magazine into the M-4. He slapped the bottom of the 30-round magazine to be sure was locked in place and that the weapon was ready to fire.

More bullets tore into the cargo box. Splinters flew. It sounded as if a high-powered weapon was being firing from the forward superstructure, probably a heavy machine gun. They couldn't stay there much longer. Encizo was rapidly stripping out of his rappelling harness. They had to do something. Bolan pointed forward at the looming superstructure. It seemed logical to try to capture the bridge, but the little Cuban knew more about ships than he did.

"The bridge?" he asked.

"Right," Encizo replied. "The wheel and the officers' quarters will be up there."

Bolan heard more firing and the sound of boots pounding across the deck. Gary Manning threw himself down behind the cargo boxes.

"They're not very good shots, Striker, but I'm not complaining."

"We have to take the bridge," Bolan said quickly. "Are you ready to blast?"

Manning patted the nylon web haversack filled with explosives he had slung over one shoulder. "Anytime, Striker."

"All right. Stand by. Rafe and I will be the artillery."

Bolan opened the M-203 grenade launcher mounted under the M-4's barrel and slipped in a 40 mm high-explosive grenade.

"Load smoke, Rafe," the Executioner ordered. "As soon as I've fired three, let them have it."

Bolan heard a click as Encizo closed the action of his M-203 grenade launcher.

"Ready. Smoke loaded, Striker."

Bolan rolled to his left and looked out around the corner of the cargo box. The machine gun was still firing short bursts. No use in waiting. There had to be people belowdecks, and they would have weapons. He aimed carefully through the grenade launcher's sight and pulled the trigger. He heard a dull *blup* and felt the recoil as his M-203 fired. The HE grenade arched through the air and struck, detonating on impact. The machine gun stopped firing abruptly. He snapped in a fresh grenade and fired, then reloaded and fired again. The shooting from the back side of the bridge stopped. The enemy seemed to be stunned by the blasts.

Encizo began firing, pouring in smoke grenades as fast as he could load and fire his M-203. Clouds of gray-white smoke billowed out from the bridge. Now or never. Bolan got to his feet and charged forward, followed by Manning, McCarter and Tanaka. They had about 150 feet to go. Someone was shooting from the bridge. Bullets struck the deck to Bolan's right and ricocheted off the hard steel into the night. Whoever was firing couldn't see through the smoke. He was simply spraying the deck at random, trying to keep the Stony Man team pinned down.

They ran forward toward the bridge as the bullets reached for them through the smoke. Bolan told himself it would be pure luck if one of them were hit, but the 150 feet seemed to stretch out forever as they ran. He heard a sharper boom as Encizo switched to high-explosive grenades and fired one into the upper structure of the bridge.

Suddenly, they were there. Bolan flattened himself against the gray steel wall that loomed up in front of him and waited for a second until the rest of the team joined him. They were relatively safe for a moment. No one could fire down on them from above unless they were willing to take a chance to expose themselves as they leaned out over the rail. Someone was willing. A burst of bullets struck the deck between Bolan and Manning. McCarter had the best shot. He snapped his M-4 carbine to his shoulder and squeezed off a burst. Bolan heard someone scream, and a man's body came tumbling down from above and smashed into the gray steel deck.

A solid steel door led into the bridge structure. Bolan tried the handle, but the door was locked. He signaled to Manning, who was already opening the nylon haversack that held his explosives. He quickly taped lengths of flexible, linear-shaped charges to the door's hinges, stepped back and pushed the button on his remote detonation box. Bolan saw several bright white flashes. The precisely focused planes of energy cut through the hinges instantly, like a hot knife through butter. The door fell outward and struck the deck with a loud clang.

Bolan wasn't foolish enough to rush through the gaping doorway. That was just as well. Someone inside was still full of fight. A burst from an AK-47 suddenly streaked through the opening. Manning didn't like unfinished business. He fused a two-and-a-half-pound block of C-4 plastique and threw it through the door. There was a one-second delay, and then the charge detonated with a sharp roar.

Bolan slipped multiple-projectile antipersonnel round into his M-203 grenade launcher and signaled to McCarter. He moved to the left edge of the door opening, and the Briton moved to the right. McCarter silently signaled that he was ready. Bolan nodded and they fired short bursts together. The high-velocity, full-metal-jacketed bullets ricocheted off the steel walls and shrieked down the passage in a lethal criss-cross pattern.

There was no reply. Bolan risked a quick look around the edge of the door. The passageway was smoking and blackened by explosions. Three men lay dead or unconscious at the far end. The steel doors on either side of the passageway were all closed.

"Cover me," he shouted to McCarter, and rushed down the passageway. He had almost reached the end when two men suddenly appeared in front of him, toting short, black submachine guns. Bolan recognized the large round drum magazines. They were the Chinese version of the old Russian burp gun. Each magazine held 71 cartridges, and each weapon could fire 15 rounds per second. They weren't accurate, but they were some of the deadliest close-quarter combat weapons ever developed. Bolan pulled the trigger of his grenade launcher. The multiple-projectile round was like a huge shotgun shell. Bolan was too close for the shot pattern to spread completely. The man on the right was struck by dozens of steel buckshot and died in his tracks.

The second man was dazed by the blast. He pulled the trigger of his submachine gun, but he wasn't aiming. The steel-jacketed bullets missed Bolan's head by six inches. He pulled the trigger of his M-4 and cut the man down where he stood. He moved forward past the bodies of the two men. Bolan could see a set of steel stairs that led toward the main bridge. The ship was controlled from there, and anyone going up the stairs would be caught in a death trap if a gunner at the top opened fire.

Bolan signaled for McCarter and Manning to move up. He pointed at the stairs. The Briton frowned and shook his head. There was no way they could provide adequate covering fire for anyone who tried to climb them. Manning grinned and reached inside his haversack. He pulled out four round objects and passed one of them to Bolan. They were U.S. Army M-61 fragmentation grenades, far better than any guns for fighting in a closed area.

The Executioner took one of the grenades in his right hand and hooked his left forefinger through the safety ring. Manning stood behind him, ready to pass him more grenades. McCarter aimed his carbine up the stairs. Before Bolan could throw one of the bombs, someone above him at the top of the stairs fired an automatic weapon. McCarter replied instantly, saturating the top of the stairs with quick, short bursts.

Bolan pulled the grenade's pin and threw the deadly egg. It landed at the top of the stairs and rolled out of sight. The bomb detonated with a dull boom, and someone on the bridge shrieked in pain. Then there was a sudden silence.

The soldier took the last two steps in a single bound and stepped on the bridge with his carbine poised in the assault position. He didn't need it. The lethal fragments from grenade had swept the bridge with deadly swarms of steel. Two men in officers' uniforms lay dead or unconscious on the floor. They had done it. The Stony Man team had seized control of the *Wuhan*.

CHAPTER SEVENTEEN

The Wuhan, *off the Coast of Sumatra*

Mack Bolan signaled for the rest of the team to move up to the bridge. Gadgets Schwarz, Meiko Tanaka and Major Salim were at the foot of the stairs, guarding the deck-level entrance. He took a quick look around. The bridge was simple. There was no exotic high-tech equipment, unless you counted a small radar display and a few instrument consoles. Encizo went to the steering wheel, lowered the body of the dead crewman to the deck and checked the helmsman's display.

"We're about twenty-five miles north of the coast of Sumatra, Striker. We're steering due south toward the coast. The other indicators are in Chinese. I can't read them. What do you want me to do?"

Chinese instruments could be a problem. He spoke into the headset of his tactical radio and asked Schwarz to send up Tanaka. He thought for a minute. The freighter was undamaged, and Encizo seemed to be able to control her movements.

"Change course, Rafe. Head us to the north toward Banda Aceh."

Encizo grinned. That wasn't exactly a precise nautical order, but he knew what Bolan wanted him to do. He spun the wheel.

The bridge's large windows provided excellent views forward or left or right. Bolan could see that the smoke was clearing. McCarter was looking toward the bow, using his binoculars. Gary Manning was checking the bodies of the two men who lay on the deck. He looked at Bolan and shook his head. The two ship's officers were dead, and he had found nothing significant on their bodies. Tanaka entered the bridge, slinging her submachine gun. Bolan pointed to the instrument consoles, and she began to examine them.

"We control the bridge. They control the aft superstructure and everything belowdecks. What can they do from down there, Rafe?" McCarter asked.

Encizo thought for a moment. "Several things, David. They could stop the engines. That would leave the ship dead in the water. They could open the seacocks and scuttle her. They could send radio messages asking for help. For all we know, there could be Chinese warships in the area. If there are military explosives in the cargo, they could rig some charges and blast us out."

"What can we do about it, Rafe?" Bolan asked.

"Not much. We wouldn't stand one chance in a million if we tried to go down below. There are more of them than there are of us. They know the ship, and we don't. It would be suicide."

"Something is happening," Tanaka said. She stared at the control console in front of her. A bright green light had come on and was pulsing steadily. "The ship's radio is transmitting." She flipped a switch.

They heard a man's voice, hoarse with excitement, speaking rapidly in an Oriental language.

"He is speaking in Chinese," Tanaka said. "He is saying, 'Emergency! Emergency! This is the cargo ship *Wuhan*. We have been attacked by heavily armed pirates off the coast of Sumatra. Pirates are on board and attempting to capture the ship. Please send assistance immediately!' Now he is repeating himself. He is giving the ship's position more accurately."

"The *Wuhan* is a merchant ship, no matter what cargo she's carrying," Bolan stated. "Any warship or coast guard vessel that picks up her message is supposed to come to her assistance. That means they'll stop and board her, arrest us and turn the *Wuhan* back over to her crew."

McCarter put down his binoculars and motioned to Bolan. "Something's going on up forward, Striker, near the bow. Three or four people came on deck. They looked around and then went back down below. They kept under cover as much as possible. They were all armed with rifles or submachine guns. One of them had binoculars. It may be that they are just trying to find out what's going on. On the other hand, they may be planning an attack.

"Take a look. See what you think."

Bolan took the binoculars and carefully scanned the bow. There was no sign of anyone. The forward section of the deck seemed deserted. Anyone on deck was well concealed and keeping very quiet. He was about to say so when a flash of movement caught his eye. Men were coming on deck and fanning out rapidly to take cover, many men armed with AK-47 rifles and Chinese submachine guns.

"Heads up! They're coming on deck," he snapped.

Bolan saw a second group of five or six men move rapidly toward the mysterious canvas-covered object and begin stripping off its cover. The Executioner stared at them intently. The CIA weapons expert had been right. As they stripped the cover off, he could see the menacing bulk of a twin-barreled automatic cannon. The gun was protected by an armored shield and was pointing forward, but as he watched, the crewmen manned the gun and began to traverse it until its long twin barrels seemed to be pointing straight at him.

"Everybody get ready! I think that they're going to rush us, and they have an automatic cannon. It looks like a Russian 23 mm for fire support. Get some people to guard the stairs, David, and bring Gadgets up here. He's too isolated down there. I'll keep an eye on them."

Bolan heard McCarter call down the stairs and Schwarz's boots pounding on the steel steps as he took them two at a time. Then things were silent as the seconds crawled by and nothing happened. Suddenly, the silence was shattered as a phone mounted near the steering wheel rang. Tanaka pointed at the phone inquiringly. Bolan nodded. There was no use pretending they weren't there. The enemy knew better than that.

She picked up the phone and said something in Chinese. She listened for a moment. Then she spoke in English.

"I am only a platoon leader. I do not have the authority to make such decisions. I will convey your insulting proposal to my commanding officer. I do not believe he will be interested in anything you have to say, but remain on the line, and I will tell you his answer.''

She carefully put her hand over the phone's speaker and spoke softly.

''It is the ship's executive officer. He is breathing fire and slaughter. If we surrender immediately, we will not be killed. If not, we will all be killed. We have one minute to decide.''

''You're a pretty good platoon leader, Meiko,'' Bolan told her. ''Keep up the good work, and I'll promote you to company commander.''

The woman still had trouble with some American idioms. She wasn't sure what ''pretty good'' meant, but Striker was sincere. She decided that it was a compliment and bowed slightly.

''I shall strive to be worthy of the honor, Striker,'' she said formally.

Bolan took a quick look around. If they were going to make any changes in their defenses, now was the time. The only way to rush the bridge was up the stairs. They had enough firepower to make that extremely hazardous for the enemy. He saw a ladder attached to one side wall that led up to a trapdoor in the ceiling.

''Where does that ladder go, Rafe?''

Encizo thought for a moment. ''Probably just gives you access to the roof of the bridge. If I remember the pictures, there are several radar and communications antennas up there.''

Bolan thought quickly. The bridge was difficult to shoot out of. The glassed windows hampered their fields of fire. They needed to get someone in a position to reach out and touch someone near the bow. He motioned to Manning. His Heckler & Koch

PSG-1 rifle was by far the best sniping weapon they had.

"Let's go up the ladder, Gary, and see if we can find some good firing positions up there."

Manning slung his rifle and moved to the ladder. He asked the sniper's classic question. "What are the target priorities, Striker?"

"Get the gun crew if they expose themselves. If the others try to rush us, kill the leaders first."

Manning nodded. It was standard operating procedure. Few things reduced attacking troops' morale faster than seeing their officers shot down in front of them. He went up the ladder slowly, carefully protecting his rifle and its scope sight. Bolan followed him up the ladder. The big Canadian opened the trapdoor and slipped through. He stayed down in a prone position and crawled slowly toward the edge of the bridge structure. Bolan followed him. The area was flat and empty except for several communications and radar antennae.

They carefully peered over the edge. The bow of the ship and the automatic cannon were about two hundred feet away. Manning smiled grimly. At that range, he could put every shot in a three-inch circle even firing rapidly. The only real problem was that the twin-barreled 23 mm cannon was well protected. With the gun pointing at the bridge, only the two long barrels protruded through the armored shield. The crew and the breeches of the weapons were out of sight behind the shield. He adjusted his scope sight to maximum magnification and studied the gun carefully.

His Heckler & Koch PSG-1 was a superbly accurate and reliable rifle. It was loaded with twenty rounds of Winchester National Match ammunition. He slipped into a rifleman's prone position, as steady as a rock, and waited for a good target, his finger pressing lightly on the trigger. Bolan slipped into a prone position beside him. His M-4 Ranger carbine was a deadly weapon and reasonably accurate, but it wasn't a tack driver like Manning's H&K. It did have one feature that Manning's rifle lacked, the 40 mm M-203 grenade launcher clipped under its barrel. Bolan loaded a high-explosive round into the M-203 and waited for Manning to finish his scan of the gun.

"It doesn't look good, Striker. The gun crew and the magazines are protected by the shield. I won't have any trouble hitting the shield, but my bullets won't be able to penetrate it. That gun was designed as an antiaircraft weapon. That shield was meant to protect it against fighter planes armed with .50-caliber machine guns or 20 mm cannon. No .308 bullet is going to get through it."

Bolan had been afraid of that. They would have to use the helicopter. He didn't like that idea. He had encountered 23 mm Russian cannons before. He couldn't remember the details precisely, but a single 23 mm could fire 800 or 900 rounds a minute. A dual mount would double that. The Black Hawk wasn't armored. A burst of HE 23 mm shells could tear it to pieces, but they were all in danger. They had to use it. He pushed the button on his tactical radio.

"Jack, this is Striker. What's your situation?"

"Sarge, I'm standing by about six miles to the south. What's your situation?"

Bolan told Grimaldi quickly. There was a short pause while Grimaldi thought it over.

"I recommend we contact the *Hornet* and request

air support. In the meantime, I'll stand by ready to attack that damned gun if you give the word.''

''All right, Jack, do it.''

GRIMALDI THOUGHT hard. It was going to be nasty. The Black Hawk had two weapons he could control from the pilot's seat, the .50-caliber M-2 Browning heavy machine gun and the 2.75-inch rocket pods under the stub wings. Both were fixed weapons. He could only aim them by pointing the helicopter's nose directly at the target. That wasn't a problem for most types of targets, but it was close to suicidal against an automatic antiaircraft cannon firing thirty shells per second straight up his flight path. Grimaldi didn't want to die for his country unless it was absolutely necessary. He believed in helping the enemy die for his. Well, Mrs. Grimaldi hadn't raised any stupid boy children. He would think of something.

He turned to Ingrid Johannsen. ''Call the *Hornet.* Tell them the situation. Tell them that our team needs air support as soon as possible!''

Johannsen keyed her transmitter and spoke urgently into her microphone. ''Hornet, Hornet. This is Viking. Come in, *Hornet.*''

For a few seconds, all she heard was the faint hiss of static. Then a man's voice with a reassuring Southern accent answered her call.

''Viking, this is *Hornet.* Reading you loud and clear.''

She sighed with relief. This was the first time she had sent a radio message in combat. It was a tremendous relief to hear that it was working.

''*Hornet,* our team has boarded the *Wuhan.* They control the bridge, but the ship has a very large crew and is organizing to retake the bridge. Request immediate air support. Repeat, immediate air support. Tell your pilots to be careful. There are automatic antiaircraft cannon mounted fore and aft.''

''Message understood. Wait one, Viking. I will relay your message to the captain.''

Johannsen waited. The seconds seemed to crawl by, then she heard a different voice.

''Received your message, Viking. Preparing to launch fast movers. Before we launch, you must authenticate. The challenge is Battle Ax.''

''Roger, *Hornet*. The authentication is Sword Blade.''

''Correct, Viking. Tell your people to hang on. We have four Harriers spotted on the flight deck. Preparing to launch in ten minutes. *Hornet* out.''

Johannsen shifted frequencies and transmitted the message to the team on the freighter.

She turned to Grimaldi. ''I guess all we can do now is wait.''

Grimaldi knew it sounded good, but it would take the Harriers fifteen minutes to get there even if there were no problems. A lot could happen in fifteen minutes.

''Oh, there's one or two things we can do to pass the time, Ingrid. Go back and strap yourself behind the door gun. You'll have a few minutes to review what I told you earlier about firing that baby.''

''I'll do what you say, Jack. But if I'm back there, who's going to work the countermeasures? Won't we be needing them if people are going to be shooting at us?''

''No, the countermeasures won't do us any good. That 23 mm gun is so low tech that they won't do any good at all. The countermeasures jam radar and infrared sensors. That gun is aimed by the gunner's eye looking through an optical sight. Countermeasures won't work against that. Okay, go strap yourself into the gunner's harness. I'm going to have to jerk her around a bit when we go in. I won't have time to warn you."

Johannsen looked a little pale, but otherwise all right. He slapped her on the shoulder.

"This is going to be a real adventure. Think of the war stories you'll be able to tell when you're back at CIA headquarters."

Johannsen nodded. Oh, yes, she would have some great stories to tell, if she got out of this alive.

FORTY MILES to the east, the USS *Hornet* turned into the wind. She looked like an aircraft carrier, but she was an amphibious assault ship. The ship lacked the steam-powered catapults and complex arresting gear required to launch conventional jet aircraft, but her attack planes weren't conventional. The flight deck had been cleared, and four of her mottled green-and-brown Marine Corps AV-8B Harriers were spotted near the stern. The Harriers could take off and land vertically if necessary, but their range and payload was increased if they taxied down the flight deck.

Major Peter Jacobs waited, strapped into the cockpit of his Harrier. The four planes in his flight were armed for an antiship mission with laser-guided bombs, Maverick missiles and the feed systems of their 25 mm Gatling guns fully loaded. Their engines were idling while his crew chiefs made a last visual check. The senior Marine sergeant nodded to Jacobs and saluted. Blue flight was ready to go.

Jacobs spoke into his flight helmet microphone. "Hornet Control, Hornet Blue ready for take off."

"Roger, Hornet Blue Leader. You are cleared for take off now. Go get 'em, tiger!"

Jacobs smiled as he pushed his throttle forward. The Harrier vibrated as its F-402 Pegasus jet engine roared and it went to full power. Jacobs released his brakes, and the Harrier rolled down the deck faster and faster until it shot over the *Hornet*'s bow. The other three planes in Blue Flight followed Jacobs off the deck. All four were airborne now. Jacobs turned smoothly on the course to intercept the *Wuhan*. Hornet Blue Flight was on the way!

BOLAN AND MANNING WAITED on the roof of the bridge with the cold patience of master snipers waiting for their targets to appear. Bolan was just as content to be waiting. The longer nothing happened, the closer they were to the fighters arriving. That should tip the balance of power decisively in their favor.

It was too good to last. Through the open trapdoor, he heard the phone ring again.

He heard Tanaka speaking in Chinese. Then she moved to the foot of the ladder and called up to Bolan.

"It was the ship's executive officer again. He is very angry. He will give us one more minute. We must wave a white flag then, or he will open fire and we will die for our stubborn behavior."

"Down!" McCarter suddenly shouted. "Everyone, down!"

Something struck the bridge like a giant sledge-hammer. Something struck a second time. The huge steel structure rang and vibrated.

"Heads up, Striker," Manning shouted. "They've started shooting."

Just two shots? Bolan knew what that meant. They were ranging in, checking their aim. As soon as the gunner was satisfied, he would be firing twenty-five shots per second.

Bolan pushed the button on his tactical radio. "They've started shooting, Jack. Attack now! Take out that damned gun if you can!"

"Roger, Striker. We're on the way."

GRIMALDI PUSHED his throttles forward and listened as the Black Hawk's two turbine engines changed from a whine to a howl at the same time they reached full power. He glanced quickly across his display panels. Green lights. Everything was working properly. The .50-caliber machine gun was loaded, and the rocket launchers were armed. He turned toward the freighter and started down in a shallow dive. He tried to remember everything he had ever heard about Russian ZU-23 mm guns. He remembered their effective range against aircraft was about 5,000 yards. He would be in range in less than two minutes.

He looked at his multifunctional display. The ZU-23's long barrels were still pointed at the bridge. Good! So far they hadn't seen him coming. It would take precious time to traverse the guns to fire at him when they did. He might even get in a burst from the side where the gun and its crew were more vulnerable. Suddenly, the infrared picture changed. The twin muzzles of the gun were wreathed in blinding light. It was firing, firing full automatic!

MCCARTER WAITED tensely on the bridge. The temptation to do something, anything, was enormous. He thought hard. Anything he might try would expose them to instant death. Abandoning the bridge might work, but that would mean turning control of the freighter back to her crew. The bridge offered very little cover against 23 mm high explosive-incendiary ammunition. He could see no alternative to staying put and hoping that Grimaldi could take out that gun.

Burst after burst of 23 mm fire slammed into the bridge and tore through its light steel structure as if it were tissue paper. McCarter saw the glowing green streaks of tracers and heard an endless stuttering roar as the 23 mm shells struck the back wall and detonated. Broken glass cascaded down from the shattered windows. He could smell the acrid odor of burning high explosives. It seemed to go on forever, but it lasted only four seconds. Then the 50-round magazines were exhausted, and the cannons stopped firing as the gun crew loaded two fresh magazines.

McCarter looked around. The team members were flat on the deck. The shells seemed to have swept the bridge two or three feet above the deck. The explosive power of a single individual 23 mm shell was limited, but the cumulative effect was staggering. He heard coughing and gasping from the fumes. No one seemed to be hit, but he didn't know how much more they could stand. Where was Grimaldi?

GRIMALDI WAS TWO MILES away, making his firing run. He was coming in at 150 miles per hour. His sights were steady on the ZU-23 mm gun mount. The long barrels were still pointing at the bridge. He didn't think they had seen him yet. The noise of their cannon firing had drowned out the sound of the Black

Hawk's engines. If he was lucky, he might get a free ride on his first attack. After that it would get hairy. He would be in firing range in thirty seconds. He set the rocket launchers to fire four rockets each and put his finger on the .50-caliber Browning's trigger.

He had no real sense of movement. The *Wuhan* seemed to be growing steadily larger in his sight. Closer, closer, just a little bit closer. Now! Grimaldi pressed the trigger. The chopper vibrated as the big M-2 Browning roared into life. He could see the blurred red streak of tracers as the big bullets shot toward the target. He saw the yellow flashes of armor-piercing bullets smashing into hardened steel. Grimaldi smiled grimly. If the gun crew hadn't seen him before, they certainly did now. He was on target. Rockets now!

The rocket launchers under the Black Hawk's stub wings were wreathed in orange fire as the eight 2.75-inch rockets shot from the launcher's tubes at two-second intervals. They streaked toward the target, trailing gray white smoke. Grimaldi fired another burst. He was on target. He could see more yellow flashes as his bullets struck the gun mount's armor. Dammit! He saw red streaks shooting away from the target. The .50-caliber bullets weren't penetrating the armor. They were ricocheting off it.

The rockets arrived, and Grimaldi saw orange flashes as their high-explosive warheads detonated. The explosions were clustered around the gun mount. The 2.75-inch rockets weren't precision weapons. They were designed to saturate an area with multiple explosions. Only luck would give him a direct hit inside the ring of armor that surrounded the gun mount. It didn't look as if he had been lucky. He

could see the 23 mm cannon barrels turning and el-
evating to point at him. Instantly, he began to make
quick left and right turns about the line of flight. He
was still moving toward the gun but never flying in
a straight line.

He waited a few seconds until his sights were on
and triggered another short burst from his .50-caliber
Browning. Even if the big bullets wouldn't penetrate
the gun's shield, they might give the gunner something to think about. Maybe that would spoil his aim.
Maybe not. Grimaldi saw blinking yellow flashes as
the dual 23 mms roared into life. Bright green tracers
flashed past the Black Hawk's canopy. To Grimaldi's
eyes, they seemed to miss by inches. He had no time
to think. He was in danger of succumbing to target
fixation and crashing into the gun mount. He pulled
back on his controls, flattened out and flashed across
the freighter's deck.

He felt the Black Hawk vibrate as Johannsen fired
a two-second burst from the door gun down the deck.
Grimaldi doubted that she would hit anything she
aimed at, but two hundred .308 bullets in two seconds
would give the Chinese sailors a burning desire to
keep their heads down. He was too close and moving
too fast for the 23 mm gunner to stay on target, but
as he cleared the deck, Grimaldi knew it was only a
matter of seconds before the gunner could fire again.

He put the Black Hawk's nose down as he cleared
the edge of the deck and went down to twenty feet.
He turned left, toward the bow, staying down. The
gun crew could hear his engines, but without being
able to see him, they couldn't be sure where he was.
That would give him the advantage of surprise when
he popped up to attack again.

MACK BOLAN WATCHED the Black Hawk streak across the deck. Gary Manning was staring intently through his telescopic sight, looking at the gun from his right side. He saw a flash of motion as two men from the gun crew turned and dashed to the side of the three-foot-high armored ring. They were snatching up large black metal objects, spare 50-round magazines. They were moving rapidly, but Manning had the crosshairs of his scope on one man's side. He squeezed the trigger, and his Heckler & Koch roared. A giant hand seemed to slap the man sideways. He dropped the magazine and crumpled to the deck.

The second man was behind cover. Manning waited patiently for someone to make a mistake. Anyone who did was going to be a dead man. The gun mount was about two hundred feet away. Manning smiled grimly. At that range, he could hit a man-sized target with every shot, even firing rapidly.

Bolan scanned the gun mount with his binoculars. He could see gouges in the armored shield where Grimaldi's bullets had struck and glanced off. There were some scorch marks on the three foot high armored ring that surrounded the gun mount where the 2.75-inch rockets had struck, but they weren't designed to penetrate armor. The gun was undamaged.

Bolan thought quickly. They couldn't go on like this. He knew Grimaldi would attack again and again, but sooner or later, the gunner would hit him. One good burst of 23 mm HE-I would tear the Black Hawk to pieces. He thought hard. All right, when your tactics weren't working, you changed them. The gun's weakness was that it could only point in one direction at a time, and its armored shield wasn't like a tank's turret. It only protected the gun crew from return fire from the direction they were shooting. If they were firing one way, they were vulnerable from the other.

If your enemy had a weakness, exploit it. He spoke into the microphone of his tactical radio.

"Jack, what's your situation?"

"I'm all right. I have 1,220 rounds of .50 caliber and thirty rockets left, and Ingrid's back there on the Gatling. I'll attack again in a minute. Keep your head down when we make our next run. I don't think Ingrid's qualified for master door gunner yet."

"She's learning on the job, Jack, but let's change our tactics. On your next run, come in as close as you can from the bow. Let them have a few rockets, and then fly down the deck. That will give Gary a few good shots, and he doesn't miss very often at that range."

"Good. If he can kill that damned gunner, the drinks are on me, Sarge."

"One other thing. Do you have any smoke left?"

"Wait one, and I'll check. Yeah. Both tanks are about half full."

"Good. Lay down a smoke screen as you fly down the deck. I'm going to pay the gun crew a call. The smoke will give me a little cover."

CHAPTER EIGHTEEN

The Wuhan *off the coast of Sumatra*

McCarter was waiting for Bolan as the soldier climbed up the ladder to the bridge. "You're going to need someone to watch your back, or you'll be shot before you get halfway to the gun."

"I'll take my chances, David. Gary has to stay here. He can cover me."

"That's not the best plan."

"What do you have in mind?"

"You and I go, and Major Salim. It's his fight, and he's a marine. He knows his way around ships. Rafe has to steer the ship, and Gadgets can help him with the electronics. Meiko wants to go, of course, but someone has to watch the stairs. I told her it is an honor to be chosen to protect the bridge and that you, personally, are counting on her. She hissed a bit, but she will do it."

"It's as good a plan as any. All we have to do now is make it work. Let's go back down and get organized. Jack may be getting a little impatient."

"Wait one, Striker," Manning said, and patted this nylon web haversack filled with explosives.

"Better take this with you. I can't blast anything from up here. It may come in handy."

Bolan slung Manning's haversack over his shoulder. Manning was right. He might need to blow something to kingdom come.

BOLAN FLATTENED HIMSELF against the side of the bridge structure and looked quickly around the corner. The deck looked deceptively peaceful. No one was in sight, but that didn't mean that they weren't there, keeping under cover with weapons ready. The 23 mm gun was trained toward the bridge. He estimated that it was about seventy yards away. In track clothes and running shoes, he could have covered that distance in eight or nine seconds. In combat boots and carrying a carbine and two heavy pistols, it was going to take longer. Bolan didn't intend to run. They had one big tactical advantage over the crew. They knew that everyone they encountered on the deck was hostile. In the limited visibility and the confusion spread by the smoke, the crew couldn't be sure. They might hesitate for a few seconds before shooting, not wanting to kill one another. That would give the team the chance to shoot first.

Bolan hoped that would be enough, but the odds were against them. Waiting wasn't going to make things any better. The smoke would dissipate in a few minutes. He glanced quickly over his shoulder. McCarter and Salim looked ready to go. The Briton gave him a thumbs-up. The team was as ready as it would ever be.

He spoke softly into the throat mike of his tactical radio.

"Jack, this is Striker. We're ready when you are."

"Roger. Attacking, now!"

Nothing happened for a few seconds. Then, Bolan heard the whine of the Black Hawk's engines. He could hear men shouting in Chinese. One man stood and pointed toward the bow. It was the last mistake he ever made. Manning's rifle cracked, and he crumpled and fell to the deck. Bolan watched intently as the dull black Black Hawk rose from behind the bow, its nose pointing down the deck. He could see the round black circles of the rocket launchers under its wings as Grimaldi hovered and fired. Yellow muzzle-flashes danced around the nose, and large red tracers streaked down the deck. Then, the rocket launchers began to spit their 2.75-inch rockets at the gun mount.

It was an impressive display, but Grimaldi couldn't stay there. The gun was traversing toward him. He put the Black Hawk's nose down and sped along the deck, trailing plumes of thick gray-white smoke. The chopper came closer and closer. At the last instant, Grimaldi turned sharply to avoid striking the bridge.

"Go, Striker, go!"

Grimaldi had quit firing. The cloud of smoke was settling on the deck. Bolan slipped a 40 mm antipersonnel round into his M-203 grenade launcher and signaled to McCarter and Salim. The smoke cloud had expanded to cover the lower part of the bridge structure. Bolan stepped around the corner and started up the deck. The thick gray smoke had an unpleasant acrid smell, but at least it provided cover. He could dimly see about ten or fifteen feet ahead. Beyond that, the rest of the ship was invisible, shrouded in the smoke.

He headed toward the bow, staring into the smoke and listening intently. Ten yards, fifteen, then he heard voices, speaking softly in Chinese. Bolan froze and motioned to McCarter. The Briton slung his M-4 carbine and drew his silenced .22-caliber Walther pistol. He moved forward silently.

Bolan followed him quietly, his M-4 up and ready. Three or four dark rectangular shapes loomed up in the smoke, wooden cargo crates stowed against one side of the rail. Bolan heard the voices again, coming from behind the crates. McCarter took a firm two-handed grip on his Walther and stepped around the edge of the nearest crate.

Someone spoke sharply. McCarter brought his pistol to eye level in one fluid motion and pulled the trigger. Bolan heard the soft hiss of the silenced pistol as McCarter fired two fast shots, pivoted slightly and fired again. Someone yelled loudly in Chinese. McCarter fired again.

Bolan rushed around the corner. One man was sprawled on the deck. The other man was trying to bring an AK-47 up to the firing position. McCarter had hit him, but he was still full of fight. The smoke kept Bolan from seeing his sights clearly. This was no time to be worrying about details. He simply looked along the barrel and pulled the trigger. The short, deadly carbine snarled and sent a burst through the man's chest. The AK-47 slipped through his hands as he fell to the deck.

It was good shooting, but it wasn't quiet. Bolan heard men shouting in the smoke, and someone was blowing a whistle repeatedly. There was no time to hesitate. They had lost the element of surprise. No time for caution. They had to strike fast before the defenders got organized.

"Go! Go! Go!" Bolan shouted, and rushed along the deck.

Salim moved up and followed, staying two strides behind the Executioner's shoulder. McCarter stopped for a second to holster his Walther and unsling his M-4 carbine, then raced after them. The smoke still clung to the deck. Bolan could hear men shouting, but the ship's crew seemed confused.

He saw something large and tall ahead, looming up through the smoke—the cargo handling masts. He was about to tell Salim to check the right-hand mast while he took care of the left-hand one when he saw flickering yellow flashes. Someone fired around the side, first from one mast, then from the other.

Bolan heard the roar of AK-47s firing on full automatic. A burst of steel jacketed .30-caliber bullets struck the steel deck two feet to his right and ricocheted away. He dived for the deck, rolled and fired a short burst at the muzzle-flashes. He heard the roar of Salim's AK-47 as he joined the firefight. Yellow flashes sparked as his bullets struck the steel mast and glanced away harmlessly. The masts were excellent cover. Rifle fire wasn't going to penetrate them.

McCarter came to the same conclusion. He snapped up his M-4 carbine and pulled the trigger of its grenade launcher. It was hard to aim precisely through the smoke, but the mast was a large target. The 40 mm HE grenade struck the mast and detonated in a flash of orange fire. Its explosive charge wasn't powerful enough to damage the mast, but its blast would discourage people from shooting accurately around its side.

Salim dropped to the deck and rolled to a prone position. He ejected the empty magazine and shoved a fresh magazine into his AK-47. "We cannot stay here much longer," he said. "They will bring up more men, and we will be trapped here. We have no weapon that can shoot through those damned masts. Cover me, and I will run between the masts and take them from behind."

Bolan shook his head. "You won't stand a chance, Major. You'll be in a cross fire when you pass between the masts. They'll cut you in two before you've gone ten feet."

"If God wills it, that may happen, but I will not just wait here for them to kill me. Still, you are right, Striker. I will not charge straight between the masts. That gives the sons of Satan too good a target. I will run at an angle toward the other mast. They will not expect that. Fire everything you have at them. With any luck, I will be on top of them before they know what is happening."

Bolan knew that Salim was determined to go. "All right. I'll fire a grenade. As soon as you hear it detonate, go. I'll try to keep their heads down."

"Fire when you are ready."

Bolan aimed just past the side of the right-hand mast and pulled the grenade launcher's trigger. The 40 mm HE projectile struck the deck fifteen feet behind the mast and detonated. He couldn't be sure whether he had hit anyone, but the blast should stun and confuse anyone behind the mast for a few precious seconds. Salim leaped to his feet and charged, yelling something in Indonesian. Bolan aimed carefully to clear the major as he charged and fired in one short burst after another.

Someone fired at Salim from behind the left-hand mast, but missed. The major sprinted around the corner out of Bolan's sight, but he heard several AK-47s firing simultaneously. The Executioner took a second to load an antipersonnel grenade into his M-203 and raced after Salim.

He rounded the edge of the mast and found himself in the middle of a fight to the death. A tall Chinese had a bayonet fixed on his AK-47. He snarled and lunged at Bolan's chest. The soldier tried to parry with his carbine, but it was too late. The sharp steel point slammed into his chest. There was an odd rasping noise as the sharp steel point grated on the trauma plate of Bolan's body armor. The crewman shrieked furiously and tried to thrust again. Too late! Bolan pulled the trigger of his grenade launcher. The 40 mm antipersonnel grenade converted his M-203 into a gigantic sawed-off shotgun, and steel buckshot struck and tore the crewman's chest to pieces.

A second man was aiming an AK-47. Bolan was looking straight into the cold black muzzle as he pivoted and pulled his carbine's trigger. He knew he had hit his target, but he saw a yellow flash at the AK-47's muzzle and something smashed him in the chest with tremendous force. The steel-jacketed bullet had nearly a ton of kinetic energy. The trauma plate of Bolan's armor held, but his body absorbed that energy in one devastating blow. He flew backward and slammed down hard on the deck. He tried to get up, but his arms and legs weren't responding properly.

He was dazed and disoriented, trying desperately to fire again. He heard a burst from an AK-47 five feet away. Major Salim was standing over the man's body, snapping a fresh magazine into his AK-47. He unsnapped a large cloth bandolier and turned to show it to Bolan.

"Look at this... What is wrong? Are you hit? Let me see."

Bolan gasped for air as the numbing effects of the blow receded.

"I'm all right, I think. My armor stopped it."

Salim opened Bolan's shirt. He stared at the base of the steel-jacketed bullet embedded in the armor.

"God be praised! You do not seem to be wounded. This is marvelous armor to stop an AK-47 bullet. Can you walk? We cannot stay here. The smoke is starting to get thinner."

Bolan rolled to get his knees under him and stood up shakily.

Salim held out the dull green bandolier. He opened one of its twelve pockets, took something out and smiled.

"Good. Now, Striker, look what I have found."

Bolan looked. He knew what it was, a Russian RDG-5 fragmentation grenade.

"We can use these," Salim said. He took out four of the grenades and hung them on his web belt. Bolan did the same.

Salim looked around. "Now, where is McCarter?"

"Coming from your left, mate," the big Englishman drawled. "I took care of these chaps behind the other mast. They were so busy shooting at you that they forgot to watch their flanks."

Bolan smiled grimly. Anyone who forgot to watch their flanks when McCarter was after them had made his last mistake. He passed the Briton the last four grenades from the bandolier.

McCarter held up his hand. "Listen! Something is going on."

Bolan listened. His ears were still ringing a bit, but he could hear whistles blowing shrilly and men shouting from the direction of the bow.

"I wish we knew what they are saying. Maybe they're going to counterattack."

"No, I know a little Chinese, not much, but I think they are saying to fall back," Major Salim said. "I think they are massing to defend the gun."

That made sense to Bolan. The Chinese crew couldn't be sure how many men were attacking them through the smoke, but as long as they held the gun mount they controlled the deck. He picked up his M-4 carbine, checked it quickly and looked along the deck toward the bow. The smoke was definitely getting thinner. They were running out of time.

"Let's go," McCarter said. He gave Bolan a quick look. "I'll take the point. You look a bit the worse for wear."

Bolan didn't argue. He could use a minute or two to shake off the effects of the direct hit on his body armor. McCarter brought his carbine to the assault position and moved out. Salim followed him, staying ten feet to McCarter's right. Bolan followed Salim, scanning the sides of the deck as they moved forward. Some sailor just might not have gotten the word. They moved forward steadily, weapons ready. Five yards, ten...

There was no warning. Suddenly, objects flashed out of the smoke ahead. Six bright green glowing streaks shot past Bolan's right arm, missing him by inches. The 23 mm projectiles were moving three times faster than the speed of sound. They were gone before Bolan heard the roar of the guns. He hurled himself down and struck the steel deck with bruising force. That burst was gone, but he knew more were on the way.

More swarms of bright green streaks flashed by as the gunner traversed his weapon and swept the decks. Bolan knew he was lucky to be alive. The 23 mm shells were nearly twice as fast as the bullets from an AK-47, and they exploded on contact. His body armor offered no protection. The 23 mm projectiles would rip through it as if it were tissue paper. If one hit his arm or leg, it would blow it off.

Bolan heard the dull boom of a 40 mm grenade launcher as McCarter fired, aiming back along the path of the projectiles. That was the right idea! He aimed quickly and emptied the magazine of his carbine in two fast bursts.

"They keep firing high. Why don't the Sons of Satan fire lower?" Salim asked.

McCarter had been thinking about that. It might be a key point.

"I don't think they can. That armored ring the gun sits in won't let them depress the barrels any lower. That means that there's a dead zone close to the gun mount they can't fire into. Now, if one of us can just get in there with a few grenades—"

"I'll go," Bolan interrupted. "I'm better with hand grenades than you are."

McCarter nodded. That was true. He unclipped two of his hand grenades and handed them to Bolan.

"Before you go, Striker, how are you fixed for carbine ammunition? I have only two full magazines left."

Bolan quickly felt his magazine pouches. "I've got

two, plus one in my carbine. Here, you take them. I'll need both hands for fast grenading.'' He handed McCarter the magazines and his carbine. If he made it to the gun mount, it would be close-quarters combat. He would depend on his pistols.

McCarter aimed along the deck. "Get ready, Striker. Any second now.''

Another swarm of green tracers flashed out of the smoke and swept across the deck as the gunner traversed. Bolan crouched, ready to go. The stream of tracers passed a foot over his head.

''Go, Striker, go!'' McCarter shouted.

Bolan sprang to his feet and charged forward. He took ten long strides and hit the deck. He could see the gun mount dimly now. Two bright yellow flashes danced on the two guns' muzzles. He took one of the RDG-5 grenades from his web belt. It had a 3.4-second delay from the time the fuse was ignited until the grenade detonated.

He hefted the grenade in his right hand, hooked his left finger in the safety ring and waited until the gun traversed past him again. Now! He pulled the pin and let the safety lever fly. He heard a pop and the soft hiss as the fuse ignited. He counted down the numbers, then threw the bomb in a fast fluid motion. He grabbed for a second grenade while the first one was still in the air. The first struck a few inches too low and started to roll down the shield. Then, it detonated. He hadn't gotten it in perfectly, but he knew the gunner was a very unhappy man.

He aimed a little higher and threw his second grenade. This time, the deadly metal egg vanished over the top edge of the gun shield. The bomb detonated, and Bolan heard men shrieking. The gun fell silent.

He drew his .44 Magnum Desert Eagle and raced toward the gun mount.

A man suddenly popped up from inside the armored ring with an AK-47 in his hands. Bolan continued to rush forward, snapping off two quick shots. The man vanished behind the armored ring, hit or just ducking, Bolan couldn't be sure. He had better stay alert. It looked like the gun crew had been reinforced by riflemen. He kept going as fast as he could. McCarter was firing a series of fast single shots, encouraging the opposition to keep their heads down. It seemed to work. Bolan was ten feet from the gun mount. He went down to the deck, sliding feet first like a baseball player stealing home.

He rolled on his back and pulled two grenades from his belt. A crewman jumped up from behind the armored ring with a submachine gun in his hands. Before he could shoot, McCarter cut him down with two quick bursts. Bolan had a grenade in each hand. With the thumb of one hand, he pulled the pin of the grenade in the other and repeated the move with his other hand. He let the safety levers fly and heard the hiss as the fuses ignited. He counted two seconds gone and quickly reached up and shoved both grenades over the edge of the armored ring. He heard two simultaneous detonations. The deadly grenade fragments swept the inside of the gun mount.

He jumped to his feet with his .44 Magnum held in a rock-solid, two-handed grip. The gun mount was crowded with eight or nine men. Some were down, dead or wounded, but two or three were still trying to fight. One man had a submachine gun. Bolan pivoted toward him and fired a fast double tap. The two heavy .44 Magnum rounds tore through his chest, and he went down. Bolan pivoted toward the other two. Before he could fire, he heard an AK-47 snarling behind him.

Salim was charging forward, firing as he came. He hit the two men with two more short bursts, and they collapsed to the deck. He reached the armored ring and emptied his magazine as he swept the inside of the gun mount with burst after burst. His AK-47 clicked on empty. He nodded at Bolan.

"I'm sure you did not need any help, Striker, but I thought you might need some backup."

"Thanks." When Bolan was fighting for his life, he was happy to have all the help he could get.

McCarter moved forward with his carbine ready, but there was no one to shoot.

"Good work, men, but we can't stay here. Let's figure some way to disable the cannons and get out of here!"

Bolan had already thought of that. He reached into Manning's haversack and drew out two oddly shaped grenades that looked like thick, oversize fountain pens. He opened the cannon's breech blocks, pulled the safety pins and shoved one of the special grenades inside. He closed the breech blocks and stepped back. He heard a hissing noise as the thermite ignited. Thermite burned at over six thousand degrees. In seconds, the breech blocks began to glow red, then an incandescent yellow. Molten metal dripped down onto the deck. McCarter raised one eyebrow.

"Well, Striker, I must say you really know how to disable a gun!"

Gadgets Schwarz's voice spoke into Bolan's headset.

"Striker, we've got trouble. They're coming up

from the stern, a lot of them, trying to recapture the bridge. Rafe has been hit. A sniper got him. I'm steering this rust bucket. Meiko is trying to hold the stairs. We need help. Get back as soon as you can.''

GRIMALDI HAD HEARD Schwarz's message. He was short of ammunition and rockets, and the smoke tanks were exhausted. He was trying to think what to do. Maybe he could make a pass down the deck and let Johannsen spray it with bullets. Then he heard a voice in his headset.

"Black Hawk, this is Hornet Blue leader. I am inbound toward your position. I have the ship in sight. I have four fast movers armed for an antiship strike. I'm here to support you. What do you need?"

"Clean off the aft deck, Hornet Blue Leader. Hit anything that moves aft of the bridge. Be careful. They have a twin 23 mm cannon mounted near the stern."

"Roger, Black Hawk. Attacking now."

THE RAIDING PARTY WAS nearly back to the bridge when Bolan heard an odd whining noise above him. He looked up and saw four green-and-brown jet fighters flying carefully along the deck at ten miles per hour. He watched in amazement as they flew up to the bridge and split smoothly, two flying around each side.

"What in God's name are those?" Major Salim asked. "I have never seen an airplane fly like that."

"Hawker Harriers, a British design, mate," McCarter said with pardonable pride.

They watched intently as the four Harriers flew slowly around the bridge.

MAJOR JACOBS LOOKED down the *Wuhan*'s deck as Hornet Blue flight came around the bridge. He could see small groups of men moving along the deck toward the bridge. He lined up his sights and pulled the trigger. The AV-8B Harrier's 25 mm Gatling gun roared into life. Jacobs squeezed the trigger for only a second, but in that second his GAU-12 gun spit sixty 25 mm high-explosive shells at the closest group of men. They seemed to disappear in a swarm of yellow flashes. Jacobs aimed at another group of men and fired again.

The remaining groups of men dissolved, as they broke and ran for cover. Jacobs led his Harriers slowly along the deck toward the aft structure near her stern. He was being careful. He hadn't forgotten Grimaldi's warning about a twin 23 mm cannon mounted near the stern. He put his sights on the aft superstructure and triggered a ripping two-second burst. Red tracers streaked toward the target, and Jacobs saw a myriad of bright yellow flashes as 120 HE 25 mm rounds struck and detonated. Target neutralized, as they said in the gunnery school.

He led his wingman around the right side of the superstructure. The other two Harriers went around to the left. He cleared the rear edge and saw the twin barrels of the aft 23 mm gun swinging toward him. He got his sights on and pulled the trigger. His wing was firing, too. His other two planes came around the superstructure and opened fire. The 23 mm gun and its crew were overwhelmed, caught in a deadly cross fire from four 25 mm Gatling guns.

"Black Hawk, this is Hornet Blue Leader. All targets on ship's deck have been neutralized. Unless you have other targets for us, we'll return to the *Hornet* to refuel and rearm.''

"Hornet Blue Leader, you did a great job. Have no further targets. Do me a favor before you leave. Go up a few thousand feet and look around. See if there's anything between us and Banda Aceh harbor.''

"We're on the way, Black Hawk.''

After a moment, Jacobs announced, "Black Hawk, this is Hornet Blue leader. There is an unidentified warship headed toward you, coming along the coast from the northwest. She appears to be on an interception course.''

"Roger, Hornet Blue Leader. Can you tell what country it's from?''

"Not from here. Wait one, and we'll go take a look.''

CHAPTER NINETEEN

USS La Jolla, *off the coast of Sumatra*

Captain John Adams was trying to get some sleep when he heard an urgent knocking at his cabin door. No rest for the wicked, particularly when he was the commander of a submarine in a combat situation. He opened the cabin door. One of his radiomen handed him a piece of paper.

"The XO said you should see this right away, sir."

Adams resisted the temptation to swear. Urgent messages almost always meant trouble. He looked at the piece of paper. The header said, "Intercept." That was interesting. *La Jolla*'s radio room had picked up a message that wasn't meant for her.

"It's from that ship we're trailing. It started about ten minutes ago, and they're sending it over and over again."

Adams scanned the message quickly. "Attacked by pirates." That was interesting.

"Anything else, Garcia?"

"No, sir. They just keep sending that message."

"Very well. Tell the executive officer I'll be there in two minutes."

Adams slipped on his shoes, put on his cap and

headed to the attack center. The walls of the long, rectangular compartment were covered with control consoles and display panels. The attack center was the brains of *La Jolla*. The duty watch sat in front of the consoles and studied the lights on their displays. The executive officer was standing in the middle of the room. The periscope was up, and he was staring intently at the image of the ocean's surface a hundred feet above.

"What's going on, Frank?" Adams asked.

The XO stepped aside so that Adams could look through the periscope.

"I'm not sure, Captain.

"We've been tracking her on sonar and taking a look through the periscope every half hour. She's been doing nothing unusual except for one thing. Her captain had been staying close to the coast of Sumatra, following the contours of the shore about twenty-five miles out. Now, she's changed course and is headed straight for the coast. It could be that they intend to turn for the shore and run her aground if they see that they're going to be intercepted by a warship.

"I took a look at her about five minutes ago, and then she broke radio silence and began sending that message about pirates. The strange thing is I don't see any sign of pirates. There are no other ships or boats in the area. Something does seem to be going on on board. There's a lot of smoke on deck, but it doesn't look like a fire to me. Damned if I can figure out what's happening. She's calling for assistance. I thought I'd better call you."

Adams thought for a moment. Something was going on, but what?

"Very well, Frank. Put us on an intercept course. Battle stations!"

Kilo-class Submarine Number 365 *off Sumatra*

KILO-CLASS SUBMARINE *365* was slipping easily and quietly through the water. She was moving slowly at three knots to run silently and conserve her battery power. She was a diesel-electric boat. Captain Tat Sun would have preferred to command one of the new Han-class nuclear-powered attack submarines, but he lacked the seniority for that. Perhaps if he completed his mission successfully, he would be promoted.

He glanced around the attack center. The men on duty were intently monitoring their display panels. There was no sign of trouble. All the boat's equipment was working normally. Sun was proud of his vessel and his crew. They were standing up well to the long days of boredom trailing the *Wuhan*. Orders were orders, of course, but Tat thought that protecting one small freighter was a poor mission for an attack submarine. He saw no reason to make any changes. He was ahead of the *Wuhan*. He would have to speed up as she went by to continue to cover her. Until then, he would continue to run as quietly as he could. Intelligence had warned him that there could be American nuclear submarines in the area. If he encountered one, it was critical that he detect the American sub before it detected him.

"Sir," the leading sonar man said suddenly, "the *Wuhan* has changed course. She is now steaming northwest along the coastline."

That was unusual, but perhaps there had been a change of plan. The *365*'s periscope and antennae weren't deployed. That made her harder to detect, but she couldn't receive or transmit radio messages. Still, he couldn't sit there while the freighter steamed away. His executive officer was standing by. The sub was already at periscope depth.

"Put us on an intercept course, Wei. Up periscope! Deploy the radio antennas!"

Lieutenant Commander Tang Wei snapped orders. Tat heard the whine of electric motors as the periscope and the antennae slid smoothly up from the conning tower and rose toward the surface. What else to do? He moved to the weapons-control console. The *365* had six 21-inch torpedo tubes, all mounted forward in her bow. All six were loaded with Type 56 wire-guided homing torpedoes. He moved back to the sonar console. The powerful Russian MGK-400 sonar was operating in the passive mode, listening but not sending out pulses of sound.

"Periscope up, sir," Tang Wei reported. "Conducting a 360-degree sweep. No other ships in sight. There is something going on aboard the *Wuhan,* however. There is a lot of gray smoke on her decks, but I see no flames. No apparent cause. Continuing to observe the freighter."

The captain smiled. A good executive officer was a blessing for which he thanked his ancestors.

A radioman dashed into the attack center. He saluted the captain and held out a message slip.

"Just received, sir. A general message from the *Wuhan.* It says she has been attacked by pirates. The pirates are on board and attempting to capture the ship. She asks for assistance immediately!"

Pirates? Tat had seen no ships or boats in the area. He glanced at Tang. Only he and the executive officer knew their secret orders. The freighter could not be allowed to fall into foreign hands. The captain disliked the thought of killing dozens of Chinese sailors, but orders are orders.

"Sound battle stations. Prepare for torpedo action!"

The alarm rang through the sub's hull. Sailors rushed to their battle stations. The XO looked at his display.

"Firing position in eighteen minutes, Captain."

The minutes crawled by.

Then the leading sonar man suddenly spoke. "Captain, I am detecting a second ship. It is coming down the coast from the north making at least twenty-five knots. If it maintains its present course, it will intercept the *Wuhan*."

Tat resisted the temptation to swear. Life was becoming complicated.

"Can you give me a range estimate?"

"That is difficult, sir, as long as we remain passive, but it is fairly close. It was screened by that group of small islands. Now, the sound is fairly loud. I believe it is a small warship, a frigate or a destroyer."

"Give me a plot, Wei," Tat said.

The executive officer studied his chart for a moment. "If we assume it just passed those islands and maintains twenty-five knots, it will intercept the *Wuhan* in six minutes. Four or five minutes before we reach firing position."

Tat considered increasing speed, but he needed to conserve battery power.

"Has he detected us?"

"Probably not, sir. At his speed, hull and propeller

noise will screen us," the sonar man said.

"Maintain present course and speed."

ON BOARD *La Jolla,* Captain Adams was also talking to his sonar man about the new contact.

"What do you make of her, Chief?"

"Destroyer or a frigate, Captain. I'm running her sonar signature through the computer now. Captain, I think I'm picking up another contact toward the *Wuhan.* I can't be sure, but it may be a submarine."

Adams knew it wasn't an American submarine. He would have been notified if another American sub was operating in his area.

"Captain, computer analysis says new track is an Indonesian Ahmad Yani class frigate. I've got better data on the second contact. It's very quiet, but I think it is a submarine, probably a diesel-electric boat."

This was getting complicated. A Chinese cargo ship, an Indonesian frigate and a mystery submarine. He didn't know how the frigate would react if it detected him. He thought his mission was to support the Indonesian government, but Adams doubted the Indonesian frigate's captain knew he was here. If he detected *La Jolla,* she would be an unidentified submarine in Indonesian waters and he might attack her. This situation involved diplomatic decisions that had to be made at higher levels.

He turned to the XO. "Take over, Frank. I'm going to the radio room and have a talk with SUBPAC."

Adams wasn't a buck passer, but he needed to know what the commanding officer of Pacific submarines wanted him to do in this confusing situation.

CAPTAIN TAT STARED at the plot board. His submarine was almost in firing position, but the frigate was within a thousand yards of her now. He didn't want to use the periscope, but he had to find out the frigate's nationality. Tang was ready with the recognition book. Probably the frigate's crew was concentrating on the *Wuhan* and wouldn't see his periscope. Tat would risk a short look.

"Up periscope!"

The periscope was already pointing at the sonar bearing of the two ships. He should see them the instant the periscope reached the surface. He waited tensely. Now! He could see the frigate clearly. Not a large ship, really no bigger than the *365*. He recognized the red-and-white Indonesian flag and saw the number 351 painted in white on her bow. That wasn't unexpected, but she was very close to the *Wuhan,* matching the bigger ship's course and speed. He could see a large group of men clustered near the frigate's bow. He switched his periscope to high magnification. The men were heavily armed. A boarding party!

"The frigate is coming alongside. She has soldiers on deck. They will board the *Wuhan.* We cannot stop them."

Tat looked at Tang. The freighter couldn't be allowed to fall into foreign hands. Everyone on board her was going to die. He was going to kill dozens of their countrymen, but it had to be done. Tat wouldn't shrink from doing his duty.

He spoke to the torpedo room through the intercom. "Open outer doors on One, Two, Three, and Four. Stand by."

Tang checked the plotting board. "In firing position now, Captain."

Tat took a deep breath. "Fire One! Fire Two! Stand by, Three and Four."

Compressed air rushed into the torpedo tubes, and two long dull green shapes slid into the water. Their propellers began to turn, and they headed toward their target, trailing their guidance wires.

The Wuhan, *off the coast of Sumatra*

MAJOR SALIM WAS jubilant as he watched the Indonesian frigate come alongside, perfectly matching the *Wuhan*'s course and speed.

"I know her," he shouted. "She is the Ahmad Yani from Banda Aceh. And look there, near the bow, see those men? Marine commandos!"

Mack Bolan was almost as happy as Salim to see the purple berets of his elite unit. They had been fighting against long odds for what seemed like forever. A company of Royal Marine Commandos should settle things quite neatly.

The marines threw up grapnels, which caught on the *Wuhan*'s rail, and began to climb up the rope ladders to the bigger ship's deck. A marine captain was the first man over the rail. He smiled broadly and saluted smartly.

"I see that you have everything under complete control, Major, but is there any way we can assist you?"

Salim smiled. "We hold the bridge and the deck. Some of the crew is still alive belowdecks. Secure the ship. They are armed. If they resist, kill them!"

The captain saluted and began snapping orders. The marines moved out, weapons ready. The last of the marines were coming over the rail.

Bolan turned to Salim, but before he could speak, he heard a tremendous roar. A huge column of water shot up from the far side of the frigate and cascaded down on both ships' decks. The *Wuhan*'s hull shuddered. Bolan heard another tremendous roar as the second torpedo struck the frigate, and its heavy warhead detonated.

The Ahmad Yani–class frigate was full of weapons and ammunition. The blasts from the torpedo's warheads triggered a series of secondary explosions that ripped through the frigate's hull like a string of giant firecrackers. A huge pillar of smoke and orange fire began to stream up from the frigate's shattered hull. It dropped away from the *Wuhan*'s side and began to sink.

Salim stared over the rail. Where in the name of God had those torpedoes come from? Then he saw a thin straight line of bubbles moving remorselessly toward the freighter's side.

"Torpedo!" he shouted.

Bolan spoke rapidly into his tactical radio.

"Gadgets, turn hard left, now!"

Schwarz wasn't sure what was happening, but he heard the urgency in Bolan's voice. He didn't waste time asking questions. He put the wheel hard over, and the bow of the freighter slowly began to swing to the left. Too late. The torpedo struck a hundred feet back from the bow.

Bolan heard a muffled roar as the warhead detonated. The freighter shuddered and shook. A huge fountain of water cascaded upward and deluged her deck. McCarter and Bolan raced toward the bridge. They pounded up the stairs, taking them two at a time. Schwarz was still steering. Encizo lay on the floor, his head propped upon a folded blanket. Meiko Tanaka had the ship's first-aid kit open and was changing the bandage on his left shoulder.

The little Cuban's face was pale, but he was conscious.

"What's going on, Striker?" he asked.

"It's a submarine. It sunk the frigate. The *Wuhan* has been hit with a torpedo up forward. We must be taking on a lot of water. Any suggestions?"

"He may not have intended to hit us, but we can't be sure. Put her back on course for Sumatra. There's no way we can stop the flooding. Let's run her ashore as fast as we can. Meiko, see those levers next to the wheel? They're used to signal the engine. Push the left-hand lever forward to full power. Good, now watch the display. Any change in engine output? No? Then call the engine room on the phone. Tell them if they want to live, give us full power now."

Tanaka picked up the phone. He heard a short intense conversation in Chinese. There was a pause, then she added a few words in an ominous tone of voice.

"Did you convince them, Meiko?" Encizo asked.

"I believe so. I told them the ship is slowly sinking. If they give us full power, we will run it ashore and they will live. If they do not, we will take the lifeboats and leave them here to drown. I think I was most convincing."

She looked at the instrument panel. "Yes, the power is building up. Speed is fourteen knots and increasing."

Encizo nodded. That was good. If the submarine didn't fire again, they ought to make the beach.

CAPTAIN TAT STARED through his periscope. He had hit the *Wuhan* near the bow. He could see that she was starting to list to port. Unless the crew applied proper damage-control procedures, she would eventually sink. Before that happened, she might reach the shore. He couldn't take that chance. He turned to his executive officer.

"Put us in firing position. We must sink her."

CAPTAIN ADAMS REENTERED *La Jolla*'s attack center. There was an air of tension. Something had happened. He spoke to the XO.

"What's going on, Frank?'

"That second contact was a submarine, Captain. She just blew the Indonesian frigate to hell and put a torpedo into the *Wuhan*."

"What's the *Wuhan*'s condition?"

"She's taking on water, but she's still moving under her own power toward the coast of Sumatra. What does SUBPAC want us to do?"

"They said we are to assist the Indonesians to capture the *Wuhan* and bring her into port. We have to prevent that other sub from hitting her again. Do you have a good track on that submarine, Chief?"

"Yes, sir. She's a diesel-electric boat, an improved Kilo class."

Adams knew what he had to do.

"Give me a firing solution, Frank. Ready Three and Four."

THE *365* WAS approaching her new firing position.

"Captain," the sonar man suddenly shouted, "torpedo running, intercept course, bearing 156, high-speed approach!"

Tat stared at his displays in horror. What was happening? There was no sign of a contact. Where in hell had the torpedo come from?

"Captain, second torpedo running! Bearing 156. High-speed approach!"

No time for thought. Tat snapped orders.

"Helmsman, turn into them, course 156! Torpedo room! Ready Five and Six for immediate firing!"

Kilo-class *365*'s blunt bow began to swing toward the oncoming torpedoes. In the torpedo room, her crew tried desperately to prepare tubes Five and Six for firing. Too late. The first torpedo struck the boat on the bow. The Mark 48's shaped-charge warhead was designed to pierce the thick, tough hulls of modern Russian submarines. The warhead detonated, and a white-hot lance of superheated gas and molten metal penetrated the hull, which rang as if she had been struck by a giant sledge hammer. Instantly, the torpedo room began to flood. Huge gouts of bubbles poured out from the hole in the hull. Water poured in, driven by the immense pressure at two hundred feet.

Desperately, the captain ordered full power. The chief engineer blasted high-pressure air into the rapidly flooding torpedo room. The men there had died almost instantly, but they were all going to die if the boat continued to flood and control was lost.

The second Mark 48 was confused by the sonar return from the vast cloud of bubbles pouring from the damaged hull. It passed over her huge gray hull, and shot on past the stricken submarine. As it emerged from the bubble cloud, its sonar had no target. Smoothly, the torpedo's computer attack logic steered the warhead into a 180-degree turn and began the target-reacquisition search pattern again. The enemy sub was very noisy, indeed, as her crew fought for survival. The Mark 48 reverted to the homing mode and sped back toward the sub.

It struck just below the conning tower. The warhead detonated. The white-hot lance of flaming gas and molten metal pierced the hull and shot into the attack center, killing some of the crew and knocking out vital equipment. Water began to pour into the attack center. Her forward compartments were flooded with hundreds of tons of water. Her crew lost control, and the huge gray hull began to go down rapidly by the bow, trailing a huge plume of bubbles. Tat took one last despairing look at his depth and pitch gauges. There was nothing he could do. Kilo-class *365* was going deeper and deeper, the angle of her dive increasing steadily, as she began her last dive to the ocean floor nine hundred feet below.

MCCARTER STARED out the gaping holes where the bridge's glass windows used to be. Through his binoculars, he could see waves breaking on a long white beach. That was good, but he could tell that the *Wuhan*'s bow was down and she was listing more and more to port as the water poured in through the hole near her bow.

"How are we doing, Rafe?" he asked quietly.

"We ought to make it in another ten minutes. Somebody go tell Salim he'd better get his marines back up on deck just in case we have to abandon ship."

The minutes crawled by.

"A red light has started blinking. It is marked depth indicator," Tanaka announced.

Encizo smiled. Good, they were approaching shallow water. Somehow he seemed to have become the captain of the *Wuhan*. He didn't want to lose his ship.

"Call the engine room. Tell them to give us half power."

After a minute or two, Encizo could feel the freighter slowing. One more minute, two, then the *Wuhan* shuddered as her keel grated on the underwater sand. She slid slowly forward and then stopped. She was safely aground.

CHAPTER TWENTY

Military Headquarters, Banda Aceh, Sumatra

The team was meeting with General Sudarso in his office. Encizo was in the hospital, but the doctors said he was doing well. The general seemed to be in a good mood. He motioned for them to be seated and offered them some steaming coffee.

"Congratulations! You did outstanding work yesterday. A major rebel base destroyed, and the *Wuhan* and all the weapons she was carrying captured. If your governments allow you to accept foreign medals, I will be happy to recommend you."

"Thank you, General. Major Salim and his Royal Marine Commandos did excellent work also. I doubt we would have succeeded without them. Where is the good Major, if I may ask?" McCarter responded.

Sudarso smiled. "He is becoming an international hero. He and his marines are guarding the *Wuhan*. He is conducting tours. There are more than a hundred members of the media there. He is showing them the Chinese weapons, convincing them that we are telling the truth when we say there is foreign intervention. He is smiling modestly when they call him a hero. He has already been filmed by CNN. In a few hours, his face will be on half the television screens in the world. Of course, the Chinese ambassador is not happy. He keeps talking about illegal seizure of a Chinese ship, but he is having trouble explaining the weapons. Major Salim will be back in an hour or so. An important delegation is coming here from Jakarta. They have asked to see him. He will probably receive a medal."

One of the general's aides entered the office.

"Sir, the American woman, Miss Johannsen, is outside. There is another American with her. She says he has important information you should hear."

"I wonder what Miss Johannsen has learned this time? Show her in."

Johannsen entered the room followed by Fred Byrnes, who was carrying two black nylon equipment cases. He looked like a multimedia reporter on the trail of a story.

"General Sudarso, this is Frank Barnes. He is an American reporter who has been working in Banda Aceh. He has picked up some valuable information I think you should here immediately."

"I am pleased to meet you, Mr. Barnes, or whatever your name really is, but I have some reservations about this story. You arrived in Banda Aceh aboard a U.S. military helicopter. Our intelligence people have been watching you. You stay in a fashionable hotel and frequent all sorts of bars and restaurants. You seem to have unlimited amounts of money. You talk to many people who are sympathetic to the rebellion. I do not think you are a reporter. Is it possible that you and Miss Johannsen work for the same organization?"

Byrnes grinned. "You see, Ingrid, I was right. He

isn't going to buy it. Well, when all else fails, tell the truth. You're right, General. I am a CIA agent. I am setting up a network of agents in Aceh Province. One of my primary objectives is to get information from inside the rebel movement. In the last few hours, I have been getting information that I think you have to know. I talked to headquarters via satcom, and they agree."

"Can you prove that what you say is true?" Sudarso asked skeptically.

"Well, it doesn't say CIA agent on my passport, but Ingrid can vouch for me and I've worked with Striker and Green before. They can tell you I'm CIA."

"Very well. What is this important information?"

"A number of my agents are saying that they should avoid being in all government buildings for the next forty-eight hours. They are telling me I should, too. They don't want me to be killed. I'm the man who pays them. They don't want to lose their meal ticket."

"Interesting, Mr. Barnes. So it will be dangerous to be inside any government building for the next forty-eight hours. Do you have any idea what the danger is?"

"No, I don't think any of the people I talked to know, but the way the warning is phrased gives us a clue. Just being inside a government building is dangerous. That sounds to me like a weapon of mass destruction, bombs or a chemical-warfare attack. I'll make a few phone calls and see what else I can find out, but it won't be easy."

Sudarso nodded. "Obviously, military headquarters is a target. Mr. Sower," he said to Gadgets Schwarz, "would you use your special equipment and make a security sweep of the building?"

Schwarz nodded and picked up his equipment.

"Thank you. Meanwhile, I will order a security alert at all government buildings in Banda Aceh. Then, let us think what else we might do."

SIX MILES AWAY in an old dilapidated warehouse, another meeting was going on. Colonel Chun was meeting with Hamed and Dr. Chang. Chun was seething. It wasn't his fault, but they had suffered a serious defeat. Red Area had been lost, but ten times worse, the Indonesians had seized the *Wuhan* and all the weapons she had on board. There were other ships, but none of them could reach Sumatra in less than a week. Without the weapons, the independence movement might falter.

Hamed was a good leader, but Chun felt he lacked imagination. All he suggested was to continue small-scale attacks in the countryside. That gave the government forces the initiative. He waited politely until the man had finished.

"That is simply not enough. We must strike the government forces heavy blows. How can we attack them here in the capital city? Do you have any ideas?"

Dr. Chang spoke smoothly. "Yes, Colonel. I agree. We must to carry the war into Banda Aceh. I am constructing several large bombs and putting them into trucks. We can use them against enemy headquarters, barracks, police stations and airfields. We can cripple their military efforts and demoralize their troops. I recommend we began immediately."

"How many weapons are ready, Doctor?" Chun asked.

"Two are ready now, and two more will be ready in ten hours. Let us use them now. I recommend we destroy the military headquarters and the governor's house. That will destroy their control of Aceh Province. Give the order, General, and we will attack."

One thing worried Chun. "You must have bought large quantities of explosives, Dr. Chang. Will this not arouse the suspicions of the police? If this happens, can the explosives be traced to you?"

Chang smiled. "I have not bought a single pound of anything that is legally a high explosive."

"Then how can you make bombs?"

"I am using ammonia-based fertilizer sensitized with diesel oil. I have added liquid propane to enhance the blast. Pound for pound it is more explosive than TNT. This is a farming area. Large amounts of all three are sold everyday. No one will be suspicious."

"Very well, then. Let us proceed."

Chun saw that Hamed was frowning.

"You do not approve of this plan, Hamed?" Chun asked.

"I would willingly destroy the military headquarters, Colonel, but the governor's house is a civilian administrative center. If we bomb it during the day, hundreds of innocent civilians will be killed. It might well turn public opinion against us. Should we do such a thing?"

Chun didn't hesitate. "Yes," he said firmly. "This is a revolution. You are fighting for your freedom. You will not achieve it unless you are willing to shed blood. Initiate the attacks immediately, Doctor."

"Very well, Colonel. You are in command. One other thing. I have been contacted by our agent inside military headquarters. He says a group of visitors from Java are coming to see General Sudarso. They will arrive shortly. He does not know their names, but they are obviously very important men."

"Good. Find out more if you can. Perhaps they will be there when we attack."

Hamed got up to leave.

"One other thing, Hamed. Assemble a strike team with at least twelve good men. If we do not kill these men one way, we will do it another."

GENERAL SUDARSO RETURNED to his office and sat down with a sigh.

"I have done everything I can to increase security, but there are dozens of government buildings in Banda Aceh. It is very difficult to guard them all when we do not know how the attack will be made."

McCarter agreed. He had faced the same problems when he served with the SAS in Northern Ireland. The enemy had the advantage of surprise.

"Is there any way we can get better intelligence, General?" McCarter asked.

"Perhaps. I have sent Mara Tharin to intelligence headquarters. They may know something."

Sudarso paused and looked around the room.

"Does anyone else have anything to say?"

Gadget Schwarz looked up from the flat black box he was studying.

"Yes, General. I'm afraid you've got a problem."

CHAPTER TWENTY-ONE

Military Headquarters, Banda Aceh, Sumatra

General Sudarso stared at Gadgets Schwarz for few seconds.

"I do not know that I need any more problems, Mr. Sower, but tell me anyway."

Schwarz smiled. He had never been particularly impressed by people in authority, but he liked Sudarso's straightforward attitude.

"Well, I just conducted a security sweep of the critical areas of the your headquarters as you requested. I found four clandestine listening devices. I neutralized them and turned them over to your people."

"Excellent work, but why is that a problem?"

"During the sweep, I detected a radio-frequency message that I'm certain was beamed at your headquarters."

"Could you read this message, or was it in code?" Sudarso asked quickly.

Schwarz frowned. "There wasn't anything to read, General. I'm using the word *message* in the broadest technical sense, the transmission of information by any means. The message I picked up was digital. It consisted of a string of ones and zeros. Now, you can easily convert a message in any language to a digital format, but this is almost certainly a computer-to-computer message. I've seen this type of message before, and there's no doubt in my mind. It's an external source communicating with an arming, fusing and firing system.''

"An arming, fusing and firing system?''

"Yes, sir. That's the part of a large bomb that triggers the explosion. I've seen this message pattern before, when I was in Lebanon a few years ago. It was designed and manufactured in China and widely distributed to terrorist groups around the world.''

"Let me be sure I understand this. You are telling me there is a bomb in the my headquarters?''

Schwarz shook his head. "Probably not in your headquarters, but close by. It's likely a very large bomb, and based on the message format, I conclude that the bomb's live and that it has been armed.''

"Exactly what do you mean when you say 'armed'?'' Sudarso asked quietly. "Do you mean that it's ready to explode?'' Sudarso's coolness had to be admired, Bolan thought. He might be staring death in the face, but if it frightened him, you couldn't tell it.

Schwarz shook his head. "No, sir. You have to be very careful with large bombs. You don't want them to explode until you have delivered them to their targets. Bomb designers who know what they are doing use what ordnance experts call an arming, fusing and firing system. When the bomb isn't armed, it is basically inert and safe to handle and transport. In theory, the bomb can't detonate when it's not armed unless it is in a fire or something explodes in contact with it. Fusing is the next step. When certain preset conditions are met, all safety features are disabled, and the bomb is ready to be fired. The firing command is the last step. It's generated by the fuse when a command initiates fuse action, and then the bomb detonates.

"That can be done in several different ways—contact, time, pressure or command. That's decided by the bomb's fuse designer. This bomb is definitely armed. It may be fused. Based on the message I intercepted, this bomb will be detonated by a remote command. Somebody will decide it's time for it to go off and will push the button. There may also be a backup timer counting down to a preset detonation time. I would have to look inside the bomb itself to determine that."

"Can you give me any idea how big the bomb is or where it's located?"

Schwarz nodded. "It's almost certainly a large car bomb containing several thousand pounds of high explosives. There is a large truck parked in front of your headquarters delivering supplies to the kitchen. I think I have detected a response to the message coming from it."

The Indonesian security officer sitting next to Sudarso spoke suddenly. "We'd better evacuate headquarters immediately, sir. I've seen what these things can do. Let's not wait. Let's get our people out now!"

"That wouldn't be a good idea," Bolan said quietly. "I'm sure all entrances and exits to the your headquarters are under continuous surveillance. If they see large numbers of people starting to leave, they'll just push the button."

"Well, what in God's name can we do? We can't

just sit here and wait for them to blow us up,'' Sudarso said angrily.

''I think I have located their observation point. The message originated from the third floor of that commercial building across the street. The transmitter will be there. If we can take that out, maybe we can move the truck,'' Schwarz said.

Sudarso liked the sound of that. He wanted to hit back, not just wait passively.

''All right, how do we do it? If they see a group of soldiers or marines heading their way, they're likely to get suspicious.''

McCarter had been sitting quietly, listening to the discussion.

''I believe a few of my associates and I can take care of it, General,'' he said. ''We won't look very military if we conceal our weapons. Mr. Barnes looks like a journalist. Meiko is just a charming young lady. We'll go out the front door as if we hadn't a care in the world, walk across the street and pay those chaps a visit.''

Sudarso and his officers stared at McCarter. They didn't like the idea of letting a foreigner they didn't know handle such an important mission. But they saw McCarter's gold lapel pin with its winged-dagger badge and the famous motto Who Dares Wins! Every special-operations officer in the world would have recognized that pin as the symbol of his famous regiment, the SAS. They were no exception.

Sudarso didn't waste time debating. ''All right, Mr. Green, take whoever you select and do it!''

McCarter thought quickly. He would like to take everyone, but that wasn't practical. Gary Manning was the best man to defuse the bomb. He needed backup in case he met resistance. Very well, Mack Bolan was a one-man battalion. He could cover Manning. Every one else would go with him. He announced his decision.

Everyone nodded and began to check their equipment. Fred Byrnes smiled.

"That's an awfully small raid team, McCarter. You need more people, I'm getting damned tired of sitting around while you guys have all the fun. Count me in."

McCarter thought for a second. It would blow Byrnes's cover, but Sudarso knew that the man wasn't really a journalist. McCarter had seen him in a fight. The CIA agent was deadly when things got up close and personal. One extra good man might make the difference.

"All right. Glad to have you with us. Do you have a rifle or a submachine gun?"

Byrnes smiled wickedly and unzipped the carryall that contained his camera equipment.

"I don't need one. Look at this baby!" He pulled out a deadly-looking dull black shotgun.

"This is one of the new Marine Corps M-1014 Combat Shotguns. It's one of the first few hundred off the production line. It's semiautomatic, 12-gauge and holds ten rounds. Loaded with buckshot, it's the best damned combat shotgun ever made!"

McCarter was impressed. "It certainly looks like it will do the job, but where did you get a gun like that?"

"You guys aren't the only ones who can get fancy guns. When the President says your mission is vital to the national security, you'd be surprised what you can get. Maybe I'll ask for an armored Rolls-Royce next week.''

''Come on. Let's go try your new toy out.''

McCarter led the raiding party quietly up the stairwell toward the building's third floor. The building had elevators, but their status panels would tell anyone who looked when the elevators were moving. Elevators made noise when they stopped on a floor, and they were a death trap if someone was standing outside with an automatic weapon when the doors started to open. Walking took longer, but they were far more likely to reach their objective alive.

They reached the top of the stairs. Slowly, gently, McCarter opened the door a crack and peered down the hall. A man was sitting in a chair sixty feet away, looking at the elevator doors. He might have been the janitor except for the AK-47 assault rifle he held across his knees. McCarter considered using his silenced .22 Walther pistol but rejected it. He couldn't be sure of a kill shot at that range. If the people on the third floor had the device that triggered the bomb, it was absolutely necessary that the guard be taken out instantly and silently. Whatever weapon they used had to kill him immediately.

McCarter motioned to Meiko Tanaka, who carried a silenced 9 mm Heckler & Koch MP-5 SD-6 submachine gun. It was as accurate as a rifle out to a hundred yards, and Tanaka was an excellent shot. McCarter opened the door a few inches more and pointed down the hall. Tanaka nodded, pushed the MP-5's selector switch to semiautomatic and took careful aim. The guard stood no chance whatsoever. He would never know what hit him, but McCarter felt no compassion. He had been fighting terrorists half his life, and he hated them with a burning passion. If a man wanted to blow up buildings full of innocent people, McCarter felt he deserved what he got.

Tanaka squeezed the MP-5's trigger twice in a fast double tap. McCarter heard a faint hissing sound as two 147-grain subsonic 9 mm bullets struck the guard in the side of the head. The guard slumped and slid to the floor as if he had fallen asleep. The only sound was made by his rifle as it dropped to the floor.

McCarter waited for a few seconds, but there was no reaction. He pushed the door open quietly and motioned to his teammates to move forward down the corridor. He could see office doors on either side of the hall. He signaled Schwarz to check the offices on the street side. The electronics wizard held his black box in both hands, placed a small, flat microphone against the walls and listened intently. Byrnes moved a few feet behind him, his 12-gauge shotgun ready for action. If anyone suddenly stepped out of an office and saw Schwarz, that would be the last thing he would ever see.

Schwarz checked three offices, then a fourth. He nodded and pointed. McCarter moved silently forward and listened. He could hear men talking in Chinese inside. He looked at Schwarz and raised one eyebrow inquiringly.

The Able Team commando listened intently and then held up four fingers. McCarter nodded. Schwarz could hear four people talking behind the door. That didn't mean that there couldn't be more. Someone might be asleep or simply sitting quietly, not talking. McCarter thought hard. He couldn't be absolutely sure the office contained the transmitter that would send the command to detonate the bomb, but it seemed likely. His attack plan had to consider that there were at least four armed men who had to be taken out before any one of them could push the button.

He considered his options. Flash-stun grenades? No, a man could be dazed and dazzled and still push a button. CS tear gas? No, it might take twenty or thirty seconds to become effective. There was really no alternative but to go in and shoot to kill. Very well, who would be the first man through the door? McCarter had been trained in the SAS tradition that an officer always leads, no matter how great the danger. It was tempting to go in first himself, but what counted wasn't how he felt but what accomplished his mission.

He looked at the three members of his team, Byrnes, Tanaka and Schwarz. The answer was obvious. In his career as a CIA field agent, Byrnes had been in dozens of room raids, and experience counted. There was one other factor. At point-blank range, his 12-gauge M-1014 shotgun was the deadliest weapon they had. McCarter pointed to Byrnes and then pumped his fist at the door. Byrnes nodded. He understood. They were going in, and he would make the initial entry.

McCarter moved to the left of the door, one pace behind Byrnes and one pace to his left. Tanaka took up a similar position to the CIA agent's right. As soon as Byrnes stepped through the door, they would be clear to fire into the far corners of the room. Schwarz moved quietly forward, staying flat against the wall. He reached carefully over and with one hand tried the doorknob. McCarter could see it turn. The door was unlocked.

He looked at Byrnes, who nodded. He was ready. McCarter brought up his left hand and then snapped it down. Go! Schwarz twisted the knob and threw open the door. Byrnes found himself looking into the face of a man less than ten feet away. He had been walking toward the door when it suddenly opened. He had an AK-47 assault rifle in his hands, the muzzle pointed across his chest. For a fraction of a second, he and Byrnes stared at each other, both surprised by the sudden, unexpected confrontation. The man tried desperately to bring his AK-47 to bear, but Byrnes's shotgun was already pointed straight at his chest. The CIA agent pulled the trigger.

The big black shotgun roared and bucked. Byrnes had loaded it with Winchester 12-gauge Magnum buckshot shells. Twelve .33-inch hardened round lead shot smashed into the man's chest. He died where he stood and fell heavily to the floor. The shotgun's report was terrible in the confined office space. The room exploded into a blur of action as the sound of its muzzle-blast echoed from the walls.

Byrnes took one long step through the door, and his cold eyes swept the room. A man was sitting, staring out the window through a large tripod camera. Behind him, a second man was sitting at a table with a telephone and two or three electronic devices. Another man was rolling off a couch to Byrnes's left, drawing a pistol as he moved. The two men near the window were the threat. One of the black boxes on the table could be the detonating device.

Byrnes pivoted from the waist, keeping his eyes, hands and shotgun muzzle in perfect alignment. The man sitting at the table lunged for something on the tabletop. The man at the telescope whirled, his hand flashing toward an automatic pistol in a holster on his belt. Byrnes pulled the shotgun's trigger three times, as fast as he could, and sent blasts of buckshot at the two men. The man at the table went down. The other man was hit. He staggered backward, but he was still on his feet, and now his pistol was in his hand.

Byrnes fought the recoil of his big shotgun and tried to bring the muzzle to bear. Too late. He and the man fired simultaneously. Byrnes felt a sharp blow on his chest like a fast jab from a good boxer as a high-velocity 9 mm bullet smashed into his body armor. Byrnes had fired a little high, but it didn't matter. Buckshot struck the man in the face, and he died instantly.

Byrnes caught a blur of motion to his right. Another man was swinging a 12-gauge pump shotgun toward him. The CIA agent knew he wouldn't be able to pivot and fire his weapon in time, but his step into the room had partially cleared McCarter's line of fire. Byrnes heard the crackling snarl of McCarter's M-4 Ranger carbine as the Englishman fired a long fast burst. Half a dozen full-metal-jacketed bullets struck the shotgunner in the head and chest. The Mossberg suddenly became too heavy for him to hold. It dropped from his nerveless hands as he slumped to the floor.

Byrnes heard Tanaka shrieking a warning. He started to pivot back to the left. Something struck him a hard, smashing blow on his side as he swung. Byrnes staggered as he completed his turn, but he was off balance and out of his firing stance. The man who had shot him was aiming again. He knew he had hit

Byrnes, but he had failed to kill him. He knew that his enemy had to be wearing body armor. The gunner took half a second to use his sights, and he was aiming at Byrnes's head.

Byrnes had no time to recover his combat stance and aim precisely. He simply shoved the barrel of his shotgun at the man who was less than fifteen feet away and fired. His 12-gauge shotgun roared and bucked as Byrnes pulled the trigger again and again, firing as fast as he could. The room seemed to shake and vibrate as the muzzle-blasts of the individual shots blended into one sustained roar and each blast sent deadly buckshot smashing into his opponent.

It wasn't pretty shooting, but it was effective. Byrnes saw the man stagger as buckshot tore into his left arm and shoulder. The shock of the impact twisted him to the left. He pulled the trigger of his big pistol, but the bullet went wide. Byrnes fired again and kept firing until his shotgun clicked on empty. The man with the pistol lay sprawled on the floor, bleeding from several wounds. He was seriously wounded, but he still held his 9 mm pistol in his right hand. He was still trying to aim at Byrnes.

Byrnes's shotgun was slow and awkward to reload. He dropped it and drew his .357 Magnum Colt Python as fast as he could, firing two fast double-action shots as soon as the big revolver cleared the holster. He saw the man's body jerk as two .357 Magnum hollowpoint rounds struck home. The big black pistol slipped from the enemy gunner's right hand, and he lay still. Byrnes swept the room with the muzzle of the big revolver. Nothing moved. The fight was over. He bent over and picked up his shotgun. He felt a sudden shudder of reaction. It had been close, too damned close!

McCarter and Tanaka were in the room now. The woman began to search the bodies. McCarter motioned to Schwarz to come forward and examine the electronic hardware on the small table.

He picked up one black box the size of a cellular telephone.

"This is it!" he said excitedly. "This is the remote detonator."

"Excellent. Secure and search the area. Gadgets, check that electronic equipment, and see if you can see what it does. Meiko, as soon as you're through checking our friends, watch the door."

He walked over to the window to get a good line of sight to the headquarters and pressed the transmit button on his tactical radio.

"Striker, this is David. The target is secure. You're free to move out."

"Roger. On the way. Striker out."

McCarter considered his options. Bolan and Manning were going to investigate the truck. He could either stay there or go back to the headquarters. They were vulnerable in their present location. They could be attacked by a superior force at any time. He would pull back to the headquarters as soon as they finished searching the bodies. They would be relatively safe there as long as the bomb didn't go off.

McCarter heard the sound of a sudden blow and a man groaning hoarsely.

"Try that again, and I'll kill you," Tanaka grated.

McCarter whirled, ready to fire, but Tanaka had the situation under control. The man who had sat at the table and reached for the detonator was alive. He was lying on the floor, grimacing in pain as Tanaka stood on his right wrist and ground down with all her 140 pounds pressing on a nerve center. The man was bleeding heavily from a wound in his left thigh. A big, black Browning pistol lay a few inches away from his right hand, but he had stopped trying to reach it. He was staring at the gaping black muzzle of the woman's 9 mm CZ-75 pistol. All the fight had gone out of him.

"Please, I am wounded. Who is in command here? I will die if I do not get to a doctor," the man gasped in perfect English. Tanaka kicked away the Browning.

"Please, I will bleed to death. Someone help me. For God's sake, help me," the man gasped.

McCarter stared down at him. The look in his green eyes was as cold as death.

"I'm in command here. It doesn't matter to me whether you live or die. Can you give me one reason why I should help you?"

"I am Dr. Chang. I am a college professor. I am merely a technical expert. I have nothing to do with these Sumatran madmen. Call the university. They will confirm everything I say."

McCarter smiled down at Chang. There was not a trace of humor in his smile. He hated terrorists. As far as he was concerned, Chang was a terrorist of the worst sort, the kind who was willing to kill masses of innocent people for his cause.

"Don't talk like a bloody fool, Chang. You helped plant a truck bomb in front of the army's headquarters."

Chang's face contorted in agony as a spasm of pain shot through his bleeding thigh.

"I have information, valuable information, about the bombings these Indonesians are planning, where the bombs are made and the targets. If I die, you will never learn this. Help me, and I will tell you everything. Everything!"

McCarter thought it over. As much as he hated terrorists, Chang's information could save thousands of innocent lives. "Very well, Doctor. I'll see that you get medical attention and get safely out of Indonesia. In return, you will tell me everything you know. If you lie to me, you can stop worrying about bleeding to death. I'll kill you personally."

McCarter turned to Tanaka. "Put a tourniquet on his leg, and keep him alive until I get back. I believe Fred Byrnes needs to talk to Dr. Chang. The CIA is used to dealing with scum like him."

MACK BOLAN and Gary Manning walked out the front door of the military headquarters building and moved casually toward the back of the parked truck. They had the truck's keys. The truck driver and his partner had been terrified when the grim-faced Indonesian paratroopers had arrested them. They swore they knew nothing about bombs. That might or might not be true, but it didn't matter. The Stony Man team had one overwhelming problem. They had to deal with a gigantic bomb in the middle of a large city.

Manning unlocked the doors, and they stepped into the back of the truck. A few boxes of canned goods were scattered here and there, but the back of the truck was almost empty. Manning pointed to the sides of the cargo compartment. Metal doors were arranged in one long solid row on either side. Manning reached out and touched a door on either side.

"Refrigerator doors, but they don't feel cold," he said very softly.

Bolan understood. There was something about knowing that you were standing *inside* an extremely large bomb that made even the bravest man quiet and cautious. Manning checked one of the doors carefully.

"No booby traps that I can detect. Here we go!"

He swung the heavy door open smoothly. Bolan looked inside. The dimly lit refrigerator compartment was filled with large plastic drums. The air inside had a strong oily smell. Manning shone his flashlight on the dull green drums. The bright beam from the mini-flashlight showed a large square label that said the drums contained ammonium nitrate fertilizer. Manning swung his flashlight beam along the compartment. Between and around the drums were silver pressurized gas cylinders. Their labels said Propane in Arabic and English.

Manning opened a second door and then a third. Each compartment was the same, row on row of the big drums and silvery cylinders. Bolan waited patiently for Manning to finish his inspection. If he had to stand inside an armed bomb, there was no one he would rather be with than Manning. The big Canadian radiated cool competence. He was an expert who was qualified in all common military and industrial explosives, particularly those used by terrorists. The commanding officer of Germany's elite GSG-9 counter-terrorist force had once described Manning as absolutely brilliant at defusing bombs.

They reached the front of the compartment. Manning shone his flashlight on a small black plastic box attached to the wall. A wire led up to the roof.

Manning nodded. "There's the fuse," he said as

he drew a small flat tool kit from his belt. Carefully, delicately, he checked the box.

"No antitamper device," he said quietly as he opened the lid of the black box. He disconnected two wires and smiled.

"Pretty simple design, Striker. Defusing it is as easy as taking candy from a baby."

Bolan discovered that he had been holding his breath, which he released as he looked around. It was a big truck, and there were an awful lot of those damned drums and cylinders.

"Just how bad does it look, Gary?"

Manning thought for a few seconds. "It's an ammonium fertilizer bomb, of course. That's very hard to detonate in the pure condition. The diesel oil sensitizes the fertilizer and makes it easy to detonate. The propane creates a fuel-air explosive effect that makes the blast much stronger. It's hard to predict the exact explosive power, but I'd say it should be somewhere between twelve thousand to twenty thousand pounds of TNT. There won't be much left of the headquarters building if this baby goes off, Striker."

He shone his flashlight slowly and carefully around the truck's cargo compartment.

"I'd better check to be sure there's not a backup fuse, Striker. I'd really be embarrassed if there was and somebody pushed the button."

"I'm with you, Gary," Bolan agreed.

Someone tapped lightly on the back doors. Bolan drew his .44 Magnum pistol and pivoted smoothly.

"Are you there, Striker?" McCarter asked cautiously. The door handles were unlocked, but he didn't touch them. Bolan was high on the list of people McCarter didn't want to startle.

"Right. Gary's just finishing defusing the bomb. Come on in," Bolan replied.

The doors swung open. McCarter, Tanaka and Byrnes stepped into the truck as Manning finished his inspection.

Byrnes stared around the interior of the truck. "This is all one big bomb?" he asked.

Manning nodded. "It's the latest thing in home-made bombs. You can buy everything they used at your friendly local hardware store except for the fuse, of course. It was made in China. You put it all together, and all you have to do is drive it to the target."

"Yes, I know. Fred and I have just concluded an interesting chat with a Dr. Chang. In exchange for a new passport, one hundred thousand dollars and transportation out of Indonesia, Dr. Chang says he has told us everything he knows. We know how the bombs were designed and the names of most of the key people involved. Chang was the expert on the bomb design and the fusing systems," McCarter said.

"What about the place where the bombs are put together and the other targets?" Bolan asked.

"He says he doesn't know that. He just designed the bombs. He wasn't involved in using them. I don't know. He may be lying, but it's hard to tell."

"That still leaves us with a problem," Byrnes said quickly. "We're standing in the middle of a tremendous disaster that's just waiting to happen. What are we going to do with this goddamned bomb?"

"If we can get it to some safe place outside the city, I could detonate it remotely," Manning said.

"I don't think so," Bolan replied. "What do you do when you get a package in the mail, Gary, and it's something you didn't order? You mark it, 'Return to sender.'"

"I'm with you, Striker, but there doesn't seem to be a return address. Where do we send it?"

Tanaka smiled. "As for that, I believe I may be of some small assistance. Mrs. Wu prepared the target list. She knows many interesting things. I will talk to her. I believe I can persuade her to help us. Let us ask General Sudarso to have her brought to his office."

Bolan nodded. They had nothing to lose by trying.

TWENTY MINUTES LATER, they were sitting in General Sudarso's office, drinking more coffee. McCarter was beginning to believe the Indonesian army ran on coffee. He would have preferred tea himself, but at least it was good coffee.

An aide knocked at the door, and two BRIMOB officers brought in Mrs. Wu. Her hands were handcuffed behind her back. There were bruises on her face, and it looked as if she had been crying. One of the BRIMOB officers took off her handcuffs and shoved her into a chair.

"Here is your little songbird, sir. If she does not tell you what you want to know, send her back to us. In an hour or two, she will be begging to tell you everything she knows."

"Wait outside," Sudarso said coldly.

Mrs. Wu shuddered. "Please do not send me back to them. They have done horrible things to me. I do not deserve to be treated like this."

"You deserve to be executed. There is a terrorist bombing campaign under way in Banda Aceh. You helped plan it. You should be shot,'' Major Salim said.

"I do not think so, Major. Perhaps she is not as guilty as she seems,'' Meiko Tanaka said smoothly.

Salim glared at Tanaka. ''Why do you defend this filthy bitch?''

"I saw her at the rebel camp, Major. She may know a few things, but she is really not an evil person, just a fool who was deceived by the rebel leaders. They kept her around to serve them. She processed maps and papers and brought them tea. She did not make policy. She was simply a glorified secretary. She is not the first woman to be deceived by men. She was stupid, but she does not deserve to die for that.''

Tanaka turned to the cowering woman and said, "Tell the general what you know, and perhaps he will spare your miserable life.''

Mrs. Wu began to cry softly. "I do not know what to do, but please do not kill me.''

"Do not be a fool,'' Tanaka said coldly. ''I am the only friend you have here. Unless you want to die for the men who deceived you, speak now!''

"Yes, yes. I will tell you everything. Give me a map of the city. I will show you where the targets are and where the bombs are assembled.''

MAJOR SALIM DROVE the bomb truck slowly and carefully through the streets of Banda Aceh. Gadgets Schwarz sat next to him and gave his remote detonating device one last check. He had replaced the original bomb detonating device with two of his own. All that was necessary to detonate the bomb now was to press two buttons. Schwarz was careful not to touch either button. The thought that he and Salim were sitting on top of twenty thousand pounds of high explosives was very sobering.

Bolan, McCarter and Manning were following a hundred yards back in another car. It was nice to have a little backup in case things went wrong.

"There it is, just ahead. See that big dilapidated warehouse surrounded by a chain-link fence? It is just as Mrs. Wu described it. All we have to do is get past the gate guards, and we will deliver our little surprise," Salim said.

He stopped the truck but left the engine running. Schwarz nodded and slid his remote detonator into his jacket pocket. He slipped out of the truck's cab and watched as Salim put the truck in gear and drove toward the gate.

A man with an AK-47 in his hands stepped out of the gatehouse.

"*Berhenti disini,*" he said, and held up his left hand.

Salim noticed there were two more men standing by the gate, pointing their AK-47s at the truck. If this was merely the local security guards, they were quite impressive.

The guard walked to the driver's door and stared at Salim suspiciously. "I do not know you. Who are you? What are you doing here?"

"I am Salim, of course. I have brought the truck back from the American Embassy because Dr. Chang said I should. Something has gone wrong with it, the arming and fusing system he said. God knows what that is, but I do not. Dr. Chang says it must be replaced."

The guard relaxed and nodded. Salim had mentioned the right name. He had no particular reason to be suspicious. If he knew Dr. Chang's name, he had to be all right. He waved his hand, and the other two guards opened the gate. Salim put the truck back in gear and drove smoothly toward the building. It was a large single-story building with several massive metal doors, big enough for large trucks to drive through. Two trucks identical to the one Salim was driving were lined up near the front wall.

"Put it next to the other trucks," a guard directed.

Salim nodded and parked the truck carefully. No one seemed to be watching them as they stepped out of the vehicle. He strolled casually back toward the gate as if he didn't have a care in the world. The guards weren't watching him. Their attention had been diverted. Tanaka had pulled up to the gate in a pale blue Honda. She was dressed to attract attention in a faded T-shirt and tight blue jeans. The guards were obviously enjoying the view.

"Do you know this woman?" one of the guards asked.

"Yes, she is my assistant. Dr. Chang gave me a message to take to headquarters. It didn't seem wise to drive the truck there. She will take me there in her car."

The guard laughed. "Would to God I had such a pretty assistant. Be on your way, and try not to stop too many times before you get to headquarters."

Salim got into the car. "As to that, friend, as God wills it, so shall it be. Drive, woman."

Tanaka pulled smoothly away from the gate and drove around the corner. She stopped, and Schwarz climbed into the back seat. She then drove rapidly down the street.

"Stop here," Schwarz said after they had gone about a thousand yards.

He took out his remote detonator and pulled out the telescoping antenna. He pushed a button. A green light came on. Ready.

He turned to Salim. "Would you like to do the honors, Major?" he asked.

Salim smiled and took the remote detonating device. He pushed the firing button, and a red light came on.

"Firing command accepted. The fusing action is under way," Schwarz said calmly.

Salim looked back toward the building and smiled coldly. He could respect men who fought for what they believed in, but he despised people who built bombs to kill innocent civilians.

He pushed the button that transmitted the firing command.

For a few seconds, nothing seemed to happen, then they heard a gigantic roaring noise like an immense clap of thunder. The car shook as the tremendous roar was repeated again and again. Salim looked out the window. Three huge balls of orange fire were rising up into the sky, followed by immense columns of dense black smoke. The bomb factory was out of business.

CHAPTER TWENTY-TWO

Military Headquarters, Banda Aceh, Sumatra

General Sudarso returned to his office, where the Stony Man team was waiting.

"I am sorry to be late, but I have received several important messages from Jakarta. They have been decoded, and I have read them, but I am not sure that I know much more than I knew before. The special delegation will be here in two hours. It is headed by Marwa Rais. He is a very powerful man, very close to the president. The American ambassador is traveling with him. That is very unusual. The third man is named Malik. I do not know him. Probably he is from intelligence or the secret police."

The general paused and poured himself a cup of coffee.

"Do you know the delegation's mission, General?" McCarter asked.

"God knows, but I do not," Sudarso said piously. "It is so secret that Jakarta will not risk discussing it even in a coded message. All they will say is that it is of critical importance. I must give the delegation any assistance they request. That is all I know except that anything that is kept this secret is bound to bring trouble. The American ambassador indicates that he may wish to speak privately with Mr. Belasko and Mr. Green. Please remain here until he arrives."

Bolan and McCarter exchanged glances. Something was up.

"We'll stay here, of course, but I'd like to check with our headquarters," McCarter said smoothly.

"Of course. Perhaps your headquarters knows what is going on. After all, I do not think the American ambassador is flying to Sumatra for a vacation."

McCarter didn't, either, but it would be interesting to hear what the ambassador had to say.

"Meiko, please keep Gary company. Who knows what trouble he might get into if we let him wander around by himself."

Tanaka understood perfectly. If military headquarters was under surveillance, it wouldn't be wise for any of them to leave it alone. She followed Manning out the door.

An aide entered the office and spoke softly to the general, who nodded, and his aide ushered in Mara Tharin. The woman looked pale and shaken, almost as if she had been crying. She spoke quietly to the general and handed him a piece of paper. He read it and glared furiously. Whether he was angry with Tharin or enraged by the paper she had shown him was hard to tell. He got up and stalked out of the room, followed by the woman.

Bolan looked at McCarter. "What the hell was that all about?"

"Major Salim is in some kind of trouble, possibly serious trouble. Mara found out about it while she was at intelligence headquarters. She wasn't supposed to tell anyone about it, but she broke the rules and told the general. He's very unhappy about it. That's all I could gather.''

''I thought you couldn't speak Indonesian, David. How come you understand most of what people say?''

''I don't speak Indonesian, Striker, but I do speak Malaysian. What you call Indonesian is really called Bahasa Indonesian. It is a dialect of the Malay language. Eighty-five percent of the words are the same, so I can understand most things Indonesians say.''

''You've been pretty closemouthed about it, David.''

''True, but it's an advantage in a foreign country when you understand the locals, but they don't think you do. It's surprising what you can learn looking like a stupid foreigner.''

Bolan sat and stared at the map on the wall. He didn't like feeling that he was in the dark. He wondered what Salim could have done to get in serious trouble. Maybe he had said something politically incorrect about Sumatran independence while he was being interviewed by the reporters. There was no use worrying about it. General Sudarso would tell them if he thought it was any of their business. Possibly Manning would learn something when he contacted Stony Man.

The office door flew open. General Sudarso stalked in, followed by Major Salim and Mara Tharin. Salim looked relaxed. If he was in serious trouble, he didn't seem to know it. Mara Tharin looked utterly miserable. The general sat behind his desk.

Salim saluted smartly. ''Major Salim reporting as ordered, sir!''

The general returned his salute formally. ''Salim, I

ordered you to report here because there is an extremely important mission that must be accomplished by you and our friends' team."

"I am a marine, sir, and marines are always ready. Give me my orders, and I will be on my way."

McCarter smiled. Whatever Major Salim might lack, it was not self-confidence.

General Sudarso looked grim. "Before I do that, Major, there is a matter we must discuss. It may affect your willingness to go on this mission. Since it is a personal matter, would you like Green and Belasko to leave the room?"

"No, sir, I trust them."

"Very well, Major. I have a copy of a directive being sent by the intelligence headquarters to all senior military commanders in Sumatra. It contains a list of seventy-two military officers of Sumatran origin who are considered probably disloyal to Indonesia. It recommends that these officers be immediately relieved of command and placed in protective custody. I am sorry to tell you that your name is on this list. When I receive this directive officially, I may be forced to take action against you."

Salim turned pale. He looked as if General Sudarso had struck him. The expression on his face changed to cold fury. "That will not be necessary, General. I will have my resignation from the Royal Marine Commandos on your desk in ten minutes. As soon as it is accepted, I will be gone. You will never see me again."

Bolan stared at Salim. He remembered what the major had said: "I will be fighting against my friends whatever I decide. If I go with Sumatra, I must fight against my friends in the army and the marines. If I stay with the government, I must fight against my friends, even my relatives, in Sumatra. It is a terrible decision. You Americans have a saying, 'I am damned if I do and damned if I don't.'"

Bolan had a sinking feeling. Some faceless bureaucrat in Jakarta had made the decision for Salim. The next time he saw Salim, they might well be shooting at each other.

"You are a marine, Salim. I cannot accept your resignation. You know that."

"Very well, let me use a radio. I will contact the marine commandant immediately. But before I do that, I would like to know just what I am accused of having done and who is my accuser."

General Sudarso frowned. "I am sorry, Major. I cannot tell you that. I simply do not know."

"So much for the constitution! I have served well and faithfully for twelve years, and now I have no rights. I am a traitor because some filthy little informer says I am one."

Salim stared around the room. His eyes stopped on Mara Tharin, who was cringing in her chair next to McCarter. Salim glared at her.

"I do not need to ask who accused me. I see the traitor sitting there. Tharin, you dirty, lying bitch. We have worked together and fought together. I have saved your miserable life more than once. I cared for you. I thought you were my friend and all the while you were writing your little reports. 'Salim is a traitor.' You are lucky you are a woman, Tharin. If you were a man, I would kill you!"

"Major Salim! You will be silent!"

General Sudarso's voice cracked like a whip. It was

the voice of a man who commanded thousands of troops. It radiated command authority.

"I understand your anger, Major. If I were accused of being a traitor when I was not, I would be angry, too. I have listened to you. Now, you will listen to me."

Major Salim's hands were still clenched into fists, but twelve years of military experience told him he had to obey.

"Very well, sir, I am listening."

"First of all, Major, everyone in this room is your friend, including Mara Tharin. I have not received this message officially. No one can prove that I have ever seen it. Miss Tharin obtained this copy when she visited the local intelligence headquarters. She is not authorized to have it or to show it to me. If her superiors find out that she has done this, her career in intelligence is over. She might well face trial and imprisonment. Why did she take this risk? Because she is your friend, and she wanted to help you.

"Stop and think, Salim. If I believed you were a traitor, I could have had a dozen armed men waiting to arrest you. You would be in prison now. You are here at liberty because I believe in your loyalty. If that were not so, I would not be considering you to lead a critically important mission. Think, and you will see that all this is true."

"Yes, sir, but what happens when the message actually arrives through channels?"

"It is awaiting the agreement of the chief of staff. If he agrees, it will still be several hours before I receive an official copy. I will send a formal protest to the chief of staff. By the time he gets it and sends me a reply, you will no longer be in Banda Aceh.

You will be gone on your critical mission, and I will not recall you.''

McCarter smiled cynically. The formal rules and regulations of army administration could be terribly annoying, but there were times when a clever man could use them to get what he wanted. General Sudarso was a clever man.

The rage seemed to have drained out of Major Salim.

''I have a coded message from Mr. Rais's office. He is intelligent enough to know that I cannot help him if I do not know what he is trying to do. The government has decided that things cannot go on as they are. A few more major incidents in Sumatra, and there will be civil war. They want to make one last attempt to have peace. Mr. Rais is carrying the government's final offer to the Free Sumatra Movement. If they accept it, there will be peace. If not, then the war has started.''

''What is this final offer, General?'' Salim asked.

''I do not know. We do not need to know that in order to accomplish our part of the mission. All we must do is get Mr. Rais and his party to the Sumatran leadership and after he has met with them, get them back safely.''

''That is easier said than done. It will not be easy to communicate with the Sumatran leadership, and if we do, I do not think they will come. They will not believe you, sir, and they will not believe me. They will suspect a trap. You are asking them to put their heads in the tiger's mouth. Who would they trust?''

''There is one man they will believe—your uncle Ismail Salim, and he will believe you, Major. If you agree, simply telephone him and ask him to arrange the meeting. If he asks them, they will come. There are few Sumatrans who will refuse a personal request from Ismail Salim.''

Bolan was startled. He remembered Salim talking about his uncle when they were flying to Aceh. He'd said that his uncle was real hero, respected by everyone in Aceh Province. He had thought at the time that Major Salim was just showing pardonable pride in his family. General Sudarso seemed to believe Salim's uncle was a national hero whose invitation no Sumatran would refuse.

McCarter interrupted. ''Excuse me, General, but I have two questions I should like to ask. Since my team will be involved in this mission, I believe I must know before I agree. First, who is Ismail Salim, and why should the rebel leadership do what he requests?''

''He is one of our last great heroes. He was twenty years old when the Japanese invaded Sumatra in 1942. He started a one-man resistance program. He was a great guerrilla leader. Many men followed him. The Japanese put a price of one hundred thousand gold coins on his head, but they never caught him. He fought the Japanese until that war was over. After that, he fought the Dutch and the British for our independence. When we finally won our independence in 1949, he was offered many things, a government post or high rank in the army. He refused them all. He said he had fought for freedom, not money or power. He went back to his land and back to farming. God knows Indonesia would be a better country if we had more men like Ismail Salim.''

''It is all true, every word of it!'' Salim said.

''I am sure he is a great man,'' McCarter said

smoothly, "but I still have one other question. Why should my team be involved? This sounds like a purely Indonesian affair."

"Because there is one serious problem, even if Ismail Salim agrees to call the meeting. There must be some way to get Rais and the ambassador to the meeting alive and, once the meeting is held, to get them back here. Think. We feel sure that military headquarters is under constant surveillance. If I send a company of paratroops or marines to escort Rais, the rebels will know this before they have gone five miles. They will be certain it is a trap and even if they do not, how can there be a secret meeting with a company of paratroops surrounding Ismail Salim's house?"

"I understand, General," McCarter said. "But then how do we solve the problem?"

General Sudarso smiled. "Simple. Major Salim will take a few days' leave. Naturally, he will go to see his uncle, and he will take his new foreign friends to meet him. No uniforms and no visible guns. What could be suspicious in this? Major Salim and his uncle are very close. It would be unusual if he did not go to see his uncle. Mr. Rais and the ambassador have never been to Sumatra before. Even if the rebels see them, it will be some time before they are identified. I believe this plan will succeed as long as our security remains tight."

"Very well, General. It is an excellent plan. We will be glad to support you."

McCarter smiled faintly as he said it. He had no better plan to suggest, but still he felt uneasy. He didn't like plans that depended on maintaining tight security. Security seemed to fail so frequently when success or failure depended on it.

"Thank you. I appreciate your support. I believe this meeting is over. Use my office as your headquarters. Major Salim, you will call your uncle. Assuming he agrees, rent civilian vehicles and prepare to depart. I will brief Mr. Rais and the ambassador."

General Sudarso left the room. Salim started to leave and then paused.

"I must apologize. I have behaved very badly. None of you has ever done anything to me, but I was furious. I lashed out at you all. I am sorry. That is all I can say."

"Think nothing of it, mate. If some intelligence twits in London accused me of being a traitor, I'd bloody well be furious. We understand."

"It is good of you to say that." Salim paused for a second and then went on.

"Mara, I must personally apologize to you. You are my friend. You have risked your career to help me, and I said terrible things to you. I did not really mean them. It was just that I was so angry I could not think. I am sorry. Please forgive me."

"I understand. I forgive you," Tharin said softly.

"Well, enough of this idle chitchat. We have work to do," McCarter said. "Let's get ready, civilian clothes and every weapon and round of ammunition you can conceal. We are likely to need them before this trip to the countryside is over."

CHAPTER TWENTY-THREE

The Salim Estate, outside Banda Aceh

McCarter drove carefully through the outskirts of Banda Aceh and into the countryside. The steel-gray BMW convertible was a beautiful vehicle, and McCarter handled it with the skill of a master driver. Salim sat next to him in the passenger seat. Bolan and Tanaka sat in the back. McCarter had chosen the BMW convertible carefully. It was true it would attract attention, but he had been in many fights in cars and he knew that most cars were easy to shoot into but difficult to shoot out of. Convertibles were the exception. With the top down, everyone had a superb field of fire. The rest of the party followed in a white Honda van.

As they drove steadily east along the coastal road toward Sigli, Bolan noticed a shift in McCarter's driving pattern He was slowing up, then increasing speed. He did this three or four times, keeping his eyes on the rearview mirror as he did it. Bolan frowned. The Phoenix Force commander never did things like that without a reason. Something was up.

McCarter frowned. "Striker, I can't be absolutely sure, but I think someone is following us."

Bolan resisted the impulse to turn in his seat and look behind him.

"Any indication that they're getting ready to attack us?"

McCarter thought for a second.

"I doubt it. It's a single car, a small red Toyota. It couldn't hold more than four men. It is probably a surveillance team, but they could have something nasty, a rocket-propelled grenade launcher, perhaps. Better get ready for them just in case."

Bolan opened the black nylon carryall beneath his feet and took out his M-4 Ranger carbine. He slipped in a 30-round magazine and chambered a round. He opened the breech of his M-203 grenade launcher and loaded a 40 mm HE grenade. If the people in the red car were hostile, he was ready.

Meiko Tanaka had noticed his movements and looked at Bolan expectantly.

"There's a car about half a mile behind us. David thinks they may be following us. Don't look back. They may be watching us through binoculars. Get your weapon out and get ready just in case."

Tanaka reached for her 9 mm Heckler & Koch submachine gun. She was looking forward to meeting Major Salim's uncle. She was always interested in meeting famous warriors, but trips through the countryside weren't Meiko's thing. She had been feeling bored. She snapped a 30-round magazine into her dull black weapon. The prospect of a little action added spice to the trip.

McCarter drove on, alternately slowing down and speeding up. The red Toyota stayed in position, but did nothing else. Bolan examined their options. They could certainly ambush the red car, but it would be embarrassing if the occupants turned out to be a Sumatran family out for a ride in the country. Better to be ready and wait and see.

Tanaka seemed disappointed that nothing was happening. She resumed staring boredly at the passing landscape. Bolan didn't mind a little boredom. This mission had been hard and continuous. He hadn't liked it from the start.

Their intelligence had been poor, and the White House just sent them in without any clearly defined tasks or objectives. They were lucky no one had been killed.

He leaned back in the comfortable seat and tried to relax. They drove on for about fifteen minutes. Then Bolan felt the BMW slow. Major Salim was pointing ahead. A narrow asphalt side road split off from the highway and wound to the left through groves of lush green trees.

"Slow down and turn left there, David. It is all my family's land past the turn," Major Salim said.

McCarter nodded and turned smoothly.

Bolan leaned forward and tapped him on the shoulder.

"Stop for a minute as soon as we're out of sight from the highway. Meiko and I are going to stretch our legs."

McCarter brought the BMW to a stop. Bolan got out and motioned to Tanaka to follow him. They took cover in a thick clump of bushes by the side of the road. The woman held her silenced 9 mm submachine gun ready. The Executioner didn't need to tell her what they were doing. If the small red car was following them, this was the perfect place to find out.

They waited quietly for a minute or two until Manning drove by in the white van. Things were quiet for another two or three minutes, but Bolan waited patiently. If the red car had been following them, it would be along shortly. Then they heard the engine of a small car. The red Toyota drove by slowly and stopped a hundred feet farther down the road.

Bolan touched Tanaka lightly on her shoulder.

"Don't shoot unless they try something or I give the signal."

Tanaka nodded and peered through her sights. Her thumb rested lightly on the safety-selector switch. It was perfectly safe, but she was less than half a second from firing her first shot if Bolan gave the signal.

Bolan watched intently the sights of his M-4 carbine perfectly aligned. A man got out and unfolded a map. He stared at it for a minute, then went to the driver's window and showed him the map. Then he got back in the car. The driver turned the Toyota around and drove back toward the highway.

They waited about five minutes, but the red car didn't come back.

"Perhaps they were not following us, Striker," Tanaka said. "Maybe it was just a coincidence."

Bolan nodded. Perhaps, but perhaps not. What was that old British army proverb that McCarter often quoted? "The first time is happenstance, the second

time is coincidence, the third time is enemy action.''
If they saw the red car again it would not be coincidence.

McCarter drove up alone in the BMW. Bolan and Tanaka climbed in.

"Salim went ahead to see his uncle. What about our friends in the red car?''

"They drove in a little ways, looked at a map and drove back to the main road. They may just have been lost,'' Bolan said.

"That's possible of course, but if they were following us, they now know where we're going. Well, we'll see.''

He turned the BMW and drove toward Ismail Salim's house.

Ismail Salim met them at the door. He was tall for an Indonesian, with dark skin and a shock of snow-white hair. Major Salim made the introductions, but Bolan would have known Ismail Salim instantly without a word being spoken. He had the subtle air, relaxed but ready, of a true fighting man. Bolan had long ago realized it took one to know one.

"This is my uncle,'' Major Salim said proudly. "My parents died when I was young. He brought me up. He is like a father to me.

"This is my friend Striker, Uncle. He is a true warrior.''

Ismail Salim smiled. "Any friend of Salim's is a friend of mine. I am sorry, but you will have to excuse me. I must greet my other guests.''

"My uncle is not fond of government officials,

Striker, but he will be polite. They are guests in his house.''

"Your uncle is a formidable man, Salim. Just so I know where I stand, how does he feel about Americans?''

"He likes Americans. They sent us weapons to fight the Japanese and never asked for anything after the war was over. Indeed, they supported Indonesia's independence. Now, come into the main hall. My uncle has ordered a simple meal. He says we must eat and relax until the men he has asked to come to the meeting arrive.''

Tanaka and McCarter were already there. The woman was staring happily at the weapons hanging on the wall. Bolan recognized a Japanese sniper's rifle and a Nambu pistol. A rising-sun battle flag and a Japanese officer's sword hung together. The brown stains on the flag looked like blood. It appeared that Ismail Salim had collected his old weapons the hard way.

Three middle-aged women came into the hall and began to place platters of food along a long table against one wall. They went out and returned with more platters of food and big brass urns of tea and coffee. Bolan stared at the table. There were platters heaped with meat, rice and exotic fruit, enough to feed a small army.

Major Salim came into the room and smiled. "My uncle apologizes for this meager meal If he had known you were coming a day or two ago, he would have prepared a feast in your honor. Alas, this is the best he could do on three hours' notice.''

McCarter smiled. "Tell your uncle that we are extremely grateful for his hospitality. We are overwhelmed by the size and variety of this magnificent meal."

"We Salims are not rich, but no guest ever leaves our house hungry. My uncle says we will hold the meeting as soon as our other guests are here."

THE SERVANTS CLEARED the table and set up two groups of chairs facing each other. Ismail Salim came into the room, followed by six men. They took one group of chairs and waited quietly. McCarter looked at the men. They ranged in age from thirty to sixty. There was nothing unusual about them. Had he passed them on the streets of Banda Aceh, he wouldn't have given them a second glance, but he knew that here he was looking at the leaders of the Free Sumatra Movement. These were the men Mr. Rais and the ambassador had come to see.

Major Salim ushered Rais's party to the other chairs. There was a pause while the two groups looked at each other. McCarter watched the Sumatrans closely. They were polite enough. They didn't glare at Rais's group, but they radiated a cool dislike. They had taken up arms to fight the central government. They didn't trust its representatives. They wouldn't have met with them if Ismail Salim had not asked them to come.

"You are all welcome in my house," he said formally. "This is Mr. Rais. He is an important man, very close to the president. He tells me that he has brought a very important message from the government in Jakarta. Please listen to his words."

Mr. Rais got to his feet and spoke solemnly. He had been in politics too long not to sense the Sumatrans' dislike. He knew he had to choose his words carefully.

"Thank you, Mr. Salim. I appreciate your arranging this critical meeting. You are wondering why I am here. I came here, because we are all at the edge of an abyss. Sumatrans, Javanese, all Indonesians are faced with a great disaster. If we do not do something, our nation and our way of life will be destroyed. I am not threatening you. I am merely stating a fact. The government in Jakarta has been meeting continuously for the last three days. They have been trying to agree on a course of action.

"There are several factions in the government, but they all agree on this. What is going on in Sumatra is a major crisis, the greatest crisis Indonesia has ever had to face. It is much worse than East Timor. East Timor was never really part of Indonesia. It was a Portuguese colony with less than two million people. We took it over when the Portuguese left it in 1975. If we lose it, it will merely be an annoyance. But Sumatra is different. If we lose Sumatra, Indonesia is finished. It will dissolve into half a dozen small weak nations. Foreigners will have the real power. So, we are all agreed. Sumatra cannot become independent."

Ismail Salim stared at Rais coldly. "You have come here to tell us that? Sumatrans do not frighten easily. By God, if you want war, you shall have it!"

"In God's name, war is the last thing the government wants. I am here to make you an offer. If you value peace, listen to me now!''

Ismail Salim nodded. ''You are a guest in my house. I will hear what you have to say.''

''Here is what I am empowered to offer you. First, an immediate and total cease-fire. Then there will be a general amnesty. All political prisoners will be freed. All those who have fought against the government are pardoned. You will have the right to elect your own legislature. Sumatra will have a high degree of autonomy within Indonesia. You will have most everything you demanded, but not independence.

''Now, I will tell you what you are not offered. Sumatra must remain a province of the Indonesian Republic. It will not be allowed to have armed forces of its own, have its own foreign policy, or allow foreign military bases on its territory. That is not negotiable.''

''If you will not negotiate, you are wasting your time and ours.''

''I cannot negotiate, Mr. Salim. Listen to me. If the government gives you more than this offer, it will fall. Many people feel even this offer gives you far too much. Many of the generals are furious. They say the rebel fighters are terrorists. They swear they will fight to the last man to keep Sumatra Indonesian. If you reject this offer, the government will be replaced by a military dictatorship. Already they are calling up the reserves and asking the Americans for more weapons. I know the Free Sumatra Movement can get weapons from China and Russia. We will have civil war. It will go on for years, and it will be fought here in

Sumatra. Your island will be ruined, and millions of people may be killed. In God's name, compromise. Accept this offer before it is too late."

Ismail Salim listened impassively. McCarter couldn't tell what he was thinking.

Ambassador Clark stood. "Gentlemen, I am Donald Clark. I am the United States ambassador to the Republic of Indonesia. You may feel that I am a foreigner interfering in a matter that must be decided by Indonesians. My President has sent me here because, since World War II, the United Sates has been a friend of the Indonesian people. We have always supported your independence. We understand that many Sumatrans are unhappy with the present situation. My government is sympathetic. Our intelligence services tell us that foreign governments are using the situation to try to break up Indonesia. That must not happen. My government urges you to accept Jakarta's offer. If you do, the United States government will use all its influence to see that its terms are carried out."

The Free Sumatra Movement leaders looked at one another for a moment. One of them stood and spoke quietly.

"Mr. Rais, we have listened to you and Ambassador Clark carefully. We understand what you have said. We must discuss the government's offer between ourselves before making a decision. If you will excuse us, we will give you our answer in an hour or two."

"I understand. God grant you wisdom."

Ismail Salim led the Sumatran group out of the room.

McCarter hoped for the best, but the history of his own country told him that when people were divided by oppression and old wars and hatreds, it was terribly hard to make peace.

McCarter's tactical radio emitted a soft electronic beep. He wasn't wearing the headset, but it was in his shirt pocket. He turned away from the people in the room and looked as if he was examining some of the weapons on the wall. He slipped on the headset and spoke into the microphone. He waited a second and then he heard Mara Tharin's voice in his ear.

"Striker, David, this is Mara. Please come in."

"David here, Mara. What's going on?"

"Two vans drove up to where they could observe the house. They are both full of armed men. Now they have pulled back a little and are unloading."

"Roger. Do you think it is an attack?"

"I am certain of it. I used my small binoculars. Their leader is Colonel Chun."

CHAPTER TWENTY-FOUR

The Salim Estate—outside Banda Aceh

Colonel Chun studied Ismail Salim's house carefully, using his binoculars, studying every detail and pondering his plan of attack. The house looked strongly built, a good place to defend. The people there didn't look as if they were alert. He saw no signs of guards or sentries, but there might be a few cleverly concealed. He hoped he would achieve complete surprise, but he couldn't count on it. He had eighteen men, fifteen armed with AK-47 rifles and hand grenades and three with Russian SVD Dragunov sniper rifles plus three RPG-7 rocket-propelled grenade launchers. They didn't need to capture the whole house to win, just get in and kill the delegates to the peace conference. He would be willing to sacrifice the entire team, including himself, to accomplish that. He signaled to his two assistant leaders and began to outline his plan of attack.

McCARTER SIGNALED Mack Bolan, who moved quickly to join him.

"Trouble?" Bolan asked.

"Party crashers, Striker. Mara says Colonel Chun and twenty of his merry men are outside getting ready to pay us a visit. Alert the rest of the team. We can't be sure which way Colonel Chun is coming. Put Gary Manning and Gadgets on the back door. Borrow a few hand grenades from Gary if he has any he can spare. We will take care of the front. Now, where is Major Salim? We kneed to know if there are any other obvious entrances."

"I will get him," Tanaka said, and dashed off.

"What do you think, Striker?" McCarter asked. "Have you any suggestions?"

Bolan thought hard for a few seconds. "Colonel Chun has to win quickly. Winning means he gets inside the house and kills the people who came to the meeting. He can't do it slowly. For all he knows, a battalion of paratroopers may drop in at any minute. I think he'll make a big attack and try to come straight in through the front door. If that doesn't work, he may try something fancy. We can't afford not to guard the back, though, but we need all the firepower we can get at the front door. Let's put Major Salim, Byrnes and Meiko there."

"I agree."

"What about Mara?" McCarter asked.

"She's probably safer outside. Dressed as she is, she looks like a farm woman. They have no reason to go after her, but if they see her trying to get back in the house, they will probably shoot her."

McCarter was about to contact Tharin when his tactical radio beeped again.

"David, be ready. They are sending some men to

the back of the house. The rest are moving closer to the front door. It looks like they will send two or three men to the front door. They will probably try to talk their way in or kill whoever answers the door. The rest are taking cover among the garden shrubs. You have five minutes at the most before they come. I will stay out here and tell you what they are doing.''

''All right, Mara. Look at the radio. Switch to channel two, then call military headquarters in Banda Aceh. Tell them where we are and that we are under attack. Ask them to send reinforcements at once. Keep watching our visitors. Call me immediately if they do anything new.''

''At once, David.''

Tanaka returned with Major Salim and his uncle. McCarter quickly explained what was happening.

''I did not ask this Colonel Chun to come here,'' Ismail Salim said with a cruel smile, ''but I will give him a warm welcome!''

''I shall welcome him, Uncle,'' Major Salim said, ''but we must remember why he is here. It is not you or I he is after. He came to kill our guests who came to the meeting. You must take them to safety while I defend the house.''

Ismail Salim's face darkened with anger. He no longer looked like an old man. When he spoke, McCarter could hear the rasp of command in his voice.

''Do not say such things to me, Nephew! This is my house. I fought the Japanese, the Dutch and the British for our land. I am not afraid of this Chinese colonel. A bullet can kill him as well as any other man. I may be old, but God knows I can still shoot well.''

He paused and took a deep breath.

''I forgive you for what you said. I know you are concerned for me, and there is wisdom in some of your words. You will take all our guests out of the house. Use the escape tunnel. Once they are safe, use your own judgment as to what to do next. Now, go with God.''

''But, Uncle—''

''Be silent! This is not a discussion! I am in command here, and I am giving you your orders. Carry them out.''

Salim stared at his uncle. Love and respect shone on his face. He snapped to attention and saluted like a Royal Marine Commando on parade.

''Yes, sir! I will carry out your orders immediately!'' He turned and quickly left the room.

Ismail Salim smiled at Mack Bolan and McCarter. ''He is really a fine young man, you know. It is just that he has a fiery temper and is sometimes a little headstrong. I fear it may run in the family.''

McCarter was far too smart to comment on that. ''Yes, sir. I understand perfectly. Now, we must get to the front door. Colonel Chun may come calling at any moment.''

''Go to the door, and organize the defenses. I will be there in a moment as soon as I get my weapons. Striker, will you stay and help me? I am not as strong as I once was. I may need help with a few things.''

''Glad to help you, sir,'' Bolan said. He admired Ismail Salim's attitude and, besides, it would be interesting to see what the old man regarded as serious weapons.

Ismail Salim went to a wall of the room and pushed aside a fine woven tapestry hanging from the wall. The wall seemed blank, but he touched two spots and slid back a panel. Bolan saw a compartment and the dull gleam of well-oiled gun metal.

"The weapons on the wall are just trophies, Striker. These are for real fighting."

Salim picked up a United States Army M-1 Garand rifle fitted with a telescopic sight.

"This is my best rifle. I once killed a Japanese colonel at eight hundred yards, but my eyes were better then. Besides, it is too powerful to use for fighting inside a house."

He picked another squat, deadly-looking weapon. Any man who really knew guns would have recognized it instantly as a Thompson submachine gun. It was one of the older Thompsons, a Model 1928, chambered to fire the .45 Colt automatic pistol cartridge. The Thompson was one of the oldest submachine gun designs in the world, but it was still amazingly effective in a close-quarters fight. The gun had seen many years of hard use. The dull blue finish was worn away in places, but it was clean and well oiled.

Ismail Salim picked up the Thompson and patted the smooth walnut stock affectionately.

"This is a fine gun, Striker. There is none better when the range is short. It is heavy to carry, but you never mind the weight when the shooting starts."

He picked up a round black 50-round drum magazine and slipped it into the Thompson's action just in front of the trigger guard and smiled as it clicked into place. He pulled back the cocking lever and pushed the safety selector lever to safe. He passed the weapon to Mack Bolan.

"Hold it for me for a moment, Striker, while I get a few more things."

Bolan hefted the Thompson. It was surprisingly heavy. With a loaded 50-round magazine, it weighed over fourteen pounds, but if groups of men were going to rush you at short range, it was hard to imagine a better weapon.

Ismail Salim fastened an old U.S. Army web belt around his waist and patted the spare magazine pouches to be sure they were full. He smiled as he took the Thompson from Mack Bolan.

"I am ready, Striker. Let us go to the front door. Your companion may need us. It would be extremely rude if I were not there to welcome Colonel Chun when he comes calling, and God knows I am a polite man."

McCARTER WAS PLANNING his defense. The house wasn't a fort or a castle, but it was strongly built with thick stone walls and heavy wooden doors. McCarter didn't think Colonel Chun had the time or the equipment to blast a hole through the thick stone walls. No, he would have to come through the wooden doors. They were the weak points. They were solidly built, but they couldn't withstand the power of modern weapons.

He told Tanaka to guard the door while he and Fred Byrnes pushed several heavy leather-covered sofas into place along the walls. They might not stop bullets, but they would provide some concealment and would stop grenade fragments. McCarter looked around and spotted Bolan and Ismail Salim. He had done everything he could think of. They were ready. Now the ball was in Colonel Chun's court. McCarter was about to take cover behind a sofa near the door when his tactical radio beeped again.

"David, they have started. Two men are walking toward the front door. They look unarmed, but they have silenced pistols. The rest of them have taken cover close to the door. Colonel Chun is there. He has a sniper's rifle."

McCarter heard a hard knocking at the door. His smile was cold, and his green eyes glittered. He was tempted to shoot through it and give whoever was on the other side a real surprise, but the longer he could delay the attack the better. He motioned to Tanaka and pointed toward the door. The woman smiled and nodded. She left her Heckler & Koch submachine gun and went to the door. McCarter drew his silenced .22-caliber Walther pistol and covered her.

Someone outside knocked again, hard and impatient.

Tanaka stood at the door, but she was careful not to stand directly in front of it. She knew that steel-jacketed bullets could penetrate many inches of the hardest wood.

"Who is it?" she asked in flawless Indonesian.

"I must speak to Ismail Salim at once. I have an important message for him from the Free Sumatra Movement."

"I am sorry, sir, but Ismail Salim is meeting with some very important guests. He left strict orders that he must not be disturbed. You cannot see him now. Leave the message by the door, and I will be sure to see that he gets it."

"This message cannot wait. Open the door, or I will see that you are punished!"

"Yes, sir, at once. Please do not be angry with me, sir. I am only a servant."

Tanaka assumed a pitiful, helpless look and unlocked and opened the door.

McCarter saw two men in civilian clothing. They looked harmless enough, but he remembered what Mara Tharin had said. The man who was nearest to the door started to force his way into the house. Tanaka stayed in front of him, her arms spread in a pleading gesture.

"Please, sir, do not—"

The man put his palm on Tanaka's chest and pushed her hard.

She exploded into action. She crossed her hands over the back of the man's hand, locking it to her chest, and suddenly bent over, driving him down toward the floor. McCarter heard the dull crack of a bone snapping and a hoarse shriek of pain as the man's locked wrist broke. Tanaka continued to hold the man's wrist and kicked him in the side of his head, not hard enough to kill him, but more than enough to take him out of the fight.

McCarter resolved never to put his hands on Tanaka unless he was sure she wanted him to. The second man was frozen by surprise for a second or two.

Then his hand moved toward his concealed pistol. The Briton's sights were already aligned. He pulled the trigger. The silenced Walther hissed and sent two hollowpoint bullets through the man's chest. He staggered and swayed, but he was still on his feet and trying to draw his weapon. McCarter shifted his aim and put two more shots through the man's head. He went down like a puppet whose strings had been cut.

The door was still open. McCarter pulled one of the hand grenades he had borrowed from Manning from his belt, pulled the pin and let the safety lever fly. He heard the hiss as the fuse began to burn and hurled the grenade out through the door. He kept down until he heard a dull boom as the grenade detonated. Then he slammed the door and locked it and took cover again.

McCarter heard snapping, crackling noises, and splinters erupted from the inside of the door as someone fired a long burst and .30-caliber steel-jacketed bullets tore through the hard wood. McCarter sneered. Bloody amateurs! They were just venting their temper. Thirty-caliber bullets would never blast open the thick old doors.

McCarter's tactical radio beeped again.

"Take cover, David! They are aiming rocket grenade launchers at the door."

McCarter didn't hesitate.

"Down, everybody! Get behind cover and stay down."

Something struck the door like a giant sledgehammer. McCarter heard a loud roaring noise. A piece of the door suddenly disintegrated, and splinters sang through the air. A five-pound 85 mm RPG-7 grenade had just struck the door and detonated. McCarter was within thirty feet of the explosion. Metal fragments and hardwood splinters ripped into the leather-covered sofa in front of him. The acrid smell of burning high explosives filled the air. He risked a quick look. The door was still on its hinges, but a gaping hole had been blasted through it. McCarter knew they would fire again.

"Stay down!" he shouted.

This time, he heard the hiss of the rocket and the ringing sound as it struck the door. The warhead detonated, and metal fragments hissed through the hall. Another rocket struck and exploded, then another. The door was split and shattered by the repeated explosions. The rain of rockets stopped, but McCarter knew that Colonel Chun was deciding whether he had done enough damage with the rocket-propelled grenades and it was time to rush the door. He heard Tharin's voice again.

"They are coming, David. They are coming now!"

McCarter snarled. He had bloody well had enough of being shot at without being able to shoot back. Let them come! If he was going to die, he would take a few of the bastards with him. He drew the last grenade from his belt and pulled the pin. He held the safety lever down and waited. He would give the first men to reach the door a real surprise. He was momentarily deafened by the explosions and wouldn't hear the attackers coming. He kept his eyes on the door opening. When he saw a flicker of movement outside, he let the grenade's safety lever fly, counted off two seconds, and hurled the grenade through the opening.

The grenade detonated. McCarter picked up his M-4 carbine and aimed at the opening in the door. Out of the corner of his eye, he saw Tanaka bring up her 9 mm submachine gun and take aim at the same target. Two men appeared at the gaping opening in the door with AK-47s in their hands. They fired long crisscrossing patterns through the door, sweeping the hallway with steel-jacketed bullets. It was classic room-entry technique. They were covering the men who would actually make the entry.

McCarter waited grimly. Suddenly, the opening was filled with armed men rushing through the gap. The Briton pushed his carbine's selector switch to full automatic and fired burst after burst at the charging men. Tanaka fired again and again. She wasn't as good as McCarter in full automatic fire, but at thirty feet some of her bullets were bound to strike her targets. Some of the charging men went down, but the others charged forward firing as they came.

McCarter saw a red dot flash toward his target as he fired the last round in his magazine. Tanaka had run dry, too. The Phoenix Force leader reached desperately for a fresh magazine, but he knew he couldn't reload in time. He and Tanaka would be overrun before they could reload. Then McCarter heard the dull, snarling roar of a Thompson submachine gun as Ismail Salim emptied a 50-round drum magazine into the attackers. The attack faltered as some of the men went down and the others sought cover against the walls.

Bolan took advantage of the momentary pause and ran forward to Tanaka's position. McCarter fired three short bursts to cover him as he ran.

"Welcome to the party, Striker!" McCarter shouted. He had nothing against Tanaka. She had done the best she could, but if he was going to have just one person beside him in a close-quarters fight, he wanted it to be Mack Bolan. Bolan grinned and fired three quick bursts at the confused attackers.

McCarter heard someone shouting in Indonesian from outside the door.

"Hold on, Colonel Chun is coming."

"Heads up, Striker, Colonel Chun is coming now!" McCarter shouted.

Bolan had never seen Colonel Chun. He would like to see him now in his M-4 carbine's sights. He aimed at the door and told Tanaka to drop back and join Ismail Salim. Someone yelled again from outside.

"Watch out, Striker, grenades," McCarter warned.

Bolan was puzzled. Grenades didn't make any sense. They would stand a better chance of hitting the attackers inside the door than he or McCarter. Two small metal objects came flying through the opening in the door, struck the floor and rolled down the hall. Bolan heard two soft pops and gray-white smoke began to pour from the grenades. He heard someone yell an order, and the men inside the hall began to fire rapidly.

He heard more shouting, and a group of men came rushing through the door and charged down the hall. The smoke prevented Bolan from aiming precisely. He aimed at the center of the hall and swept it with three long bursts. He could hear McCarter firing, too. It slowed them, but it didn't stop them. No time to reach for a fresh magazine and reload. Bolan dropped his carbine and drew his .44 Magnum pistol and took a firm two-handed grip.

Three men came rushing through the smoke. Bolan saw the man in the middle was wearing a khaki uniform. He knew it was Chun, but the man on the colonel's left was charging straight at Bolan firing his AK-47 from the hip as he came. It was brave, but not very smart. It was almost impossible for him to hit anything shooting that way. Bolan leveled his .44 at the man's chest and pulled the trigger twice. The two heavy bullets struck the man in the heart and he went down. McCarter had hit the man on Chun's right, but the colonel had rushed past them and was charging down the hall.

Ismail Salim saw him coming and fired a short burst. The big, heavy, full-metal-jacketed bullets struck Chun in the chest. He staggered from the force of the repeated blows, but his soft body armor stopped the slow-moving bullets. Chun leveled his AK-47 and fired a burst at Ismail Salim. Bolan saw the Thompson drop from his hands as he fell heavily.

Chun started to swing his AK-47 toward Bolan, but the Executioner was already pivoting smoothly from the waist. He fired the instant he saw his front sight against Chun's chest. His big .44 bucked and roared as Bolan fired a fast double tap. The two heavy high-velocity .44-caliber bullets smashed through Chun's body armor. Chun was still alive, but he knew he was going to die. He wanted to take his killer with him.

He tried to pull the trigger of his rifle again, but Bolan fired another round. Colonel Chun went down and lay still.

Without thinking, Bolan slipped a fresh magazine into his pistol and stared out through the shattered door. The enemy seemed to have vanished. Fred Byrnes was yelling gleefully.

"Listen, Striker, listen," he yelled.

For a moment, Bolan couldn't hear anything. His ears were ringing from the repeated muzzle-blasts of powerful weapons fired indoors. Then he heard it, the sound of helicopter rotors, many helicopters. The troops from Banda Aceh were arriving.

He looked around. McCarter was bleeding from a gash on his forehead, but he looked as if he would be all right. Perhaps they had all made it through.

"Striker," Tanaka called. "Please come here. I need help."

Bolan turned. She was kneeling by Ismail Salim, trying desperately to stop the blood that was welling from the wounds in his chest.

"I need more bandages, Striker. I cannot stop the bleeding."

Bolan snapped open the first-aid kit on his belt and handed her two trauma dressings. He didn't think it would be enough, but that was all they had.

Ismail Salim looked up at her and smiled, but he was starting to bleed from one corner of his mouth. Tanaka wiped the blood away, but more came.

"Do not waste your time, child. I know that am dying."

Bolan thought he was right, but there might still be a slight chance.

"Hang on, we'll get you to a doctor. You'll be all right," he said.

"Do not try to deceive an old man, Striker. We have both seen enough men shot to know I am going to die. Where is my nephew? I must speak to him before I go."

McCarter raced out the door shouting for Major Salim. He was back in a few seconds with Salim and General Sudarso. Major Salim stared down at his uncle.

"Who did this?" he asked, his voice shaking with fury.

"Colonel Chun," Bolan said quietly. "He's dead. I shot him."

"I thank you for that, but I wish you had left him for me!"

"Come here, Nephew," Ismail Salim said. "I have no time to waste. Now, listen to me. All this land is yours. You must fight for it as I have. There is one other thing you must do, boy. Find a nice Muslim girl and marry her. Have many children. Carry on our family name."

Major Salim took his uncle's hand. "But, Uncle—"

Ismail Salim stared at him. For the last time, they heard the rasp of command in his voice.

"Be silent! I am not asking you. I am telling you! I am still in command here, and I am giving you your orders. Carry them out."

Salim stared down at his uncle. "Yes, sir! I will carry out your orders immediately!"

He felt his uncle's hand go limp. He stared at Tanaka. She shook her head.

"I am sorry, Major. I did all I could, but it was not enough. He is gone."

General Sudarso put his hand on Major Salim's shoulder.

"He is with the Prophet in Paradise, Salim. I am fortunate to have known such a man."

CHAPTER TWENTY-FIVE

The Main Airport, Banda Aceh

McCarter and Bolan watched as the crew of the Air Force C-17 finished loading the aircraft. The rest of the Stony Man team and Fred Byrnes were already on board. Major Salim and Mara Tharin had escorted them to the airport. McCarter was smiling as he listened to General Sudarso on the airport's PA system. The general was announcing the cease-fire on radio and TV. Salim smiled at Bolan as an Air Force sergeant signaled that it was time for him to board.

"Goodbye, Striker. We have done some great things together. Do not forget us. Go with God."

They shook hands, and Bolan and McCarter went up the ramp and into the C-17's huge interior. They took their seats with Byrnes and the team as the pilot started the four huge engines and began to taxi out. In a minute, they were airborne. Bolan looked back out the window as the C-17 turned out over the sea and Banda Aceh vanished in the distance.

Fred Byrnes was jovial. "Well, we made it. We did the job, and we all got out alive."

He reached into his attaché case and pulled out a bottle of Jack Daniel's. He poured the whiskey into small metal cups and passed them around.

"Here's to you and your team, Striker. I've said it before, and by God, I'll say it again. It's a pleasure to work with you. If we had enough men like you, we could save the whole damned world."

Bolan didn't really want a drink, but the toast was important to Fred. He drank it slowly and sat thinking. Tanaka wasn't used to drinking straight whiskey. She didn't care much for the taste, but she understood that it was a warrior's after-battle ritual. She was honored to be invited to participate. She smiled and sipped her drink.

"What's the matter, Striker? You don't look happy," McCarter observed.

"I just didn't like the mission. Our intelligence was lousy, and the White House just threw us in, sink or swim. We were lucky we got out alive."

McCarter sipped his drink. "I know how you feel, Striker, but we can't fix the intelligence problems. We don't make national policy or plan the wars. We just fight the battles. We accomplished every task we were handed. We did our duty and perhaps more than that. We helped stop a war. A million people's lives may be saved by what we helped to do. I must say I feel proud of that, and you should, too."

Bolan nodded. He knew McCarter was right. They had gone in and done their job, and everyone on the team had made it out alive. That made it a good mission. Now he could relax until the next one.

The Marshal's Situation Room, Beijing, China

FOUR THOUSAND MILES away, two other men were discussing the situation. A large map of the South China Sea hung on one wall of the situation room. The marshal sat at his desk. He poured two cups of hot, bitter tea and offered one to the general.

"Give me your assessment, General. How do you evaluate the latest events in Indonesia?"

The general stared at his cup, but he could think of no words that would alter the program's failure and his own disgrace.

"I regret to report that Colonel Chun was killed while leading the attack on the peace conference. The Free Sumatra Movement has accepted the central government's offer of a cease-fire and increased Sumatran autonomy within the Indonesian Republic. It will be years before we could mount another major effort in Indonesia. I am sorry to say it, sir, but we have lost the war."

The marshal sipped his tea and stared at the general for a minute. It was hard to read his expression.

"Lost the war, General? We have only lost the first battle. I have been a soldier for fifty years. I fought the Japanese, the Americans, in India and in Vietnam. Do you think I have never lost a battle? I have lost many battles, but China won every war I fought in. We are a great power because we take the long view. The Americans are different. They are a powerful nation, but in some ways they are childish. They cannot think beyond their next election. They have won a battle in Indonesia, and they think they have won the war. They will go home and celebrate, but we are still here and the war for Asia goes on. It will go on until we win.''

The general knew that the marshal was right. He had made the mistake of becoming emotionally involved in the Indonesian operation. He wouldn't let that happen again. When the time came to activate phase two, he would proceed.

**In a ruined world, the past and future clash
with frightening force...**

JAMES AXLER

DEATH LANDS®

Sunchild

Ryan Cawdor and his warrior companions come face-to-face with
the descendants of a secret society who were convinced that
paradise awaited at the center of the earth. This cult is inexorably
tied to a conspiracy of twentieth-century scientists devoted to
fulfilling a vision of genetic manipulation. In this labyrinthine ville,
some of the descendants of the Illuminated Ones are pursuing the
dream of their legacy—while others are dedicated to its nightmare.

Even in the Deathlands, twisted human beliefs endure....

Available in December 2001 at your favorite retail outlet.

James Axler

OUTLANDERS®

PRODIGAL CHALICE

The warriors, who dare to expose the deadly truth of mankind's destiny, discover a new gateway in Central America—one that could lead them deeper into the conspiracy that has doomed Earth. Here they encounter a most unusual baron struggling to control the vast oil resources of the region. Uncertain if this charismatic leader is friend or foe, Kane is lured into a search for an ancient relic of mythic proportions that may promise a better future…or plunge humanity back into the dark ages.

In the Outlands,
the shocking truth is humanity's last hope.

DON PENDLETON'S

STONY

AMERICA'S ULTRA-COVERT INTELLIGENCE AGENCY

MAN

DON'T MISS OUT ON THE ACTION
IN THESE TITLES!